D0838458

BODIES FROM THE LIBRARY

Lost tales of mystery and suspense by
Agatha Christie
and other Masters of the Golden Age

Selected and introduced by

TONY MEDAWAR

COLLINS
CRIME
CLUB

COLLINS CRIME CLUB
An imprint of HarperCollins*Publishers*
1 London Bridge Street
London SE1 9GF
www.harpercollins.co.uk

This edition 2018
3

For copyright acknowledgements, see page 323.

A catalogue record for this book
is available from the British Library

ISBN 978-0-00-828922-5

Typeset in Minion Pro 11/15 pt by
Palimpsest Book Production Ltd, Falkirk, Stirlingshire

Printed and bound in Great Britain by
CPI Group (UK) Ltd, Croydon CR0 4YY

MIX
Paper from
responsible sources
FSC™ C007454

This book is produced from independently certified FSC™
paper to ensure responsible forest management.

For more information visit: www.harpercollins.co.uk/green

CONTENTS

INTRODUCTION

'Death in particular seems to provide the minds of the Anglo-Saxon race with a greater fund of innocent amusement than any other single subject.'

Dorothy L. Sayers

In the beginning was Poe. It all begins with him. An alcoholic American critic who created, among other things, the detective story. And for that, if for nothing else, God bless Edgar Allan Poe.

Poe's detective was the Chevalier C. Auguste Dupin, a brilliant if patronising bibliophile of independent means who appeared in 'The Murders in the Rue Morgue', a long short story published in 1841, and in two other short stories. For these and other mysteries, Poe created the concept of a detective story—a story in which murder or some other crime is solved by observation and deduction—and Poe also created many of the tropes of detective fiction: the 'impossible crime', the notion of an amateur investigator from whom the professionals seek advice, the least likely suspect as murderer . . . Quite simply, before anyone did anything, Poe did everything. Or *almost* everything.

While Poe's stories were popular, and prompted others to try their hand at detective fiction, it would be nearly twenty years before the first novel-length detective story was published. This was *The Notting Hill Mystery* (1862–63) by Charles Warren Adams, writing as Charles Felix. Though other detective novels appeared, most notably *The Moonstone* (1868) by Wilkie Collins, detection remained generally subordinate to romance and suspense, and it would be a further twenty years before the next landmark in detective fiction, Fergus Hume's *The Mystery of a Hansom Cab*, published in 1886. And then, in 1887, readers were introduced to the greatest detective of them all, Arthur Conan Doyle's Sherlock Holmes. As well as that first novel, *A Study in Scarlet*, Holmes appeared in three more novels, but it is principally because of the fifty-six short stories about Holmes, published in the *Strand* magazine, that the character has endured. While Holmes had other 'rivals' in the 1880s and '90s, most notably Arthur Morrison's investigator Martin Hewitt, none has survived to the present day.

The popularity of detective fiction, especially in the short story form, continued into the Edwardian Age, although only two characters from that period approach Holmes in terms of the quality of the stories in which they appear: G. K. Chesterton's Father Brown, a Catholic priest with an eye for paradox and a soul for the guilty, who featured in more than fifty stories; and Dr John Thorndyke, R. Austin Freeman's preternaturally intelligent forensic investigator, although his novel-length cases are more satisfying than the forty-one short stories in which he appears.

While the puzzles set by Chesterton and Freeman were for the most part very much in the tradition of the Sherlock Holmes mysteries, E. C. Bentley's 1913 novel *Trent's Last Case* was a game-changer, its publication often regarded as marking the beginning of what has become known as the Golden Age of crime and detective fiction. In *Trent's Last Case*, Bentley presented a clear problem, the shooting of a millionaire; but he turned convention on its head by allowing Trent to fall in love with a suspect—commonplace now but far from so at that time—and Bentley further confounded readers' expectations because Trent does *not* solve the case.

Trent's Last Case was immensely popular and remains in print today, along with Bentley's second Trent novel and a volume containing all thirteen of the Trent short stories, *Trent Intervenes* (1938). The novel prompted a boom in detective fiction in Britain, and for the best part of the next twenty years a detective short story appeared in almost every issue of almost every magazine: in long-lost titles like *The Red*, *Pearson's*, *The Bystander*, *The Sphere*, *The Corner*, *Britannia and Eve*, as well as others that have endured like *Harper's* and *The Tatler*. Detective stories—and episodic mystery serials—also became a standard feature in national weekly newspapers like the *News of the World*, and they could also be found in regional weeklies like the *Yorkshire Weekly Post* and the *Sheffield Weekly Telegraph*. These and countless other titles quickly became a strong, diverse and seemingly sustainable market for detective fiction, especially stories that turned on a twist or which featured an impossible crime, an unusual weapon or an unbreakable alibi, and they provided a complementary source of income for many of the best-known Golden Age authors as well as for some opportunistic hacks.

As the First World War ended, a steady trickle of novels that have come to be recognised as classics of the genre began to appear. In 1920, the Irish engineer Freeman Wills Crofts published *The Cask*, a sturdy police procedural whose mystery carried it through multiple editions. The same year, Agatha Christie, unquestionably the most popular writer of the Golden Age, had her first detective novel, *The Mysterious Affair at Styles*, serialised over eighteen weeks in the weekly edition of *The Times*, providing a retired Belgian police officer, Hercule Poirot, with his first case, and his first published book in Britain in 1921. In 1923, Dorothy L. Sayers' first Lord Peter Wimsey novel, *Whose Body?*, was published, while 1924 saw the publication of *The Rasp*, the first of Philip Macdonald's Colonel Gethryn novels. In 1925, John Rhode's Dr Priestley and Anthony Berkeley's Roger Sheringham took their first bow in, respectively, *The Paddington Mystery* and *The Layton Court Mystery*.

And so on. The trickle became a flood . . .

By the mid-1920s the appetite for crime fiction was enormous in Britain, as well as in much of the English-speaking world. As well as the many weekly and monthly magazines that carried crime and detective stories, daily newspapers also published mysteries, often basic puzzle stories in which the object was simply to spot the murderer's error before the detective. And when radio came along, in the form of 2LO, the precursor to the BBC, it provided a new outlet for detective fiction, a tradition that continues—thankfully—to this day.

In 1928, with his tongue (as often) firmly in his cheek, Father Ronald Knox set out ten rules for anyone considering writing a detective story; in America, the crime writer S. S. Van Dine did much the same, albeit at greater length. And in late 1929, Anthony Berkeley founded the Detection Club, a dining club to allow the elite of the genre to gather together and at the same time distinguish themselves from the mass of writers then working to meet the enormous demand for mysteries.

With hindsight, the 1930s can be seen as the high-point of the Golden Age, with many of the greatest writers in the genre producing their finest work, carefully constructed novels in which generally bloodless crimes are committed by consistently ingenious means; criminals are protected by unbreakable alibis and seemingly impenetrable mysteries are resolved by unmatchable detectives.

The Golden Age can be regarded as having ended in 1937 with the publication of Dorothy L. Sayers' final Wimsey novel, *Busman's Honeymoon*, which she described as 'a love story with detective interruptions', despite previously having said that 'sloppy sentiment' had no place in detective stories. However, it is important to acknowledge that there is much debate about dates. Some consider that the Golden Age continued into the 1940s, while others argue that it did not end until well into the second half of the twentieth century. Nonetheless, after *Busman's Honeymoon* came the Second World War, and nothing was ever the same again. The magazines and newspapers that had survived paper rationing continued to carry mysteries, including the *London Evening Standard*, which published a detective story almost every day through to the early 1960s. While Dorothy L. Sayers and Anthony Berkeley had abandoned writing in the genre in the late 1930s, other Golden Age writers continued, with some like Agatha Christie and Ngaio Marsh writing into the '70s and '80s. As Berkeley and others had predicted, the focus of crime fiction moved away from detective puzzles, which focused for the most part on 'Who?' and 'How?', to more psychologically nuanced mysteries in which 'Why?' was the driving question.

Dating from as far back as 1917, most of the stories and plays in this collection, all of them by writers active in the Golden Age, have either been published only once before—in a newspaper, a rare magazine or an obscure collection—or have *never* been published until now. They hark back to a gentler time, when murder was committed by simpler means and solved without forensic science. And yet, if the psychological thriller and police procedurals reign supreme today, there are still stories and television series that have their roots firmly in the Golden Age—writers like Elly Griffiths, Ann Cleeves or, in a delightfully mad way, Christopher Fowler; and programmes like *Death in Paradise* and *Midsomer Murders*, as well as others of mixed lineage like *Shetland*, *Broadchurch* and *River*. There are also a small number of continuation novels, which aim to sustain the traditions of the Golden Age by reviving some of its best-loved characters—the Wimsey novels by Jill Paton Walsh, Sophie Hannah's Poirot series, Mike Ripley's Campion novels and unquestionably the best of its kind, *Money in the Morgue* by Ngaio Marsh and Stella Duffy, published in 2018. And, happiest of all, many of the classics of the Golden Age remain in print or are available as e-books thanks to publishers like HarperCollins, the British Library and small press imprints like Crippen & Landru, which has published many new short story collections by individual Golden Age authors.

Finally, there is the annual *Bodies from the Library* conference, held each year since 2015 at the British Library in London and attracting an audience from around the world. The event brings together writers, readers and academics to consider and discuss the themes and character of the books of the Golden Age and to focus on particular authors or publishers and their unique contributions. Among other topics, the conference has highlighted the existence of a frustratingly large number of uncollected short stories, forgotten radio and stage plays, and even unpublished material by some of the best-remembered writers of the period. For most of the individual writers concerned there are insufficient stories to assemble new dedicated collections, but there is ample material for volumes such as this, bringing together 'lost' works by different writers for their keenest admirers as well as for collectors and new readers who have an insatiable appetite for murder and the innocent amusement of a bygone age.

The Golden Age is dead; long live the Golden Age!

Tony Medawar
April 2018

BEFORE INSULIN

J. J. Connington

'I'd more than the fishing in my mind when I asked you over for the weekend,' Wendover confessed. 'Fact is, Clinton, something's turned up and I'd like your advice.'

Sir Clinton Driffield, Chief Constable of the county, glanced quizzically at his old friend.

'If you've murdered anyone, Squire, my advice is: Keep it dark and leave the country. If it's merely breach of promise, or anything of that sort, I'm at your disposal.'

'It's not breach of promise,' Wendover assured him with the complacency of a hardened bachelor. 'It's a matter of an estate for which I happen to be sole trustee, worse luck. The other two have died since the will was made. I'll tell you about it.'

Wendover prided himself on his power of lucid exposition. He settled himself in his chair and began.

'You've heard me speak of old John Ashby, the iron-master? He died fifteen years back, worth £53,000; and he made his son, his daughter-in-law, and myself executors of his will. The son, James Ashby, was to have the life-rent of the estate; and on his death the capital was to be handed over to his offspring when the youngest of them came of age. As it happened, there was only one child, young Robin Ashby. James Ashby and his wife were killed in a railway accident some years ago; so the whole

£53,000, less two estate duties, was secured to young Robin if he lived to come of age.'

'And if he didn't?' queried Sir Clinton.

'Then the money went to a lot of charities,' Wendover explained. 'That's just the trouble, as you'll see. Three years ago, young Robin took diabetes, a bad case, poor fellow. We did what we could for him, naturally. All the specialists had a turn, without improvement. Then we sent him over to Neuenahr, to some institute run by a German who specialised in diabetes. No good. I went over to see the poor boy, and he was worn to a shadow, simply skin and bone and hardly able to walk with weakness. Obviously it was a mere matter of time.'

'Hard lines on the youngster,' Sir Clinton commented soberly.

'Very hard,' said Wendover with a gesture of pity. 'Now as it happened, at Neuenahr he scraped acquaintance with a French doctor. I saw him when I was there: about thirty, black torpedo beard, very brisk and well-got-up, with any amount of belief in himself. He spoke English fluently, which gave him a pull with Robin, out there among foreigners; and he persuaded the boy that he could cure him if he would put himself in his charge. Well, by that time, it seemed that any chance was worth taking, so I agreed. After all, the boy was dying by inches. So off he went to the south of France, where this man—Prevost, his name was—had a nursing home of his own. I saw the place: well-kept affair though small. And he had an English nurse, which was lucky for Robin. Pretty girl she was: chestnut hair, creamy skin, supple figure, neat hands and feet. A lady, too.'

'Oh, any pretty girl can get round you,' interjected Sir Clinton. 'Get on with the tale.'

'Well, it was all no good,' Wendover went on, hastily. 'The poor boy went downhill in spite of all the Frenchman's talk; and, to cut a long story short, he died a fortnight ago, on the very day when he came of age.'

'Oh, so he lived long enough to inherit?'

'By the skin of his teeth,' Wendover agreed. 'That's where the trouble begins. Before that day, of course, he could make no valid will. But now a claimant, one Sydney Eastcote, turns up with the claim that Robin made a will the morning of the day he died, and by this will this Eastcote scoops the whole estate. All I know of it is from a letter this Eastcote wrote to me giving the facts. I referred him to the lawyer for the estate and told the lawyer—Harringay's his name—to bring the claimant here this afternoon. They're due now. I'd like you to look him over, Clinton. I'm not quite satisfied about this will.'

The Chief Constable pondered for a moment or two.

'Very well,' he agreed. 'But you'd better not introduce me as Sir Clinton Driffield, Chief Constable, etc. I'd better be Mr Clinton, I think. It sounds better for a private confabulation.'

'Very well,' Wendover conceded. 'There's a car on the drive. It must be they, I suppose.'

In a few moments the door opened and the visitors were ushered in. Surprised himself, the Chief Constable was still able to enjoy the astonishment of his friend; for instead of the expected man, a pretty chestnut-haired girl, dressed in mourning, was shown into the room along with the solicitor, and it was plain enough that Wendover recognised her.

'You seem surprised, Mr Wendover,' the girl began, evidently somewhat taken aback by Wendover's expression. Then she smiled as though an explanation occurred to her. 'Of course, it's my name again. People always forget that Sydney's a girl's name as well as a man's. But you remember me, don't you? I met you when you visited poor Robin.'

'Of course I remember you, Nurse,' Wendover declared, recovering from his surprise. 'But I never heard you called anything but "Nurse" and didn't even hear your surname; so naturally I didn't associate you with the letter I got about poor Robin's will.'

'Oh, I see,' answered the girl. 'That accounts for it.'

She looked inquiringly towards the Chief Constable, and Wendover recovered his presence of mind.

'This is a friend of mine, Mr Clinton,' he explained. 'Miss Eastcote. Mr Harringay. Won't you sit down? I must admit your letter took me completely by surprise, Miss Eastcote.'

Wendover was getting over his initial astonishment at the identity of the claimant, and when they had all seated themselves, he took the lead.

'I've seen a copy of Robin's death certificate,' he began slowly. 'He died in the afternoon of September 21st, the day he came of age, so he was quite competent to make a will. I suppose he was mentally fit to make one?'

'Dr Prevost will certify that if necessary,' the nurse affirmed quietly.

'I noticed that he didn't die in Dr Prevost's Institute,' Wendover continued. 'At some local hotel, wasn't it?'

'Yes,' Nurse Eastcote confirmed. 'A patient died in the Institute about that time and poor Robin hated the place on that account. It depressed him, and he insisted on moving to the hotel for a time.'

'He must have been at death's door then, poor fellow,' Wendover commented.

'Yes,' the nurse admitted, sadly. 'He was very far through. He had lapses of consciousness, the usual diabetic coma. But while he was awake he was perfectly sound mentally, if that's what you mean.'

Wendover nodded as though this satisfied him completely.

'Tell me about this will,' he asked. 'It's come as something of a surprise to me, not unnaturally.'

Nurse Eastcote hesitated for a moment. Her lip quivered and her eyes filled with tears as she drew from her bag an envelope of thin foreign paper. From this she extracted a sheet of foreign notepaper which she passed across to Wendover.

'I can't grumble if you're surprised at his leaving me this

money,' she said, at last. 'I didn't expect anything of the kind myself. But the fact is . . . he fell in love with me, poor boy, while he was under my charge. You see, except for Dr Prevost, I was the only one who could speak English with him, and that meant much to him at that time when he was so lonely. Of course he was much younger that I am; I'm twenty-seven. I suppose I ought to have checked him when I saw how things were. But I hadn't the heart to do it. It was something that gave him just the necessary spur to keep him going, and of course I knew that marriage would never come into it. It did no harm to let him fall in love; and I really did my very best to make him happy, in these last weeks. I was so sorry for him, you know.'

This put the matter in a fresh light for Wendover, and he grew more sympathetic in his manner.

'I can understand,' he said gently. 'You didn't care for him, of course . . .'

'Not in that way. But I was very very sorry for him, and I'd have done anything to make him feel happier. It was so dreadful to see him going out into the dark before he'd really started in life.'

Wendover cleared his throat, evidently conscious that the talk was hardly on the businesslike lines which he had planned. He unfolded the thin sheet of notepaper and glanced over the writing.

'This seems explicit enough. "I leave all that I have to Nurse Sydney Eastcote, residing at Dr Prevost's medical Institute." I recognise the handwriting as Robin's, and the date is in the same writing. Who are the witnesses, by the way?'

'Two of the waiters at the hotel, I believe,' Nurse Eastcote explained.

Wendover turned to the flimsy foreign envelope and examined the address.

'Addressed by himself to you at the institute, I see. And the postmark is 21st September. That's quite good confirmatory evidence, if anything of the sort were needed.'

He passed the two papers to Sir Clinton. The Chief Constable seemed to find the light insufficient where he was sitting, for he rose and walked over to a window to examine the documents. This brought him slightly behind Nurse Eastcote. Wendover noted idly that Sir Clinton stood sideways to the light while he inspected the papers in his hand.

'Now just one point,' Wendover continued. 'I'd like to know something about Robin's mental condition towards the end. Did he read to pass the time, newspapers and things like that?'

Nurse Eastcote shook her head.

'No, he read nothing. He was too exhausted, poor boy. I used to sit by him and try to interest him in talk. But if you have any doubt about his mind at that time—I mean whether he was fit to make a will—I'm sure Dr Prevost will give a certificate that he was in full possession of his faculties and knew what he was doing.'

Sir Clinton came forward with the papers in his hand.

'These are very important documents,' he pointed out, addressing the nurse. 'It's not safe for you to be carrying them about in your bag as you've been doing. Leave them with us. Mr Wendover will give you a receipt and take good care of them. And to make sure there's no mistake, I think you'd better write our name in the corner of each of them so as to identify them. Mr Harringay will agree with me that we mustn't leave any loophole for doubt in a case like this.'

The lawyer nodded. He was a taciturn man by nature, and his pride had been slightly ruffled by the way in which he had been ignored in the conference. Nurse Eastcote, with Wendover's fountain pen, wrote her signature on a free space of each paper. Wendover offered his guests tea before they departed, but he turned the talk into general channels and avoided any further reference to business topics.

When the lawyer and the girl had left the house, Wendover turned to Sir Clinton.

'It seems straight enough to me,' he said, 'but I could see from the look you gave me behind her back when you were at the window that you aren't satisfied. What's wrong?'

'If you want my opinion,' the Chief Constable answered, 'it's a fake from start to finish. Certainly you can't risk handing over a penny on that evidence. If you want it proved up to the hilt, I can do it for you, but it'll cost something for inquiries and expert assistance. That ought to come out of the estate, and it'll be cheaper than an action at law. Besides,' he added with a smile, 'I don't suppose you want to put that girl in gaol. She's probably only a tool in the hands of a cleverer person.'

Wendover was staggered by the Chief Constable's tone of certainty. The girl, of course, had made no pretence that she was in love with Robin Ashby; but her story had been told as though she herself believed it.

'Make your inquiries, certainly,' he consented. 'Still, on the face of it the thing sounds likely enough.'

'I'll give you definite proof in a fortnight or so. Better make a further appointment with that girl in, say, three weeks. But don't drag the lawyer into it this time. It may savour too much of compounding a felony for his taste. I'll need these papers.'

'Here's the concrete evidence,' said the Chief Constable, three weeks later. 'I may as well show it to you before she arrives, and you can amuse yourself with turning it over in the meanwhile.'

He produced the will, the envelope, and two photographs from his pocket-book as he spoke and laid them on the table, opening out the will as he put it down.

'Now first of all, notice that the will and envelope are of very thin paper, the foreign correspondence stuff. Second, observe that the envelope is of the exact size to hold that sheet of paper if it's folded in four—I mean folded in half and then doubled over. The sheet's about quarto size, ten inches by eight. Now look here. There's an extra fold in the paper. It's been folded in four and then it's been folded across once more. That struck me as soon as I had it in my hand. Why the extra fold, since it would fit into the envelope without that?'

Wendover inspected the sheet carefully and looked rather perplexed.

'You're quite right,' he said, 'but you can't upset a will on the strength of a fold in it. She may have doubled it up herself, after she got it.'

'Not when it was in the envelope that fitted it,' Sir Clinton pointed out. 'There's no corresponding doubling of the envelope. However, let's go on. Here's a photograph of the envelope, taken with the light falling sideways. You see the postal erasing stamp has made an impression?'

'Yes, I can read it, and the date's 21st September right enough.' He paused for a moment and then added in surprise, 'But where's the postage stamp? It hasn't come out in the photo.'

'No, because that's a photo of the impression on the back half of the envelope. The stamp came down hard and not only cancelled the stamp but impressed the second side of the envelope as well. The impression comes out quite clearly when it's illuminated from the side. That's worth thinking over. And, finally, here's another print. It was made before the envelope was slit to get at the stamp impression. All we did was to put the envelope into a printing-frame with a bit of photographic printing paper behind it and expose it to light for a while. Now you'll notice that the gummed portions of the envelope show up in white, like a sort of St Andrew's Cross. But if you look carefully, you'll see a couple of darker patches on the part of the white strip which corresponds to the flap of the envelope that one sticks down. Just think out what they imply, Squire. There are the facts for you, and it's not too difficult to put an interpretation on them if you think for a minute or two. And I'll add just one further bit of information. The two waiters who acted as witnesses to that will were given tickets for South America, and a certain sum of money each to keep them from feeling homesick . . . But here's your visitor.'

Rather to Wendover's surprise, Sir Clinton took the lead in the conversation as soon as the girl arrived.

'Before we turn to business, Miss Eastcote,' he said, 'I'd like to tell you a little anecdote. It may be of use to you. May I?'

Nurse Eastcote nodded politely and Wendover, looking her over, noticed a ring on her engagement finger which he had not seen on her last visit.

'This is a case which came to my knowledge lately,' Sir Clinton went on, 'and it resembles your own so closely that I'm sure it will suggest something. A young man of twenty, in an almost dying state, was induced to enter a nursing home by the doctor in charge. If he lived to come of age, he could make a will and leave a very large fortune to anyone he choose: but it was the merest gamble whether he would live to come of age.'

Nurse Eastcote's figure stiffened and her eyes widened at this beginning, but she merely nodded as though asking Sir Clinton to continue.

'The boy fell in love with one of the nurses, who happened to be under the influence of the doctor,' Sir Clinton went on. 'If he lived to make a will, there was little doubt that he would leave the fortune to the nurse. A considerable temptation for any girl, I think you'll agree.

'The boy's birthday was very near, only a few days off; but it looked as though he would not live to see it. He was very far gone. He had no interest in the newspapers and he had long lapses of unconsciousness, so that he had no idea of what the actual date was. It was easy enough to tell him, on a given day, that he had come of age, though actually two days were still to run. Misled by the doctor, he imagined that he could make a valid will, being now twenty-one; and he wrote with his own hand a short document leaving everything to the nurse.'

Miss Eastcote cleared her throat with an effort.

'Yes?' she said.

'This fraudulent will,' Sir Clinton continued, 'was witnessed by two waiters of the hotel to which the boy had been removed; and soon after, these waiters were packed off abroad and provided with some cash in addition to their fares. Then it occurred to the doctor that an extra bit of confirmatory evidence might be supplied. The boy had put the will into an envelope which he had addressed to the nurse. While the gum was still wet, the doctor opened the flap and took out the "will", which he then folded smaller in order to get the paper into an ordinary business-size envelope. He then addressed this to the nurse and posted the will to her in it. The original large envelope, addressed by the boy, he retained. But in pulling it open, the doctor had slightly torn the inner side of the flap where the gum lies; and that little defect shows up when one exposes the envelope over a sheet of photographic paper. Here's an example of what I mean.'

He passed over to Nurse Eastcote the print which he had shown Wendover and drew her attention to the spots on the St Andrew's Cross.

'As it chanced, the boy died next morning, a day before he came of age. The doctor concealed the death for a day, which was easy enough in the circumstances. Then, on the afternoon of the crucial date—did I mention that it was September 21st?—he closed the empty envelope, stamped it, and put it into the post, thus securing a postmark of the proper date. Unfortunately for this plan, the defacement stamp of the post office came down hard enough to impress its image on *both* the sheets of the thin paper envelope, so that by opening up the envelope and photographing it by a sideways illumination the embossing of the stamp showed up—like this.'

He handed the girl the second photograph.

'Now if the "will" had been in that envelope, the "will" itself would have borne that stamp. But it did not; and that proves that the "will" was not in the envelope when it passed through the post. A clever woman like yourself, Miss Eastcote, will see the point at once.'

'And what happened after that?' asked the girl huskily.

'It's difficult to tell you,' Sir Clinton pursued. 'If it had come before me officially—I'm Chief Constable of the county, you know—I should probably have had to prosecute that unfortunate nurse for attempted fraud; and I've not the slightest doubt that we'd have proved the case up to the hilt. It would have meant a year or two in gaol, I expect.

'I forgot to mention that the nurse was secretly engaged to the doctor all this while. And, by the way, that's a very pretty ring you're wearing, Miss Eastcote. That, of course, accounted for the way in which the doctor managed to get her to play her part in the little scheme. I think, if I were you, Miss Eastcote, I'd go back to France as soon as possible and tell Dr Prevost that . . . well, it hasn't come off.'

J. J. CONNINGTON

Alfred Walter Stewart, alias J. J. Connington, was born in Glasgow in 1880. A clever child with an enquiring mind, he attended Glasgow High School and graduated in 1902 from Glasgow University with honours in chemistry, mathematics and geology. While Stewart could have pursued almost any of the sciences he decided to focus on chemistry. After completing his doctorate in 1907, he took up an appointment at Belfast University where in 1919, after spells working for the Admiralty and lecturing at the universities of London and Glasgow, he became Professor of Chemistry, occupying this chair until his retirement in 1944. He had been suffering for many years from a debilitating illness, and he died in 1947.

Stewart had begun writing novels in the 1920s, adopting the pseudonym J. J. Connington doubtless to distance what he saw as a hobby from his academic career. His first book, *Nordenholt's Million* (1923), dealt with a Wellsian apocalypse, brought about by scientific error and ended—in the Clyde valley—by scientific genius. His second, *Almighty Gold* (1924), was a more prosaic tale of adventure and crime in the world of high finance. Both books sold well, and were well received critically, but this was the 1920s and what John Dickson Carr would later describe as 'the lure of detective fiction' was too great. For his first detective story, *Death at Swaythling Court* (1926), Stewart wrote an entertaining village mystery in which a blackmailing butterfly collector is poisoned *and* stabbed. This was quickly followed by *The Dangerfield Talisman* (1926), an 'old dark house' mystery with many characters and almost as many clues.

For *Murder in the Maze* (1927), Stewart created his first recurring character, Sir Clinton Driffield, an atypically misanthropic policeman who would appear in seventeen novel-length mysteries. Driffield is generally aided, and sometimes hindered, by his Watsonian friend Squire Wendover, a local landowner in the county where Driffield is the chief constable. Driffield is a far more active chief constable than is customary in fiction—or in real life—and, while he can tend to be didactic, he is one of only a handful of detectives in the Golden Age willing to admit, occasionally, that he is unable to explain every aspect of a case. And Driffield can also proceed in unorthodox ways, never more so than in the extraordinary *Nemesis at Raynham Parva* (1929).

As might be expected from a scientist, Stewart's mysteries are careful and methodically written and, while some contemporary critics felt the author could sometimes be long-winded, the majority found him adept at constructing ingenious plots, entertaining and imaginative, and above all scrupulous at playing fair with the reader. His novels often feature memorable elements, such as the sinister legend of the Green Devil in *Death at Swaythling Court*, the hedge maze of *Murder in the Maze*, the lottery tontine of *The Sweepstake Murders* (1931) or the 'fairy houses' and weaponry museum in *Tragedy at Ravensthorpe* (1927).

'Before Insulin', the only short story to feature Driffield and Wendover, was first published in the *London Evening Standard* on 1 September 1936 as the final story in *Detective Cavalcade*, a series of stories selected by Dorothy L. Sayers.

THE INVERNESS CAPE

Leo Bruce

You'd think I was used to violence, wouldn't you? *asked Sergeant Beef, rhetorically*, after all the crime and horror I've seen. But there was one crime of violence, I remember, which shocked me more than any of your sneaking poisoners could do. It happened some years ago now. One old lady was clubbed to death in full view of her crippled sister. The most brutal case I ever had to tackle.

I knew the old ladies well; nice kind old parties who would do anyone a good turn. They lived together in a big house overlooking their own park. The only thing that anyone could have against them was that they were rich.

Miss Lucia was the older of the two and must have been over seventy. She was active, though: moved like a young woman and loved her garden, which was kept 'just so' by two gardeners and a lad. Miss Agatha was a few years younger and no one had ever seen her out of her invalid chair since the bad hunting accident she had as a young girl. She would be wheeled out on to the terrace on fine days and sit there watching her sister in the garden. They were very fond of one another and very happy.

Then their nephew came to live with them, young Richard Luckery, and I didn't much take to him. It was known that he hadn't any money of his own and he must have had a lot from the old ladies because he spent like a madman. Motor-cars, racing, racketing about—an extravagant young devil who cared only for himself.

Perhaps what I didn't like was that he used to dress in the most extraordinary clothes; eccentric, that's what he looked. And when he started wearing one of those Inverness capes and a deerstalker hat, like Sherlock Holmes, I thought it downright silly.

He had friends to play up to him, though, like anyone else who throws money about. One of these, Cuthbert Mireling, lived right opposite to the old ladies' home, and another, Gilly Ponstock, had rooms at the local pub where Richard Luckery used to drink, sometimes with one of his aunt's gardeners, Albert Giggs.

On a Saturday in June, Miss Lucia said at lunch that she was going to spend the afternoon taking cuttings of pinks and pansies in one of the borders. The gardeners would have gone home and she liked having the garden to herself. In fact, she never missed her Saturday afternoon's gardening.

Agatha asked her nephew to wheel her out on the terrace from which she would be able to watch her sister. This he did, then went up to his own room for a sleep.

At about half-past two, in full blazing sunlight, Miss Agatha was horrified to see a man walk furtively out of the shrubbery with a heavy bar of wood and crash it down on her sister's head. The first blow may have been enough to kill her, but he struck again and again.

Miss Agatha screamed, but it was some minutes before Katie, the only servant then in the house, came running out and a few minutes more before Richard Luckery appeared. He seemed rather dazed, and said afterwards that he had been asleep.

Miss Agatha then did something which shocked and astounded the servant. She turned to Richard in great horror and shouted, 'Keep away from me! You killed Lucia!'

Richard protested: he had been upstairs. His aunt was hysterical, he said. He was as shocked as she was. Then he told the servant to telephone for a doctor. The old lady would not be left alone with Richard. It was some time before she became coherent enough to tell the servant exactly what had happened.

By now people began to gather. Giggs, the gardener, whose cottage was across the stable yard, appeared and Cuthbert Mireling arrived at the front door, having heard the screams from his home. A doctor was sent for and so was I, and between us we examined Miss Lucia, who was quite dead, and managed to calm her sister a little.

It was not until the evening, however, that I could get a statement from her. I had been over the ground by then and seen that the murder had happened about 200 yards from the terrace and that it was possible to reach the shrubbery from the house without being visible from where Miss Agatha had sat. Or, as I thought, to reach the house from the shrubbery for that matter.

The first thing that Miss Agatha said was that her nephew must be arrested at once.

'I saw him do it!' she kept repeating.

I pointed out that it was 200 yards away and asked how she could be sure.

'I watched him. He was wearing his deerstalker hat and that cape of his.'

'But did you see his face?'

She would not or could not give a clear answer to that question. She *knew* it was Richard. She could see him quite clearly. The cape . . . the hat . . . it *was* Richard. I was to arrest him; not leave him in the house with her. Question her as I might, I could get no more from her.

Then I tackled the nephew. Before lunch he had been in the local pub playing darts with his two friends and Giggs, the gardener. He had left his aunt on the terrace and gone upstairs to sleep. He had heard the screams and come down. He could not account for Miss Agatha's accusations.

When I asked him about the Inverness cape he said he had

found a stuffy little outfitter's shop in London which had some old stock of things long out of fashion—spats, fancy waistcoats, Norfolk suits and these capes. He gave me the name and address. He said that he had thought it would be amusing to wear something so dated. Yes, his friends knew where he had purchased it. I asked him to go and fetch it, and he did so, but took a long time over it.

'Katie had it,' he explained. (Katie was the servant.) 'She was mending a tear in it.'

There was no sign of a stain or anything unusual about the thing.

I sent for Katie and found out, as I half-expected by then, that she had taken the cape to her room after lunch that day to repair it and that it had actually been in her hands while the murder was committed.

It was easy to understand which way the case was developing now, and when I went to the little shop and found that they had sold two of these Inverness capes in the last few months I could see daylight. The shopkeeper could not help me much over the two purchasers. He remembered the first fairly well and his description fitted Richard Luckery, but about the second he was uncertain. He remembered it was a young man, but nothing much more except that he had seemed in a hurry.

Next, of course, I cross-examined the two friends, but neither of them had much of an alibi. Cuthbert Mireling had been at home reading, he said, in a deck-chair on the lawn when he had heard screams coming from the old ladies' house. He had gone across to see what was the matter and whether he could be of any help. Gilly Ponstock had remained in his room at the inn asleep. He knew nothing about the murder till he came down to tea at half-past four and was told by the innkeeper. The gardener had been alone in his cottage.

It was a puzzler. Someone had bought one of these capes with which to impersonate Richard Luckery, had put it on in the shrubbery, murdered the old lady and made off. Giggs and Mireling had some sort of motive because each had fair-sized legacies, Giggs as an old employee, Mireling as a son of old friends. Either could have done it, but there was not a shred of real evidence against them.

My wife said that case would be the death of me. I couldn't sleep for worrying over it. I'd tried all the ordinary things that should have provided clues—fingerprints, footprints, the weapon used, but none of them gave me an inkling. If I ever commit murder, I said, it will be like this, in the open where everyone can see me do it. Then I know I'll never be found out.

Then suddenly I had an idea. I searched Richard Luckery's room, then came downstairs and arrested him. He was charged, tried and, I'm glad to say, in due course hanged.

The explanation? Well, he had found what he thought was a very clever way of committing murder. A double bluff. He decided to impersonate someone impersonating him. Perhaps it was by chance that he came on that old stock of Edwardian clothes, or perhaps he was actually looking for something of the sort. He chose that Inverness cape as a garment easily distinguishable, bought another with which to impersonate himself, made a habit of wearing the first one, then waited his moment. He chose a Saturday afternoon because he knew that Miss Lucia would be gardening then, asked Katie to mend his first cape, went down to the shrubbery where he had hidden the second, put it on, murdered his aunt and returned to the house, which he entered while the servant was on the terrace. He had a perfect witness in Miss Agatha, who would swear it was him, because of the cape, and a perfect alibi in that *his* cape would be in Katie's room. He knew I should soon find out about the purchase of the second cape by someone who did not resemble the purchaser of the first—some simple disguise, I guessed. The more Agatha swore it was him, the more sympathy he would gain for being impersonated.

But, of course, he made his one mistake. They all do, thank heavens, or I don't know what would become of detectives. He forgot to plan the disposal of the second cape. I found it between the mattresses on his bed.

LEO BRUCE

Rupert Croft-Cooke, who wrote detective fiction under the pen name of Leo Bruce, was born in 1903. He was brought up in south-east England, an aesthete in a family of athletes, and attended Tonbridge School and what is now known as Wrekin College in Shropshire, where he did well both academically and at the game of darts, at which he excelled.

Croft-Cooke published his first work, a slim booklet of verse entitled *Clouds of Gold*, at the age of 18. Aged 19, after a brief period working as a private tutor, he decided to go in search of what he would later describe as 'adventure, romance and excitement'. He secured a teaching post in Argentina and travelled throughout South America, taking in Brazil and even the Falkland Islands. After two years he returned to England, and began working as a freelance journalist and writer, as well as broadcasting on 2LO, one of the first radio stations in Britain, which would go on to become part of the BBC.

In 1940, Croft-Cooke enlisted in the Intelligence Corps, serving first in Madagascar and later in India. On returning to civilian life, he settled in Ticehurst, Sussex, where he continued to write. In 1953, as part of a 'war on vice'—defined as encompassing prostitution and homosexuality—initiated by the then Commissioner of the Metropolitan Police, Croft-Cooke and his Indian companion and secretary were charged with indecency and convicted. After serving his sentence, he sold up and moved to Tangier, where he spent the next fifteen years writing and playing host to visiting writers including Noël Coward.

Over a career lasting more than fifty years, Rupert Croft-Cooke was amazingly prolific. He authored nearly thirty volumes of autobiography, including *The World is Young* (1937) on his experiences in South America, as well as collections of verse, memoirs of his extensive travels and biographies of Lord Alfred Douglas—Oscar Wilde's Bosie—and of the entertainers Charles 'Tom Thumb' Stratton and Colonel 'Buffalo Bill' Cody. Croft-Cooke also wrote widely on subjects that interested him, including his beloved darts and the circus, as well as the importance of freedom of the press and the problems caused by 'petty' regulation. After his conviction and subsequent imprisonment, he argued for greater tolerance of homosexuality and in support of improvements to the penal system. His writing was highly regarded by critics up to the early 1950s, but after his conviction, reviews tended to be more negative and even favourable ones were marred by obscurely worded but plainly homophobic allusions.

As well as his extensive writing under his own name, Croft-Cooke also wrote detective stories using the pseudonym of Leo Bruce. His first mystery novel, *Case for Three Detectives*, was published in 1936. While the titular detectives parody Lord Peter Wimsey, Hercule Poirot and G. K. Chesterton's Father Brown, the case is solved by a cockney policeman, Sergeant William Beef, who would go on to appear in seven other novels. In the early 1950s, Croft-Cooke abandoned Beef and created another amateur sleuth, Dr Carolus Deene, a history teacher who would appear in more than twenty novels. As Bruce and under his own name, Croft-Cooke wrote many short stories including a round-robin novella with Beverley Nichols and Monica Dickens, author of the *Follyfoot* series of children's novels. His last book was published in 1977 and Rupert Croft-Cooke died in 1979.

One of four uncollected stories to feature Sergeant Beef, *The*

Inverness Cape was first published in *The Sketch* on 16 July 1952. The text in this collection is taken from the original manuscript of the story in the author's papers, where it was located by Curtis Evans, author of *Masters of the 'Humdrum' Mystery* and *The Spectrum of English Murder*.

DARK WATERS

Freeman Wills Crofts

For years Weller, the solicitor, had handled Marbeck's affairs, and when he received the old man's letter saying that he wanted to realise some securities, it struck him like a sentence of death.

For the securities were gone. In order to recoup some unlucky operations on the Stock Exchange, he had sold the lot. Marbeck was no business man, and as his dividends continued to be paid with unfailing regularity he had suspected nothing.

For Weller discovery would mean the end of everything. He would not escape prison. His business in the nearby town, his charming house on the Thames, his position and his friends—all would be gone. He could look forward to nothing but poverty and misery.

But there was an alternative. He scarcely dared to put it into words, but if Marbeck were dead he could undoubtedly produce papers which would convince the executors that he had sold at the old man's request and paid him the money.

He saw very clearly how the deed could be done, and with complete safety. The Thames! What was the river for, if not to meet the problems of those who lived on its banks? A little care, an unpleasant five minutes, and then—

Weller's house was on the north bank. He was not married, but his sister kept house for him, helped by a woman who came morning and evening to clean and cook. He would have to choose a time when his sister was away from home, as he must have the home to himself in the late evening.

On Wednesday nights for years past he and three friends had met at each other's houses for a rubber of bridge. There was a dentist, an architect and Marbeck, who was a retired professor of music. The first two lived near Weller on the north bank, but—and this was where the river came in—Marbeck's house was on the south bank almost immediately opposite. There was no bridge close by, and all four had light skiffs which in suitable weather they used as ferries, preferring to scull directly across rather than to get out cars and drive some miles round.

This was Thursday and on the coming Wednesday the meeting was to be at Weller's. Till then he could easily put Marbeck off with assurances that the sale of the stock was in hand. Wednesday indeed would suit from every point of view, for his sister was going to some friends in Torquay for that entire week.

Two small preliminaries required attention. At a London chemist's Weller bought some of those 'safe' sleeping tablets obtainable without a medical prescription. The shop was large and full of customers and he was satisfied that the purchase had attracted no attention.

On Wednesday evening he dissolved two tablets in a little whisky, then destroying the remainder. It was the custom for the four men to have drinks when breaking up at the end of the game, and as usual Weller set out the decanter, siphon and four glasses. Into one of the glasses he poured the prepared whisky. While standing at the side table he could see the liquid, but it would be invisible to his seated guests.

The other preliminary Weller dealt with shortly before his friends were due. Going to his boathouse, he made sure that his boat was ready for instant use, with rowlocks and oars in place and water gate open.

In due course the men arrived and settled down to their game. Weller threw himself desperately into the play, partly as the best way of passing the time, partly lest he should make some error which might later give rise to comment.

The evening, the longest he had ever spent, came to an end at last. He and his partner had lost, but without, he felt sure, any suggestion of carelessness on his part. They settled up their few shillings' debt and then he turned to the glasses. Marbeck was the senior and Weller poured the whisky for him first.

After interminable delays the whisky was drunk, second helpings being offered and, as usual, refused. Further delay followed as the guests made their way to the hall and put on their coats in the most leisurely manner. But finally they left and strolled off together down the drive. Weller stood watching them, then slowly closed the door.

Now he could drop the pretence of composure. In the hall cloakroom he put on a cap and dark waterproof. Hurrying to a side door, he let himself out and made his way noiselessly towards the Thames.

It was not completely dark. More by sound than sight he located Marbeck. The old man was on his, Weller's, boat slip, a tiny pier adjoining, but outside, his boathouse. Marbeck had moored his skiff, as usual, at the slip. Weller heard him getting in and unchaining his sculls. His movements were slow and fumbling, the result, no doubt, of the dope. But at last he cast off and floated out, a shadow of deeper jet on the dark waters.

Weller now worked frantically. In less than a minute his boat was following the other. He tried to steady the thumping of his heart, reminding himself that everything was going perfectly. He overtook Marbeck in mid-stream just as he had intended. 'Marbeck!' he called softly.

'Yes, Yes? Who is it?'

'Weller. A small matter I forgot. Ease up a moment.'

The other held water and the boats drew together. Weller unshipped his sculls, laying them parallel to the gunwale at either side. Then, as the skiffs touched, he gripped the gunwale of

Marbeck's, pushed it downwards, and then raised it with all his strength. The skiff rolled violently and then righted itself. Marbeck was overboard.

The victim's single cry would not invalidate Weller's plan; in fact it would help it. But further cries might give him away, he swung his skiff round to where Marbeck was struggling, and leaning over the gunwale, seized the figure and pushed it under.

His waterproof caught somewhere, impeding him, and he jerked it roughly free. He was counting on the dope making the old man stupid. It appeared to have done so, for his feeble struggling soon ceased.

One more point and Weller had finished. A glance showed him that Marbeck's boat was as he wanted it: one oar caught in the rowlock, the other overboard. What had occurred would be obvious to everyone. Some slight indisposition or carelessness and Marbeck had lost an oar. He had made a sudden effort to recapture it before it floated away. The light skiff was unsteady in the water and its sudden roll had taken the old man unawares.

Weller now moved at top speed, though still silently. He rowed to his boathouse, replaced the boat, and hurried to the house. There he had a wash and brush up. He thought another whisky permissible while he waited for the next development.

Half an hour later it came, just as he had intended it should. Mrs Marbeck rang up to ask if her husband had left.

'Yes, Mrs Marbeck,' Weller hastened to reply. 'He left at his usual time, nearly an hour ago.'

'Well, he hasn't arrived here and I'm rather anxious.'

'I'll come across at once,' Weller declared and rang off.

This call was really part of his scheme. The wet oars, the drippings in his boat, the damp sleeves of his waterproof: all such awkward items would be explained by the speed with which he had hastened across.

Everything continued to go exactly to plan. He made his report to Mrs Marbeck, they rang up several houses at which the old man might have called. Then at Weller's suggestion they telephoned the police.

Inspector French was at the house within minutes. He listened to statements and said he would start an immediate inquiry. Then came a period of waiting.

Mrs Marbeck urged Weller to go home, but his sickening anxiety prevented him. Fortunately his presence was not suspicious since politeness also required him to stay. At length, two hours later, the inspector returned. To Mrs Marbeck he broke his news with genuine kindness. Her husband's body had been found lower down the river. He had evidently fallen overboard while making the crossing. Then he turned to Weller.

'I'd like, sir, to go over to your house to get some further details about Mr Marbeck's start. If you'll take me over in your boat, I'll send the car round.'

'Right,' Weller answered. He put on his waterproof and said he was ready.

But the inspector was looking at him very strangely. Weller's heart missed a beat. All had been going perfectly; what could now be wrong? 'I said I was ready,' he repeated shortly.

Inspector French bent forward. 'Excuse me, sir. I see you've lost a button from your coat.'

Weller glanced down. This was what he had felt. No doubt it had jammed under the oar. 'My own fault, inspector,' he said with truth. 'It was loose and I omitted to have it resewn.'

French took something from his pocket. 'It's not lost, sir. I think this is it. Yes: colour, shape, size and even thread are the same. And do you know where I found it? Gripped in Mr Marbeck's fingers: I could hardly get it out.'

FREEMAN WILLS CROFTS

Born in Dublin in 1879, Freeman Wills Crofts would go on to become one of Britain's best loved writers of detective fiction. After leaving school, Crofts joined the Belfast and North Counties Railway, rising to Chief Assistant Engineer. In 1912 he married and, in his early 30s, wrote a novel during a long period of convalescence. In homage to Charles Dickens, this first attempt was entitled *A Mystery of Two Cities* but by the time it was published in June 1920, by Collins, it had been retitled *The Cask* after a rewrite that saw the final section of the novel, largely comprising a trial, excised altogether.

Fired by this success, Crofts wrote a second novel, *The Ponson Case*. And then a third . . . For his fifth novel, *Inspector French's Greatest Case*, he created Joseph French, the Scotland Yard detective who would go on to appear in a total of thirty novels, countless radio plays and three stage plays. As Crofts described him, '*Soapy Joe* [is] *an ordinary man, carrying out his work, in an ordinary way . . . He makes mistakes but goes ahead in spite of them.*'

More books followed and Crofts was soon recognised as one of the best practitioners in the genre. The railway engineer and part-time organist and choirmaster retired in 1929 to take up writing full time, and in 1930 Crofts was invited by Anthony Berkeley to become a founding member of the Detection Club, based in London. Partly because of this, Crofts and his wife Mary moved to

Blackheath, a pretty village in Surrey where their first home was a house, *Wildern*, which has since been re-named after its most famous owner. Over the next twenty years Crofts would produce many books including *The Hog's Back Mystery* (1933), *Crime at Guildford* (1935) and *The Affair at Little Wokeham* (1943), all of which are set in Surrey.

An active member of the Detection Club, Crofts also contributed to several of their collaborative ventures, including the 1931 novel *The Floating Admiral*, which he wrote together with Agatha Christie and other members of the Detection Club. During the Second World War, Crofts produced dozens of radio plays for the BBC, many of which he later turned into short stories for the Inspector French collection *Murderers Make Mistakes* (1947). Throughout the war and in the years immediately afterwards, Crofts continued to write but his output gradually declined and he died in 1957 after a stubborn battle with cancer.

Croft's obituarist in *The Times* praised the writer for his 'logically contrived' plots and his close attention to detail, especially in the construction and breaking down of superficially cast-iron alibis. Crofts' novels often feature railway travel and the alibis of his criminals often turn on the complexities of pre-internet timetabling. His shorter fiction is similarly precise with the majority turning on what he would style 'the usual tiny oversight' or an inconsistency in a suspect's statement so that they offer the reader an opportunity to outwit the criminal before French.

Sixty years after his death, the work of Freeman Wills Crofts is having something of a resurgence. Several of his novels are once again in print and a celebratory collection is in preparation bringing together previously uncollected short stories and some of his unpublished stage and radio plays.

'Dark Waters' was first published in the *London Evening Standard* on 21 September 1953.

LINCKES' GREAT CASE

Georgette Heyer

I

The chief paused and glanced sharply across the table to where Roger Linckes sat facing him, listening to his discourse.

'It is a big job,' Masters said abruptly. 'So much is at stake. It's not like some stage robbery, where Lady So-and-So's pearls are stolen. It's—well, the whole country—perhaps all Europe—is implicated. Maybe I'm wrong to set you on to it. You're very young; you've had very little experience.'

The younger man flushed slightly under his tan.

'I know, sir.'

Masters looked him over thoughtfully, from his grave young eyes to his brogued shoes. He smiled a little.

'Anyhow, right or wrong, I'm going to let you see what you can do. I must admit I haven't much hope. Where Tiffrus and Pollern have failed, a comparative tyro isn't likely to succeed. But you did exceedingly well over that Panton affair, and it's just possible you might hit on a solution to this mystery.' He drummed on the table, frowning. 'I've known it happen before. I suppose the big detectives get stale, or something approaching it. Let's hope you'll bring fresh ideas into the business. How much do you know about it?'

Linckes crossed his legs, clasping his hands about one knee.

'Precious little, sir. You've seen to that, haven't you? Nothing known to the papers, I mean. All I know is that there's a leak in the Cabinet. Knowledge of our doings is being sold to Russia and to Germany. You say it has been going on for some time. The Soviets got wind of our new submarines. Hardly anyone in England knew about 'em, and yet Russia discovered the secret! Someone must have duplicated the plans and sold them—probably he's done it many times before—and that someone must be one of those in the small circle of people who knew all the details of the new subs. In fact, he must have been a pretty big man. It only remains for us to find out which one.'

'Very easy,' Masters grunted. 'It might have been a secretary.'

'It might,' conceded Linckes.

'You don't think so?'

'I don't know. It doesn't seem likely. Who was in that circle?'

'The Government knew all about the submarines,' Masters answered. 'But the actual plans at the time of the betrayal had been seen only by Caryu, the Secretary for War, Winthrop, the Under-Secretary, and Johnson for the Admiralty, and the inventor, of course, Sir Duncan Tassel. That rather dishes your theory, doesn't it? Naturally, Tassel is above suspicion; so is Caryu; so are the other two.'

'Are you sure that no one else knew of the plans?'

'No, I'm not sure. I'm convinced that someone else did know—must have known. Winthrop swears no one could have known, but he can't supply a counter-theory. He's more or less running the investigation, you know.'

'What does he say?'

'He's terribly worried, of course. We thought at first that his secretary was the man, but we can't find the slightest grounds for suspicion against him, and Winthrop's had him in his employ for years. It's the greatest mystery I've struck yet. We've been working to discover the betrayer for months, and we're no nearer a solution now than we were when we began. And still it goes on. Take the affair of the negotiations with Carmania. They leaked into Russia, we know. Or take the case of the submarines. Those plans weren't stolen, they were just copied. The only person, seemingly, who could have done it, was Winthrop. He alone knows the secret of Caryu's safe. The plans were with Caryu for three days. All the rest of the time they were with Tassel, and they never left him for a moment. The thing must have been done during those three days that they were in Caryu's safe, because before that date they were incomplete, and dates show that they can't have been copied after they were returned to Fothermere. Now, having whittled the date down to three days, how much nearer the solution are we? Of course, everything points to Winthrop.'

'Or Caryu,' said Linckes quietly.

'My good youth, are you seriously accusing Mr Caryu? Even supposing that he is the man we're after—which he isn't—would he have copied the plans while they were in his house? He's not a fool, you know.'

'Where was he during those three days?'

'At home. Winthrop went round to his house, and together they examined the plans. That was on the first day, and Winthrop left the house soon after nine in the evening. Shortly after he had gone Caryu put the plans into his safe. He had them with him next day at the War Office, and put them into the safe when he came home. Not even his secretary knew of their existence. They were returned to Tassel on the following afternoon.'

Linckes' forehead wrinkled in perplexity.

'When did Johnson see them?'

'Before. He worked with Tassel, you see.'

'Um! And where did Sir Charles Winthrop go when he left Caryu's house that night?'

'He went straight down to his place in the country—Millbank. Took Max Lawson with him. He was there for the rest of the week, with a small house-party. That wipes him off the list.'

'What sort of a man is Winthrop?' Linckes asked. 'All I know is that he's fairly young, very clever, and good-looking, rich, and an orphan.'

'He's an awfully decent chap. Everybody likes him. Son of old Mortimer Winthrop, the railwayman. Mortimer separated from his wife when Charles was a kid. You know Charles' history. She went abroad with the other child, I believe, and Mortimer kept Charles. Did awfully well in the Secret Service during the war, and rose like a rocket. He'll be a big man before long, if this awful business is cleared up. Of course, he feels pretty badly about it. Means he'll perhaps have to resign his post.'

'Yes, I suppose so. What about Tassel?'

'Tassel? My dear Linckes, if you're going to shadow him I shall begin to regret I ever put you on to the case. Why, you might just as well suspect Caryu!'

'Ah!' said Linckes, and saw the chief's lips twitch.

The telephone-bell rang sharply before Masters had time to speak again. He unhooked the receiver.

'Hallo! What? Sir Charles? Yes, put him through to me at once, will you?' He nodded at Linckes. 'I thought Winthrop would ring up. I told him about you. Our White Hope. Yes? Hallo! Is that Sir Charles? Good morning! Yes, he's here now. Yes, I've told him all I know. No. I don't think so. Well, he hasn't had much chance to yet. What? Yes, certainly! Now? All right, Sir Charles, I'll send him along. What! Oh, I see! Yes, all right. Goodbye!'

He put the receiver back.

'Sir Charles wants you to go along to his house now, Linckes—16, Arlington Street. Get along there as quickly as you can, will you? I want you to put every ounce of your brain into this. It's a big chance for you, you know.'

Linckes rose, and drew a deep breath.

II

Half an hour later he stood in the library of No. 16, Arlington Street, taking in his surroundings with appreciative eyes. He was examining a fine old chest by the window when Winthrop came in.

Linckes turned. He beheld a tall, slim man of perhaps thirty-five years old, with an open, handsome face, in which sparkled a pair of dark eyes, singularly expressive, and fringed by long black lashes. Winthrop held Linckes' card in his hand, and he came forward, smiling. The smile dispersed the slight sternness about his mouth, and left it boyish and charming. Very simply he told Linckes all that he knew, while the young detective listened intently, occasionally putting a question.

'And that's all,' Winthrop ended ruefully. ''Tisn't much to go on, is it?'

'No; very little. You don't suspect anyone yourself?'

'I don't. I admit it looked like the work of an outsider, but I just don't see how it can be. Masters first suspected Ruthven, my secretary; but that's impossible. I can account for all his movements, and I know that he didn't go near Caryu's place during the three days that the plans were there, for the simple reason that he was with me at Millbank.'

'There might be an accomplice.'

Winthrop screwed up his nose, perplexed.

'Well, of course there might be. But, considering that Ruthven himself doesn't know the key to the safe, I don't see how that helps. Besides, Caryu has a most elaborate alarm thing in his safe-room. Only he and I know the workings to it. Either of us could enter the room without disturbing it, provided we did not try to get in at the window, or any funny trick like that, but no one else could. Whoever did it must have watched the place for months; might even have been in the household. Probably was, because there were no signs of burglary. We had no idea anything had been tampered with until we had ample proof that Russia had learnt the secret of those new subs. I tell you, it's absolutely incomprehensible!'

Linckes pulled out his cigarette-case, frowning. He started to tap a cigarette on it absent-mindedly.

'The servants have been accounted for, I suppose?'

Winthrop's white teeth gleamed in an infectious laugh.

'Oh lor', yes! They're all being watched and interrogated, and Heaven knows what besides. We don't think they have anything to do with it. It's too big a thing.'

'I may act as I think fit?' Linckes asked.

'Absolutely! Interview all the servants, or anyone else you like. I say, don't smoke your own cigarette. Have one of mine.'

Linckes suddenly became aware of the cigarette in his hand.

'I beg your pardon!' he exclaimed. 'I ought to have asked you if you minded smoking. Well, thanks very much!' He took a cigarette from the box Winthrop held out to him, and inspected it. ''Fraid I don't usually indulge in this brand. I smoke gaspers as a general rule.'

He lit the cigarette, smiling.

'Do you? I only smoke these. Sometimes, but very rarely, a cigar.'

'Of course, I really prefer a pipe to anything,' Linckes remarked.

Winthrop shook his head.

'Can't rise to that. I think they're ghastly things. Look here! Have I told you enough? I mean, ask me any question you like.'

'I think I've got enough to keep me occupied for a few days, thanks. I'll be getting along now, if you don't mind.' He rose and held out his hand.

Winthrop jumped up.

'Right-ho! And try your damnedest, Won't you? We're trying to keep a brave front. But—well, it's serious. Just as serious as it can be. And until the mystery is solved Caryu and the rest of us are in a pretty sultry position. And—and it happens to mean rather a lot, to me especially, to have the thing cleared up.'

'You may be quite sure that I shall do my best,' Linckes told him. He gripped Winthrop's hand, and as he did so the door opened.

' Charlie, it really is too bad of you!' chided an amused voice. 'I suppose you've quite forgotten that you asked me to lunch with you at the Berkeley? Oh, I beg your pardon! I'd no idea you were engaged. Daddy, he's deep in business.'

'Well, you shouldn't burst in on him in that unceremonious way,' answered Caryu. He came leisurely into the room and cast a quick glance at Linckes. 'Sorry to intrude like this, Charles. Autonia's fault!'

'How was I to know that he was engaged?' demanded Miss Caryu aggrievedly. She sauntered forward, bowing to Linckes.

'I'm not engaged, I'm sorry to say,' retorted Winthrop. 'I hadn't forgotten, Tony, honestly. I was detained, but I was just coming. Caryu, may I introduce Mr Linckes?'

Linckes found himself the object of a keen scrutiny.

'Very pleased to meet you!' said Caryu, and shook hands. 'You're not Tom Linckes' son, by any chance?'

'Yes, I am, sir. Do you know him?'

'Very well. We were at college together. Hope you'll be able to help us in this business.'

Tony, who had just seated herself on the table, looked up.

'Oh, are you the new detective, Mr Linckes?' she asked interestedly.

'Autonia!'

'Well, all right, daddy. You can't help my knowing. How do you do?'

She extended a small gloved hand to Linckes, who took it, and stammered something that seemed to him inane.

'I hope you'll solve the mystery,' Tony said. 'You don't look frightfully Sherlock Holmes-y, you know!'

She smiled mischievously. It was then that Linckes' heart changed hands.

Then he took his leave of them and went out, all thoughts obscured for the moment by the picture of Miss Autonia Caryu sitting on a table with her slim ankles crossed, and a friendly smile on her beautiful red lips.

III

Nearly three months slipped by, and found Linckes disgruntled. Caryu had been very kind to him. So, too, had Caryu's daughter.

He was a little puzzled by Winthrop. He had been drawn to him from the very first, but he was at a loss to understand his moods. One day Sir Charles would be flippant and gay, the next irritable and restless; he was sometimes most inconsequent and absent-minded. Yet with all this nervous temperament he was undoubtedly clever, always charming, and an eminently responsible person. Once Linckes spoke tentatively to Tony about him, and the girl had laughed.

'Oh, Charlie's an extraordinary man!' she had said. 'A perfect darling, but quite mad! They think an awful lot of him at the War House, you know. Under that flippant manner of his there's heaps and heaps of brain. Everybody loves him, but he's a dreadful trial!'

'A trial?' had asked Linckes. 'Why?'

'Well, he's so—so moody. And he will forget things. Sometimes he'll say a thing to me and contradict it within an hour. When I tease him about it, he just laughs and says, "Oh, did I? That was just hot air, then." It's a pose, I think. He used not to do it so much.'

Linckes eyes narrowed.

'Funny! Doesn't seem quite to fit in with his reputation, somehow.'

'That's why I say it's a pose,' Tony had answered triumphantly.

''Cos really he's a most capable person. Daddy says he's got a huge grip on affairs. And—and now this beastly traitor business has cropped up, and if you can't solve the mystery it means Charlie and daddy'll be under a sort of cloud, and it's—it's such a *shame*! I mean, everyone who knows Charlie knows that he's such a—such a splendid man! Why, look at the things he did during the war! Daddy says he was simply wonderful! Mr Linckes, *please* do try and solve the mystery! I'd—I'd like to put the man who did the thing in *boiling* oil! I *would*!'

'Of course I'm going to try my hardest to get to the bottom of it all,' Linckes said. He tried to speak carelessly. 'I—I suppose you're awfully fond of Sir Charles?'

At that Tony had opened her eyes wide.

'Well, naturally. He's like a dear elder brother, and I've known him ever since I was a kid.'

Linckes' depressed spirits suddenly soared high. A little colour stole up to the roots of his brown hair.

'You bet I'll never rest till I've found the man who's doing the dirty on us all!' he said impulsively. 'Would you—er—Would you be pleased if *I* discovered who it is, Miss Caryu?'

Tony had become suddenly interested in her shoe-buckles.

'I—I hope you'll do the deed, certainly,' she answered.

Linckes took his courage in both hands.

'I mean to. And—and if I do succeed I'm going to ask you a question, Tony.'

'Oh—oh, are you?' had said Tony in a small voice.

Not many days after his conversation with Tony, Linckes presented himself at Winthrop's house, with nothing at all to report. He found Sir Charles writing at his desk. He barely looked up at Linckes' entry, and the detective knew that one of his black moods was upon him.

'Oh, hallo!' said Sir Charles. 'Sit down! Any news?'

'Not much. The butler is now wiped off the list of possibles.'

'Well, I never thought he was a possible.' Winthrop pushed

his chair back impetuously. 'I'm dead sick of the whole business! The wretched culprit, whoever he is, is just one too many for us.'

'I'm dashed if he is!' Winthrop's ill-humour seemed to react on Linckes. 'Hang it all, he must give himself away *some* time!'

'Why? He hasn't done it so far.'

'Pretty soon he'll be trying to bring off another little coup,' said Linckes savagely, 'and then I'll get him!'

'Hope you will, that's all I can say. Help yourself to a cigarette.'

Winthrop pushed the box across to Linckes, taking out a cigarette himself. He lit it, and began to smoke in silence.

Linckes glanced at him idly, and suddenly a furrow appeared between his brows. It struck him that Winthrop was smoking in a curious way, rather as though he were puffing at a pipe. Usually he inhaled with almost every breath, sending the smoke out through his delicately chiselled nostrils.

'If I didn't know you loathed pipes, I should say you were in the habit of smoking one,' remarked Linckes.

The dark eyes looked an inquiry.

'You're treating that unfortunate cigarette as though it were one,' Linckes explained.

Winthrop laughed, throwing the cigarette into the fire.

'Am I? Well, I'm worried. I suppose it's a nervous trick. I feel inclined to do something desperate. If only there were a clue!'

Linckes sighed.

'It's all so hazy,' he complained. 'You can't even know for certain that the plans of the submarines *were* sold. You, can't prove it.'

'Well, if the fact that Germany is building submarines almost in accordance with those plans isn't proof enough, I'd like to know what is!' Winthrop retorted irritably.

'Oh, I believe they were sold all right, but it can't be proved. 'Twasn't as though the plans were stolen. There wasn't even a sign of anyone having tampered with the safe. The room—'

'For goodness' sake don't let's go all over it again!' Winthrop begged. 'We've torn it to bits. Oh, yes, I'm getting peevish, aren't I?' He smiled reluctantly. 'You'd be peevish in my place.'

'You're certainly a bit morose,' admitted Linckes, 'What a mercurial sort of chap you are! A fortnight ago you were perfectly cheerful, and then you were suddenly plunged in despair!'

'Can't help it. Made that way.' Winthrop picked up his pen, and started to address an envelope. 'Oh, now the beastly pen won't write! Damn! I hate quills!'

'Then why use them?'

'Heaven knows! I used to like them awfully. Yes, John?'

The butler had entered the room.

'Mr Knowles to see you, sir.'

Winthrop's brow cleared as if by magic.

'Knowles? Show him in, will you? I say Linckes, do you mind if I interview this man? I won't be many minutes.'

Linckes rose at once.

'Rather not! I'll clear out for a bit, shall I? Can you give me a little time when you've finished? There are one or two questions I want to ask you.'

'Of course! Show Mr Linckes into the drawing-room, please, John.'

Linckes went to the door just as Winthrop's visitor entered. As he went out Linckes cast him a passing glance, and noted that he was an elderly man with grizzled black hair and a short beard and moustache. He bowed slightly, received a pleasant smile in return, which vaguely reminded him of someone, and went out.

He had not to wait long. Presently, from the drawing-room window, he saw Knowles descend the steps of the house and hail a passing taxi. As the vehicle drew up beside the kerb, he turned and saw Linckes. He nodded slightly, smiling, and after speaking to the taxi-driver got briskly into the cab. He let down the window, and as the taxi moved forward looked up at Linckes with a strangely mocking expression in his eyes.

Then the butler came to tell Linckes that Sir Charles was at liberty.

Winthrop was standing with his back to the fire when Linckes came in, smoking, and he greeted the detective with his old, sunny smile.

'I say, I'm awfully sorry to have turfed you out like that!' he exclaimed. 'My time's not my own, you know. What do you want to ask me especially? Didn't you say there were one or two questions?'

Something about him was puzzling Linckes. The frown had quite disappeared from Winthrop's face; the nervous, irritable movements had left him. He was smiling in his own peculiarly charming fashion, and as he looked at Linckes he sent two long columns of smoke down through his nose.

'Every track turns out to be the wrong one,' Linckes answered bitterly. 'I begin to think we shall never get to the bottom of it all.'

Winthrop went to his desk and picked up the despised quill. He held it poised, smiling at Linckes.

'Oh, come! Don't lose hope, Linckes! Something must leak out soon.'

Linckes stared at him.

'Well, I like that! Only half an hour ago you were groaning that nothing would ever be discovered!'

'Yes, but that *was* half an hour ago,' Winthrop explained. 'I've taken a turn for the better since then.'

'You certainly have. You've cheered up wonderfully. Did your visitor bring you good news, or what?'

'Knowles? Nothing to speak of. Now, who on earth has been mucking about with my pen? Beastly thing won't write.'

Linckes leaned forward a little in his chair, eyes narrowed suddenly.

'You said how well it *did* write a moment ago,' he said deliberately.

Winthrop turned the pen round in his hand, and for an instant their eyes met.

'I don't remember saying any such thing,' he replied.

A tiny smile hovered about the corners of his mouth, as if of triumph.

'But you did!' insisted Linckes. 'What an appalling bad memory you've got!'

Winthrop looked back at his hand, scrutinising the bent nib-end that bore unmistakable evidence of having been jabbed down into some hard substance.

'My dear Linckes, it's your memory that's at fault. I believe I cursed the pen.'

He glanced up again, one eyebrow raised quizzingly.

'Did you?' Linckes laughed. 'I must be going to pieces. Yes, I think you did. Still, you *did* say that you always liked a quill, didn't you?'

'Of course I did! It's true, too. Well, I'll see what I can do for you in the matter of Fortescue, Caryu's secretary, that you were asking about. Anything else?'

'No, not at present, thanks. I must be getting along.'

Winthrop laughed, and held out his hand.

'I'll see you tomorrow, I suppose?'

'Oh, I'm sure to come along to report,' Linckes answered, and went out, his temples throbbing with excitement.

IV

A month later Linckes was shown into Caryu's study. Caryu looked at him hopefully, for there was a glitter in Linckes' eyes, and a very purposeful look.

'You've got a fresh suspicion?' he said, with the glimmer of a smile.

Linckes sat down opposite him.

'Yes, sir, I have. And I've come to ask your help.'

'Have you, indeed? I'm sure I have to imitate the famous Watson, haven't I? I shall meekly do your bidding, being myself quite in the dark.'

Linckes laughed.

'That is about the size of it, sir,' he confessed. 'But I really believe I've got on to the right track at last.'

'Any clue?'

'No, sir. Pretty strong suspicion, though.'

A shadow crossed Caryu's face.

'Only a suspicion, Linckes? I seem to have listened to so many.'

'This time it amounts to a conviction, sir. And, because I'm practically certain in my own mind, I'm going to have the cheek to ask you to do something that'll seem quite insane to you.'

Caryu moved a paperweight uncertainly.

'I'm not at all sure that I shall comply, then. What is it?'

Linckes clasped and unclasped fingers rather nervously.

'Sir, you've got the plans of the new plane here, haven't you?'

The elder man smiled a little.

'You ought to know, Roger. You and your colleagues are supposed to be keeping an eye on them. But if you imagine they can be taken out of this new safe, you're wrong. No one knows the secret of the combination except myself.'

'I know, sir. I don't expect the thief to attempt it. I want you to tell Sir Charles, when you see him tomorrow, that you have made one or two suggestions on the plans, and are sending them by your secretary to his house for him to see.'

Caryu reddened.

'What are you driving at?' he asked levelly. 'What do you mean?'

'Just that, sir. I think Mr Fortescue carries documents to Sir Charles' house fairly often? Minor documents, I mean.'

'Certainly. But I do not understand—'

'I know, sir. I want you to give Mr Fortescue a package containing blank sheets. Keep the plans in your safe.'

Caryu drew himself up.

'Linckes, you must please explain yourself. I don't know what crack-brained notion you have got into your head, but if you are insinuating that Sir Charles is the criminal, I may as well tell you that it is an impertinent and foolish suggestion.'

'I'm not insinuating anything, sir. I can't even tell you who I suspect. But I do beg of you to just do as I ask without mentioning my name. It can't do any harm, and I believe it'll enable me to find the man who's betraying us all.'

Caryu's face softened a little.

'You think that whoever is doing it will try to intercept Fortescue on his way to Winthrop's house? It is rather improbable, isn't it? He has only a few yards to go.'

'That's just what I'm counting on, sir. It's too short a distance for him to take a taxi. He doesn't, I know, for I've often been with Winthrop when he has come over with a letter for you, or, as I said, some minor document.'

Caryu was silent for a moment. He looked Linckes over, frowning.

'And when Fortescue comes to Winthrop and gives him a package of blank sheets,' he said sarcastically, 'what am I to say to Winthrop? You don't seem to understand that if that happens my action in sending blank sheets amounts to a very serious insult.'

'No, sir. If Fortescue does arrive, unmolested, and with the blank sheets, you can explain why it was done. You don't suspect Sir Charles. I haven't said that I do. It's quite simple.'

Caryu smiled faintly.

'Very well. I will tell Winthrop that among other things I am sending him the plan of the new 'plane. Are you satisfied?'

'Yes, sir. Thank you!'

Linckes rose and prepared to depart.

'What happens if Fortescue is sand-bagged?' inquired Caryu. 'What will he think of your little plot?'

'Not much chance of that, sir,' Linckes grinned. 'From Park Lane to Arlington Street isn't a far cry, and it's never exactly deserted. But don't tell Fortescue anything, will you? Not even that you are supposed to be sending plans. Send him off at the usual time.'

'"The usual time" covers a wide margin,' remarked Caryu. 'I shall send him at about six in the evening. That is the most usual time.'

'Then tell Winthrop, sir, casually. And thanks awfully!'

He shook Caryu's outstretched hand, and went to the door.

'Mind you, I think you've got a bee in your bonnet,' Caryu warned him. 'If you haven't—well, it'll be a fairly large feather in the bonnet instead.'

V

'Got another fit of the blues, Winthrop?'

Sir Charles looked up, smiling.

'Getting rather frequent, aren't they? Sorry I'm such a surly brute. It's very nice of you to consent to stay and dine with me.'

Linckes leaned back in his chair, crossing his legs.

'It's jolly nice of you to ask me,' he retaliated. 'I don't wonder you're feeling depressed.'

Winthrop gave a short sigh.

''Tisn't very surprising, is it? We don't seem to get any forrader, do we? Since Masters' ingenious butler theory there haven't been any fresh suspicions, have there?'

Linckes turned sharply. Caryu's secretary had just come into the room. Linckes looked him over quickly, conscious of a sinking sensation of disappointment somewhere in the region of his stomach.

'Good evening, Sir Charles! Mr Caryu sent me with one or two things for you to sign.'

Winthrop had risen.

'Yes, that's right. Oh, don't go, Linckes! It's nothing private.'

Dully, Linckes watched Fortescue lay his dispatch-case on the table and insert a key into the lock. After a moment's twisting and turning he drew it out again and looked up at Winthrop, rather white about the mouth.

'Funny!' he said uneasily. 'It won't open!'

Linckes' heart leapt. He lounged back at his ease, outwardly careless, but his eyes never left Winthrop's face.

'Won't open? Perhaps you've got hold of the wrong key?'

'No; it's a special lock and key.'

Fortescue's eyes were rather wide.

'Then something must have gone wrong with the lock,' said Winthrop impatiently. 'You must force it.'

'Ah!' Relief sounded in the secretary's voice. 'That's it, of course. I got hung up on one "island" in the middle of Piccadilly, and when half the people surged forward into the road there was a bit of a scrum, and I dropped the case. I suppose that did it.'

'You dropped it?' Winthrop asked. 'Rather careless, surely!'

Fortescue flushed.

'Yes, Sir Charles. But it fell at my feet, and I'd picked it up in a flash.'

'I see.'

Breathlessly Linckes watched the secretary burst open the lock.

'Mr Caryu told me to ask you to run through his memorandum concerning the Crosstown Barracks, sir. Here it is!'

He was turning over some long envelopes. One of these he handed to Winthrop, who took it and pulled out several folded sheets.

There was a moment's silence, broken only by the crackle of paper as Winthrop spread open the papers. Then Linckes saw Sir Charles look up sharply at Fortescue, the lines about his mouth suddenly grown stern.

'Ah, yes!' he said quietly. 'Anything else?'

'Yes, sir. Mr Caryu placed several documents in the case. I don't know what they were, but he told me to give—'

'Give them to me, please. Thank you!'

Winthrop cast a hurried glance at each of the sealed documents handed to him. Then he laid the whole sheaf down upon his desk, and shot the secretary a long, keen look. Lastly he turned to Linckes.

'This is a case for you, I think,' he said.

'Oh!' Linckes sat up. 'What is the matter?' He looked inquiringly from Winthrop's impassive countenance to the secretary's surprised, vaguely nervous expression. 'Anything wrong?'

'A very great deal. Come and look at these documents. You too, Fortescue.'

Linckes went to the table and spread open the various sheets. Looking over his shoulder, the secretary gave a startled gasp. But Linckes' heart was beating madly. Every sheet was blank.

'Good heavens!' he said.

'Exactly!' Winthrop turned to Fortescue. 'Mr Fortescue, I saw Mr Caryu this morning. He informed me that he was sending certain important papers. Did you know this?'

'No, Sir Charles. Oh, heavens! Surely—'

He broke off, staring blankly at Winthrop.

Winthrop sat down at his desk.

'Your case was stolen, Mr Fortescue. Presumably when you dropped it in Piccadilly.'

'But—but, Sir Charles, it was only on the ground for an instant. Besides, who *could* know that the case contained anything important?'

'I'm afraid I cannot tell you that,' Winthrop said coolly. 'Will you please try and remember the exact circumstances of your dropping it?'

'I—I crossed to the "island", Sir Charles, and waited for the stream of traffic to pass. There—there were a good many people on the "island", and, as I said, there was a lot of pushing and barging. There was a stout woman who rather lost her head and tried to make a dash for the other side of the road, and had to get back again to the "island" in a hurry. She must have pushed the man standing next to me. Anyway, he fell against me, and I lost my balance, and—and I dropped the case.'

'And this man,' said Winthrop. 'Was he by any chance carrying a dispatch-case?'

The secretary moistened his lips.

'I—I'm afraid I didn't notice, sir. I dare say he was. It was at an hour when most men are coming away from business, and—Oh, heavens!' He ended on a stricken note. 'What a *fool* I am! What a damned fool! If only I'd known that there were important papers in the case! Sir Charles, it—they—they weren't the new plans?'

'That is precisely what they were,' Winthrop answered.

He unhooked the receiver from the telephone and called a number. While he was waiting to be connected he glanced at Linckes, smiling rather wearily.

'Well, here's your chance, Linckes. And he's got away with it, the scoundrel! Hallo! Is that Mr Caryu's house? Put me through to him, please. Winthrop speaking. Thanks!'

Again there was a pause. Then he began to speak into the telephone. Quite calmly he told Caryu all that had happened. At the end he hung up the receiver and nodded to Fortescue.

'Mr Caryu wants you to go back, Fortescue.'

Some of the pallor left Fortescue's face.

'Mr—Mr Caryu doesn't suspect me, sir?'

'No. You'd better get along as fast as possible. Tell Mr Caryu that I shall come round at once.'

'One moment!' interposed Linckes.

'Can you remember what the man who fell against you looked like?'

'Just—just ordinary,' answered the unhappy secretary. 'He was middle-aged, I think, but I won't swear to it.'

'I see. Thank you! Winthrop, I won't stay to dinner, if you'll excuse me. I'll get right on to this at once.'

Winthrop nodded.

VI

It was close on eleven o'clock that same evening, and Arlington Street was very quiet. One or two people passed down the road, and presently someone left Winthrop's house and went away in a large limousine. Several people had visited Sir Charles that evening, and he himself had returned from Caryu's house shortly after eight.

For some time after the last visitor had departed there was silence in the street, and then the chunk-chunk of a London taxi made itself heard, and in a few moments a car drew up outside No. 10. A man in an overcoat and opera hat got out, paid the driver, and mounted the steps to the front door. He pressed the bell, and stood waiting to be admitted. He was a medium-sized man, inclined to stoutness, and with a short, grizzled beard. The butler opened the door.

'Is Sir Charles in?' asked the newcomer. His voice was rather hoarse and guttural.

'Yes, sir. But I don't think he's seeing anyone else today.'

'Would you ask him if he will give me a moment?'

The man handed John a card. The butler read it.

'Oh, Mr Knowles, sir! I beg your pardon! Will you come in while I see if Sir Charles is still up?'

Knowles entered the house, and the door closed again.

From the shadowy depths of the area two men rose stealthily, and crept up the steps to the street.

'Got him!' Linckes whispered. 'Your revolver ready, Tomlins?'

His companion nodded.

'Yes, it is. Wish I knew what you're about.'

'You soon will know,' said Linckes grimly. 'Your men are prepared?'

'Inspector Gregory's at the back of the house, Mr Linckes, and Inspector Marks is just down the road. He'll come up to the house with Sergeant O'Hara as soon as we get in.'

'All right. Don't forget that all you've got to do is to follow me and to do as I say instantly.'

'No, sir. Carry on!'

Linckes ran lightly up the steps of the house and rang the bell. After a short pause the door was opened.

'John, is Sir Charles up?'

'Yes, sir. Oh, is it you, sir? Come in!'

Linckes walked into the hall, followed by the other detective. John looked at Tomlins surprisedly.

'Sir Charles is engaged just at the moment, sir. But if you'll wait—'

'Oh, is he? We'll just wait here, then. Don't bother to stay, John.'

He turned to Tomlins.

'The library is at the bottom of this passage. It'll be locked, and we shall wait in absolute silence outside. There are two men in the room, and when they come out you are to cover Sir Charles Winthrop. Leave the other to me. See?'

'Can't say I do, sir. But I'll do as you say, of course.'

'Then follow me. Not a sound, remember!'

In perfect silence the two men took up their stations on either side of the library door, revolvers held ready. The murmur of conversation could be heard within, and although neither Linckes nor Tomlins could distinguish any word spoken, they could hear that the talk was worried.

Then, after what seemed an interminable time, the key scraped in the lock, and Winthrop opened the door. Behind him stood the man Linckes had seen entering the house a few minutes ago.

For a moment there was dead silence as Winthrop stared haughtily from one levelled revolver to the other. Even now Linckes could not but admire the indomitable courage and sang-froid that Sir Charles displayed.

'Really, Mr Linckes!' he said, faintly amused. 'May I ask what you think you are doing?'

'Hands up, please!' Linckes said sternly. 'If you attempt to escape I shall shoot!'

Winthrop shrugged slightly, and raised his hands. Still he preserved that air of haughty bewilderment. But the man beside him had grown very pale, and was biting his under-lip. The hands that he held up were trembling.

Linckes advanced into the room, covering his man.

'I may be doing you a grievous injury, Sir Charles, but I do not think so.' With his free hand he drew a silver whistle from his pocket and blew three shrill blasts upon it. 'Mr Winthrop, will you be so good as to remove your wig and your beard? Your make-up is excellent!'

Disregarding Tomlins' levelled revolver, Sir Charles lowered his hands. He sank down into his chair, and regarded Linckes with a twinkle in his eye. His fine lips smiled generously.

'Do tell me how you found out,' he said pleasantly. 'Take the wig off, Alec. The game's up!'

With starting eyes Tomlins watched the pseudo Mr Knowles tear off his wig and beard. Night black hair with a faint crinkle in it was revealed, and when the man had rubbed his face with his handkerchief, removing most of the cunning make-up, the detective's jaw dropped.

'Sir—Sir Charles!' he gasped.

A little, low laugh came from Winthrop.

'Wonderful, isn't it? Quite difficult to tell us apart.' He paused, listening to the sudden pandemonium without. 'Well, you've roused the whole household, Linckes, and I suppose your assistants are even now invading my house. You must allow me to congratulate you. I never thought you'd discover me. And I've had a fair run for my money, haven't I? I don't regret it a bit. Poor Alec's looking rather glum. But then he always was rather peevish That was what made you suspect me in the first place, wasn't it? Jolly clever of you to think of that blank sheet scheme. I ought to have guessed, of course. Fact of the matter is, you took me in. I didn't think you suspected me.'

VII

Tony dabbed at her eyes, and gave a tiny sob.

'It's so awful, Roger! I c-can't bear to think of Charlie doing such a thing. I—I just can't realise it. It—it seems impossible!'

Linckes patted her shoulder uncomfortably.

'And—and somehow I can't feel angry with him. He was always such a dear!'

'I know. He was just one of those people who couldn't run straight? 'Twasn't altogether his fault. And one must admire his courage.'

Tony was silent for a moment, still mopping her eyes.

A pair of soft arms stole round his neck.

'No; and I can't help admiring you!' whispered Tony.

GEORGETTE HEYER

Georgette Heyer, unquestionably one of Britain's best-loved historical novelists, was born in 1902. She began her career as an author at the age of 19 with the novel *The Black Moth*, an exciting story about highwaymen set in the eighteenth century, which Heyer had expanded from a short story written to entertain her brother. It was the first of what would eventually be more than fifty novels, the vast majority of which dealt with the Georgian and Regency periods of British history.

While views differ as to the extent to which her books trod new ground rather than reviving scenarios and ideas from Jane Austen, Georgette Heyer was extremely popular and she remains so today, loved in particular for her lively and compelling characters and for the comedy and humour with which her novels are peppered. As a critic put it in 1929, Heyer's historical novels 'are not historical [and] they are not novel, but they are very good fun'.

The same can be said for the dozen novel-length 'thrillers', as she called them. The crimes with which these are concerned were considered by some contemporary critics, among them Dorothy L. Sayers, to be largely unoriginal but, as with her much more popular historical fiction, Heyer's crime fiction was consistently praised for her rich characterisation, vivid dialogue and warm humour. Her dozen detective mysteries are regularly reprinted and some in particular have real merit, in particular *A Blunt Instrument* (1933),

Death in the Stocks (1935) and *Envious Casca* (1941), a clever locked room mystery. Unlike her historical novels, Heyer's detective mysteries did not require extensive research, and they were for the most part based on plot outlines provided by her husband, the eminent lawyer George Rougier. Heyer's interest lay mainly in the characters and she would routinely seek Rougier's advice when it came to unravelling the mystery in the final chapters and ensuring she had 'played fair' throughout the novel.

Heyer was a very private person, once saying that her readers would find all they needed to know about her in her books, which she considered as, 'unquestionably, good escapist literature'. A heavy smoker, she died from lung cancer in 1974.

Georgette Heyer's only uncollected detective short story, 'Linckes' Great Case', was first published in the very rare magazine, *Detective*, on the 2nd of March 1923, and I am very grateful to the bookseller Jamie Sturgeon for providing a copy.

'CALLING *JAMES BRAITHWAITE*'

Nicholas Blake

CHARACTERS

LADY ALICE BRAITHWAITE . . . wife of Sir James, daughter of Greer.

LAURENCE ANNESLEY . . . junior partner in Sir James Braithwaite's firm.

LAURA ANNESLEY . . . his sister.

SIR JAMES BRAITHWAITE . . . shipowner.

NIGEL STRANGEWAYS . . . private detective.

CAPTAIN GREER . . . master of the '*James Braithwaite*'.

MR MACLEAN . . . first mate of the '*James Braithwaite*'.

SMITH . . . a seaman.

PART I
THE CRIME

ALICE: I hate him! There, I've said it at last, I hate him.

LAURENCE: But, Alice—

ALICE: No, I'm not being hysterical. I won't—sometimes I think that's what he wants—to drive me mad.

LAURENCE: Now you *are* exaggerating, my dear. James is not—well, not one of the world's leading charmers. But—

ALICE: Hate. I wonder if you know what it's like. Real hate. Oh, Laurence, what's going to happen? I've stood it for nearly three years. The humiliations, the scenes, the horrible little pinpricks, all the things he does to break down my pride. You can't imagine—

LAURENCE: Perhaps I can, my dear. Remember, I have to work with him.

ALICE: It's like having a—a huge toad sitting across the path, blocking it, blocking it, blocking out the whole future. Oh God, I—

LAURENCE: There's one way out, Alice?

ALICE: One way out.

LAURENCE: My darling. I love you. You must know that. Come away with me. Leave him.

ALICE: I wonder if you mean that. Do you realise—? No, listen. It would be the end of your partnership in the firm. Daddy would be sacked too, and James would see he never got another ship. I couldn't do it.

LAURENCE: My sweet, do you love me?

ALICE: I—oh, I don't know, Laurence. I'm fond of you. You've been so kind to me all these months—

LAURENCE: Kind!

ALICE: No, please don't make it more difficult for me. You know I can't. If it was just ourselves—but there's Daddy. He set all his hopes on me. He wanted me to have the world—and he thinks I've got it. Lady Braithwaite! No, it'd break his heart. I am grateful to you, my dear—

LAURENCE: Very well. I understand. I'll not say a word more about it. For the present. Perhaps James will fall overboard during the voyage or something.

ALICE: The voyage. I'm dreading it. Do you know why I'm so upset this morning? Why James is bringing you and Laura and me on the voyage? Do you realise what this Mr Strangeways is for?

LAURENCE: Strangeways? He's coming as a temporary secretary, your husband told me.

ALICE: Secretary! Laurence, it's vile. James suspects—shh—oh, it's Laura.

LAURA: Hello, you two. You look very cheerful, I must say. I've just been laying in some Mother Siegel's. Where's James?

(*Fade. Sound of subdued voices. Voice of Page-boy growing louder.*)

PAGE-BOY: Calling Sir James Braithwaite. Room 15. Calling Sir James Braithwaite. Room 15. Calling Sir James Braithwaite. Room—

(*Snapping of fingers.*)

JAMES: Here, boy. Haven't you got eyes in your head? What is it, now?

PAGE-BOY: Mr Nigel Strangeways to see you, sir. In the lobby, sir.

(*Sir James rises. As he goes out, the murmur of voices is heard again. Above it, three voices rise.*)

VOICE I: Who's that old bird, Reggie?

VOICE II: Sir James Braithwaite. The shipowner. Sailing on one of his own ships next tide, I believe.

VOICE III: Jimmy Braithwaite sailing on one of his own ships? Crikey! Is he tired of life, or what?

(*Fade. A door closes.*)

JAMES: Morning, Strangeways. So you've decided to take on the job, eh?

NIGEL: Yes, Sir James. I—

JAMES: Just step out on the terrace with me a moment. It'll be quieter out there.

(*Sound of swing-door. Lobby noises cut off.*)

NIGEL: (*brisk, cheerful, not at all overawed by Sir James*) Yes. You made such a mystery of it over the telephone. And I just can't refrain from poking my nose into mysteries.

JAMES: (*very frigid*) Indeed? It is understood that you will be sailing as my employee, my secretary?

NIGEL: (*faintest note of amusement in voice*) Yes, Sir James.

JAMES: Very well, As I think I told you, we are to sail on one of my own ships: the '*James Braithwaite*'. She's a freighter of some 2,500 tons, with accommodation for a few passengers. My wife—Lady Alice; Laurence Annesley and his sister, Laura—he's a junior partner in my firm—will be coming as well. We go out on the evening tide.

NIGEL: And where does the—er—secretary come in?

JAMES: Your job is to keep your eyes open, Strangeways—and your mouth shut.

NIGEL: Hmm. A sea trip and a nice fat fee for—keeping my eyes open.

JAMES: When I need a job doing, young man, I can afford to pay for it.

NIGEL: So you've purchased the best detective that money can buy, to keep his eyes open. Open for what, Sir James? . . . Are you anticipating an attempt on your life, for instance?

JAMES: Don't be ridiculous . . . I'll tell you more when we get on board. There's several kinds of treachery, young man.

NIGEL: Just one thing, Sir James. Why the '*James Braithwaite*'? Why have you decided to sail on a small, uncomfortable cargo-steamer, when—

JAMES: That's my affair. Nothing wrong with my ships, let me tell you—

(*Fade out. Fade in to quayside. Sound of seagulls, winches, commands. Voices, Tyneside accent, are of two stevedores and one seaman.*)

VOICE I: Got the owner sailing with you, Geordie, eh?

VOICE II: Aye, the old—(*loud expectoration*). And a cargo of skirts. Women on board! I don't like it. It's not lucky.

VOICE III: Won't be the first time a Braithwaite boat's been unlucky, mate.

VOICE II: Aye, and for why? Look at the way he sorts them out. Ruddy suicide ships, that's all they are.

VOICE I: Reckon your owner doesn't worry. He gets the insurance, see?

VOICE II: Too true he does. (*lowers voice*) I was on the '*Mary Garside*', chum. Gaw, she was a packet! Chuck a cupful of water at her, and she'd start her rivets. And roll! Jees, we was hardly off soundings, and she rolled so you could see passing ships through the ventilators. When she went down—

VOICE III: Pipe down, Geordie. There's the master going aboard.

GREER: Morning, Mr Maclean.

MACLEAN: Good day to you, Captain.

GREER: Got your loading done?

MACLEAN: There's just those crates for Number 3 hold to go in. She's trimmed by the head a wee bit, I'm thinking.

GREER: Step this way a minute, mister. Let Mr Cafferty attend to it.

(*Steps along deck, down companionway. Noises shut off as they enter the captain's saloon. The two men relax.*)

GREER: A-Ah. Well, Donald, they'll be aboard presently, it's a great day for me—Alice and Sir James sailing with us.

MACLEAN: I don't grudge it to you, John. I wish he might have picked on some other ship, though.

GREER: I know. But ye must let bygones be bygones.

MACLEAN: Bygones be bygones! I could forgive him for sailing out the '*Mary Garside*' ill-found that voyage. Maybe I'd find it in my heart to forgive him that. But when he sets on his lawyers at the inquiry to make out it was my fault, when he loses me my master's ticket—na, na, John, flesh and blood wilna endure that.

GREER: I know, Donald. But he had to save his face. And he kept you on in the company's service.

MACLEAN: Wasn't that great! A robber steals your reputation and allows ye to keep your badge-cap! And now he's coming aboard to gloat over it. I'm wondering how I'll keep my hands off the blasted wee runt. Why must he choose the '*James Braithwaite*'?

GREER: You know that as well as I do. (*lowers voice*) It's a nice bit of eyewash, sailing on one of his own fleet. After the '*Triton*' and the '*Mary Garside*', well, there was nasty talk going about. So he's sailing with us just to show the Braithwaite ships are all right. And he chose this ship because he knows she's the soundest in the fleet. He's got his head screwed on all right.

MACLEAN: He's a damned hypocrite, John, and you know it.

GREER: Eh, well, you don't get on in this world without a bit of that, and he's good to Alice. Remember that, Donald. He's made her happy. You should see the letters she writes me. She's got everything she wants, everything I wanted for her—money, a grand position, hobnobbing with the swells—

MACLEAN: *Everything* she wants?—

GREER: Eh, it's a fair knock-over. To think of my little Alice riding about in a Rolls-Royce—and me who started life a deck-side Geordie. Lady Braithwaite. Her mother'd be proud if she could see her now. And I'm to be a grandfather next year. What d'ye say to that, Donald? A grandfather . . . No, I'll not deny he gave you a bad deal: but he's not as bad as he's painted—not when he makes my little girl so happy . . .

(*Fade out. Fade in to dockside noises and approaching voices*)

ALICE: Hello, Daddy, here we are.

GREER: Well, isn't this great! Why, you're looking pale, lass. She needs the sea air to put some roses in those cheeks, doesn't she, Sir James?

JAMES: Evening, Greer. Everything ready for us? You know Mr Annesley. This is his sister—Captain Greer, Miss Annesley. My secretary, Mr Strangeways.

GREER: Welcome aboard, Miss Annesley. Gentlemen. Hope you'll enjoy your trip. This way, please. The steward'll show you your cabins.

LAURA: Steward! Oh, it makes me feel quite queer already. Stewards and basins do seem to go hand in hand, if you follow me, don't they? Oh, Captain Greer, I do hope this is a steady boat. I always . . .

(*Fade out with receding footsteps. Fade in to general conversation.*)

GREER: This is my saloon. You must make yourselves at home here. There's a radio set: and you'll find playing-cards, and—

NIGEL: And dominoes? Do you play dominoes, Captain, during the long dog-watches? That's a game I—

LAURA: Oh, Captain, what's that perfectly dinky contraption over there?

GREER: That's the radio telephone. You can talk to your friends ashore.

LAURA: Well, isn't that sweet?

(*Knock at door. Door opens*)

GREER: My first mate. Mr Maclean.

MACLEAN: Good evening, ladies. Evening, Sir James—and gentlemen. Pilot's come aboard, sir.

GREER: Very well. Carry on, mister.

(Deck and bridge sounds. Orders. Casting away the hawsers. Sound of telegraph. Steam-whistle. Pulse of engines grows louder, quicker. Presently its rhythm is mixed into a different sound—the tapping of a pencil on a table. We are in James' and Alice's cabin.)

ALICE: James. Please stop tapping with your pencil. It—it gets on my nerves . . . Why are you looking at me like that?

JAMES: Aren't you a little overwrought, my dear? I was just thinking, you've a nice long sea-voyage before you. A nice long voyage with—your husband.

ALICE: Yes, James.

JAMES: And with young Laurence Annesley. You don't seem so very pleased with the prospect. Two admirers, and no competition.

ALICE: Can't you say straight out what you mean? Isn't it rather cowardly—this perpetual hissing?

JAMES: Of course, he's a younger man than I am, isn't he? A good-looking young fellow, too.

ALICE: James, this is contemptible. I—

JAMES: And sea air does bring 'em up to scratch, doesn't it? These shipboard romances. The moon, a lonely deck, the waves swirling past . . . But of course you wouldn't encourage anything like that. You're faithful to your husband, who has—the money. Yes. But you'd be glad of a little extra protection, I'm sure. Strangeways will help to keep an eye on you, and see that nothing—

ALICE: So that's it. I *was* right. You've hired him to spy on me. You admit it.

JAMES: Indeed no. I admit nothing. Ask him, if you like.

ALICE: You haven't even got the courage of your own vileness. You have to get somebody else to do your dirty work.

JAMES: But perhaps it's a case of shutting the stable door after the horse is out. This child you're going to have. It *is* mine? You're quite sure?

ALICE: (*breaks down: sobbing*) Oh! How dare you say—? Oh God!

(*Slam of door. Sobbing fades; then grows louder again, more intermittent, mixed with sea-sounds. We are on deck.*)

LAURENCE: Darling, what is it? Tell me. Has he been—?

ALICE: (*during this conversation she gradually controls herself, till towards the end her voice has the flat finality of despair*) He—no, I can't tell you, it's too horrible for words.

LAURENCE: Tell me. You'll feel better for it.

ALICE: He said—he accused me of—that the child I'm going to have isn't his.

LAURENCE: Not his? But that's—

ALICE: He hinted things—about you and me. That's what he's got Mr Strangeways for. To spy on us. He's a detective.

LAURENCE: The swine. That settles it. I'm going to have to talk with Sir James Braithwaite.

ALICE: No. Stop. It's no good. You don't understand, Laurence. I don't mind the things he says. Not now. I'm broken in, I suppose. One gets used to anything, even the misery he's made of my life. Yes, I've forgotten what happiness feels like. But when he talked about my child, it came to me—what sort of life would it have with him for a father? I can put up with his bullying, his meanness, his suspicions: but I won't let my baby—

LAURENCE: You must leave him, my dear. You must.

ALICE: He'd never let me go . . . (*very flat, speaking half to self*) Unless . . . yes, there is one way . . . Perhaps I shall leave him . . . Sooner than he—

(*Cough. Footsteps*)

GREER: Well, lass, sharpening up your appetite? That's right. But what's this? Tears? Well now, this won't do.

ALICE: It's nothing, Daddy. I—this baby makes me feel weak and silly. It's nothing, really.

GREER: Come now, that's better, take my arm. We'll go into the saloon. It's just on dinner-time.

(*Footsteps recede. Noises of sea. Then fade into general conversation*)

LAURA: Well, that's what I call a slap-up dinner. I only hope I will be able to keep it inside me. Is it going to be very rough tonight, Captain?

GREER: Don't you worry, Miss Annesley. Weather reports say we may run into a bit of local fog. Nothing worse than that. She'll not jump about much till we get into the Bay, and you'll have your sea-legs by then.

LAURENCE: Well, Strangeways, how's the—secretarial work going?

NIGEL: O.K., thank you kindly.

JAMES: Mr Strangeways is a *confidential* secretary, Annesley?

LAURENCE: yes. To be sure. A formidable responsibility—to be the repository of Sir James Braithwaite's secrets.

(*Embarrassed pause*)

LAURA: I'm sure it'll be very nice for Mr Strangeways to have something to do—to keep his mind occupied, I mean. I mean, there are limits to one's capacity for playing deck-quoits. I say—that reminds me—where are all the sailors, Captain?

GREER: The sailors?

LAURA: Yes. I was on the deck quite a long time before dinner, and I never saw a single one. I thought there'd be dozens of them—polishing the binnacle and letting the bullgine run, and so on.

LAURENCE: Bad luck, Laura. All your beautiful cruise-wear wasted.

GREER: A modern cargo vessel pretty well runs itself, Miss Annesley. You'll not find seamen on the deck, except when the watches are being changed. We've nothing to do but squirt oil into the engine now and then; the rest of the time we spend knitting socks for our nippers.

LAURA: Knitting socks?—He's pulling my leg, isn't he, Sir James?

JAMES: The modern seaman certainly has an easy time of it, compared with the man of thirty years ago.

GREER: Aye. All that brass we had to clean. Wherever they could put a bit of brass on those old tramps, they did.

JAMES: —And nowadays he doesn't know when he's well off. Better food, more comfortable quarters, overtime pay.

MACLEAN: He'll have an easy time, maybe—till the ship starts to go down under his feet.

(*Another embarrassed pause*)

LAURA: Oh but how gruesome you are, Mr Maclean. Have you ever been in a shipwreck? Do tell us all about it.

GREER: Well, if you ladies and gentlemen will excuse me, I'll just see if the shore agent has got anything to tell me. He rings me up at 8.30. You see, Miss Annesley, I just put on these headphones, and turn this switch, and—

(*Pause. Faintly we hear, as over the radio telephone—*)

VOICE: '*James Braithwaite*'. '*James Braithwaite*'. '*James Braithwaite*'. Cullercoats radio calling. Cullercoats radio calling. Cullercoats radio calling the '*James Braithwaite*'. Over to you.

GREER: '*James Braithwaite*' answering. '*James Braithwaite*' answering Cullercoats radio. Over to you.

(*Sound of switch being put over. The others begin to talk quietly, so that we now only hear the captain's end of the conversation. His sudden excitement, however, soon stops their talk.*)

GREER: Hello, Tom . . . How's the wife keeping? . . . That's fine. Anything for me? *What's that?* (*Long pause: the passengers' talk dies out: we hear squeaky unintelligible noises through the radio telephone.*) Well, that's a nice thing. Why can't they keep a better look-out? . . . Eh? . . . And what am I supposed to do about it: I haven't got a padded cell on my ship, have I? . . . Oh, get out with you! . . . Oh, he is, is he? Yes, I see. I'll take action. Yes, I'll take action. Goodbye, Tom.

(*Pause. They are expecting the captain to speak*)

JAMES: Well, Greer, what is it? What was all that about?

GREER: I've had a rather disagreeable message . . . A warning, you might say.

ALICE: 'Warning', Daddy? What—?

GREER: it seems a chap escaped from that lunatic asylum at Newcastle last night.

LAURA: Oo-er. Is he swimming after the ship?

GREER: They've just had a report that someone answering to this chap's description was seen hanging round the docks early this morning, near the '*James Braithwaite*'. A big chap, with a limp—a sort of shuffling walk—is the way they describe it. An ex-seaman, he is.

JAMES: (*sharply*) Well, what about it?

GREER: Well, it seems this chap has delusions. He's what they call a homicidal maniac.

ALICE: Oh!

GREER: Now don't upset yourself, lass. No reason to suppose the fellow got aboard. We'll have the ship searched, just to make sure he's not here. Mr Maclean, take a search-party if you please, and go right over her.

MACLEAN: Very good, sir.

(*Gets up: sound of door closing*)

GREER: Lucky we've got a detective on board. May come in useful.

LAURA: Detective? Well, I'll say this is a surprise packet. First we get a loony, then a detective—what'll you give us next?—the Grand Lama of Tibet? Where is this mysterious detective?

GREER: (*quickly*) Now I think we'll rearrange the cabins a bit. Miss Annesley won't want to sleep alone. We'll put her in with Alice: and Sir James can shift into Number 2 cabin—that's the single one next to mine. Mr Annesley and Mr Strangeways stay as they are in Number 4. Just an extra precaution. No need to fret yourselves. Mr Maclean will find this chap, if he is on board.

(*Fade. Fade into forecastle. Talk. An accordion or mouth-organ playing*)

MACLEAN: Tumble out, the watch. Search-party. Stowaway aboard. Evans, take three men and search the deck—lifeboats and everything. Watch yourselves, he may show fight. Escaped lunatic. The rest, follow me.

(*Someone whistles. Feet running up ladder, dispersing. Voices. We follow footsteps along deck, down iron ladder into engine-room. Sound of engines grows louder. Following conversation carried on fortissimo*)

MACLEAN: Evening, Chief.

VOICE: This is an unexpected pleasure. What can I do for you, Mr Maclean?

MACLEAN: Search-party. There's a lunatic escaped. He may have come on board last night.

VOICE: Indeed? If you're looking for lunatics, ye'd better try the bridge, Mr Maclean. Ye'll not find them in the engine room.

MACLEAN: Sorry, Chief. Captain's orders.

VOICE: Lunatics! In my engine room! T'chah!

(*Sounds of search. Noise of engines fades into noise of sea. On deck. Footsteps*)

VOICE I: He's not in this lifeboat, any road.

VOICE II: I always said it was unlucky, bringing women aboard.

VOICE III: My sister's husband went balmy. Used to see angels walking about in t'back yard, in nightgowns. Fair knock-off, he was. They had to put him away.

(*Voices and steps approaching*)

VOICE I: He's nowhere on deck, sir.

MACLEAN: Very well, Evans. Follow me, you men. Number 1 hold first.

(*Sound of steps: then of hatch-cover being removed. Fade into comparative silence of hold, where men are bumping about in search.*)

MACLEAN: Show a light over here.

VOICE II: Jees, look at that, chum! The man with the glaring eyes!

VOICE III: It's a rat, you silly bleeder!

VOICE II: What I say is, no luck ever came from having women aboard.

VOICE I: We heard yer. Talk about a needle in a haystack. Chap could stay hidden for days in this stuff. What I say—

(*Fade. Fade in to saloon*)

GREER: I didn't want to say it in front of the ladies. But I don't mind telling you gentlemen, with all this cargo we've got below hatches, a chap might stay hidden for a long time—search-party or no search-party. He's an ex-seaman. He'd know his way about.

JAMES: Why wasn't a better watch kept while she was tied up at the quay? Who's responsible?'

GREER: You can't allow for escaped loonies running about loose on the docks.

JAMES: You'd better put about, Greer. We're only four hours out.

GREER: (*with cheerful authority. Throughout this scene, James is made to sound peevish and insignificant, in contrast with the assurance of the two ship's officers. We must realise that he is a rather nasty, frightened little businessman, quite out of his element*) No need for that, Sir James.

JAMES: May I remind you that you're in my employment?

GREER: And you're in my ship, Sir James. I'm master of this ship, and my authority holds till we're on soundings again . . . No, I'll not make a laughing stock of us both by putting back to port just on the strength of a rumour.

JAMES: You may regret this, Greer.

NIGEL: We mustn't get excited. After all, even if he is on the ship, it doesn't necessarily mean he's going to run amok and stab us right and left. Homicidal maniacs are like volcanoes—dormant most of the time. Unless this chap's delusions are centred on someone on board, he—

(*sharp knock at door*)

JAMES: (*frightened*) What's that?

GREER: Come in.

MACLEAN: Ship searched. No sign of a stowaway, sir.

JAMES: (*breathes audible sigh of relief*)

GREER: Well, Mister Maclean?

MACLEAN: I was just thinking, Sir. Ye said this escaped lunatic was reported to be an ex-seaman—a big chap with a limp, a sort of shuffling walk—didn't ye?

GREER: That's so. What about it? . . . Come on, man.

MACLEAN: Well, e-eh, there was a seaman aboard the '*Mary Garside*' when she went down, A big chap. His leg was crushed when the falls of the starboard lifeboat parted. As you know, we were in an open boat for six days. What with the pain of his leg, and—well, he went off his head.

JAMES: Poor fellow. Very tragic. But I scarcely see—

MACLEAN: They put him in an asylum. The asylum at Newcastle. (*Pause*)

JAMES: (*whispers to self*) At Newcastle?

NIGEL: Ah. This gets more interesting. Perhaps the fellow's delusions *are* centred upon someone in this ship. In which case—

JAMES: (*wildly*) What the devil is this nonsense?

MACLEAN: The poor chap, in his crazed mind, may be holding one of us responsible for the injuries he—

JAMES: Are you suggesting?—

MACLEAN: Maybe it's myself. I was captain of the '*Mary Garside*'. Maybe you, Sir James. Maybe he holds one of us responsible for the parting of that lifeboat's falls, for the ship going down, and—

JAMES: I advise you to be careful, Maclean.

MACLEAN: But we're agreed it's just a delusion the poor fellow has. Neither of us could have wanted the '*Mary Garside*' to founder. Eh, Sir James?

GREER: Well, I'll be turning in for an hour or two. My watch at midnight. As you're sleeping alone, Sir James, perhaps you'd like the loan of a revolver. I've got a spare one here—

(*Sound of drawer being opened, revolver taken out and loaded*)

—not that I think you'll need it. The chances are twenty to one against the chap being on board. And remember there's a communicating door between your cabin and mine, in case you—(*voice drowned by bellow of steam-whistle overhead*)

JAMES: Presumably some sort of watch will be kept on the decks?

GREER: Surely. But if this fog thickens, it may not be so easy to—

JAMES: Lot of damned poppycock. You're all talking like a pack of old women. I'm off to bed. Tell the steward to call me at 7.30 sharp, Strangeways . . . You and your lunatics!

(*Door slams*)

NIGEL: I suppose the women have locked their door all right.

GREER: I told them to, Mr Strangeways. Just to be on the safe side.

(*Fade in to women's cabin. Stirring of bunks. Prolonged blast of steam-whistle overhead.*)

LAURA: Rocked in the bosom of the deep. What life! (Yawns) I wish I could go to sleep. You did lock the door, darling, didn't you?

ALICE: Yes, Laura. We're quite safe in here. I wish Daddy hadn't to go on the bridge tonight, though.

(*Faint sound of telegraph. Steam-whistle again.*)

LAURA: These marine noises get in my hair. Why must they keep blowing that hooter? We might as well be sleeping in the Zoo.

ALICE: It's not that. It's because we're afraid. I know Daddy told us they'd searched the ship and couldn't find anyone: but we don't really believe it yet. That's why we can't go to sleep.

LAURA: You've said it, darling . . . Should we shut the port-hole, do you think? Just to be on the safe side?

ALICE: If you like . . . No. No, please don't. I hate feeling as if I was in prison.

LAURA: Snap out of it, duckie—this is sheer claustrophobia.

ALICE: Claustrophobia? (*slight laugh*) Is that what you call it? (*half to herself*) You don't know what it's like to be in prison. No hope of escape . . . Ever . . . But there is a way out—

LAURA: Darling, what is it? Won't you tell me? I know you're unhappy. I've felt it for a long time. Is it—about Laurence?

ALICE: I'm sorry. I can't tell you. It's my own trouble. I asked for it, and I've got it. Perhaps it will be over soon. Try and go to sleep, Laura.

LAURA: I—oh well. (*begins to yawn. Yawn is taken up by long blast on steam-whistle. As this fades, we hear Laurence muttering*)

LAURENCE: Damn this fog! (*stirs restlessly*) You awake, Strangeways?

NIGEL: (*grunts*)

LAURENCE: (*yawning*) I always used to yawn like this before house-matches. Nerves, I suppose . . . What's the time?

NIGEL: Just after eleven. Are you nervous now?

LAURENCE: I suppose I am. Maniacs wandering about the ship, and all. You seem to take it very calmly. Quite the imperturbable detective.

NIGEL: Who told you I was a detective?

LAURENCE: Alice did. And as we're on the subject, I must say, it's not a job I'd fancy—spying on an innocent woman. Still, every man to his taste.

NIGEL: That's not exactly what Sir James engaged me for, you know. He said he wanted me to keep my eyes open.

LAURENCE: Huh! Open for what?

NIGEL: That's just what I asked him. He was waiting till he got me aboard the lugger before informing me about my—duties.

LAURENCE: You have to hand it to the old swine.

NIGEL: Was it you or Lady Braithwaite who told Captain Greer I was a detective?

LAURENCE: I certainly didn't. And I'm sure Alice wouldn't—*What's that?*

(*Faint sound of scuffle overhead, cut off at once by roar of steam-whistle*)

NIGEL: Steam-whistle.

LAURENCE: I thought I heard something else. On the deck overhead. A sort of scuffling noise.

NIGEL: You're very much on edge tonight, Annesley. Something on your mind?

LAURENCE: What the devil should I—(*obvious attempt at*

self-control) I've just got a feeling that something's going to happen. That's all. Silly of me—

(*Fade. Sound of telegraph and steam-whistle. Sound of waves. Hold this a little. Then a bell rings clearly, for change of watch*)

LAURA: (*wearily*) Bells now, What'll they do next to keep us awake? (*stirs in bunk*) Only twelve o'clock. I feel as if I'd been awake for—Alice! ALICE! Listen. Can't you hear something?

(*We begin to hear a shuffling, dragging footstep approach: it passes along the deck overhead; and recedes. As it approaches, Laura screams*)

LAURA: A sort of shuffling walk! That's what they said—Alice, it's that man—the lunatic!

ALICE: Oh God, it's going towards the bridge. Daddy. Quick, we must—

(*Knocking on door*)

NIGEL: Is anything the matter?

(*Door opens*)

ALICE: Quick! We heard footsteps overhead. Shuffling footsteps—going towards the bridge. Oh, do hurry!

NIGEL: All right. We'll find him. Don't worry. You two get inside and lock the door again.

ALICE: No, I'm coming with you.

LAURA: I'm not staying here alone.

(*Confused footsteps running up companionway towards bridge. Distant Voices. Noise of sea getting louder*)

GREER: Now what's all this? Alice, you'll catch your death.

ALICE: Oh, Daddy, are you all right? Thank God!

NIGEL: Lady Braithwaite heard footsteps on the deck. Going aft. Dragging footsteps. She thought it was—

GREER: There's no one come up on the bridge. Bar myself, I've just come to relieve Mr Cafferty. And Smith, of course.

NIGEL: Smith? Who's Smith?

GREER: Seaman. Didn't you hear the bell for change of watch?

Smith came aft to take his trick at the wheel. Did you see anyone on deck, Smith?

SMITH: No, sir.

ALICE: He must be hiding somewhere.

GREER: Mr Cafferty. Will you and Mr Annesley just take a look round? Here's my revolver.

NIGEL: No, wait a minute. Just a minute . . . Smith, you haven't by any chance got a wooden leg?

SMITH: No, sir.

LAURENCE: Big gun misfires.

NIGEL: Hmm. But I see you're wearing—. May I borrow this man a moment, Captain?

GREER: I don't see—Very well. Take the wheel, if you please, Mr Cafferty.

NIGEL: Now, Smith. Kindly walk up and down on the bridge outside.

SMITH: Yes, sir.

(*Footsteps. They are exactly like those we heard before, only louder*)

LAURA: Oh! But that's what we heard. How?—

NIGEL: That'll do, Smith, thank you.

SMITH: Yes, sir. (*Returns into wheel-house*)

VOICE: Keep her as she's going.

SMITH: As she's going, sir.

NIGEL: It's quite simple, really. You see, Smith is wearing slippers. That accounts for the shuffling noise. And they're not a pair: one's too big for him: hence the drag in his step. Storm in teacup now blown itself out.

ALICE: Oh, I'm so glad! I was afraid—

GREER: There, there, lass. No need to fret now. It's all over. All over. Supposing you go and take a glass of spirits in the saloon, before you turn in. You deserve one, Mr Strangeways. Very smart it was of you.

LAURENCE: Before we start celebrating our narrow escape from

Jack the Ripper, there's one thing I'd like to point out. One thing the eminent detective seems not to have noticed . . . Why is Sir James Braithwaite not in our midst? We made enough shindy to wake him.

(*Confused outbreak of voices*)

ALICE: —but he *is* a heavy sleeper.

GREER: Go along round and knock at his door, then.

(*Voices and footsteps: we follow them down companionway, along short passage. They halt.*)

ALICE: (*whispers uncertainly*) He'll be terribly angry if we wake him up.

LAURENCE: Let him.

NIGEL: No need. Listen.

(*We hear sound of snoring*)

LAURA: No doubt about *that*. He's a heavy sleeper all right.

LAURENCE: So that's that. No maniacs. No casualties. Run along and get to sleep, girls. Tomorrow's another day.

(*Noise of doors opening and shutting. Bunks creaking*)

LAURENCE: Well, I fancy we'll be able to go to sleep now.

NIGEL: Yes. Reaction after strong excitement. Better than morphia.

LAURENCE: Though I don't know why. We've still no proof this lunatic isn't on board.

NIGEL: For that matter, we've no *proof* there ever was a lunatic.

LAURENCE: But that's crazy. Why—

NIGEL: We only heard the captain's end of that little chat over the radio telephone.

LAURENCE: But why on earth should he want to start a scare, especially with his own daughter on board?

NIGEL: Why indeed? If I knew that, I'd know the answer to quite a few—

LAURENCE: Oh you're dreaming! If Cullercoats really transmitted no message about an escaped lunatic, it'd be bound to come out before long. And then Braithwaite would take the hide off Captain Greer—father-in-law or no father-in-law.

NIGEL: Damn! That reminds me. I forgot to tell the steward to call Sir James. I'll have to do it myself. 7.30 he said, didn't he? I'll set my alarm-clock.

(*Sound of setting clock, drowned by crescendo of sea and engine noises. They are held for a few moments, then fade, and we hear the alarm-clock ringing.*)

NIGEL: (*stops alarm: yawns*) 7.30. Ugh, what an hour to get up!

(*We hear him getting out of bunk, putting on dressing-gown, leaving cabin. As he does so, he is singing quietly to himself, in Dowland's setting,* 'Come, heavy sleep, thou image of true death.' *He knocks on Sir James' door*)

NIGEL: Sir James! . . . *Sir James!* . . . Half past seven, sir! SIR JAMES!

(*Rattles door handle*)

NIGEL: Bolted inside. He certainly is a heavy sleeper. Better try the other door.

(*We follow his footsteps*)

NIGEL: Oh, it's you, Captain. I can't make Sir James hear. The other door is bolted. May I try the one through your cabin?

GREER: Surely. I'll come with you.

(*Footsteps. Door opening*)

NIGEL: Not here. That's funny . . . And his bunk. Look, Captain . . . Blankets crushed and rumpled, as if he'd been lying *on* them, but didn't actually get inside. You've not seen him this morning?

GREER: He's not in the saloon. May be on deck, or in the engine room. I'll take a look round.

(*We hear him climb the companionway. Presently Nigel, humming same tune, follows. Noise of sea.*)

NIGEL: Hello, Mr Maclean. You looking for something too?

MACLEAN: (*startled; wary*) Me? What's that? No.

NIGEL: Well, I am. Sir James seems to have disappeared.

(*Sound-track quickly through ship. Clatter of plates and knives *in forecastle. Sound of engines. Stokers at furnaces. These natural sounds punctuated by an accelerating rhythm of footsteps and occasional snatches of conversation:* 'Anyone seen Sir James about?' . . . 'Owner's disappeared.' . . . 'Hope the old sod's chucked himself over t'rail.' . . . 'Ye'll not find him in my engine room.' . . . 'I always said it weren't lucky to have women on board.' . . . 'Anyone seen Sir James Braithwaite?' . . . 'Talk about death-ships! Now he's got a bit of—' *fade back to sound of sea.*)

MACLEAN: But it's ridiculous. He couldn't disappear. Not on a ship.

NIGEL: (*dreamily*) There's all that sea, remember. All round us. Perhaps that's where he's hiding. (*sharply*) The ship has been painted recently, hasn't she?

MACLEAN: Aye. Specially for this voyage.

NIGEL: A whited sepulchre. But someone's been scratching it. Look at those long scratches on the deck. Just where you're standing. And here are some more marks, on the rail.

MACLEAN: What?—

NIGEL: Can't you see it? Feet dragging, kicking? And then a splash . . . Mr Maclean. I want you to radio the shore at once. Find out if there's any more news of that escaped lunatic. Quick, it's urgent.

MACLEAN: (*doubtfully*) Well, I'll ask Captain Greer—

(*Voice and footsteps receding. Nigel begins to whistle his tune through his teeth. The sound is mixed into the ziz-ziz-ziz of radio sender. Hold radio sound for a few moments, then back to Nigel whistling. He begins to sing, very softly,* 'Come, heavy sleep, thou image of true death,' *as he moves about deck in search of something. Breaks off sharply, and mutters the words to himself*)—

NIGEL: Come, heavy sleep . . . thou image of true death . . . Is that it? . . God, what a nerve! . . . Yes, it might have been done like that . . . If only I could find what Maclean was looking for . . .

(*Crawls about deck again, whistling through teeth. After a while, exclaims* 'Ah!' *Whistles again. Mix into ziz-ziz of radio sender. Pause. Sea-sounds as Maclean emerges from wireless room. Follow his footsteps along deck.*)

MACLEAN: Here's your answer.

(*Rustle of sheet of paper*)

NIGEL: 'Escaped lunatic recaptured near docks late last night.'

MACLEAN: He wasn't on the ship after all, ye see.

NIGEL: But there *was* a lunatic. Yes, I—

(*Approaching footsteps*)

GREER: No sign of Sir James anywhere. I'm afraid it looks as if—

NIGEL: No, we shan't find him now. Not alive. There's something I have found, though. It had got underneath that lifeboat. Look.

GREER: A button.

NIGEL: Yes, gentlemen. A little brass button.

(*Noise of sea increases: gradually fades out*)

PART II
THE SOLUTION

(*Sound of engines and sea. Fade into Nigel talking. Almost throughout this scene his voice remains patient and dispassionate, like that of a doctor in his consulting room—in contrast with the nervousness, caginess etc. of the others*)

NIGEL: . . . so that's the set-up. Just after midnight Lady Braithwaite and others heard her husband snoring in his cabin. At 7.30 he wasn't there. It was during that period then, on the face of it, that he was thrown overboard.

LAURENCE: Thrown overboard? But, damn it all, Strangeways, you've just told us the escaped lunatic was recaptured on shore. Are you suggesting that someone on this ship—?

GREER: That's a serious statement, Mr Strangeways. Have you not considered the possibility of suicide?

NIGEL: Suicide? You can't seriously mean that, Captain? With those scratches on the deck and rail—signs of a struggle? No, it won't do, I'm afraid. Why should he anyway? He had power, money, reasonable health. Lady Braithwaite, can you imagine any reason why he should want to kill himself?

ALICE: No . . . No, I can't.

NIGEL: On the other hand, everyone here with the exception of Miss Annesley and myself had remarkably strong reasons for killing him.

(*General outrcry and tohu-bohu*)

ALICE: No, that's not true! Daddy had no reason. He never knew—

NIGEL: Never knew how wretchedly unhappy your husband made you? Is that so, Captain Greer? . . . Look here, this is a miserable business for us all. Can't we finish it quickly? If the one who killed Sir James would confess, it'd save the rest of us a great deal of pain. (*pause*) No? Well, I'm afraid I must go through with it, then. Mr Maclean, where were you between midnight and 7.30?

MACLEAN: In my cabin asleep, till four o'clock. Then I went on watch. Mind you, I can't prove I was below asleep, but—

LAURENCE: Well, it couldn't have been Alice or Laura or myself. We were in double cabins. None of us could have got out without waking the other.

NIGEL: Oh, but I think you could. Remember the alarm we had at midnight. None of us had been able to go to sleep before that. The reaction was a big one. We'd all sleep very sound after it—unless one of us wanted to keep awake.

LAURENCE: If you're suggesting that Alice—

NIGEL: She had the strongest motive for getting rid of Sir James. She said more than once—so Miss Annesley has told me—that there was 'only one way out—'

LAURA: I'm sorry, darling. He—he sort of wormed it out of me. I didn't mean.

ALICE: When I said there was only one way out, I was thinking of something else.

GREER: Alice!

ALICE: I was going to kill myself. I couldn't stand it any— (*she breaks down*)

NIGEL: You'd better take her out, Miss Annesley.

(*They go out*)

NIGEL: Lady Braithwaite couldn't have done it, of course. She's not nearly strong enough to throw a man overboard.

LAURENCE: Then why did you bully her into—

NIGEL: Control yourself. I said this was going to be a painful business for us all, if the murderer didn't confess. He still has the chance. (*pause*) Oh well. Now, have any of you asked yourselves how the murderer got Sir James out on deck at all? He wouldn't be apt to go for a constitutional round the deck in the early hours of the morning, especially when he believed there might be a maniac sloping around, out for his blood. Would he, Annesley?

MACLEAN: That's a verra interesting point.

NIGEL: I suggest the one thing strong enough to master Sir James' fear was his jealousy. He was insanely jealous of his wife and Annesley. Now supposing Annesley somehow conveyed to Sir James that he had made an assignation with Lady Braithwaite to meet him on the deck when everyone was asleep—allowed Sir James to intercept a note, perhaps; or—

LAURENCE: This really is fantastic, Strangeways. If he had intended to catch me out, as you suggest, would he have been snoring away at midnight?

NIGEL: It might have been a—pretence of snoring.

GREER: Oh, come now, Mr Strangeways. A pretence of snoring. That's a bit too clever, isn't it?

LAURENCE: (*shaky*) But what motive could I have had? I was sorry for Alice—well, fond of her, if you like. But to kill her husband on the strength of—damn it, that'd be carrying chivalry a bit far.

NIGEL: Motive? There's more than that to it, Annesley. With Sir James dead, your own position in the firm would be stronger, and you'd stand an excellent chance of marrying the widow—and the fortune which her husband leaves her.

LAURENCE: Why, damn you, Strangeways! I—

NIGEL: And what's more. Just after eleven o'clock last night, you claimed to hear a scuffling noise on the deck above our cabin—

GREER: What's this?—

NIGEL: Was that to give yourself an alibi? A bit unlucky for you we had that false alarm at midnight, otherwise we'd not have heard the snoring in Sir James' cabin, and we'd have assumed he was thrown overboard at eleven o'clock, when you claimed to hear sounds of a struggle on deck—yes, and just on the spot where there are marks of a struggle, where you crept out later, when I was dead asleep, and killed him.

LAURENCE: (*shouting*) Shut up! Stop it! I tell you, you're all wrong! You—

NIGEL: Motive. You're the only one with a motive strong enough—

LAURENCE: You're wrong. Listen to me. Captain Greer—Soon after we came aboard, Alice ran out on deck. I was there. She was crying. Her husband had been bullying her again. She told me James had hired you to spy on her. She—I thought then, from something she said, that she might be going to kill herself. She said she couldn't face it any longer, because of the baby she's having. And her father came up, while she was talking. He may have heard everything she—

NIGEL: Is this true, Captain?

GREER: Aye, I heard them. That's how I knew you were a detective.

NIGEL: Well, I've got that out in the open at last. It's taken a long time.

MACLEAN: If ye think Captain Greer has anything to do with it, ye're making a fool of yerself. He was on watch from midnight till four of the morning. After that, I came on watch, and he stayed on the bridge chatting with me till about half seven.

NIGEL: Till 7.30, when I found you—looking for something on deck. Your watch didn't end till eight o'clock. Why weren't you on the bridge? Just what were you looking for on deck, at the spot where Sir James went overboard?

GREER: Steady now, Mr Strangeways, steady.

NIGEL: Was it this?

(*We hear sound of button thrown down on top of table*)

Was it a little brass button, torn off the sleeve of a uniform coat—during a struggle?

LAURENCE: Your methods really are intolerably dramatic.

NIGEL: Still feeling the strain a bit, Annesley? Relax, man, relax. Well, Mr Maclean?

MACLEAN: Anyone might lose a brass button, I'm thinking. There's three mates on this ship—

NIGEL: And a captain. Yes. But you've not answered my question . . . very well. Leave that aside a moment. You were captain of the '*Mary Garside*' when she foundered. At the inquiry you lost your ticket: Braithwaite's counsel managed to fasten the blame for losing the ship on you. Right? But she went down because Braithwaite had sent her out ill found. You had a grudge against him since then. He ruined your career.

MACLEAN: I'll not deny it'd have been a pleasure to me to see him roasting in hell. But that doesn't mean I murdered him.

NIGEL: Indeed no. Tell me, what were you and Captain Greer talking about on the bridge?

(*Perceptible pause*)

MACLEAN: On the bridge? When?

NIGEL: You said he stayed chatting with you on the bridge after his watch was over, till nearly 7.30. Three hours and a half. A longish chat. Must have been cold out on the bridge. But, if you'd gone into the wheel-house, the helmsman would have heard what you were saying, eh? What were you talking about?

MACLEAN: (*not hysterical, like Laurence: grim*) Damn and blast your impertinence! By what right—

GREER: Steady on, Donald. Maclean and I are old friends, Mr Strangeways. We just got talking about old times.

NIGEL: Old friends? Old friends might give each other alibis.

MACLEAN: If one of us had left the bridge, you fool, the man at the wheel would have noticed it. Just ask him.

NIGEL: I have. I'm satisfied that neither of you did. And the man is certain that Captain Greer was in the wheel-house with him from midnight till four a.m. You have no alibi for that period, Mr Maclean.

MACLEAN: I'm verra well aware of that.

NIGEL: You've also got a brass button missing from the sleeve of your great coat—the one you were wearing last night.

LAURENCE: (*gasps*) What's that? Is that true?

NIGEL: You see, Mr Maclean? Motive, opportunity, and the one damning clue—they're all against you. What have you to say?

MACLEAN: I'm saying nothing.

NIGEL: Well, Captain. What are we to do about it? The case is out of my hands now. It's up to you.

GREER: (*heavily*) Up to me, eh? Aye, you're right. But have done without all this tomfoolery. I could see what you were driving at, Mr Strangeways. I'd best—

MACLEAN: (*shouts*) All right, John, all right! I'll admit it. I killed Sir James. For God's sake stop this havering and put me under arrest!

GREER: Nay, Donald, I'll not let you do it.

NIGEL: I'm sorry about this, Captain, But there it is. It had to be you or Maclean. The button is damning evidence. And Sir James would never have stirred out of his cabin for Maclean; he'd be too suspicious of him, after the '*Mary Garside*' episode.

LAURENCE: Look here, what is all this? Haven't you just admitted that Captain Greer has an alibi for the period from midnight till 7.30?

NIGEL: He has. But Sir James was killed before midnight. He was killed just after eleven o'clock. You heard it happening. That scuffle on the deck overhead.

MACLEAN: Ah'm thinking we have got a lunatic on board now. Sir James was heard snoring in his cabin at midnight. Ye heard him yourself, Mr Strangeways.

NIGEL: That was Captain Greer we heard snoring . . . I'd better start at the beginning. The escaped lunatic. It's a captain's responsibility to prevent panic spreading on board his ship. So why, when he got that message over the radio telephone, did Captain Greer announce it publicly, in front of two women, his own daughter one of them? He could so easily have instituted a quiet search without alarming them. But he wanted to establish an atmosphere of panic.

LAURENCE: But why?

NIGEL: First, because it enabled him to shift round the cabins—to put Sir James in a single cabin, with a communicating door leading to his own. Second, to get Sir James' nerves on the jump. You'll remember he lent him a revolver.

GREER: Aye. Ye're too smart for me, Mr Strangeways. I can see ye know it all.

NIGEL: Except what went wrong with your original plan.

GREER: I'll tell ye. I overheard what Alice was saying to Mr Annesley before dinner last night. It was—a terrible shock to me. You see, I'd encouraged her to marry him. I wanted her to have everything I couldn't give her. I firmly believed she was happy with him. And then to find out—well, it near broke my heart. I could see she was at the end of her tether. Aye, and it was a tether: Sir James'd never have let her go. I was afraid she meant to—end it. Then that message came through. And I saw what I could do.

NIGEL: It was to have been an accident of some sort, wasn't it?

GREER: That's right. I told him—I'd overheard Alice appointing to meet Mr Annesley on deck at eleven o'clock. I knew that'd get him out. I put on carpet slippers. It was foggy, ye remember. I was going to stalk him along the deck, make him think I was the lunatic, put the fear of God into him. He'd lose his nerve and fire at me with the revolver I lent him. I'd fire back . . . It sounds a daft sort of plan now. But I had to . . .

NIGEL: You'd be able to say afterwards that you'd assumed it was the lunatic, and you'd shot him in self-defence after he'd fired at you? What went wrong?

GREER: I'll tell ye. It was like this . . .

(*Fade into sea sounds. Blast of steam-whistle. Stealthy pad of feet. We hear Sir James mutter,* 'What's this? I can't see . . . Damn this fog.' *Limping shuffle of footsteps.* 'Oh God, it's—No, no! Keep away! Oh God, I' . . . 'It's you, Greer. What the'—*choking scream. Sound of struggle, cut off by blast of steam-whistle. Fade*)

GREER: Ye see. I meant him to lose his nerve. But not all that much. He was so frightened, he couldn't even yell or use his revolver. When I came up with him, he was cowering behind a ventilator, frozen there, like a rabbit with a stoat after it. But he'd seen me by then. I had to go through with it. I clapped my hand over his mouth and dragged him along the deck. Then he did begin to struggle. I dragged him to the rail and tipped him over. The steam-whistle had been blowing a lot. I hoped it'd drown the noises he made, and the splash. But Mr Maclean was on deck, forward. He saw enough to—. That's what he and I were talking about on the bridge.

NIGEL: Yes. I see. And when we had that false alarm at midnight, you saw how it could give you an alibi. Annesley noticed that Sir James was not present. You told us to go round and knock at his cabin door. The moment we left the wheel-house, you hurried through your own cabin into Sir James', lay down on the bed, and began to snore . . . Yes—'Come, heavy sleep, thou image of true death.'

MACLEAN: Don't believe a word he's said. It's not true. He's trying to protect me. It was I—

NIGEL: No, Maclean, it won't do. You've done your best for him. Yes, when you discovered last night a sleeve-button was missing from Captain Greer's greatcoat, you tore one off your own. I found that coat, as you meant me to. But I also searched Captain Greer's cabin: and I found a button had recently been sewn on his greatcoat—the thread was new. You were searching for the missing button on deck this morning, weren't you? Well, Captain, I'm sorry about this, but there's no help for it. I'll have to—

(*Sharp sound of drawer being opened*)

GREER: No. Not that way. Keep back, all of you! I'll have some use for this revolver after all . . . Donald, look after her, old friend. She'll be alone now.

MACLEAN: I will, John, goodbye.

GREER: You'll get your master's ticket back now, Donald, maybe . . . Good luck.

(*Footsteps slowly receding during this conversation. Door slams and is locked. General movement in the saloon. Pause. A distant splash. Cry of* 'Man overboard!' *Sharp ring of telegraph and roar of reversed engine. Running of feet on deck. Orders. Boat is being swung out. All fade to sound of wind and waves*)

NICHOLAS BLAKE

'Nicholas Blake' is the pen name of Cecil Day Lewis, who was born in Ballintubbert, Ireland, in 1904. He was educated at Sherborne and at Wadham College, Oxford, where he became friends with W. H. Auden, Louis MacNeice and Stephen Spender.

Day Lewis was primarily a poet. His first collection of verse, *Beechen Vigil*, was published in 1925, and several other collections appeared to wide acclaim over the next ten years. However, poetry paid so poorly that, to supplement his income and specifically to pay for the repair of a leaking tiled roof, Day Lewis decided to turn his hand to 'commercial prose' and what he later called 'the most popular of modern blood sports', detective fiction. His first mystery, *A Question of Proof*, was published in 1935 and appeared under the pseudonym Nicholas Blake, the surname taken from his mother's maiden name. The detective is Nigel Strangeways, a charismatic amateur investigator and gentleman sleuth, superficially in the tradition of Lord Peter Wimsey and Albert Campion but based, at least initially, on Day Lewis's Oxford friend W. H. Auden. Conveniently for Strangeways, his uncle is an Assistant Commissioner at Scotland Yard.

His second mystery, *Thou Shell of Death*, was published in 1936, and in 1937 the growing stature of 'Nicholas Blake' was recognised by his election to the Detection Club, the writers' dining club founded by Anthony Berkeley, who had also attended Sherbourne.

Day Lewis found it very easy to write detective stories, unlike his 'straight' books, and the 'Nicholas Blake' books were immensely popular. They are characterised by strong, innovative set ups and careful, fair play detection. Moreover, as might be expected, they are very well written, with fully realised characters and insightful commentary on social mores.

In all 'Nicholas Blake' wrote twenty novels and Day Lewis also used the pseudonym for reviewing detective fiction in *The Spectator* magazine. Fifteen of the mysteries feature Strangeways who over time became less like Auden and more like the author, although aspects of Day Lewis's life are apparent from the outset, particularly his complicated love life. The first 'Blake', *A Question of Proof*, is set at a public school very much like Cheltenham College, where Day Lewis had been teaching at the time of its publication; so much so that the novel almost cost the author his job when the chairman of the board of governors became convinced—wrongly—that the novel amounted to a confession of adultery with the head teacher's wife. Another of the Strangeways series, *Minute for Murder*, is as much a satire as a detective story and was inspired by Day Lewis's experience working for the Ministry of Information during the Second World War. In another, *Head of a Traveller*, the central character is a well-known poet suffering writers' block. Of the series, the finest is *The Beast Must Die*, which was inspired by an incident involving Day Lewis and one of his sons. It is an ingeniously structured novel of revenge and was filmed in 1969 as *Que la Bête Meure*, directed by Claude Chabrol.

In 1951, Cecil Day Lewis was appointed Professor of Poetry at Oxford, and in 1962 he was appointed to a similar position at Harvard. On 1 January 1968 he was appointed Poet Laureate by H.M.Queen Elizabeth II, on the advice of Prime Minister Harold Wilson, but his tenure ended prematurely in 1972 with his death from cancer.

'Calling *James Braithwaite*' was first broadcast on the BBC Home

Service on 20 and 22 July 1940 as part of a series of two-part plays by members of the Detection Club produced by John Cheatle. The script is published here for the first time.

THE ELUSIVE BULLET

John Rhode

'By the way, professor, there's something in the evening paper that might interest you,' said Inspector Hanslet, handing over as he spoke the copy he had been holding in his hand. 'There you are, "Prominent City Merchant Found Dead". Read it, it sounds quite interesting.'

Dr Priestley adjusted his spectacles and began to read the paragraph. The professor and myself, Harold Merefield, who had been his secretary for a couple of years, had been sitting in the study of Dr Priestley's home in Westbourne Terrace, one fine June evening after dinner, when Inspector Hanslet had been announced. The inspector was an old friend of ours, who availed himself of the professor's hobby, which was the mathematical detection of crime, to discuss with him any investigations upon which he happened to be engaged. He had just finished giving the professor an outline of a recent burglary case, over which the police had confessed themselves puzzled, and had risen to go, when the item in the newspaper occurred to him.

'This does not appear to me to be particularly interesting,' said the professor. 'It merely states that on the arrival of the 3.20 train this afternoon at Tilbury Station a porter, in examining the carriages, found the dead body of a man, since identified as a Mr Farquharson, lying in a corner of a first-class carriage. This Mr Farquharson appears to have met his death through a blow on the side of his head, although no weapon capable of inflicting such a blow has so far been found. I can only suggest that if the facts are as reported, there are at least a dozen theories which could be made to fit in with them.'

'Such as?' inquired Hanslet tentatively.

The professor frowned. 'You know perfectly well, inspector, that I most strongly deprecate all conjecture,' he replied severely. 'Conjecture, unsupported by a thorough examination of facts, has been responsible for more than half the errors made by mankind throughout the ages. But, to demonstrate my meaning, I will outline a couple of theories which fit in with all the reported facts.

'Mr Farquharson may have been struck by an assailant who left the train before its arrival at Tilbury, and who disposed of the weapon in some way. On the other hand, he may have leant out of the window, and been struck by some object at the side of the line, or even by a passing train, if he was at the right-hand side of the carriage, looking in the direction in which the train was going. Of course, as I wish to emphasise, a knowledge of all the facts, not only those contained in this brief paragraph, would probably render both these theories untenable.'

Hanslet smiled. He knew well enough from experience the professor's passion for facts and his horror of conjecture.

'Well, I don't suppose the case will come my way,' he said as he turned towards the door. 'But if it does I'll let you know what transpires. I shouldn't wonder if we know the whole story in a day or two. It looks simple enough. Well, good-night, sir.'

The professor waited till the front door had closed behind him. 'I have always remarked that Hanslet's difficulties are comparatively easy of solution, but that what he calls simple problems completely baffle his powers of reasoning. I should not be surprised if we heard from him again very shortly.'

As usual, the professor was right. Hanslet's first visit had been on Saturday evening. On the following Tuesday, at about the same time, he called again, with a peculiarly triumphant expression on his face.

'You remember that Farquharson business, don't you, professor?' he began without preliminary. 'Well, it did come my way after all. The Essex police called Scotland Yard in, and I was put on to it. I've solved the whole thing in under 48 hours. Not a bad piece of work, eh? Mr Farquharson was murdered by—'

Dr Priestley held up his hand protestingly. 'My dear inspector, I am not the least concerned with the murderer of this Mr Farquharson. As I have repeatedly told you, my interest in these matters is purely theoretical, and confined to the processes of deduction. You are beginning your story at the wrong end. If you wish me to listen to it you must first tell me the full facts, then explain the course of your investigations, step by step.'

'Very well, sir,' replied Hanslet, somewhat crestfallen. 'The first fact I learnt was how Farquharson was killed. It appeared at first sight that he had been struck a terrific blow by some weapon like a pole-axe. There was a wound about two inches across on the right side of his head. But at the post-mortem, this was found to have been caused by a bullet from an ordinary service rifle, which was found embedded in his brain.'

'Ah!' remarked the professor. 'A somewhat unusual instrument of murder, surely? What position did the body occupy in the carriage when it was found?'

'Oh, in the right-hand corner, facing the engine, I believe,' replied Hanslet, impatiently. 'But that's of no importance, as you'll see. The next step, obviously, was to find out something about Farquharson, and why anyone should want to murder him. The discovery of a motive is a very great help in an investigation like this.

'Farquharson lived with his daughter in a biggish house near a place called Stanford-le-Hope, on the line between Tilbury and Southend. On Saturday last he left his office, which is close to Fenchurch Street Station, about one o'clock. He lunched at a restaurant nearby, and caught the 2.15 at Fenchurch Street. As this was the train in which his dead body was found I need hardly detail the inquiries by which I discovered these facts.'

The professor nodded. 'I am prepared to take your word for them,' he said.

'Very well, now let us come to the motive,' continued Hanslet. 'Farquharson was in business with his nephew, a rather wild young fellow named Robert Halliday. It seems that this young man's mother, Farquharson's sister, had a good deal of money in the business, and was very anxious that her son should carry it on after Farquharson's death. She died a couple of years ago, leaving rather a curious will, by which all her money was to remain in her brother's business, and was to revert to her son only at her brother's death.'

The professor rubbed his hands. 'Ah, the indispensable motive begins to appear!' he exclaimed with a sarcastic smile. 'I am sure that you feel that no further facts are necessary, inspector. It follows, of course, that young Halliday murdered his uncle to secure the money. You described him as a wild young man, I think? Really, the evidence is most damning!'

'It's all very well for you to laugh at me, professor,' replied Hanslet indignantly. 'I'll admit that you've given me a line on things that I couldn't find for myself often enough. But in this case there's no possible shadow of doubt about what happened. What would you say if I told you that Halliday actually travelled in the very train in which his uncle's body was found?'

'Speaking without a full knowledge of the facts, I should say that this rather tended to establish his innocence,' said the professor gravely.

Hanslet winked knowingly. 'Ah, but that's by no means all,' he replied. 'Halliday is a Territorial, and he left London on Saturday afternoon in uniform, and carrying a rifle. It seems that, although he's very keen, he's a shocking bad marksman, and a member of a sort of awkward squad which goes down occasionally to Purfleet ranges to practise. Purfleet is a station between London and Tilbury. Halliday got out there, fired a number of rounds, and returned to London in the evening.'

'Dear, dear, I'm sorry for that young man,' remarked the professor. 'First we have a motive, then an opportunity. Of course, he travelled in the same carriage as his uncle, levelled his musket at his head, inflicted a fearful wound, and decamped. Why, there's hardly a weak link in the whole chain.'

'It wasn't quite as simple as that,' replied Hanslet patiently. 'He certainly didn't travel in the same carriage as his uncle, since that very morning they had quarrelled violently. Farquharson, who was rather a strict old boy, didn't approve of his nephew's ways. Not that I can find out much against him, but he's a bit of a young blood, and his uncle didn't like it. He travelled third-class, and swears that he didn't know his uncle was on the train.'

'Oh, you have interviewed him already, have you?' said the professor quietly.

'I have,' replied Hanslet. 'His story is that he nearly missed the train, jumped into it at the last moment, in fact. Somewhere after Barking he found himself alone, and that's all he told me. When I asked him what he was doing scrambling along the footboard outside the train between Dagenham and Rainham he became very confused, and explained that, on putting his head out of the window, he had seen another member of the awkward squad a few carriages away, and made up his mind to join him. He gave me the man's name, and when I saw him he confirmed Halliday's story.'

'Really, inspector, your methods are masterly,' said the professor. 'How did you know that he had been on the footboard?'

'A man working on the line had seen a soldier in uniform, with a rifle slung over his back, in this position,' replied Hanslet triumphantly.

'And you immediately concluded that this man must be

Halliday,' commented the professor. 'Well, guesses must hit the truth sometimes, I suppose. What exactly is your theory of the crime?'

'It seems plain enough,' replied Hanslet. 'Halliday had watched his uncle enter the train, then jumped into a carriage close to his. At a predetermined spot he clambered along with his loaded rifle, shot him through the window, then, to avert suspicion, joined his friend, whom he had seen enter the train, a little farther on. It's as plain as a pikestaff to me.'

'So it appears,' remarked the professor drily. 'What steps do you propose to take in the matter?'

'I propose to arrest Halliday at the termination of the inquest,' replied Hanslet complacently.

The professor made no reply to this for several seconds. 'I think it would be to everybody's advantage if you consulted me again before doing so,' he said at last.

A cloud passed for an instant over Hanslet's face. 'I will, if you think it would do any good,' he replied. 'But you must see for yourself that I have enough evidence to secure a conviction from any jury.'

'That is just what disquiets me,' returned the professor quickly. 'You cannot expect the average juryman to have an intelligence superior to yours, you know. I have your promise?'

'Certainly, if you wish it,' replied Hanslet rather huffily. He changed the subject abruptly, and a few minutes later he rose and left the house.

In the course of our normal routine I forgot the death of Mr Farquharson entirely. It was not until the following afternoon, when Mary, the parlourmaid, entered the study with the announcement that a Miss Farquharson had called and begged that she might see the professor immediately, that the matter recurred to me.

'Miss Farquharson!' I exclaimed. 'Why, that must be the

daughter of the fellow who was murdered the other day. Hanslet said he had a daughter, you remember.'

'The balance of probability would appear to favour that theory,' replied the professor acidly. 'Yes, I'll see her. Show Miss Farquharson in please, Mary.'

Miss Farquharson came in, and the professor greeted her with his usual courtesy. 'To what do I owe the pleasure of this visit?' he inquired.

Miss Farquharson hesitated a moment or two before she replied. She was tall and fair, dressed in deep mourning, with an elusive prettiness which I, at least, found most attractive. And even before she spoke, I guessed something of the truth from the flush which suffused her face at the professor's question.

'I'm afraid you may think this an unpardonable intrusion,' she said at last. 'The truth is that Bob—Mr Halliday—who is my cousin, has heard of you and begged me to come and see you.'

The professor frowned. He hated his name becoming known in connection with any investigations which he undertook, but in spite of all his efforts, many people had come to know of his hobby. Miss Farquharson took his frown for a sign of disapproval and continued with an irresistible tone of pleading in her voice.

'It was only as a last hope I came to you,' she said. 'It's all so awful that I feel desperate. I expect you know that my father was found dead last Saturday in a train at Tilbury, while he was on his way home?'

The professor nodded. 'I am aware of some of the facts,' he replied non-committally. 'I need not trouble you to repeat them. But in what way can I be of assistance to you?'

'It's too terrible,' she exclaimed with a sob. 'The police suspect Bob of having murdered him. They haven't said so, but they have been asking him all sorts of dreadful questions. Bob thought perhaps you might be able to do something—'

Her voice tailed away hopelessly under the professor's unwinking gaze.

'My dear young lady, I am not a magician,' he replied. 'I may as well tell you that I have seen Inspector Hanslet, who has what he considers a convincing case against your cousin.'

'But you don't believe it, do you, Dr Priestley?' interrupted Miss Farquharson eagerly.

'I can only accept the inspector's statements as he gave them to me,' replied the professor. 'I know nothing of the case beyond what he has told me. Perhaps you would allow me to ask you a few questions?'

'Of course!' she exclaimed. 'I'll tell you everything I can.'

The professor inclined his head with a gesture of thanks. 'Was your father in the habit of travelling by the 2.15 train from Fenchurch Street on Saturday afternoons?'

'No,' replied Miss Farquharson with decision. 'Only when he was kept later than usual at the office. His usual custom was to come home to a late lunch.'

'I see. Now, can you tell me the reason for the quarrel between him and your cousin?'

This time Miss Farquharson's reply was not so prompt. She lowered her head so that we could not see her face, and kept silence for a moment. Then, as though she had made up her mind, she spoke suddenly.

'I see no harm in telling you. As a matter of fact, Bob and I have been in love with one another for a long time, and Bob decided to tell my father on Saturday morning. Father was rather old-fashioned, and he didn't altogether approve of Bob. Not that there was any harm in anything he did, but father couldn't understand that a young man liked to amuse himself.

'There was quite a scene when Bob told him, and father refused to hear anything about it until Bob had reformed, as he put it. But I know that Bob didn't kill him,' she concluded entreatingly. 'It's impossible for anybody who knew him to believe he could. You don't believe it, do you?'

'No, I do not believe it,' replied the professor slowly. 'If it is any consolation to you and Mr Halliday, I may tell you in confidence that I never have believed it. When is the inquest to be?'

A look of deep thankfulness overspread her features. 'I am more grateful to you than I can say, Dr Priestley,' she said earnestly. 'The inquest? On Saturday morning. Will you be there?'

The professor shook his head. 'No, I shall not be there,' he replied. 'You see, it is not my business. But I shall take steps before then to make certain inquiries. I do not wish to raise your hopes unduly, but it is possible that I may be able to divert suspicion from Mr Halliday. More than that I cannot say.'

Tears of thankfulness came to her eyes. 'I can't tell you what this means to Bob and me,' she said. 'He has been terribly distressed. He quite understands that things look very black against him, and he cannot suggest who could have wanted to kill my father. Father hadn't an enemy in the world, poor dear.'

'You are sure of that?' remarked the professor.

'Quite,' she replied positively. 'I knew every detail of his life; he never hid the smallest thing from me.'

And after a further short and unimportant conversation, she took her leave of us.

The professor sat silent for some minutes after her departure. 'Poor girl,' he said at last. 'To lose her father so tragically, and then to see the man she loves accused of his murder! We must see what we can do to help her, Harold. Get me the one-inch map of the country between London and Tilbury, and a timetable of the Southend trains.'

I hastened to obey him, and for an hour or more he pored over the map, working upon it with a rule and a protractor. At the end of this period he looked up and spoke abruptly.

'This is remarkably interesting, more so than I imagined at first it would be. Run out and buy me the sheets of the six-inch survey which cover Rainham and Purfleet. I think we shall need them.'

I bought the maps he required and returned with them. For

the rest of the day he busied himself with these, and it was not until late in the evening that he spoke to me again.

'Really, my boy, this problem is beginning to interest me,' he said. 'There are many points about it which are distinctly baffling. We must examine the country on the spot. There is a train to Purfleet, I see, at 10.30 tomorrow morning.'

'Have you formed any theory, sir?' I inquired eagerly. The vision of Miss Farquharson and her conviction of her cousin's innocence had impressed me in her favour.

The professor scowled at me. 'How often am I to tell you that facts are all that matter?' he replied. 'Our journey tomorrow will be for the purpose of ascertaining facts. Until we know these it would be a waste of time to indulge in conjecture.'

He did not mention the subject again until the next morning, when we were seated in the train to Purfleet. He had chosen an empty first-class carriage, and himself took the right-hand corner facing the engine. He said nothing until the train was travelling at a good speed, and then he addressed me suddenly.

'You are a good shot with a rifle, are you not?' he inquired.

'I used to be pretty fair,' I replied in astonishment. 'But I don't think I've had a rifle in my hand since the war.'

'Well take my stick and hold it as you would a rifle. Now go to the far end of the carriage and lean against the door. That's right. Point your stick at my right eye, as though you were going to shoot at it. Stand like that a minute. Thank you, that will do.'

He turned away from me, took a pair of field-glasses from a case he was carrying, and began to survey the country through the window on his side. This he continued to do until the train drew up at Purfleet and we dismounted on to the platform.

'Ah, a lovely day!' he exclaimed. 'Not too warm for a little walking. We will make our first call at Purfleet ranges. This was where young Halliday came to do his shooting, you remember.'

We made our way to the ranges, and were lucky enough to

find the warden at home. Dr Priestley had, when he chose, a most ingratiating way with him, and he and the warden were very shortly engaged in an animated conversation.

'By the way,' inquired the professor earnestly, 'was there any firing going on here between half-past two and three on Saturday last?'

The range-warden scratched his head with a thoughtful expression on his face. 'Let me see, now, last Saturday afternoon? We had a squad of Territorials here on Saturday afternoon, but they didn't arrive till after three. Lord, they was queer hands with a rifle, some of them. Much as they could do to hit the target at all at three hundred. They won't never make marksmen, however hard they try.'

'Isn't it rather dangerous to allow such wild shots to fire at all?' suggested the professor.

'God bless your heart, sir, it's safe enough,' replied the range-warden. 'There's never been an accident the whole time I've been here. They can't very well miss the butts, and even if they did there's nobody allowed on the marshes when firing's going on.'

'That is comforting, certainly,' said the professor. 'Apart from this squad, you had nobody else?'

The range-warden shook his head. 'No, sir, they was the only people on the range that day.'

'I suppose it is part of your duty to issue ammunition?' inquired the professor.

'As a rule, sir. But, as it happens, this particular squad always bring their own with them.'

The professor continued his conversation for a little longer, then prepared to depart.

'I'm sure I'm very much obliged to you,' he said as he shook hands. 'By the way, I believe there are other ranges about here somewhere?'

'That's right, sir,' replied the range-warden. 'Over yonder, beyond the butts. Rainham Ranges, they're called.'

'Is there any objection to my walking across the marshes to them?'

'Not a bit, sir. There's no firing today. Just keep straight on past the butts, and you'll come to them.'

The professor and I started on our tramp, the professor pausing every hundred yards or so to look about him through his field-glasses and to verify his position on the map. We reached the Rainham ranges at last, discovered the warden, who fell under the influence of the professor's charm as readily as his colleague at Purfleet had done, and opened the conversation with him in much the same style.

'On Saturday afternoon last, between half-past two and three?' replied the warden to the professor's inquiry. 'Well, sir, not what you might call any shooting. There was a party from Woolwich, with a new sort of light machine-gun, something like a Lewis. But they wasn't shooting, only testing.'

'What is the difference?' asked the professor.

'Well, sir, by testing I mean they had the thing held in a clamp, so that it couldn't move. The idea is to keep it pointing in exactly the same direction, instead of wobbling about as it might if a man was holding it. They use a special target, and measure up the distance between the various bullet-holes on it when they've finished.'

'I see,' replied the professor. 'I wonder if you would mind showing me where they were firing from?'

'Certainly, sir, it's close handy.' The range-warden led us to a firing-point nearby, and pointed out the spot on which the stand had been erected.

'That's the place, sir. They were firing at number 10 target over yonder. A thousand yards it is, and wonderful accurate the new gun seemed. Shot the target to pieces, they did.'

The professor made no reply, but took out his map and drew a line upon it from the firing-point to the butts. The line, when extended, led over a tract of desolate marshes until it met the river.

'There is very little danger on these ranges, it appears,' remarked the professor, with a note of annoyance in his voice. 'If a shot missed the butts altogether, it could only fall into the river, far away from any frequented spot.'

'That's what they were laid out for,' replied the range-warden. 'You see, on the other side there's a house or two, to say nothing of the road and the railway. It wouldn't do to have any stray rounds falling among them.'

'It certainly would not,' replied the professor absently. 'I see by the map the Rainham station is not far beyond the end of the ranges. Is there any objection to my walking to it past the butts?'

'None at all, sir, it's the best way to get there when there's no firing on. Thank you, sir, it's been no trouble at all.'

We started to walk down the ranges, a puzzled frown on the professor's face. Every few yards he stopped and examined the country through his glasses, or pulled out the map and stared at it with an absorbed expression. We had reached the butts before he said a word, and then it was not until we had climbed to the top of them that he spoke.

'Very puzzling, very!' he muttered. 'There must, of course, be some explanation. A mathematical deduction from facts can never be false. But I wish I could discover the explanation.'

He was looking through his field-glasses as he spoke, and suddenly his attention became riveted upon an object in front of him. Without waiting for me he hurried down the steep sides of the butts, and almost ran towards a flagstaff standing a couple of hundred yards on the far side of them. When he arrived at the base of it, he drew a couple of lines on the map, walked half round the flagstaff and gazed intently through his glasses. By the time I had caught up with him he had put the glasses back in their case, and was smiling benevolently.

'We can return to town by the next train, my boy,' he said cheerfully. 'I have ascertained everything I wished to know.'

He refused to say a word until our train was running into Fenchurch Street Station. Then suddenly he turned to me.

'I am going to the War Office,' he said curtly. 'Will you go to Scotland Yard, see Inspector Hanslet, and ask him to come to Westbourne Terrace as soon as he can?'

I found Hanslet, after some little trouble, and gave him the professor's message.

'Something to do with the Farquharson business, I suppose?' he replied. 'Well, I'll come if the professor wants to see me. But I've got it all fixed up without his help.'

He turned up, true to his promise, and the professor greeted him with a pleasant smile.

'Good evening inspector; I'm glad you were able to come. Will you be particularly busy tomorrow morning?'

'I don't think so, professor,' replied Hanslet in a puzzled voice. 'Do you want me to do anything?'

'Well, if you can spare the time, I should like to introduce you to the murderer of Mr Farquharson,' said the professor, casually.

Hanslet lay back in his chair and laughed. 'Thanks very much, professor; but I've met him already,' he replied. 'It would be a waste of your time, I'm afraid.'

'Never mind,' said the professor, with a tolerant smile. 'I assure you that it will be worth your while to spend the morning with me. Will you meet me by the book-stall at Charing Cross at half-past ten?'

Hanslet reflected for a moment. The professor had never yet led him on a wild-goose chase, and it might be worth while to humour him

'All right,' he replied, reluctantly. 'I'll come. But, I warn you, it's no good.'

The professor smiled, but said nothing. Hanslet took his leave of us, and the professor appeared to put all thought of the Farquharson case out of his head.

We met again at Charing Cross the next day. The professor had taken tickets to Woolwich and we got out of the train there and walked to the gates of the arsenal. The professor took an official letter out of his pocket, which he gave to the porter. In a few minutes we were led to an office, when a young officer rose to greet us.

'Good morning, Dr Priestley,' he said. 'Colonel Conyngham rang me up to say that you were coming. You want to see the stand we use for testing the new automatic rifle? It happens to be in the yard below, being repaired.'

'Being repaired?' repeated the professor quickly. 'May I ask what is the matter with it?'

'Oh, nothing serious. We used it at Rainham the other day, and the clamp broke just as we were finishing a series. We had fired 99 rounds out of 100, when the muzzle of the gun slipped up. I don't know what happened to the round. I suppose it went into the river somewhere. Beastly nuisance, we shall have to go down and start all over again.'

'Ah!' exclaimed the professor, in a satisfied tone. 'That explains it. But I wouldn't use No.10 target again if I were you. Can we see this stand?'

'Certainly,' replied the officer. 'Come along.'

He led us into the yard, where a sort of tripod with a clamp at the head of it was standing. The professor looked at it earnestly for some moments, then turned to Hanslet.

'There you see the murderer of Mr Farquharson,' he said quietly.

Of course Hanslet, the officer and myself bombarded him with questions, which he refused to answer until we had returned to London and were seated in his study. Then, fixing his eyes upon the ceiling and putting the tips of his fingers together, he began.

'It was, to any intelligent man, perfectly obvious that there are half a dozen reasons why young Halliday could not have shot his uncle. In the first place, he must have fired at very close range, from one side or other of the carriage, and a rifle bullet fired at such a range, although it very often makes a very extensive wound of entry, does not stay in a man's brain.

'It travels right through his head, with very slightly diminished velocity. Next, if Halliday fired at his uncle at all, it must have been from the left-hand side of the carriage. Had he fired from the right-hand side, the muzzle of the weapon would have been almost touching his victim and there would have been signs of burning or blackening round the wound. Do you admit this, inspector?'

'Of course?' replied Hanslet. 'My theory always has been that he fired from the left-hand side.'

'Very well,' said the professor quickly. 'Now Halliday is notoriously a very bad shot, hence his journey to Purfleet. Harold, on the contrary, is a good shot. Yet, during our expedition of yesterday, I asked him to aim at my right eye with a stick while the train was in motion. I found that never for an instant could he point the stick at it. I find it impossible to believe that a bad shot, firing from the footboard and therefore compelled to use one hand at least to retain his hold, could shoot a man on the far side of the carriage exactly on the temple.'

The professor paused, and Hanslet looked at him doubtfully.

'It all sounds very plausible, professor, but until you can produce a better explanation I shall continue to believe that my own is the correct one.'

'Exactly. It was to verify a theory which I had formed that I carried out my investigations. It was perfectly obvious to me, from your description of the wound, that it had been inflicted by a bullet very near the end of its flight, and therefore possessing only enough velocity to penetrate the skull without passing through it. This meant that it had been fired from a considerable distance away. Upon consulting the map, I discovered that there were two rifle ranges near the railway between London and Tilbury. I could not help feeling that the source of the bullet was probably one of these ranges. It was, at all events, a possibility worth investigating.

'But at the outset I was faced with what seemed an insuperable objection. I deduced from the map, a deduction subsequently verified by examination of the ground, that a round fired at any of the targets on either range would take a direction away from the railway. I also discovered that the only rounds fired while the train in which Mr Farquharson's body was found was passing the ranges were by an experimental party from the arsenal. This party employed a special device which eliminated any inaccuracy due to the human element. At this point it occurred to me that my theory was incapable of proof, although I still adhered to my view that it was correct.'

The professor paused and Hanslet ventured to remark:

'I still do not see how you can prove that the breakage of the clamp could have been responsible,' he said. 'The direction of the bullet remained the same, and only the elevation was affected. By your own showing, the last shot fired from the machine must have landed in the marshes or the river.'

'I knew very well that notwithstanding the apparent impossibility, this must have been the bullet which killed Mr Farquharson,' replied the professor equably. 'I climbed the butts behind the target at which the arsenal party had been firing, and while there I made an interesting discovery which solved the difficulty at once. Directly in line with number 10 target and some distance behind it was a flagstaff. Further, upon examination of this flagstaff, I discovered that it was made of steel.

'Now the map had told me that there was only a short stretch of line upon which a train could be struck by a bullet deflected by this flagstaff. If this had indeed been the case, I knew exactly where to look for traces, and at my first inspection I found them. High up on the staff is a scar where the paint has recently been removed. To my mind the cause of Mr Farquharson's death is adequately explained.'

Hanslet whistled softly. 'By Jove, there's something in it!' he exclaimed. 'Your theory, I take it, is that Farquharson was struck by a bullet deflected by the flagstaff?'

'Of course,' replied the professor. 'He was sitting on the right-hand side of the carriage, facing the engine. He was struck on the right side of the head, which supports that theory of a bullet coming through the open window. A bullet deflected in this way usually turns over and over for the rest of its flight, which accounts for the size of the wound. Have you any objection to offer?'

'Not at the moment,' said Hanslet cautiously. 'I shall have to verify all these facts, of course. For one thing, I must take the bullet to the arsenal and see if it is one of the same type as the experimental party were using.'

'Verify everything you can, certainly,' replied the professor. 'But remember that facts, not conjecture, are what should guide you.'

Hanslet nodded. 'I'll remember, professor,' he said. And with that he left us.

Two days later Mary announced Miss Farquharson and Mr Halliday. They entered the room, and Halliday walked straight up to the professor and grasped his hand.

'You have rendered me the greatest service one man can render to another, sir,' he exclaimed. 'Inspector Hanslet tells me that all suspicion that I murdered my uncle has been cleared away, and that this is due entirely to your efforts.'

Before the professor could reply, Miss Farquharson ran up to him and kissed him impulsively. 'Dr Priestley, you're a darling!' she exclaimed.

The professor beamed at her through his spectacles. 'Really, my dear, you make me feel quite sorry that you are going to marry this young man,' he said.

JOHN RHODE

The writer best known as 'John Rhode' was born Cecil John Charles Street in 1884 in the British territory of Gibraltar, where his father was Colonel-in-Chief of the second battalion of Scottish Rifles.

At the age of 16, Street left school to attend the Royal Military Academy at Woolwich and, on the outbreak of war, he enlisted. His main contribution to the war effort concerned the promulgation of allied propaganda for which he was awarded the Order of the British Empire in the New Year Honours List for 1918 and also the prestigious Military Cross. As the war came to an end, Street moved to a new role in Dublin Castle in Ireland, where he was responsible for countering the campaigning of Irish nationalists.

During the 1920s, Street seems to have spent most of his time at a typewriter, producing a fictionalised memoir and various political studies, biographies and a wartime romance, as well as short stories and articles on subjects as diverse as piracy and peasant art. While his early books found some success, the Golden Age of detective stories was well underway, so he decided to try his hand at the genre. He created Doctor—or rather Professor—Lancelot Priestley, a former academic whose first case was *The Paddington Mystery*, published in 1925 as by 'John Rhode'. Under this pseudonym he wrote nearly eighty novels and one of the first full-length studies of the trial of Constance Kent. But one pen name wasn't enough for this astonishingly prolific writer. Street also became

'Miles Burton', as whom he wrote over sixty novels, and 'Cecil Waye', whose four books featured sibling investigators Christopher and Vivienne Perrin.

John Street was also a member of the Detection Club and edited *Detection Medley* (1939), arguably the best anthology of stories by members of the Club. He had also contributed to the Club's first two round-robin detective novels, *The Floating Admiral* (1931) and *Ask a Policeman* (1933), as well as one of the Club's series of radio plays for the BBC and the excellent true-crime anthology *The Anatomy of Murder* (1936). Street also helped other Club members with scientific and technical aspects of their own work including Dorothy L. Sayers and also John Dickson Carr, who later made Street the inspiration for his character Colonel March, head of *The Department of Queer Complaints* (1940).

Street was as ingenious as he was prolific, devising seemingly impossible crimes in locked houses, locked bathrooms and locked railway compartments, and even—in *Drop to his Death*, co-authored with Carr in 1939—a locked elevator. And as well as unusual settings he was adept at devising unusual means of murder, including a hedgehog *[sic]*, a marrow and a hot water bottle; even bed-sheets, soda syphons, car batteries and pyjamas could be lethal in Street's hands. His books are particularly noteworthy for their humour and social observations and he also defies some of the expectations of the genre, with one novel in which Dr Priestley allows a murderer to go free and another in which the guilty party is identified and put on trial . . . . . . but acquitted.

John Street died in 1964.

'The Elusive Bullet' was published in the *London Evening Standard* on 10 August 1936 as part of a series *Detective Cavalcade* edited by Dorothy L. Sayers.

THE EUTHANASIA OF HILARY'S AUNT

Cyril Hare

Hilary Smyth came of what his father was fond of calling 'a good old family'. How old the family actually was might have been open to doubt, but Mr Smyth's standards of behaviour were certainly old-fashioned enough to satisfy any Victorian aristocrat.

So it came about that as the result of the merest peccadillo, relating to a few dishonoured cheques, Hilary had found himself summarily exiled to Australia, a place of which Mr Smyth knew little except that it provided a convenient dumping-ground for the black sheep of good old English families.

Hilary had not liked Australia, nor had Australia liked Hilary, and he took the earliest opportunity to return to England. Owing to his congenital incapacity to earn enough money to pay for his passage home, the opportunity only occurred when the simultaneous deaths of his father and elder brother put him in possession of the good old family's fortune.

The fortune was disappointingly small—old fashioned standards having proved sadly unremunerative of recent years—and Hilary, in the first flush of recovered liberty, ran through it in a matter of months. He was reduced to the ugly alternatives of destitution or looking for employment when he fortunately recollected that he was not alone in the world. He possessed an aunt.

Hilary knew little enough of his father's only sister, and for this the late Mr Smyth's outdated code was again responsible. 'Your Aunt Mary disgraced herself,' was all that the old gentleman would ever say when her name was mentioned.

So far as Hilary could ascertain, however, the disgrace consisted merely in the fact that she had chosen to throw in her lot with a man who, so far from belonging to a good old family, was involved in a low activity known as 'trade', and, it was hinted, 'retail trade' at that. From the time that Mary Smyth became Mrs Prothero, she was as one dead so far as her brother was concerned, and not even the demise of Mr Prothero, waving her very comfortably off with no encumbrances, could suffice to bring her to life again.

Hilary got in touch with his aunt through the family solicitor—to whom, fortunately, she had, despite her downfall, remained faithful—and the sun shone for him once more. The old lady appeared to take to him. Hilary, when on his best behaviour, could be excellent company, and, from being a frequent visitor, it was not long before he became an inmate of the comfortable Hampstead house that the profits of retail trade had provided.

Hilary unpacked his battered suitcase in his new home with the relief of a sailor who makes harbour just before the onset of a gale. He had brought it off, but only just in time, for he was down almost to his last sixpence.

Before very long he realised that in another sense he had been only just in time effecting his reunion with his aunt. The old lady, although she put a brave face on things, was gravely ill.

A confidential chat with her doctor alarmed Hilary very much. Stripped of technical phrases, his report amounted to this: Mrs Prothero's illness was incurable and inoperable. She might live for some considerable time to come, but the end was certain. 'Her condition may begin to deteriorate at any moment,' the doctor concluded. 'When it gets beyond a certain stage—well, it's not really a kindness to want her to live very long.'

Not unnaturally, Hilary felt thoroughly aggrieved that fate, after seeming to relent, should now be preparing to turn him adrift in the world once more. He took the obvious course for a man in his position. He chose an evening when his aunt was feeling better than usual, and then, very tactfully, raised the question of her will.

Mrs Prothero laughed outright when the subject was mentioned.

'Have I made a will?' she said. 'Bless you, child, yes! I left all my money to—let me see, what was it?—missions to China, I think—or it may have been Polynesia. I can't remember, but I know it was missions of some sort. Blenkinsop, the lawyer, will tell you which. He has it still I suppose. I was very keen on missionaries when I was a girl. I nearly married one, as a matter of fact.'

'You made this will when you were a girl, Aunt Mary?'

'The day I was twenty-one. It was your grandfather's idea that everyone should make a will on coming of age. Not that I had anything to leave—then.'

Hilary's heart, which had sunk at the mention of Polynesian missions, leaped again.

'Didn't you make another will when you married?' he asked.

His aunt shook her head, 'There was no need for it,' she said. 'I had nothing and Johnny had everything. Then after Johnny went, I had plenty to leave and nobody to leave it to.' She looked at Hilary deliberately. 'Perhaps now I'd better see Mr Blenkinsop again,' she suggested.

Hilary assured her that there was no need for anything to be done in haste and changed the subject. A visit to the local public library next confirmed him in his belief that by marrying Mr Prothero his aunt had effectually destroyed the efficacy of her early will. As her only living relative, his future was assured.

Within a few months, however, it was not so much the future as the problems of the present that were weighing upon Hilary.

The change in his aunt's condition foretold by the doctor had occurred. She took to her bed, and it was morally certain that she would never rise from it.

At the same time, he was more than usually in need of cash. He had expensive tastes and presuming on Aunt Mary's kindness he had run up some accounts which, taken together, came to a staggering sum.

Unfortunately, with increasing illness, Mrs Prothero became more and more difficult to approach on matters of money. Racked with pain and able to sleep only with the aid of soporifics, she was positively querulous when the subject was mentioned.

Finally, they had something approaching a quarrel over a mere matter of £10, in the course of which she accused him outright of being 'after her money'.

Aunt Mary, Hilary reflected, was not herself. He bore her no ill will. Her selfish attitude was the result of her sad condition. Remembering the doctor's words, he asked himself whether it was a kindness to her to wish her to go on living.

He slept on that problem and when, the next morning, his aunt told him that she had decided to send for Mr Blenkinsop, he came to the clear conclusion that the greatest possible kindness he could do to the poor old soul—and incidentally to himself—would be to double the strength of her sleeping draught that night.

It proved more easy than he had dared to hope. As though anxious to fall in with his plans, Mrs Prothero herself suggested to the old servant who was nursing her that she should take the evening off to attend to her own affairs, leaving her nephew to give her the drug which the woman was to prepare before she went out.

All that Hilary had then to do was to dissolve another two tablets in the glass which already contained the prescribed dose. lt would be simple to explain—if explanation were ever called for—that he had misunderstood the arrangement and made an unfortunate mistake. Nobody would suspect a devoted nephew.

Mrs Prothero took the glass from her nephew's hand with a look of gratitude.

'Thank you, Hilary,' she said. 'I am longing for sleep. To sleep and not wake up again would be the happiest thing for me.'

She looked at him fixedly. 'Is that what you intend me to do, Hilary? I have given you your chance. Forgive me if my suspicions of you are wrong. Old invalids get these ideas, you know. I shall make amends tomorrow, if I am alive then. Mr Blenkinsop is coming here and I shall make my will in your favour.

'If I die tonight, I am afraid you will be disappointed, and some mission or another will be the richer. You see, Johnny Prothero never married me. He had a wife who wouldn't divorce him. That was what shocked your silly old father so much . . .

'No, Hilary, don't try to take the glass away. That would tell me too much, and I'd rather not be told. Good-night, Hilary . . .'

Then, very deliberately, she raised the glass to her lips and drank it off.

CYRIL HARE

Cyril Hare, whose real name was Alfred Alexander Gordon Clark, was born in 1900 in Surrey. In 1920, after graduating with a First in Modern History from Oxford, Clark was admitted to the Inner Temple, one of the prestigious Inns of Court, and he was called to the Bar in 1924. While he had written short pieces for *Punch* and other magazines, his first substantial criminous work was a play, *Murder in Daylesford Gardens*; it is unclear if this was performed but it was possibly written for a dramatic society within the Temple.

A few years later Clark revised the play but again no details of any performances have been confirmed; and he then used it as the basis of his first novel, *Tenant for Death*, published in 1937 in which the detective is Inspector Mallett, a policeman drawn more realistically than most of his fictional contemporaries but with a prodigious appetite and as blunt as his name suggests.

Tenant for Death appeared under the nom de plume of Cyril Hare, a pseudonym derived from two London addresses: his home in Cyril Mansions in Battersea, and his place of work, Hare Court Chambers. While continuing to practise as a barrister in Kingston and in London, Clark also carried on writing crime fiction. His most famous novel *Tragedy at Law*, was published in 1942 and drew on his pre-war experience as a judge's marshal. The novel introduced Francis Pettigrew, a witty and capable barrister who helps to unravel mysteries in a casual and generally reluctant way. Pettigrew appears in five novels, in three alongside Mallett, and both appear alone in novels and short stories.

The law provided Clark with background and ideas for other detective novels as did his squirearchical hobbies, hunting and fishing and one, the slyly satirical *With a Bare Bodkin*, draws on his wartime work in the Ministry of Economic Warfare. He wrote one radio play, *Murder at Warbeck Hall*, first broadcast in 1948, and he later turned this into first a novel, *An English Murder*, and then a stage play, *The House of Warbeck*, a 'political thriller' that had its first performance in September 1955. Clark also wrote many short stories for a variety of magazines including *The Sketch* and *The Illustrated London News* as well as for the *London Evening Standard*, which carried daily short stories for over forty years, and other newspapers.

In 1946, Clark was elected a member of the Detection Club and, despite contracting tuberculosis around this time, he played an active part in its social activities, for example portraying Sherlock Holmes in a playlet by John Dickson Carr.

In 1950, Clark was appointed a County Court Judge on the Surrey circuit, which is where he had lived as a child and was the setting for some of his books, including *That Yew Tree's Shade* (1954). He died at his home in 1957.

'The Euthanasia of Hilary's Aunt' was first published in the *London Evening Standard* on 4 December 1950.

THE GIRDLE OF DREAMS

Vincent Cornier

The elderly lady had a withered and weasel aspect; a sandy and bloodless look. Her air and attitude engendered the curious impression that here was something out of the hedgerows' dust, frightened and about to squeak. A narrow and beady eyed personage—the very pince-nez through which she flickered her glinting hazel glances seemed set across her nose to stridulate its bony string with a tarnished golden bow.

Her dress was horrific comedy. She wore a gabardine and a sealskin tippet. A turmoil of saffron velvet, maybe an old-fashioned toque, was on her nodding head. And she had a veil; a lugubrious downfall of maroon netting spotted with grey chenille. Her face was rather alarmingly framed by its poke of rusty shadows, like something ceraceous in a cowl. Mr Lionel Blayne, senior partner of the firm Messrs Blayne, Ridley and Cowperthwaite, Court Jewellers, of New Bond Street, happily refused to believe in it . . .

'Now my dear sir,' he chuckled richly. 'I am quite prepared to contribute my mite—but I can't resist taking the wind out of your sails. You've just to say overdone it, my lad.'

Rodent teeth were revealed by the elderly lady's open mouth. She had lifted her veil to speak, and Mr Blayne was suddenly horrified. This was certainly not a man's mouth. Those moles and that sparse hairiness of the upper lip were in no sense masculine. Mr Lionel Blayne realised he had made a frightful mistake.

And this was a woman's voice: 'I beg your pardon. Am I to understand you are addressing me?'

'I—I am terribly sorry, madam,' Mr Blayne stammered and went white, 'but—but I thought you were—'

He stopped at that, mortified and more sick at heart than he had ever been. He could not even explain. How could he tell this eccentric dame that he had mistaken her for one of the fantastically garbed and turned out medical students who were thronging the West End, making a Christmas collection for their particular hospital? He had seen them when he arrived for business. Most of them wore operating-theatre gowns and caps, but quite a number were daubed with grease paint and decorated with false hair and decked in hideous caricatures of bye-gone fashion. He had honestly erred in thinking the elderly lady was one of these jovial masqueraders.

Looking anywhere but into those scintillant hazel eyes, Mr Blayne saw the stolid form of Sergeant Everard, the commissionaire, standing at steady ease in the fan-lighted Georgian doorway. He had the same peculiar 'set' about him that he reserved completely for the duchesses, the marchionesses and the occasional 'royals' who patronised the discreet and sombrely quiet old shop; for these and none less. Therefore, argued the spinning mind of Mr Lionel Blayne, the elderly lady's atrocious ensemble must have impressed Everard with its authenticity—he would have been the first to pounce on a glad-ragged student. Then Mr Blayne chanced to glimpse the magnificent drop pearl earrings worn by the elderly lady . . . Everard would know a pearl of price when he saw one; maybe they had convinced his sober mind.

'Whoever you thought I was, Mr—Mr—?'

'Blayne.'

'Mr Blayne—is immaterial to my purpose in coming here.'

The elderly lady talked with precision but in the magical music which must have held the wedding guest, apart from the ancient mariner's glittering eye: a cold, light, silken voice. 'We may discard the incident, don't you think?'

Now the elderly lady smiled. Smile was as voice. Mr Blayne blinked and felt a gentle caress go under his scanty hair—a lovely touch of interest. Maybe the lady was not so incongruous as he had at first supposed; maybe Sergeant Everard had no reason for amaze. He was driving at a decision that she was far better looking and far better dressed than he instantly realised . . .

'With my apologies, madam,' bowed Mr Blayne, 'and in what way might I be of use to you?'

The elderly lady looked around the simply lighted shop. Not a soul save Mr Blayne was visible. Only Mr Blayne, and great grave glowings of gold, the fierce and frozen rainbows of diamonds and the evenings of emerald and sapphire, the dawns of turquoise and of pearl, with a touch of discreet Christmas decorations. The elderly lady smiled like a warm cat. The mesmeric potency of her eyes was also feline.

'I seem to have come at the wrong hour,' she said. 'I often heard that Bond Street has only one hour in a day for business. I'm sure this can't be it.'

'As a matter of fact,' Mr Blayne was very anxious to be pleasant, 'I was about to leave for luncheon. But, of course, that doesn't very much count—can I show you anything?'

'I rather wanted to show you something,' the elderly lady replied. 'I would like to sell you'—she fumbled in the capacious pockets of her sizeable gabardine and pulled out a clanking line of gold—'this.'

Mr Lionel Blayne was so highly trained in his craft that he had the piece identified before the elderly lady had freed it from her coat. And so swiftly thinking was Mr Blayne, he had a thick chamois leather swept across the glass top of the counter to receive the careless dumping. It would never do to have a treasure of this sort injured.

'A sixteenth century chiavacuore,' he breathed, 'of Italian workmanship, I think.'

'Mr Blayne,' the elderly lady still smiled, 'if you are capable of such a feat of identification as that, you might also be capable of perfectly open dealings. I hope so—otherwise I must take this elsewhere. Of Italian workmanship, indeed.'

My Lionel Blayne picked up the bridal girdle and let its weight soothe his unsteady hands. His eyes feasted on its beauty. It was a small belt formed of intaglio medallions, all jewelled and profoundly chased, linked together by diamond-studded chain-rings. Its clasp was a bulbous foam of silver-gilt and gems representing lilies and roses enshrouding a tiny heart. The heart was cloven by a trifling blade—a lean silver crescent like a scimitar—and the two parts concealed the minute engine of the cunning locks which kept the girdle closed.

Only one man could have fashioned the exquisite work. Mr Blayne quite reverently breathed his name:

'Benvenuto Cellini, without a doubt—'

'And wrought when he was at the height of his powers,' the elderly lady gently insisted, 'after his return from the French Court. This example was probably executed in Florence, in the hey-day of Cosimo the First.' There was a faint suggestion of 'and that's that' in the lady's otherwise impeccable survey.

'A golden chiavacuore without parallel, I am beginning to believe, and, Mr Blayne, I think I've examined every museum piece extant.' She laughed. 'You see, I have been curious.'

In the last analysis Mr Blayne was a shrewd man of business. He was slightly afraid he had trapped himself, by a devotee enthusiasm, to the detriment of the communal pocket of Messrs Blayne, Ridley and Cowperthwaite. This elderly lady was no fool. Her bargaining, he surmised, was going to be hard driven; since she knew exactly what her treasure was, it was certain she had its uttermost price in mind as well. Mr Blayne became prim and non-committal.

'If you wouldn't mind going forward, madam,' he insinuated, 'I'll run my lens over this in my private room. One cannot traffic with such rarities in the usual way, over the counter, you know.'

'I quite appreciate that,' said the elderly lady. 'I haven't the slightest objection to your taking up the whole day with your examination. You'll find this girdle genuine.'

'Now, madam, in here if you please.' Mr Blayne put on his most courtly air. He opened a door and the elderly lady swept forward into the dim inner office. 'I don't for a second doubt but what we'll determine the piece as a veritable Cellini,' he hastened to say, 'yet there remains the—er—valuation, don't you know.'

The elderly lady did not reply to that. She took her seat before Mr Blaine's big desk and clasped her gloved hands.

She watched Blayne manipulate a telescopic apparatus which centred, at last, above a grey agate slab. Then the expert touched a switch and the telescopic instrument poured green-grey and violet fire on to the chiavacuore.

'Do you object'—the elderly lady suddenly asked, and startled Mr Blayne with her question—'if I smoke while you are occupied?'

A teaser this. Clients did not usually smoke in Mr Blaine's sanctum . . . but the lady was bringing a supreme asset to the holdings of Messrs Blayne, Ridley and Cowperthwaite, an occasion when eccentricities would not matter.

'Why—why not at all, madam,' gasped Mr Blayne, 'not the slightest objection I assure you.' He darted to his pockets. 'Do let me get you some matches.'

'I have an automatic lighter, thank you, Mr Blayne. And I'm afraid I must warn you—you'll perhaps forgive the herby smell of my cigarettes. I'm subject to asthma. I smoke stramonium.'

Mr Blayne managed to give a smile to that. He felt very

martyred, but then, he again consoled himself, it was all in the interests of the firm. The elderly lady began her stenchy smoking. Mr Blayne tried to ignore it and examined the bridal girdle under the ultra-violet radiance of the Hebbison-Caicroft light.

It appeared that the chiavacuore had been taken from a haphazard storage place. It had not been cleaned for scores of years. This last was not surmise. Blayne knew as much about the oxygeneous faculties of gold that he was aware it had taken upwards of a century to form this sullen 'skin' it possessed. In the crevices of the ornamentations and chases were granulations of wood and paper; he envisaged the girdle, neglected and almost forgotten, wrapped in tissues and hidden in a wormy box. Through his optical glasses he could see more than these things magnified—the quadrified wards of the secret lock, for instance, were netted by spider threads.

The precise 'heart's key'—the true 'chiavacuore'—was the pippin hilt of the little scimitar. It was a cabochon diamond of peculiarly wicked lambency, like myrrh in water and like the chilly circles-cenele of the elderly lady's curious eyes. It was all as cruel as the silvern sliver of that blade which menaced among the roses and the lilies . . .

Mr Lionel Blayne suppressed a grave-tread shudder. He did not care for that baleful stone; it reminded him, oddly enough, of dead lips seen in morning light. He certainly did not like it, but he knew it was the master of the whole. And very much charmed by his knowledge, Mr Lionel Blayne let the two chasms of the golden heart come together. They met and lazily locked, with the sound of a kiss. Then Mr Lionel Blayne, more than ever cheered by his knowledge, magnificently rejected the obvious—did not finger the waiting blade—but revolved the evil diamond in its place. The scimitar rose and hovered and struck . . . and the girdle of the bride was opened.

Mr Blayne felt a tiny sting as the precious hilt twitched beneath his touch and he was conscious that its apex had lanced his flesh. That was a trifling matter. Stones cut en cabochon often did that; a faceted diamond never. It served him right for being careless. He should have remembered—especially so in this case, where the bulb of the stone was rested on metal while its needle crown jutted up in no wise guarded . . . Mr Blayne looked at the wet point of blood and rubbed it away. He was rather surprised, however, at the angry ache which had taken the tactile buds of his finger end in possession. He hoped to goodness the diamond was clean. But then a craftsman's fervour made him busy with the uncannily complicated inner workings of the lock, and he did not trouble any more about the pain. He blew upon the quadridentate miracle in steel which responded to the diamond hilt—he blew into the hollows of the heart to dispel the cobwebbings. They were so very old that they resolved into grey and vicious follicles of dust at his breath.

He sighed at last and put the treasure down.

'Yes, veritable Cellini,' he decided, 'and madam, as you say, of his best period.' He drew a writing pad across the desk. 'And now for the—ah—formalities, shall we say? They must precede any transaction, as you'll agree, madam. Might I have your card, and you can tell me anything you know of this girdle's previous history?'

The elderly lady deliberately squashed her stramonium cigarette on mahogany belonging to Messrs Blayne, Ridley and Cowperthwaite.

'I am sorry, Mr Blayne, but I cannot answer either question. What is to be learned of the chiavacuore's history you must discover from other sources. And my name won't convey anything to you—I do not intend to give it. All I want to do is to sell the piece at the best possible price.'

Although it cut Mr Blayne to the quick, he got to his feet and pushed the jewelled girdle across the desk.

'The firm of Blayne, Ridley and Cowperthwaite never buy

blind, madam. I, too, am sorry, but I must ask you to take this to some less scrupulous or more careless firm—'

'A moment, Mr Blayne,' the elderly lady squeaked at last. 'Give me a moment, if you please. Perhaps you haven't stopped to consider that there might be reasons of gravest policy underlying my apparent brusquerie. I am in no immediate hurry. Keep the girdle as long as you like; let your partners examine it and assess it . . . Make what inquiries you wish, and where you wish.' Her head nodded almost sorrowfully, certainly reproachfully. 'That ought to suffice, instead of my name and so forth, oughtn't it?'

'I really don't care to . . .'

'Do as I suggest, Mr Blayne.' The lady was shrill and headlong in her pleading. 'Please do—when you've decided to buy or not to buy, put an advertisement in the personal column of the *Times* newspaper—merely "Cellini, call", and I'll come here again for your attention.'

Mr Lionel Blayne looked up, puzzled, yet half smiling. His austere and handsome face looked in calculating stillness above his smooth black clothing. 'You have had all this matter prearranged, then?' He was reluctant, but becoming convinced that the elderly lady hinted at the truth; that she really was in a quandary, and that the girdle was being disposed of for 'reasons of policy'. 'Dear me, it's—it's all so very odd and unconventional, but you know, I'm half inclined to take you at your word, madam.'

'By all means do so.' Now the elderly lady rose, and she spoke in a tune of words, fascinating. 'I do not want to waste any more of your time—all I ask is that you will accept my position and be so kind as to—help me out in the way I suggest.' She laughed gently and winningly. 'I hope you don't think I've come by the girdle dishonestly—'

'Oh, no! My dear madam. No!' That little laughter had tipped the beam. 'Of course not!' Mr Blayne touched his teeth with the forefinger he had cut—very strange how it pained him. 'I think I will do as you ask. Tell me, what's that message again?'

'"Cellini, call", that's all that is necessary.' The elderly lady pulled her tippet closer to her dun-coloured shoulders. 'Only one more thing, Mr Blayne.' The jeweller raises his grey eyebrows and waited. 'Might I see you put the girdle away? Frankly, it's not my sole responsibility. I will have to recount to someone else every incident of this interview. I cannot very well say I came away and left the girdle lying on your desk. Then, if you'll be so good, I shall have to have a receipt.'

'Why, certainly—certainly, my dear madam.' Blayne was fully convinced at last, hence indulgent. 'You are in the right.' He went to the door of a big green safe and selected two keys from a bunch he took out of his pocket. 'I shall put the piece in here for the time being and give you your receipt. Then there will be insurance—but we'll have to talk about that later.'

Strange, thought Mr Blayne, how throbbing was that puncture in his forefinger. It seemed to be getting worse.

'Ah, yes, I'd not thought of insurance.' This was never the silken cold and level voice of the elderly lady, Mr Lionel Blayne decided. He confusedly told himself it was the honeyed crooning of some lithe houri—a talking down, a world of feathery bliss. 'Certainly a point to be taken into consideration.'

Mr Blayne was able to feel his well-known keys in hand, but was not conscious of seeing them. He felt extraordinarily blithe. What the devil did seeing things after—he had that crooning and the satin crash of daffodils within the noise of spring winds for his hearing. He had a wine warmth in his body and great laughter in his mind. Who the hell cared for the damned keys he would like to know—symbols of his pruned and rigid former life. He opened the door of the big green safe without knowledge of the act. What had he to do with safes in this existence? Why bother about keys and locks and metal caverns and such, when a pavilion of Tyrian flame and bat-hour shadows welcomed him to a languorous forgetfulness . . .

Queer how a faint recollection started into his mind at the

thought-sound of the word 'key'. Somewhere (he was not concerned enough to determine where and when) a woman—a rodent-mouthed creature with a leprous veil—had tried to sell him a chiavacuore, the gemmed and golden 'heart key' of a bride long dead and of the dust of centuries. Whoever that bride had been she surely could not have had one-tenth of the radiantly faery beauty of the one who waited for him there—among the secrecies of shade and luscious peace in this pavonine pavilion where the sound of zephyred blossoms and warm music lived.

He would give her all she asked of him. A belt of tawdry gold? Pah!—what was that to him? Why, of course she could have it—here, he laughed and waved his hands—she might have her choice of these as well—of these diamonds and pearls and emeralds and sapphire stones . . . Here . . . Let her take them while she may.

And she took them.

The fantastic robbery consummated on the premises of Messrs Blayne, Ridley and Cowperthwaite, Court Jewellers, of New Bond Street, West., bade fair to become a classic when it was referred to his Britannic Majesty's Intelligence Service, Political—the Secret Service departments. Scotland Yard had routed it curiously throughout police 'informations'. Its classification read:

'M.O. 3–2,—Query—M.O. 2–3. (Shop) Jewellery
Midday, December 16th.
Stolen by: Shopbreaking: Trick.
Particulars of property: Twenty-seven unmounted diamonds, one hundred and fourteen mounted diamonds, ninety-three single unmounted sapphires, eight emeralds, two necklaces of large and graduated pearls . . .'

'You see,' Professor Gregory Wanless, F.R.S., gently tapped on the flimsy report and smiled across at Major Helmerdyne, 'the police cannot make up their minds about the job. You notice that they've listed it "Modus Operandi", department three, class two. Then they've queried it as being a "two-two" crime. They don't know, according to that, whether it was a larceny with violence or not.'

'In other words,' Major Helmerdyne spoke lazily, 'poor old Lionel Blayne, despite his lifetime's integrity and standing, is suspected of complicity—what?'

'I wouldn't go so far as to say that. Still, his yarn was so fantastic that he has never been wholly admitted as non-suspect.'

'I don't follow you in your finer shades, Professor; I'm sorry. However, that to one side, what's your opinion? You've had tons of time to go through those reports,' he indicated the complete dossier of the case, 'and what have you to suggest?'

Professor Wanless looked around his cosy chamber. Its dim lighting and serried books rather overawed Helmerdyne, the man of action. Wanless found it all an inspiration.

'In my considered opinion, Helmerdyne, Mr Blayne had told the truth, and nothing but the truth. Think of the agony of mind he must have endured when he had to retail to smug and hard-headed police officers all the sensuous traffic of his mind which held them impotent while the actual theft was committed. If he were inventing surely he would not have chosen such a peculiar line? I'm not going to labour the point—I accept it as cold truth, therefore my basis.'

'Of course he had credence for his tale at first while his finger was poisoned—'

'Admittedly. That's certainly quite a boggle in one's path, as I recognise. Naturally the theory arose that a subtle poison the needle-tip of that pip of a diamond, that scimitar hilt, had affected his mind . . . a Borgia touch which rendered him incapable for the time being. But when it was proved that no poison was in his blood-stream, despite the appearance of the finger, the theory simply had to collapse.'

'Granted.' Helmerdyne sat back and closed his eyes. 'I take it that you are working down, by process of elimination, to arrive at the cause of his state of mind.'

'I am. The stramonium cigarette was the next item to be considered. As the woman had pressed it out in the mahogany top of the desk the fused varnish held quite enough ash for analysis. Stramonium and nothing else—bang goes any theory of hashish or opium drugging by inhalation.'

'Oh, that's cut out, don't you agree, by the fact that the sinister dame smoked the cigarette herself . . . Doesn't it follow that she would have been the one to suffer had it contained a powerful hypnotic and opiate drug?'

Professor Wanless smiled and shook his head.

'Not at all, my dear fellow—not at all! It's far too complicated and wearing a subject to go into now, but it is quite possible for an habitual opiate smoker to be immune from fumes sufficiently potent to render a non-indulgent person, chancing to inhale them, unconscious. Take that as read and by the same token rid your mind of any suspicion attaching to that medicinal cigarette.'

'It's hard to accomplish. By closing down the avenues of the poisoned gem theory, and the drugged smoke theory, one is left, comparatively speaking, helpless.'

'On the contrary, Helmerdyne, one is helped tremendously. Lionel Blayne was doped. He was suddenly possessed by a devil of a morality which confused his brain to its temporary ruin. That woman deliberately chose that one hour of the Bond Street day to make certain she would only have one victim to subdue. I believe her fantastic dress was also as deliberately chosen . . .

'You mustn't lose sight of the fact that she was a caricature. She had transgressed the bounds of mere eccentricity. Nor must you forget those medical students were holding a rag which provided her with a background of uncommonly useful kind. She was effaced, in general incongruity, by her particular—

disguise.' Wanless shot out the word. 'It was only that—a perfect and baffling disguise.'

'All right, have your way, Professor.' Major Helmerdyne shrugged his shoulders. 'You're eliminating to zero, aren't you? What's going to be left to work on?'

'Loads of stuff! Good heavens, Helmerdyne, you don't mean to tell me you're exhausted of data already?'

'Carry on!' Helmerdyne laughed. 'Take your pretty triumph, Wanless! I'm exhausted . . . what have you still in hand?'

Professor Wanless fiddled with the papers of the dossier. He withdrew a water-coloured representation of a heraldic crest.

'Here, have a look at this,' he advised. 'That's from the College of Heralds—the armorial bearings of the family which once owned the chiavacuore, my lad.'

Helmerdyne discarded his careless and listless attitude. He stifled an exclamation and sat bolt upright. His eyes shone, and once again he was caught in that thrill of admiration he held for this subtle master of intelligence work—Professor Gregory Wanless, sometime professor of physics and reader in natural philosophy . . .

'Damn it!' He took the Whatman paper from the scientist. 'Are you going to swoozle us all again, Professor?' Wanless chuckled and coughed. 'I'm all agog, but I can't make much out of this—whose crest is it?'

'It is the crest of a girl of 15 years of age who proudly, let us hope, snapped that chiavacuore from the workshops of the master, Cellini, around her waist . . . on her marriage morning—on October the fourth, fifteen-hundred and fifty-five.'

'The devil!' Helmerdyne had difficulty in remaining in his chair. 'You're not going to tell me next that you've trodden out the history of that—that girdle?'

'I'm afraid I had to,' Wanless quietly stated. 'It was definitely necessary.'

'But—but how? Hang it all, man, it baffled the whole blessed guild of goldsmiths, let alone Museum people and what-not!'

'Most of them forgot,' Wanless cryptically and slowly murmured; 'the world is very wide and also rather old. And, I'm afraid, hardly one of them paused to consider the sentimental side of the history of any chiavacuore—not this one in particular. I would also wager that none of them paid the slightest heed to Blayne's signed statement to the effect that it's "skin" showed by oxygeneous inference a century of negligence.

'The sentiment I speak of has it that to allow the bridal girdle of an ancestress to pass out of the keeping of a family is a deadly and fateful thing. Working on that supposition I granted myself that this chiavacuore, out of its sheer perfection and unknown history, must have belonged to a family of tremendous rank and wealth and exclusiveness, suddenly—or, rather, recently—suffered in fortune. I postulated an Italian family.

'You see, I couldn't get out of my mind Blayne's report of the woman's placing on the girdle—"after Cellini's return from the foreign Court" and "in the hey-day of Cosimo the First". Now, the woman wanted to show Blayne she knew as much of the piece as he could tell her. Natural vanity . . . but it led me to go into matters deeply. Cellini went to Florence from the French Court in fifteen-hundred and fifty-five, to be under the patronage of the Medicis, and to work for Cosimo.

'Thinking of the Medicis, I remembered the heart and the jewel-hilted scimitar. A little research and I was made aware of an amazing fact: Here, in the girdle clasp, was the ornate heart of the Medici family crest, cloven by an alien scimitar—undoubtedly the crest of some other great house. Records again, Helmerdyne—records again. Soon I struck a change of arms, where the escutcheon of Medici was impaled with the arms of another family; a natural heraldic ordinance to portray legitimate marriage.

'Here I had working space. I traced a marriage of the date I have mentioned: a Medici girl with a foreign prince. I investigated the result of the union. Only one member of descending family survives—a man. Now I was in a fix. Recalling the doom which is supposed to fall on anyone selling or otherwise disposing of a chiavacuore—even allowing it to go out of personal possession for one hour—I had to argue that the visitor to Blayne's shop on December the sixteenth—was that man!'

'Oh, no!—no!—no! Wanless! Why, hang it all, that's impossible! Hasn't Blayne sworn to the moles and the slight hairs of the upper lip and the voice of an ugly elderly woman? Going by the book there can't be any doubt about that!'

'Mr Blayne, like the majority of us, is used to dealing with mankind in the ordinary. The fellow I have in mind is one of the most extraordinary persons alive today. He is of the wrong century; all wrong, in fact.' Wanless regarded his cigar and once again glanced at the clock. 'He is completely atavistic; a throwback to his Medici ancestry. He is delicately made yet exceptionally strong. He suffers from the historic Medici asthma and has the double voice of the breed—the man's bass and the woman's shrill treble—recall that from olden history, too.

'Our suspect has had an extraordinary career as well. When he hasn't been big game hunting he's used up his peculiar energy in trekking the hinterlands of Borneo and the Fiji Islands. He knows a lot about—the hinterlands of Fiji . . .'

Wanless broke off; the telephone had buzzed. He picked up the handpiece and held a quiet conversation with the downstairs offices. He smiled at length and turned to Major Helmerdyne.

'Mr Lionel Blayne to see me, Helmerdyne. A man with a sense of punctuality. Dead on time.' Again he troubled himself with inserts to the dossier of the strange case. 'I won't keep him long.'

Mr Blayne had aged. His kindly and ascetic face had thickened and coarsened a little. His eyes were very dull and weary. But they did not remain so long after Wanless handed to him a photograph taken from the dossier.

'You'll notice I've done some tinkering with that, Mr Blayne—such as drawing a toque-shaped hat for its head, a pair of drop earrings and a pair of pince-nez. But tell me, do you recognise the general ensemble with some certainty?'

There was no mistaking the effect the likeness had on Mr Blayne. He shot up in his place and went purple.

'This is she,' he shouted. 'This is the woman—'

'Thank you, Mr Blayne.' The Professor carefully retrieved the card and as carefully filed it away. 'Now sit down and don't get so flurried. I believe we are on the verge of recovering your lost property, so it behoves you to be calm. My next question is equally simple.' Blayne sat down again and regained his normal composure. 'You state here,' Wanless put on his spectacles and found the place, 'that you found spiders' webbing in the heart lock of this chiavacuore. Is that adhered to?'

'Why, of course, Professor Wanless. I wouldn't say—'

'Are you absolutely certain these foulings were cobwebs?' Wanless was cold and inexorable. 'Would you swear, for instance, on oath that they were these and nothing other?'

'What—what else could they be?' Mr Blayne was troubled. 'They appeared to me to be cobwebs, anyway.'

'You also state' (another paragraph was found) 'you blew these "cobwebbings" out of the mechanism of the secret lock. Had they been cobwebs, Mr Blayne, could you have blown them out of that intricate and tiny machinery? I really doubt it.'

'I blew out what was in the lock. That's all I can tell you.'

'Ah, that's heaps better!' Wanless was satisfied. He opened a little box and passed the bottom half of a padlock to the jeweller. 'That's an ordinary lock,' he said, 'but spiders' threads are in it. Blow them out, Mr Blayne—please try.'

After a while Blayne had to admit the feat was impossible. The Professor smiled and took back the padlock.

'And now, Major Helmerdyne, prepare to sacrifice a modicum of your intelligence to the cause of pure science.' Wanless twitted his friend and took a walnut from the box. 'You have a blow at this: only a trifling blow, mark you.' He pulled at the walnut and its shell came into two parts. In each was a webbing, grey and dusty, yet viscous; a webbing such as spiders make. 'And you, Mr Blayne, might recognise this contrivance as a simple model of the cleft heart of the chiavacuore—and its contents.'

Blayne was emphatic, without doubt, he said, he was looking once again at the stuff he had seen in the heart lock.

'Now, Major—blow!'

After a minute or two—'My God,' sighed Helmerdyne, deep with awe, 'what an uncanny experience to undergo! Music and—and—oh, all sorts of—'

'Detail is not necessary,' Wanless curtly told him. 'We'll pass the test. Get yourself a drink . . . Maybe you'll take one as well, Mr Blayne?'

They were drinking when the butler magnificently announced to them: 'Prince Erick von Hodenburg-Sturmheim.'

'This,' said Professor Wanless, coldly, 'is His Highness the Rogue, Mr Blayne. Pray do not exert yourself to rise and batter him—sit down, Mr Blayne—sit down! With the addition of a woman's costume, a lot of greasepaint and some veiling, here you have the lady who negotiated with you over the Hodenburg-Sturmheim chiavacuore—a girdle made for Beatrice Giola de'Medici in fifteen fifty-five. This is, also, of course, the person who stole fourteen thousand pounds' worth of the property of Messrs Blayne, Ridley and Cowperthwaite.'

The slight figure of the prince would have been seated. His deadly hazel eyes calculated, but his lips smiled.

'Keep on your feet, young man; keep on your feet!' Wanless was terrific. 'How dare you?'

'I believe you have the right,' His Highness of Hodenburg-Sturmheim bowed mockingly. He spoke in perfect English. 'By the way, about this affair of the jewels . . . I quite acknowledge my game has come to loss. I also appreciate I must return to this good jeweller the property of his I am—ah—detaining at present. Your rather too explicit command for me to present myself here tonight, Professor, leaves me no option.'

'That, or ruin throughout Europe, Prince. There are ways and means, you know . . .'

'I abhor details; so tedious, don't you think?' Self-confessed rogue as he was, the Prince did not lack for assurance. 'However—what I should like to learn is how you managed to get on my track. I had thought my little scheme a faultless thing; disguise, action and everything.'

'Every criminal makes his one mistake,' Wanless icily stated. 'Yours was four centuries old—it waited for you.' Hodenburg-Sturmheim looked puzzled. 'You never realised that your heart-lock of the chiavacuore was suggested to Cellini by your Medici ancestress's crest, the scimitar by the Hodenburg-Sturmheim crest . . . The tiniest of clues, to me, but all sufficient.'

'The devil take it.' The Prince's face worked in sheer anguish. 'I—I certainly hadn't dreamed of that.' He was furiously quiet for a time, then he shot out, arrogantly: 'I congratulate you on your patient work, Herr Professor! But how the good Blayne was trapped into opening his silly safe and into handing me part of his firm's wealth together with my own chiavacuore—most deferentially escorting me to his shop door afterwards and bowing me out under the nose of his commissionaire—will never be told. That's a secret trick I'll try on the next fool I decide to loot. For loot I must, or sink.'

Professor Wanless then showed to His Highness the Prince of Hodenburg-Sturmheim two half shells of an emptied walnut. In one half was cobwebbing. In the other, Helmerdyne had breathed his breath. 'Would you like a dissertation?' he asked.

'Ach, nein—nein!' The Prince was confounded into his mother tongue. 'Das ist Sache . . . Herr Professor, das weiβ ich schon auswendig!' He grasped and controlled himself: his look was grey murder. 'I—I really must have under-estimated the profound British Intelligence Corps,' he finally drawled.

'You have travelled extensively in the Fijian Islands, Prince.

You would doubtless utilise that cunning brain of yours to some evil purpose; you couldn't help. You would not miss the kau-karo tree, the "itchwood tree" as we call it. And you would learn, trust you to do that, about the essences of the tree: so potent that a tiny drop exuded from one oblong leaf can cause intense irritation and, occasionally, blindness. And you would inform yourself all about the sap's distillation into a drug of the mydriatic genus—a powerful hypnotic causing the mind to conceive and imagine all kinds of erotic nonsenses.

'And, my scion of the Medici breed, being atavistic out of the failure of that breed,' the listener writhed, 'your uncanny intellect seized on the human element of the stuff. Probably you knew that medicinal men had tried it, along with atropine, and the rest, but had abandoned it because of its loathsome effect on the brain. Yet you did not scruple to employ it against an innocent subject like Mr Blayne.

'The Fiji islanders crudely tap the kau-karo, whereupon its sap coalesces into a cobwebby substance which again resolves in such gases as the human respiratory system can exude. My idea is that you took this process of coalescence to its Nth degree—prepared a pure and most powerful substance, almost instantaneous in its horrible effects. I also argue that you introduced this substance to the four-fold lock of the girdle and to the razor spicule of the cabochon diamond pip. You had Mr Blayne both ways.

'He did all you wanted him to do. Not only did he cut himself and so introduce the poison for a time to his bloodstream but he vaporised it and inhaled it. After that he was your helpless creature—like a drugged and dreaming Fiji islander, helpless in the undergrowth, a clod. Then you commanded him and robbed him. Whatever you told him was transmogrified into tiny ecstasies. He joyfully obeyed.' The fascinated eyes of the Prince answered all this. 'And now,' snapped Professor Wanless, 'remains your restitution.'

'I have—I have no choice in the matter. Blayne will get his jewellery back in the morning, intact.'

'More than that is required . . . Mr Blayne has suffered in many other ways,' Wanless purred. 'Seven days of agony of mind and business loss have passed since you visited him. You will pay Mr Blayne five hundred guineas a day for all that period—and a thousand guineas you will have to find for some charity.' Wanless still purred. 'It's no use looking like that—you are still comparatively speaking, wealthy, for all your talk of poverty and sinking. You'll do as I say.'

Prince Erick von Hodenburg-Sturmheim drew himself up and clicked his heels together. His rodent mouth snapped like a trap.

'I am a player in the game of the world,' he said, 'and I know how to lose.'

'Good enough!' Wanless waved him away. 'Glad to hear it—a Merry Christmas to you and—now clear off!' He turned to Major Helmerdyne. 'Do you mind,' he questioned, 'opening the window?'

VINCENT CORNIER

From the late 1920s to the early 1950s short stories of crime and detection were phenomenally popular throughout the whole of the English-speaking world. As well as magazines, many daily and weekly newspapers carried fiction, and while many of those who wrote primarily for this market were no better than hacks, paid by quantity rather than quality, some stood out—and none more so than Vincent Cornier. In a career spanning over forty years Cornier produced more than a hundred puzzles of crime and the supernatural as well as some stories of romance and adventure.

Born with the rather plainer surname of Corner in 1898 in what was then the North Riding of Yorkshire, the writer who would become Vincent Cornier started at an early age. Indeed, he once told Frederick Dannay, half of the 'Ellery Queen' partnership, that he had sold his first fiction while still a teenager, although none of these early works has yet been found.

In 1915, Corner was called up and joined the Royal Flying Corps, serving in northern France. After apparently being invalided out, he married and, rather than returning to his pre-war employment as a 'dental improver', he joined the *Yorkshire Post*, one of the oldest newspapers in the country.

Happily, an inheritance allowed him to become a freelance writer, for which he adopted the surname Cornier, and produced dozens of articles on subjects as diverse as Satanism and the impact on

Britain of rising numbers of American tourists. His fiction also began to be published widely in British and Australian newspapers, with early works including 'The Waiting House', a lightly criminous 'yuletide yarn' published in an Adelaide newspaper in 1925, and a series of *Secret Service Stories* featuring Sir Richard Thorreston Brantyngham. More stories followed—dozens and dozens of them, some reworking the same ideas and situations—and Cornier introduced new series characters including Home Office pathologist Michael Featonby and, in the early 1930s, Barnabas Hildreth, known as 'The Black Monk' and, like Brantyngham, an intelligence officer. Foremost among Cornier's sleuths is the partnership of Professor Wanless and Major Helmerdyne, who appeared in several novella-length stories including 'The Girdle of Dreams'.

Cornier's unusual plots and outlandish titles suggest an eccentric turn of mind and his work is characterised by extensive knowledge of arcana and the occult as well as plots that rely on bizarre murder methods or which turn on obscure aspects of geology and other aspects of the natural world. Cornier uses out of the way knowledge to create 'impossible' crimes, such as a shooting inside a locked room in which no weapon can be found, or extraordinary events such as a worldwide outbreak of spontaneous combustion or the resurgence of mediaeval plagues. Often implausible, sometimes preposterously so, Cornier's work is nonetheless always entertaining. While his career as a writer declined after the Second World War, when he took up teaching journalism, Cornier continued to produce new fiction from time to time, mainly for the American mainstay of short crime and detective stories, *Ellery Queen's Mystery Magazine*. He died in 1976.

'The Girdle of Dreams' was first published in the *Sheffield Daily Independent*'s *Christmas Budget for 1933*, where it was discovered by the Cornier scholar Stephen Leadbeatter.

THE FOOL AND THE PERFECT MURDER

Arthur Upfield

This story was written in the late 1940s, and some characters behave in a way that reflects the prejudices and insensitivities of the period.—T.M.

It was Sunday. The heat drove the blowflies to roost under the low staging that supported the iron tank outside the kitchen door. The small flies, apparently created solely for the purpose of drowning themselves in the eyes of man and beast, were not noticed by the man lying on the rough bunk set up under the veranda roof. He was reading a mystery story.

The house was of board, and iron-roofed. Nearby were other buildings: a blacksmith's shop, a truck shed, and a junk house. Beyond them a windmill raised water to a reservoir tank on high stilts, which in turn fed a long line of troughing. This was the outstation at the back of Reefer's Find.

Reefer's Find was a cattle ranch. It was not a large station for Australia—a mere half-million acres within its boundary fence. The outstation was forty-odd miles from the main homestead, and that isn't far in Australia.

Only one rider lived at the outstation—Harry Larkin, who was, this hot Sunday afternoon, reading a mystery story. He had been quartered there for more than a year, and every night at seven o'clock, the boss at the homestead telephoned to give orders for the following day and to be sure he was still alive and kicking. Usually, Larkin spoke to a man face to face about twice a month.

Larkin might have talked to a man more often had he wished. His nearest neighbour lived nine miles away in a small stockman's hut on the next property, and once they had often met at the boundary by prearrangement. But then Larkin's neighbour, whose name was William Reynolds, was a difficult man, according to Larkin, and the meetings stopped.

On all sides of this small homestead the land stretched flat to the horizon. Had it not been for the scanty, narrow-leafed mulga and the sick-looking sandalwood trees, plus the mirage which turned a salt bush into a Jack's beanstalk and a tree into a telegraph pole stuck on a bald man's head, the horizon would have been as distant as that of the ocean.

A man came stalking through the mirage, the blanket roll on his back making him look like a ship standing on its bowsprit. The lethargic dogs were not aware of the visitor until he was about ten yards from the veranda. So engrossed was Larkin that even the barking of his dogs failed to distract his attention, and the stranger actually reached the edge of the veranda floor and spoke before Larkin was aware of him.

'He, he! Good day, mate! Flamin' hot today, ain't it?'

Larkin swung his legs off the bunk and sat up. What he saw was not usual in this part of Australia—a sundowner, a bush waif who tramps from north to south or from east to west, never working, cadging rations from the far-flung homesteads and having the ability of the camel to do without water, or find it. Sometimes Old Man Sun tricked one of them, and then the vast bushland took him and never gave up the cloth-tattered skeleton.

'Good day,' Larkin said, to add with ludicrous inanity, 'Travelling?'

'Yes, mate. Makin' down south.' The derelict slipped the swag off his shoulder and sat on it. 'What place is this?'

Larkin told him.

'Mind me camping here tonight, mate? Wouldn't be in the way. Wouldn't be here in the mornin', either.'

'You can camp over in the shed,' Larkin said. 'And if you pinch anything, I'll track you and belt the guts out of you.'

A vacuous grin spread over the dust-grimed, bewhiskered face.

'Me, mate? I wouldn't pinch nothin'. Could do with a pinch of tea, and a bit of flour. He, he! Pinch—I mean a fistful of tea and sugar, mate.'

Five minutes of this bird would send a man crazy. Larkin entered the kitchen, found an empty tin, and poured into it an equal quantity of tea and sugar. He scooped flour from a sack into a brown paper bag, and wrapped a chunk of salt meat in an old newspaper. On going out to the sundowner, anger surged in him at the sight of the man standing by the bunk and looking through his mystery story.

'He, he! Detective yarn!' said the sundowner. 'I give 'em away years ago. A bloke does a killing and leaves the clues for the detectives to find. They're all the same. Why in 'ell don't a bloke write about a bloke who kills another bloke and gets away with it? I could kill a bloke and leave no clues.'

'You could,' sneered Larkin.

''Course. Easy. You only gotta use your brain—like me.'

Larkin handed over the rations and edged the visitor off his veranda.

The fellow was batty, all right, but harmless as they all are.

'How would you kill a man and leave no clues?' he asked.

'Well, I tell you it's easy.' The derelict pushed the rations into a dirty gunny sack and again sat down on his swag. 'You see, mate, it's this way. In real life the murderer can't do away with the body. Even doctors and things like that make a hell of a mess of doing away with a corpse. In fact, they don't do away with it, mate. They leave parts and bits of it all over the scenery, and then what happens? Why, a detective comes along and he says, "Cripes, someone's been and done a murder! Ah! Watch me track the bloke what done it." If you're gonna commit a murder, you must be able to do away with the body. Having done that, well, who's gonna prove anythink? Tell me that, mate.'

'You tell me,' urged Larkin, and tossed his depleted tobacco plug to the visitor. The sundowner gnawed from the plug, almost hit a dog in the eye with a spit, gulped, and settled to the details of the perfect murder.

'Well, mate, it's like this. Once you done away with the body, complete, there ain't nothing left to say that the body ever was alive to be killed. Now, supposin' I wanted to do you in. I don't, mate, don't think that, but I's plenty of time to work things out. Supposin' I wanted to do you in. Well, me and you is out ridin' and I takes me chance and shoots you stone-dead. I chooses to do the killin' where there's plenty of dead wood. Then I gathers the dead wood and drags your body onto it and fires the wood. Next day, when the ashes are cold, I goes back with a sieve and dolly pot. That's all I wants then.

'I takes out your burned bones and I crushes 'em to dust in the dolly pot. Then I goes through the ashes with the sieve, getting out all the small bones and putting them through the dolly pot. The dust I empties out from the dolly pot for the wind to take. All the metal bits, such as buttons and boot sprigs, I puts in me pocket and carries back to the homestead where I throws 'em down the well or covers 'em with sulphuric acid.

'Almost sure to be a dolly pot here, by the look of the place. Almost sure to be a sieve. Almost sure to be a jar of sulphuric acid for solderin' work. Everythin' on tap, like. And just in case the million-to-one chance comes off that someone might come across the fire site and wonder, sort of, I'd shoot a coupler kangaroos, skin 'em, and burn the carcasses on top of the old ashes. You know, to keep the blowies from breeding.'

Harry Larkin looked at the sundowner, and through him. A prospector's dolly pot, a sieve, a quantity of sulphuric acid to dissolve the metal parts. Yes, they were all here. Given time a man could commit the perfect murder. Time! Two days would be long enough.

The sundowner stood up. 'Good day, mate. Don't mind me. He, he! Flamin' hot, ain't it? Be cool down south. Well, I'll be movin'.'

Larkin watched him depart. The bush waif did not stop at the shed to camp for the night. He went on to the windmill and sprawled over the drinking trough to drink. He filled his rusty billy-can, Larkin watching until the mirage to the southward drowned him.

The perfect murder, with aids as common as household remedies. The perfect scene, this land without limits where even a man and his nearest neighbour are separated by nine miles. A prospector's dolly pot, a sieve, and a pint of soldering acid. Simple! It was as simple as being kicked to death in a stockyard jammed with mules.

'William Reynolds vanished three months ago, and repeated searches have failed to find even his body.'

Mounted Constable Evans sat stiffly erect in the chair behind the littered desk in the Police Station at Wondong. Opposite him lounged a slight dark-complexioned man having a straight nose, a high forehead, and intensely blue eyes. There was no doubt that Evans was a policeman. None would guess that the dark man with the blue eyes was Detective Inspector Napoleon Bonaparte.

'The man's relatives have been bothering Headquarters about William Reynolds, which is why I am here,' explained Bonaparte, faintly apologetic. 'I have read your reports, and find them clear and concise. There is no doubt in the Official Mind that, assisted by your black tracker, you have done everything possible to locate Reynolds or his dead body. I may succeed where you and the black tracker failed because I am peculiarly equipped with gifts bequeathed to me by my white father and my aboriginal mother. In me are combined the white man's reasoning powers and the black man's perceptions and bushcraft. Therefore, should I succeed there would be no reflection on your efficiency or the powers of your tracker. Between what a tracker sees and what you have been trained to reason, there is a bridge. There is no such bridge between those divided powers in me. Which is why I never fail.'

Having put Constable Evans in a more cooperative frame of mind, Bony rolled a cigarette and relaxed.

'Thank you, sir,' Evans said and rose to accompany Bony to the locality map which hung on the wall. 'Here's the township of Wondong. Here is the homestead of Morley Downs cattle station. And here, fifteen miles on from the homestead, is the stockman's hut where William Reynolds lived and worked.

'There's no telephonic communication between the hut and the homestead. Once every month the people at the homestead trucked rations to Reynolds. And once every week, every Monday morning, a stockman from the homestead would meet Reynolds midway between homestead and hut to give Reynolds his mail, and orders, and have a yarn with him over a billy of tea.'

'And then one Monday, Reynolds didn't turn up,' Bony added, as they resumed their chairs at the desk.

'That Monday the homestead man waited four hours for Reynolds,' continued Evans. 'The following day the station manager ran out in his car to Reynolds' hut. He found the ashes on the open hearth stone-cold, the two chained dogs nearly dead of thirst, and that Reynolds hadn't been at the hut since the day it had rained, three days previously.

'The manager drove back to the homestead and organised all his men in a search party. They found Reynolds' horse running with several others. The horse was still saddled and bridled. They rode the country for two days, and then I went out with my tracker to join in. We kept up the search for a week, and the tracker's opinion was that Reynolds might have been riding the back boundary fence when he was parted from the horse. Beyond that the tracker was vague, and I don't wonder at it for two reasons. One, the rain had wiped out tracks visible to white eyes, and two, there were other horses in the same paddock. Horse tracks swamped with rain are indistinguishable one from another.'

'How large is that paddock?' asked Bony.

'Approximately two hundred square miles.'

Bony rose and again studied the wall map.

'On the far side of the fence is this place named Reefer's Find,' he pointed out. 'Assuming that Reynolds had been thrown from his horse and injured, might he not have tried to reach the outstation of Reefer's Find which, I see, is about three miles from the fence whereas Reynolds' hut is six or seven?'

'We thought of that possibility, and we scoured the country on the Reefer's Find side of the boundary fence,' Evans replied. 'There's a stockman named Larkin at the Reefer's Find outstation. He joined in the search. The tracker, who had memorised Reynolds' footprints, found on the earth floor of the hut's veranda, couldn't spot any of his tracks on Reefer's Find country, and the boundary fence, of course, did not permit Reynolds' horse into that country. The blasted rain beat the tracker. It beat all of us.'

'Hm. Did you know this Reynolds?'

'Yes. He came to town twice on a bit of a bender. Good type. Good horseman. Good bushman. The horse he rode that day was not a tricky animal. What do Headquarters know of him, sir?'

'Only that he never failed to write regularly to his mother, and that he had spent four years in the Army from which he was discharged following a head wound.'

'Head wound! He might have suffered from amnesia. He could have left his horse and walked away—anywhere—walked until he dropped and died from thirst or starvation.'

'It's possible. What is the character of the man Larkin?'

'Average, I think. He told me that he and Reynolds had met when both happened to be riding that boundary fence, the last time being several months before Reynolds vanished.'

'How many people besides Larkin at the outstation?'

'No one else excepting when they're mustering for fats.'

The conversation waned while Bony rolled another cigarette.

'Could you run me out to Morley Downs homestead?' he asked.

'Yes, of course,' assented Evans.

'Then kindly telephone the manager and let me talk to him.'

Two hundred square miles is a fairly large tract of country in which to find clues leading to the fate of a lost man, and three months is an appreciable period of time to elapse after a man is reported as lost.

The rider who replaced Reynolds' successor was blue-eyed and dark-skinned, and at the end of two weeks of incessant reading he was familiar with every acre, and had read every word on this large page of the Book of the Bush.

By now Bony was convinced that Reynolds hadn't died in that paddock. Lost or injured men had crept into a hollow log to die, their remains found many years afterward, but in this country there were no trees large enough for a man to crawl into. Men had perished and their bodies had been covered with wind-blown sand, and after many years the wind had removed the sand to reveal the skeleton. In Reynolds' case the search for him had been begun within a week of his disappearance, when eleven men plus a policeman selected for his job because of his bushcraft, and a black tracker selected from among the aborigines who are the best sleuths in the world, had gone over and over the 200 square miles.

Bony knew that, of the searchers, the black tracker would be the most proficient. He knew, too, just how the mind of that aborigine would work when taken to the stockman's hut and put on the job. Firstly, he would see the lost man's bootprints left on the dry earth beneath the veranda roof. Thereafter he would ride crouched forward above his horse's mane and keep his eyes directed to the ground at a point a few feet beyond the animal's nose. He would look for a horse's tracks and a man's tracks, knowing that nothing passes over the ground without leaving evidence, and that even half an inch of rain will not always obliterate the evidence left, perhaps, in the shelter of a tree.

That was all the black tracker could be expected to do. He would not reason that the lost man might have climbed a tree and there cut his own throat, or that he might have wanted to vanish and so had climbed over one of the fences into the adjacent paddock; or had, when suffering from amnesia, or the madness brought about by solitude, walked away beyond the rim of the earth.

The first clue found by Bonaparte was a wisp of wool dyed brown. It was caught by a barb of the top wire of the division fence between the two cattle stations. It was about an inch in length and might well have come from a man's sock when he had climbed over the fence.

It was most unlikely that any one of the searchers for William Reynolds would have climbed the fence. They were all mounted. and when they scoured the neighbouring country, they would have passed through the gate about a mile from this tiny piece of flotsam. Whether or not the wisp of wool had been detached from Reynolds' sock at the time of his disappearance, its importance in this case was that it led the investigator to the second clue.

The vital attribute shared by the aboriginal tracker with Napoleon Bonaparte was patience. To both, Time was of no consequence once they set out on the hunt.

On the twenty-ninth day of his investigation Bony came on the site of a large fire. It was approximately a mile distant from the outstation of Reefer's Find, and from a point nearby, the buildings could be seen magnified and distorted by the mirage. The fire had burned after the last rainfall—the one recorded immediately following the disappearance of Reynolds—and the trails made by dead tree branches when dragged together still remained sharp on the ground.

The obvious purpose of the fire had been to consume the carcass of a calf, for amid the mound of white ash protruded the skull and bones of the animal. The wind had played with the ash, scattering it thinly all about the original ash mound.

Question: 'Why had Larkin burned the carcass of the calf?' Cattlemen never do such a thing unless a beast dies close to their camp. In parts of the continent, carcasses are always burned to keep down the blowfly pest, but out here in the interior, never. There was a possible answer, however, in the mentality of the man who lived nearby, the man who lived alone and could be expected to do anything unusual, even burning all the carcasses of animals which perished in his domain. That answer would be proved correct if other fire sites were discovered offering the same evidence.

At daybreak the next morning Bony was perched high in a sandalwood tree. There he watched Larkin ride out on his day's work, and when assured that the man was out of the way, he slid to the ground and examined the ashes and the burned bones, using his hands and his fingers as a sieve.

Other than the bones of the calf, he found nothing but a soft-nosed bullet. Under the ashes, near the edge of the splayed-out mass, he found an indentation on the ground, circular and about six inches in diameter. The bullet and the mark were the second and third clues, the third being the imprint of a prospector's dolly pot.

'Do your men shoot calves in the paddocks for any reason?' Bony asked the manager, who had driven out to his hut with rations. The manager was big and tough, grizzled and shrewd.

'No, of course not, unless a calf has been injured in some way and is helpless. Have you found any of our calves shot?'

'None of yours. How do your stockmen obtain their meat supply?'

'We kill at the homestead and distribute fortnightly a little fresh meat and a quantity of salted beef.'

'D'you think the man over on Reefer's Find would be similarly supplied by his employer?'

'Yes, I think so. I could find out from the owner of Reefer's Find.'

'Please do. You have been most helpful, and I do appreciate it. In my role of cattleman it wouldn't do to have another rider stationed with me, and I would be grateful if you consented to drive out here in the evening for the next three days. Should I not be here, then wait until eight o'clock before taking from the tea tin over there on the shelf a sealed envelope addressed to you. Act on the enclosed instructions.'

'Very well, I'll do that.'

'Thanks. Would you care to undertake a little inquiry for me?'

'Certainly.'

'Then talk guardedly to those men you sent to meet Reynolds every Monday and ascertain from them the relationship which existed between Reynolds and Harry Larkin. As is often the case with lonely men stationed near the boundary fence of two properties, according to Larkin he and Reynolds used to meet now and then by arrangement. They may have quarrelled. Have you ever met Larkin?'

'On several occasions, yes,' replied the manager.

'And your impressions of him? As a man?'

'I thought him intelligent. Inclined to be morose, of course, but then men who live alone often are. You are not thinking that—?'

'I'm thinking that Reynolds is not in your country. Had he been still on your property, I would have found him dead or alive. When I set out to find a missing man, I find him. I shall find Reynolds, eventually—if there is anything of him to find.'

On the third evening that the manager went out to the little hut, Bony showed him a small and slightly convex disc of silver. It was weathered and in one place cracked. It bore the initials J.M.M.

'I found that in the vicinity of the site of a large fire,' Bony said. 'It might establish that William Reynolds is no longer alive.'

Although Harry Larkin was supremely confident, he was not quite happy. He had not acted without looking at the problem from all angles and without having earnestly sought the answer to the question: 'If I shoot him dead, burn the body on a good fire, go through the ashes for the bones which I pound to dust in a dolly pot, and for the metal bits and pieces which I dissolve in sulphuric acid, how can I be caught?' The answer was plain.

He had carried through the sundowner's method of utterly destroying the body of the murder victim, and to avoid the million-to-one chance of anyone coming across the ashes of the fire and being made suspicious, he had shot a calf as kangaroos were scarce.

Yes, he was confident, and confident that he was justified in being confident. Nothing remained of Bill Reynolds, damn him, save a little greyish dust which was floating around somewhere.

The slight unhappiness was caused by a strange visitation, signs of which he had first discovered when returning home from his work one afternoon. On the ground near the blacksmith's shop he found a strange set of boot tracks which were not older than two days. He followed these tracks backward to the house, and then forward until he lost them in the scrub.

Nothing in the house was touched, as far as he could see, and nothing had been taken from the blacksmith's shop, or interfered with. The dolly pot was still in the corner into which he had dropped it after its last employment, and the crowbar was still leaning against the anvil. On the shelf was the acid jar. There was no acid in it. He had used it to dissolve, partially, buttons and the metal band around a pipestem and boot sprigs. The residue of those metal objects he had dropped into a hole in a tree eleven miles away.

It was very strange. A normal visitor, finding the occupier away, would have left a note at the house. Had the visitor been black, he would not have left any tracks, if bent on mischief.

The next day Larkin rode out to the boundary fence and on the way he visited the site of his fire. There he found the plain evidence that someone had moved the bones of the animal and had delved among the ashes still remaining from the action of the wind.

Thus he was not happy, but still supremely confident. They could not tack anything on to him. They couldn't even prove that Reynolds was dead. How could they when there was nothing of him left?

It was again Sunday, and Larkin was washing his clothes at the outside fire when the sound of horses' hoofs led him to see two men approaching. His lips vanished into a mere line, and his mind went over all the answers he would give if the police ever did call on him. One of the men he did not know. The other was Mounted Constable Evans.

They dismounted, anchoring their horses by merely dropping the reins to the ground. Larkin searched their faces and wondered who was the slim half-caste with, for a half-caste, the singularly blue eyes.

'Good day,' Larkin greeted them.

'Good day, Larkin,' replied Constable Evans, and appeared to give his trousers a hitch. His voice was affable, and Larkin was astonished when, after an abrupt and somewhat violent movement, he found himself handcuffed.

'Going to take you in for the murder of William Reynolds,' Evans announced. 'This is Detective Inspector Napoleon Bonaparte.'

'You must be balmy—or I am,' Larkin said.

Evans countered with: 'You are. Come on over to the house. A car will be here in about half an hour.'

The three men entered the kitchen where Larkin was told to sit down.

'I haven't done anything to Reynolds, or anyone else,' asserted Larkin, and for the first time the slight man with the brilliant blue eyes spoke.

'While we are waiting, I'll tell you all about it, Larkin. I'll tell it so clearly that you will believe I was watching you all the time. You used to meet Reynolds at the boundary fence gate, and the two of you would indulge in a spot of gambling—generally at poker. Then one day you cheated and there was a fight in which you were thrashed.

'You knew what day of the week Reynolds would ride that boundary fence and you waited for him on your side. You held him up and made him climb over the fence while you covered him with your .32 high-power Savage rifle. You made him walk to a place within a mile of here, where there was plenty of dry wood, and there you shot him and burned his body.

'The next day you returned with a dolly pot and a sieve. You put all the bones through the dolly pot, and then you sieved all the ashes for metal objects in Reynolds' clothes and burned them up with sulphuric acid. Very neat. The perfect crime, you must agree.'

'If I done all that, which I didn't, yes,' Larkin did agree.

'Well, assuming that not you but another did all I have

outlined, why did the murderer shoot and burn the carcass of a calf on the same fire site?'

'You tell me,' said Larkin.

'Good. I'll even do that. You shot Reynolds and you disposed of his body, as I've related. Having killed him, you immediately dragged wood together and burned the body, keeping the fire going for several hours. Now, the next day, or the day after that, it rained, and that rainfall fixed your actions like words printed in a book. You went through the ashes for Reynolds' bones before it rained, and you shot the calf and lit the second fire after it rained. You dropped the calf at least two hundred yards from the scene of the murder, and you carried the carcass on your back over those two hundred yards. The additional weight impressed your boot prints on the ground much deeper than when you walk about normally, and although the rain washed out many of your boot prints, it did not remove your prints made when carrying the dead calf. You didn't shoot the calf, eh?'

'No, of course I didn't,' came the sneering reply. 'I burned the carcass of a calf that died. I keep my camp clean. Enough blow-flies about as it is.'

'But you burned the calf's carcass a full mile away from your camp. However, you shot the calf, and you shot it to burn the carcass in order to prevent possible curiosity. You should have gone through the ashes after you burned the carcass of the calf and retrieved the bullet fired from your own rifle.'

Bony smiled, and Larkin glared.

Constable Evans said, 'Keep your hands on the table, Larkin.'

'You know, Larkin, you murderers often make me tired,' Bony went on. 'You think up a good idea, and then fall down executing it.

'You thought up a good one by dollying the bones and sieving the ashes for the metal objects on a man's clothes and in his boots, and then—why go and spoil it by shooting a calf and burning the carcass on the same fire site? It wasn't necessary. Having pounded Reynolds' bones to ash and scattered the ash to the four corners, and having retrieved from the ashes remaining evidence that a human body had been destroyed, there was no necessity to burn a carcass. It wouldn't have mattered how suspicious anyone became. Your biggest mistake was burning that calf. That act connects you with that fire.'

'Yes, well, what of it?' Larkin almost snarled. 'I got a bit lonely livin' here alone for months, and one day I sorta got fed up. I seen the calf, and I up with me rifle and took a pot shot at it.'

'It won't do,' Bony said, shaking his head. 'Having taken a pot shot at the calf, accidentally killing it, why take a dolly pot to the place where you burned the carcass? You did carry a dolly pot, the one in the blacksmith's shop, to the scene of the fire, for the imprint of the dolly pot on the ground is still plain in two places.'

'Pretty good tale, I must say,' said Larkin. 'You still can't prove that Bill Reynolds is dead.'

'No?' Bony's dark face registered a bland smile, but his eyes were like blue opals. 'When I found a wisp of brown wool attached to the boundary fence, I was confident that Reynolds had climbed it, merely because I was sure his body was not on his side of the fence. You made him walk to the place where you shot him, and then you saw the calf and the other cattle in the distance, and you shot the calf and carried it to the fire.

'I have enough to put you in the dock, Larkin—and one other little thing which is going to make certain you'll hang. Reynolds was in the Army during the war. He was discharged following a head wound. The surgeon who operated on Reynolds was a specialist in trepanning. The surgeon always scratched his initials on the silver plate he inserted into the skull of a patient. He has it on record that he operated on William Reynolds, and he will swear that the plate came from the head of William Reynolds, and will also swear that the plate could not have been detached from Reynolds' head without great violence.'

'It wasn't in the ashes,' gasped Larkin, and then realised his slip.

'No, it wasn't in the ashes, Larkin,' Bony agreed. 'You see, when you shot him at close quarters, probably through the forehead, the expanding bullet took away a portion of the poor fellow's head—and the trepanning plate. I found the plate lodged in a sandalwood tree growing about thirty feet from where you burned the body.'

Larkin glared across the table at Bony, his eyes freezing as he realised that the trap had indeed sprung on him. Bony was again smiling. He said, as though comfortingly, 'Don't fret, Larkin. If you had not made all those silly mistakes, you would have made others equally fatal. Strangely enough, the act of homicide always throws a man off balance. If it were not so, I would find life rather boring.'

ARTHUR UPFIELD

Born in England in 1890, Arthur William Upfield is probably Australia's best known writer of detective fiction. He landed in Adelaide, Australia, in 1911 intending to become a surveyor but ending up working on a pineapple plantation. He enlisted in the Australian military in August 1914, fighting in Gallipoli and in France, from time to time selling short stories and articles to the press back home about the experiences of the Australian. In 1915, he married an Australian nurse with whom he had one child, and after the war, he returned to work in England as secretary to the chairman of an ordnance factory.

But the pull of Australia was too strong and the Upfields returned in 1920. He travelled extensively throughout Australia, working in a variety of jobs—'droving, rabbiting, kangaroo-hunting, prospecting, opal-gouging and anything else that was going.' In 1925, Upfield started writing in his spare time 'working in camel carts, station kitchens, in tents, on tucker-boxes under the mulgas—anywhere I could use pencil and paper.' He wrote more short stories and six novels, one of which was published in book form, a thriller entitled *The House of Cain* (1928). Its success prompted him to try his hand at a detective story, and in *The Barrakee Mystery* (1929) he introduced Detective Inspector Napoleon 'Bony' Bonaparte of the Queensland police, the son of an aboriginal mother and a white father.

Around this time, Upfield had started working on the infamous 'No. 1 Rabbit Fence' in Western Australia. His third book, *The Beach of Atonement* (1930), was a thriller but did not feature Bony. However, the detective returned in *The Sands of Windee* (1931), which led to Upfield's giving evidence against a man on trial for murdering three transient labourers. While writing the novel, Upfield had discussed the plot with other labourers on the rabbit-proof fence, including the man accused of the murders who had realised how he could exploit the 'perfect' murder method that Upfield planned to use in the book. The trial led to the novel's being serialised in countless newspapers across the country and, never one to miss an opportunity himself, Upfield also wrote a book on the case, *The Murchison Murders* (1934).

Later in the 1940s, Upfield joined the Australian Geological Society and led an expedition to northern and western parts of Australia, including the Wolfe Creek Crater, the setting for the Bony novel *The Will of the Tribe* (1962). Bony remained very popular, appearing in 28 novels, all of which draw on the author's experiences of outback life and one of which had been left unfinished at the time of his death in 1964. Upfield also wrote an autobiography which, curiously, appeared under the name of his long-time companion, Jessica Hawke, for whom Upfield had left his wife in 1945.

He wrote 'The Fool and the Perfect Murder', the only short story to feature Bony, in 1948 when it was submitted to *Ellery Queen's Mystery Magazine* for a short story contest. Astonishingly it was mislaid and not published until 1979, when it appeared in the magazine under the title 'Wisp of Wool and Disk of Silver', a title not coined by Upfield.

BREAD UPON THE WATERS

A. A. Milne

'Kindness doesn't always pay,' said Coleby, 'and I can tell you a very sad story which proves it.'

'Kindness is its own reward,' I said. I knew that nobody else would say it if I didn't.

'The reward in this case was the hangman's rope. Which is what I was saying.'

'Is it a murder story?'

'Very much so.'

'Good!'

'What was the name of the kind gentleman?' asked Sylvia.

'Julian Crayne.'

'And he was hanged?'

'Very unfairly, or so he thought. And if you will listen to the story instead of asking silly questions, you can say whether you agree with him.'

'How old was he?'

'About thirty.'

'Good-looking?'

'Not after he was hanged. Do you want to hear this story or don't you?'

'Yes!' said everybody.

So Coleby told us the story.

Julian Crayne (he said) was an unpleasantly smooth young man who lived with his Uncle Marius in the country. He should have been working, but he disliked work.

He disliked the country, too; but a suggestion that he should help the export drive in London with a handsome allowance from Marius met with an unenthusiastic response; even when he threw in an offer to come down regularly for week-ends and bring some of his friends with him.

Marius didn't particularly like his nephew, but he liked having him about. Rich, elderly bachelors often become bores, and bores prefer to have somebody at hand who cannot escape.

Marius did not intend to let Julian escape. To have nobody to talk to through the week, and then to have a houseful of rowdy young people at the weekend, none of whom wanted to listen to him, was not his idea of pleasure. He had the power over his nephew which money gives, and he preferred to use it.

'It will all come to you when I die, my boy,' he said, 'and until then you won't grudge a sick old man the pleasure of your company.'

'Of course not,' said Julian. 'It was only that I was afraid you were getting tired of me.'

If Marius had really been a sick old man, any loving nephew such as Julian might have been content to wait.

But Marius was a sound 65, and in that very morning's newspaper there had been talk of somebody who had just celebrated his 105th birthday at Runcorn.

Julian didn't know where Runcorn was, but he could add 40 years to his own age and ask himself what the devil would be the use of this money at 70; whereas now, with £150,000 in the bank and all life to come—well, you can see for yourself how the thing would look to him.

I don't know if any of you have ever wondered how to murder an uncle; I mean an uncle whose heir and only relation you are.

As we all know, the motives for murder are many. Revenge,

passion, gain, fear, or simply the fact that you have seen the fellow's horrible face in the paper so often that you feel it to be almost a duty to eliminate it.

The only person I have ever wanted to murder is—well, I won't mention names, because I may do it yet.

But the point is that the police, in their stolid unimaginative way, always look first for the money motive, and if the money motive is there, you are practically in the bag.

So you see the very difficult position in which Julian was placed. He lived alone with his uncle's heir, and his uncle was a very rich man.

However subtly he planned, the dead weight of that £150,000 was against him. Any other man might push Marius into the river, and confidently wait for a verdict of Accidental Death; but not Julian.

Any other man might place a tablet of some untraceable poison in the soda-mint bottle, and look for a certificate of 'Death from Natural Causes'; but not Julian.

Any other man might tie a string across the top step of the attic stairs—but I need not go on. You see, as Julian saw, how terribly unfair it was. The thing really got on his mind. He used to lie awake night after night thinking how unfair it was; and how delightfully easy it would be if it weren't for this £150,000.

I have said that Uncle Marius was a bore. Bores can be divided into two classes: those who have their own particular subject, and those who don't need a subject.

Marius was in the former, and less offensive, class. Shortly before his retirement (he was in the tea business) he had brought off a remarkable double. He had filled in his first football pools form 'just to see how it went', distributing the numbers and the crosses in an impartial spirit, and had posted it 'just for fun'; following this up by taking over a lottery ticket from a temporarily embarrassed but rather intimidating gentleman whom he met in the train.

The result being what it was, Marius was convinced that he had a flair, or, as he put it, 'a nose for things.'

So when he found that through the long winter evenings—and, indeed, during most of the day—there was nothing to do in the country but read detective stories, it soon became obvious to him that he had a nose for crime.

Well, it was this nose which poor Julian had had to face. It was bad enough, whenever a real crime was being exploited in the papers, to listen to his uncle's assurance that once again Scotland Yard was at fault, since it was obviously the mother-in-law who had put the arsenic in the gooseberry tart; it was much more boring when the murder had taken place in the current detective story, and Marius was following up a confused synopsis of the first half with his own analysis of the clues.

And it was at just such a moment as this that Julian was suddenly inspired.

'You know, Uncle Marius,' he smiled, '*you* ought to write a detective story.'

Marius laughed self-consciously and said that he didn't know about that.

'Oh, I daresay I should be all right with the deduction and induction and so on—that's what I'm really interested in—but I've never thought of myself as a writer. There's a bit of a knack to it, you know. More in your line than mine, I should have thought.'

'Uncle, you've said it!' cried Julian. 'We'll write it together. Two heads are better than one. We can talk it over every evening and criticise each other's suggestions. What do you say?'

Marius was delighted with the idea . . . So, of course, was Julian. He had found his collaborator.

Yes (went on Coleby, wiping his mouth), I know what you are expecting.

Half of you are telling yourselves that, ironically enough, it was Uncle who thought of the fool-proof plan for murder which

Nephew put into execution; and the rest of you are thinking what much more fun it would be if Nephew thought of the plan, and, somewhat to his surprise, Uncle put it into execution.

Actually it didn't happen quite like that.

Marius, when it came to the point, had nothing much to contribute. But he knew what he liked.

For him one murder in a book was no longer enough. There must be two, the first one preferably at a country house-party, with plenty of suspects.

Then, at a moment when he is temporarily baffled, the Inspector receives a letter inviting him to a secret rendezvous at midnight, where the writer will be waiting to give him important information.

He arrives to find a dying man, who is just able to gasp out 'Horace' (or was it Hoxton?) before expiring in his arms. The murderer has struck again!

'You see the idea, my boy? It removes any doubt in the reader's mind that the first death was accidental, and provides the detective with a second set of clues. By collating the two sets—'

'You mean,' said Julian, 'that it would be taken for granted that the murderer was the same in the two cases?'

'Well, of course, my dear boy, of course,' said Marius, surprised at the question. 'What else?'

'The poacher, or whoever it was, had witnessed the first murder, but had foolishly given some hint of his knowledge to others—possibly in the bar of the local public-house. Naturally the murderer has to eliminate him before the information can be passed on to the police.'

'Naturally,' said Julian thoughtfully. 'Yes . . . Exactly . . . You know,' and he smiled at his uncle. 'I think something might be done on those lines.'

For there, he told himself happily, was the fool-proof plan. First, commit a completely motiveless murder, of which he could not possibly be suspected.

Then, which would be easy, encourage Uncle Marius to poke his 'nose for things' into the case; convince him that he and he alone had found the solution; and persuade him to make an appointment with the local Inspector.

And then, just before the Inspector arrives, 'strike again'.

It may seem to some of you that in taking on this second murder Julian was adding both to his difficulties and his moral responsibility.

But you must remember that through all these months of doubt he had been obsessed by one thing only, the intolerable burden of motive; so that suddenly to be rid of it, and to be faced with a completely motiveless killing, gave him an exhilarating sense of freedom in which nothing could go wrong.

He had long been feeling that such a murder would be easy. He was now persuaded that it would be blameless.

The victim practically selected himself, and artistically, Julian liked to think, was one of whom Uncle Marius would have approved.

A mile or two away at Birch Hall lived an elderly gentleman of the name of Corphew. Not only was he surrounded by greedy relations of both sexes, but in his younger days he had lived a somewhat mysterious life in the East.

It did not outrage credibility to suppose that, as an innocent young man, he might have been mixed up in some secret society, or, as a more experienced one, have robbed some temple of its most precious jewel; and though no dark man had been seen loitering in the neighbourhood lately, at least it was common knowledge that Sir George had a great deal of money to leave, and was continually altering or threatening to alter his will.

In short, his situation fulfilled all the conditions which Uncle Marius demanded of a good detective story.

At the moment Julian had no personal acquaintance with Sir George; and though, of course, they would have to be in some sort of touch with each other at the end, his first idea was to remain discreetly outside the family circle.

Later reflection, however, told him that in this case it would be better to be recognised as just a friendly acquaintance; obviously harmless, obviously with nothing to gain, even something to lose, by Sir George's death.

In making this acquaintance with his victim Julian was favoured by fortune. Rejecting his usual method of approach to a stranger (an offer to sell him some shares in an oil-well in British Columbia) he was presenting himself at the Hall as the special representative of a paper interested in eastern affairs, when he heard a cry for help from a little coppice which bordered the drive.

Sir George, it seemed, had tripped over a root and sprained his ankle. With the utmost good will Julian carried him up to the house.

When he left an hour later it was with a promise to drop in on a bed-ridden Sir George the next day and play a game of chess with him.

Julian was no great chess-player, but he was sufficiently intimate with the pieces to give Sir George the constant pleasure of beating him.

Between games he learned all he could of his host's habits and the family's dispositions. There seemed to him to be several admirable candidates for chief suspect, particularly a younger brother of sinister aspect called Eustace, who had convinced himself that he was to be the principal legatee.

Any morbid expectations you may now have of a detailed assessment of the murder of Sir George Corphew will not be satisfied. It is enough to say that it involved the conventional blunt instrument, and took place at a time when some at least of the family would not be likely to have an alibi.

Julian was not at this time an experienced murderer, and he would have been the first to admit that he had been a little careless about footprints, finger-prints and cigarette ash. But as he would never be associated with the murder, this did not matter.

All went as he had anticipated. A London solicitor had produced a will in which all the family was heavily involved and the inspector had busied himself with their alibis, making it clear that he regarded each one with the liveliest suspicion.

Moreover, Uncle Marius was delighted to pursue his own line of investigation which, after hovering for a moment round the Vicar, was now rapidly leading to a denunciation of an under-gardener called Spratt.

'Don't put anything on paper,' said Julian kindly. 'It might be dangerous. Ring up the Inspector, and ask him to come in and see you tonight. Then you can tell him all about it.'

'That's a good idea, my boy,' said Marius. 'That's what I'll do.'

But, as it happened, the Inspector was already on his way. A local solicitor had turned up with a new will, made only a few days before. 'In return for his kindness in playing chess with an old man,' as he put it, Sir George had made Julian Crayne his sole legatee.

Very unfair.

A. A. MILNE

Alan Alexander Milne was born in 1882. While he is best known for his stories for children about a certain teddy bear, A. A. Milne also wrote a number of detective stories and one novel, which in its day was something of a sensation.

A. A. Milne began his career writing for the school magazine at Westminster and he went on to edit *Granta* at Cambridge. In his twenties, despite his parents' hopes that he would join the Civil Service or become a teacher, he joined the staff of the satirical magazine *Punch*. During the First World War, Milne served with the Royal Warwickshire Regiment until he was invalided out after being injured in the battle of the Somme. After recuperating, he joined Military Intelligence in which capacity his role consisted mainly of writing propaganda articles until he was discharged in 1919.

This was around the beginning of what was to become the 'Golden Age' of detective fiction and, in addition to writing a number of successful comedy plays, Milne fulfilled what he called his 'passion' for the genre and wrote a detective story himself. The result, first serialised in the *Daily News*, was *The Red House Mystery*, in which an amateur sleuth investigates a mysterious shooting. The novel was widely praised and it was heralded by one eminent critic, with a *slight* qualification, as 'the most vivacious detective story, I think, that I have ever read'.

Despite—or perhaps because of—the tremendous artistic and commercial success of his first attempt, Milne did not write another novel-length mystery. He did however write some criminous plays, including *The Fourth Wall*, in which a pair of 'bright young things' prove that an apparent suicide is murder. The play was first produced in 1928, by which time Milne had become internationally famous for *Winnie-the-Pooh*, a volume of short stories first published in book form in 1926. *Winnie-the-Pooh* was followed by *The House at Pooh Corner* and both books feature a small boy called Christopher Robin, named for Milne's son who had been born in 1920.

Milne continued to write plays, including an adaptation of Kenneth Grahame's *The Wind in the Willows*, and essays on war and pacifism. However, his wider writing remained very much in the shadow of Pooh and his friends in the Hundred Acre Wood, whose popularity grated on Milne much as Sherlock Holmes eventually became a curse for Conan Doyle. During the Second World War, Milne served as a Captain in the Home Guard, but in 1952 a stroke effectively brought his writing career to an end, and he died in 1956.

One of only a small number of short detective stories by Milne, 'Bread upon the Waters' was first published in the *London Evening Standard* on 10 April 1950.

THE MAN WITH THE TWISTED THUMB

Anthony Berkeley

I

To smack the face of one's employer's husband, even under the severest provocation, cannot be considered good policy for a nursery-governess. Exactly three hours after neatly imprinting a small red splodge on M. Duchateau's sallow cheek, Veronica Steyning found herself stepping into a taxi in front of the trim Duchateau villa on the outskirts of Nice, with her trunk on the roof and a month's salary in her purse.

And did she return sorrowing to England, to seek humbly for a respectable post in Sutton or Surbiton? She did not. She took the next train to Monte Carlo, which in all her two years' guardianship over the stout but virtuous Duchateau offspring she had never yet visited, and spent the whole month's salary and the salary of more than one month before it, in buying all the clothes which she had always longed for and never before had the courage to acquire. It is very soothing at times to be utterly, violently and improvidently mad.

Not, however, that Veronica was quite so mad as she pretended to herself. She had saved money during those two years and she knew quite well that she could afford a holiday before beginning to look out for another post. But at twenty-two one must pretend to oneself to be rather mad sometimes.

Seated on a bench overlooking the blue sea in the Casino gardens two days later, Veronica was finding that life, for once in a while, was good. She was wearing some of the new clothes and that helped life to be good. Veronica was still wondering at the strange feeling of positively enjoying life, when she became aware of a large black shadow between herself and the sun. She looked up.

The shadow belonged to a tall young man, with a tanned, lean face and remarkably blue eyes, who was coughing in a deprecatory sort of way. 'I beg your pardon,' he said, 'but did you know you'd dropped this?'

Veronica pounced gladly on the handkerchief that he was offering her. She had bought some handkerchiefs only yesterday and they had been regrettably expensive. She felt most grateful to the tall young man for retrieving this one and thanked him warmly. So warmly, it seemed, that the young man appeared to consider her tone an invitation to sit down on the bench beside her, which he promptly did.

Veronica, who had been a little taken aback, smiled at herself. This after all was Monte Carlo, where acquaintances were as easily made as forgotten. Besides, she had been a little lonely these last two days. Half-an-hour's chat would not come at all amiss.

To her surprise she found herself, long before the half-hour was up, giving the young man, who had introduced himself by now under the name of Geoffrey Grant, a vivid account of her ejectment from the Duchateau villa. It wasn't a good story and Veronica realised now that she had been spoiling for an audience to hear it. She made the most of it.

Mr Grant seemed much impressed by the recital. The more so, it appeared, because Mr Grant himself had done almost exactly the same thing. Only a few days ago Mr Grant had been secretary to a highly unpleasant millionaire. The millionaire had been even more unpleasant than usual and Mr Grant with manly dignity had told him a few facts which somebody ought to have told him years ago and then rapidly followed them with his resignation before the millionaire could recover enough breath to dismiss him. And then, instead of returning humbly to England to seek another post, just like Veronica, Mr Grant had taken a room at an expensive hotel and proceeded to take a holiday worth having.

'This,' said Veronica solemnly, 'is fate.'

'It is,' agreed young Mr Grant, no less solemnly.

Veronica, who a few minutes ago had looked on this encounter as a chance affair with no sequel once the two of them had said good morning and parted, began to wonder. One might not believe in fate, but one cannot fail to recognise coincidence.

'Have you been to the Casino yet?' asked Mr Grant. 'No? Then we go there tonight.'

Veronica nodded her agreement. It seemed the least one could do, to celebrate such an admirable coincidence.

She opened her bag to stow away the handkerchief which all this time she had been holding in her hand and from the inside another handkerchief innocently confronted her.

'Hullo! This isn't my handkerchief after all.'

Mr Grant looked slightly embarrassed. 'Isn't it? Are—are you sure you didn't have two? Lots of people do, you know.'

'Where did you find it?' Veronica asked severely.

'Well, if you must know,' said Mr Grant with reluctance, 'on the beach at Cannes yesterday afternoon. Were you in Cannes yesterday afternoon?' he added hopefully.

Veronica smiled. 'I don't think I ought to come to the Casino with you tonight.'

'But you will,' said Mr Grant with confidence.

Mr Grant's confidence was justified; Veronica did go to the Casino with him that evening, but Mr Grant did not know how near she came during the afternoon to not going. It was only her sense of humour, which told her that a young man who would go so far as to buy a handkerchief in order to scrape an acquaintance really deserved to have his enterprise rewarded, that brought her to the meeting place.

The Casino, with its rococo magnificence, had not attracted Veronica; the gaming-rooms themselves definitely disappointed her. The highly-coloured fiction that has made a legend of this rather dreary spot, raises one's expectations altogether too high. Veronica had to admit that the throng around her differed in no particular, except in its cosmopolitan composition, from the sort of audience one might expect to see at a smart Wagner concert in Brighton.

She explored the place under Mr Grant's guidance, watched the play for a time at one or two tables, not at all sure who was winning and who losing, risked a few ten-franc throws herself without any sensational result, sat on a settee and drank some coffee and then professed herself ready to go. They separated in the vestibule to go to their respective cloakrooms, and met again on the steps outside. Mr Grant proposed a stroll through the gardens before he took her back to her hotel, and Veronica agreed.

When they had reached the sea-front Mr Grant, looking slightly triumphant, asked her if she had missed anything.

'No,' said Veronica, puzzled.

With the air of a conjurer producing the rabbit from the top-hat Mr Grant drew a small black and silver moiré bag from his pocket. 'Then what about this?' he asked. 'You left it on the settee.'

Veronica looked at it in bewilderment. 'That isn't my bag. I've got mine here, under my cloak.'

II

It was Geoffrey Grant's turn to look bewildered.

'Not your bag? But . . .'

'Here's mine, look,' said Veronica. 'Why, how extraordinary! They're almost the same, aren't they?'

Geoffrey Grant took the bag she was holding out to him and compared the two. Except for some small differences in the filigree work they were identical.

'Well, then,' he said, 'whose is this one?'

'It must belong to that woman who was sitting on my left. Do you remember? A handsome, Spanish-looking person in a black velvet frock and a little hat with ospreys. Her husband came up to her, or some man, and she went off with him. I expect she's still in the Casino. You ought to take this back there at once, Mr Grant. I'll stay here.'

The Casino was only a couple of minutes away, but in a hurried inspection of the crowd round the tables Geoffrey could not see the Spanish-looking lady in black velvet or her escort, whose face he only dimly remembered. Leaving the bag at the bureau, with an explanation of how it had come into his possession, he hurried back to Veronica.

She greeted him with an exclamation of relief. 'Oh, Mr Grant, thank goodness you're back. I don't much like being here alone. I've had an adventure.'

'An adventure?' Geoffrey echoed, leaning his elbows on the stone balustrade beside her.

'Yes. What do you think? A man came up to me just after you'd gone and said, most politely, that he feared there'd been a mistake over my handbag, and would I kindly give him the one that had been inadvertently taken by my—by you,' Veronica corrected herself hastily. 'I said you'd gone back to the Casino with it and he faded away.'

'Quick work,' Geoffrey commented in surprise. 'The husband, I suppose?'

'No, that's the funny thing. It wasn't the husband.'

'That's odd. And in any case, how on earth did he know that we'd come here?'

'That's just what I wondered. And, Mr Grant!'

'Hullo?'

'He was quite polite, and all that, but somehow—I don't know—he frightened me. He made me positively shiver, just like the snake-house in the zoo.' She looked at him with a face that still retained traces of fright.

If Geoffrey was impressed, he took care not to show it. 'Nerves!' he said robustly. 'Nerves and Monte Carlo combined. What a ridiculous fuss about a simple matter of two handbags. What does a handbag contain? What does your handbag contain? A handkerchief, a lip-stick and a powder puff. What you need, young woman, is a cup of strong coffee. Come along.'

Veronica let him lead the way. Her recent encounter had shaken her even more than she had admitted. As Geoffrey Grant said, it was absurd to imagine that the man had really set much store on the restitution of an insignificant handbag and even more absurd to feel that there had been an undercurrent of purposeful menace beneath his perfectly courteous manner. Of course it was nerves. A good cup of black coffee and perhaps a sip of brandy would set all that right in a moment. For the first time in her life Veronica felt she really needed such a stimulant if she were not to faint or do something else equally ridiculous.

Seated a minute or two later at a small open-air table before the café which borders the famous open space in front of the Casino, Veronica felt some compunction as she observed the care with which Geoffrey was ordering the very best brandy that the place could supply.

'Are you sure you can afford it?' she asked frankly, when the waiter had gone.

Geoffrey looked a little surprised. 'Why not?'

'I should hate to think I'd cut short your holiday by a day for the sake of a glass of brandy,' Veronica smiled. 'Your own glass, I mean. Of course, I shall pay you for mine.'

'You'll do nothing of the kind.'

'Indeed I shall,' Veronica said firmly. 'We're both in the same boat, so we'll pull equally at the oars. Otherwise I shall feel I can't go out with you again.'

'Independent sort of girl, aren't you?'

'Yes, I am.'

Geoffrey smiled. 'I like independence. Very well, you shall pay. I suppose,' he added, with a casual air, 'if I were a bloated millionaire myself instead of only the ex-secretary of one, you wouldn't be with me now?'

'No,' said Veronica without hesitation. 'And I should have been very much annoyed about your trick with the handkerchief, Mr Grant. But being in the same boat does make a difference. I don't know why, but it does.'

'Kindred spirits,' suggested Mr Grant.

'Something like that, perhaps,' admitted Veronica.

The arrival of the waiter put a stop to any possible development of this theme. While he was serving them Veronica let her eyes roam over the brilliantly lighted scene and the other small tables around them. Suddenly she uttered a low exclamation.

Geoffrey looked up. 'What is it?'

'Don't look round now, but that Spanish woman is here, a few tables away behind your left shoulder. I'm quite sure she wasn't there when we sat down. I noticed those tables as we came over.'

'Curious coincidence,' Geoffrey said lightly. 'Well, we haven't got her bag, so we can't help her.'

Veronica sipped her coffee. She had not mentioned it to Geoffrey, but it had seemed to her that the Spanish woman had been watching them intently. She was looking away now, but only after she had caught Veronica's eye. Nerves again, Veronica told herself impatiently, and set herself to be interested only in Geoffrey's conversation.

She was interested and it was not long before she forgot the

Spanish woman and her strange friend; Geoffrey could be very charming when he liked and he was obviously liking now. When the two got up to go, nearly an hour later, their friendship had made a considerable stride. Christian names had been exchanged and Veronica was already beginning to feel that for the rest of her stay Monte Carlo would be a still more pleasant place for her.

But the incident of the bag had not passed quite from her mind. As Geofirey was seeing her back to her hotel she stopped once and looked back. Geoffrey asked her what was the matter.

'It's silly of me,' Veronica said, with a rather nervous little laugh, 'but I had an idea that we were being followed.'

Geoffrey smiled indulgently. 'What you want is eight hours solid sleep. Take it from me, there'll be none of these fancies tomorrow.'

'I hope not,' said Veronica, with a slight shiver.

III

When Geoffrey Grant reached his own hotel it was, for the penniless ex-secretary of a millionaire, a strangely sumptuous bedroom into which he walked from the lift, just as it was a strangely sumptuous dressing-gown which he proceeded to exchange for his dinner-jacket.

The time was not late, as lateness in Monte Carlo goes, but Geoffrey felt disinclined to go out again. Neither, however, did he feel like staying alone in his bedroom. An odd restlessness had come over him, not in any way connected with the incident of the wrong bag, for he had attached little importance to Veronica's very small adventure. After standing for a moment in doubt in the middle of the floor, he went out of the room, crossed the passage and tapped at a door opposite.

A loud voice told him to enter, in French of an almost incredibly execrable accent. Geoffrey went in.

'Hullo, Archie, this is a bit of luck; I never expected to find you in.' Geoffrey threw himself into a chair and crossed his long legs. 'Well, how's things? I rather wanted to see you before dinner, but you were out.'

'I was,' agreed the other, an exquisite young man in evening clothes, with a monocle dangling from a silk ribbon round his neck. 'The Ransomes turned up here and I couldn't get away.' He inspected his friend critically. 'What have you been doing with yourself, Geoffrey? You look uncommonly pleased with life.'

'I am,' Geoffrey agreed. 'Give me a gasper—no, not a Turkish abomination; a real gasper—and I'll tell you the whole 'orrible story.'

'Been at it again?' sighed the exquisite young man. 'Really, you ought not to be let out without a keeper, Geoffrey. I don't want to hear your story in the least.' But he produced the required gasper nevertheless.

'This,' said Geoffrey, as he lit it, 'is the real thing.'

'It always is.'

'Listen,' Geoffrey said equably. 'Listen while I get it all off my chest or I'll burst your shirt-front in. Which will you have?'

'Go ahead,' said the exquisite young man, with resignation.

Geoffrey went ahead. Swinging his legs precariously from a small table, Archie listened.

When Geoffrey had finished, he shook his head. 'Poor girl! *Poor* girl! Little does she know what fate has brought her. The world's prize idiot, studded with diplomas a yard long; or ought to be.' He dodged a cushion aimed at his head and drew at his cigar. 'And what on earth made you tell her that rigmarole about being a newly-sacked profiteer's valet or whatever it was?'

'Because I had an idea that she wouldn't go on knowing me unless she thought I was in the same boat as herself,' Geoffrey pointed out patiently. 'And I was right. She said as much this evening.'

'I see. "Unhahnd me, Sir Jahsper. I may be but a poo-er maiden, but I have my pri-hide. Never let your riches darken my private bench in the Casino gardens again." That sort of girl, is she? Humph!'

'Yes. She *is* that sort of girl, Archie.'

'Quite so, old man,' Archie agreed hastily. 'I'm sure she is, if you say so. You know that what you say goes with me. I was only thinking that—well, that this is Monte Carlo, after all, you know.'

'I don't care a hang what you were thinking,' Geoffrey growled, 'but don't think it again.'

'It's unthought already,' said Archie generously.

There was a meditative silence, during which it was palpable that Archie was trying hard not to think it again.

Geoffrey yawned and stretched. His restlessness seemed to have gone now. He had an appointment with Veronica the next morning. Time to think about getting his beauty-sleep.

Suddenly Archie lifted his head and cocked an ear in the direction of the passage.

'Hullo,' he said. 'Someone in your room?'

'Not that I know of. Why?'

'I heard a bump and I'd have sworn it came from your room or as near as dash it.'

'Chambermaid, I suppose.'

'It's too late for chambermaids.'

'Good heavens,' Geoffrey grumbled, 'have you begun getting nerves now? All right, little boy, Uncle Geoffrey will go and catch the naughty burglar.'

He heaved himself out of his chair and stole noiselessly across the passage. Archie crept behind him. With a sudden jerk Geoffrey threw open his bedroom door. Inside the room, peering into a drawer in the dressing-table, was a man. He turned sharply round and Geoffrey recognised him at once as the (problematical) husband of the lady with the ospreys.

'Wanting to borrow a spare sponge or something?' he asked pleasantly. 'I keep them on the wash-stand.'

The intruder did not seem in the least disconcerted.

'I owe you an apology, sir,' he said, in perfect English, flavoured only with a very slight foreign accent of undistinguishable nationality. 'I came to ask if you would be good enough to restore to me my wife's bag, which you inadvertently took from the couch in the Casino, and getting no answer to my knock, took the liberty of looking round for it myself. Perhaps you will overlook my intrusion and hand me the bag.'

'I must say,' Geoffrey replied stiffly, 'that I don't much care about having my room invaded by a complete stranger, sir, even in search of his own property. As for the bag, you'll find it at the Casino bureau, where I left it as soon as I discovered the mistake, for which I apologise.'

The man's eyes narrowed. 'Is that all you have to say?' he asked curtly.

'Absolutely,' Geoffrey agreed in surprise. What more after all can one do than apologise? Did the fellow want him to buy another bag? Geoffrey would be quite willing to do so if the first one was really lost. But it was at the Casino bureau. 'Absolutely,' he repeated.

'Then you'll be sorry!'

Without a further word the man turned on his heel and swung out of the room and down the corridor, a square, burly figure, exuding unmistakable annoyance at every pore.

IV

'Well, can you beat that?' demanded the astonished Geoffrey of his no less astonished companion. 'What on earth did he mean?'

'The man doesn't seem to like having his wife's handbag rescued,' Archie remarked. 'And I may be wrong, but I'll swear he never knocked at your door.'

The two stared at one another.

'There's something fishy going on somewhere,' Geoffrey pronounced.

'Well, what's it all about, anyhow?' Archie asked plaintively. 'I don't remember anything about handbags in that story of young love you were telling me just now. Have you been trying to steal some woman's bag, my dear chap? There really wasn't any need. You can always borrow from me while the funds hold out.'

'Don't be funny, Archie. I'm beginning to think this is serious.' As shortly as possible Geoffrey explained how he had picked up a bag from the couch in the Casino, thinking that it was Veronica's and slipped it into his pocket to produce later with triumph when she missed it and it had not been Veronica's bag at all.

'But why all this fuss?' he concluded. 'Women don't keep anything in their evening bags but a lipstick and a mirror. Veronica seemed to think we were being followed back to our hotels and upon my word, it looks as if she were right. Why?'

Archie carefully closed the door of Geoffrey's bedroom and relit the stump of his cigar. 'I'm so glad I came to Monte Carlo,' he remarked. 'Well, obviously, my dear old lad, if you'd only make some use of the little grey cells instead of standing there and bleating, you'd realise that there was something more than a lip-stick and a mirror in this particular bag. And from the anxiety shown by the parties of the other side to recover it, something dashed valuable too.'

'Yes, of course; I know that. But why should I be "sorry" that all I had to say was that I'd left the thing at the Casino bureau?'

Archie raised his eyebrows. 'Put in words of one syllable, the chap did not think you had done so. And why? Because someone else stepped in during the interim and claimed it. And the husband of your Spanish friend thinks you've still got it. So let's sit down and make ourselves comfortable while we wait for the fireworks.' Archie dropped into an armchair, crossed one leg over the other and prepared to wait intelligently.

'You think that chap really is going to follow up?'

'From the look of him,' Archie returned languidly, 'I should say he'd follow anything up. A boy of the bulldog breed, was friend Fritz.'

Geoffrey grinned. 'I'm glad I came to Monte Carlo, too.'

They waited.

Nothing happened.

'It doesn't look as if he's coming back tonight,' suggested Geoffrey.

'Give him a chance, give him a chance,' Archie urged. 'He hasn't had time to collect his reinforcements yet.'

'By jove, you may be right,' Geoffrey exclaimed, remembering Veronica's 'adventure' in the Casino gardens. 'The fellow who spoke to Veronica wasn't the same as our man. There are two of them in it besides the woman.'

'And probably plenty more behind the scenes,' Archie said, comfortably. 'Yes, it looks quite like a scrap. I wonder what's behind it all. What'll you bet on a supply of dope?'

'Or a stolen diamond necklace?'

'Or a packet of Woodbines?'

Geoffrey stretched himself slowly. Though spare he was well-muscled. He flexed a tentative forearm. 'Well, I wish they'd come along, while we're ready for them.'

'Like me to sleep in here with you tonight?' Archie grinned. 'Or across your threshold, like a Great Dane?'

'I suppose one doormat's as good as another. By the way, are you going to scrap in a white waistcoat and tails?'

Archie looked down at his perfectly fitting coat not without pleasure. 'Why not?' His eyes wandered to the gaudy garment which covered his companion. 'Are you going to scrap in a dressing-gown?'

Geoffrey yawned. 'To tell you the truth, I don't believe there's going to be a scrap at all. Our friends will take the sensible course and complain to the police in the morning. That is, if those grey cells of yours were right and they genuinely think I've been trying to steal that bag.'

'Oh, that's what they think all right,' Archie said carelessly.

There was a moment's silence. Then Geoffrey uttered an exclamation and slapped his thigh.

'Caught it?' Archie asked sympathetically.

'Archie, a great light has broken on me. You and your rotten grey cells are off the track altogether. That isn't what they think at all. You see, they've been to the Casino, and they *have* got the bag. That's what the trouble is.'

'My dear old boy, why?'

Geoffrey beamed. 'Because it was the wrong bag.'

'What?'

'I had both bags in my hands, you see. I don't know which is which, but obviously I must have given Veronica theirs and taken hers back to the Casino. So naturally they think I've double-crossed them. That is the expression, isn't it?'

But Archie was not smiling. 'Ah! Then do you know what friend Fritz has been doing while we've been waiting here? Scurrying along to your young woman's hotel as fast as his legs will carry him.'

'By Jove, Archie, that's the first sensible thing you've said tonight. I'd better ring up the Magnificent at once, and warn her.'

Geoffrey went to the telephone by his bedside, demanded and got the Magnificent and asked to be put on to Miss Steyning's room. There was a pause of at least two minutes. Then Geoffrey muttered something into the mouthpiece, hung up the receiver and turned to Archie with undisguised alarm in his voice.

'The chap says he can't get any reply. I'm going round there at once.' He was moving towards the door as he spoke.

'And so am I,' said Archie, with some indignation.

V

The night-clerk at the Magnificent was a man whom very little in this world could surprise; yet even he forgot himself so far as to raise his eyebrows when there burst suddenly through the imposing main entrance a tall young man clad in a vivid purple dressing-gown. The fact that under it he wore the stiff shirt and black tie of ordinary evening dress detracted nothing from the glory of the dressing-gown. The night-clerk could not but feel that the companion who followed close on the heels of the dressing-gown in the more conventional white waistcoat and tails, however exquisite, was something of an anti-climax.

Geoffrey wasted no time on the night-clerk's musings. He had covered the quarter-of-a-mile from the Hermitage, his own hotel, in something under two minutes; in any case he never allowed petty considerations of etiquette to stand in his way when he was in a hurry. As he strode up to the counter, behind which the night-clerk's eyebrows still formed a cold note of interrogation, he gave an impression of such purpose that the night-clerk, who had had every intention of translating the query of his eyebrows into frigid speech, hastily reconsidered this decision.

'I was speaking to you on the telephone just now,' Geoffrey said shortly, in excellent French. 'You told me there was no answer from Miss Steyning's room. Try to get her again, please.'

Once more as he looked at the dressing-gown across his counter, words rose tumultuously to the night-clerk's lips; once more his eyes rose to Geoffrey's face and he thought better of it. Confining himself to a pointed shrug of his thin shoulders, he turned to the telephone at his elbow.

'There is no reply from Miss Steyning's room, sir,' he remarked a minute later.

'What's its number?' Geoffrey demanded.

This time the night-clerk did give way to his feelings. 'Monsieur, this is highly irregular,' he burst out, with a jaundiced glance at the offending dressing-gown. 'It is quite impossible for me to give you the number of Mademoiselle Steyning's room. I must ask you please to leave the hotel at once, or I shall be compelled—'

A large hand shot out and grabbed the back of his neck.

'What's the number of Miss Steyning's room?' Geoffrey repeated pleasantly. 'Quick—before I bump your nose on the counter.'

'Number three hundred and twenty-seven, third floor,' hurriedly squeaked the night-clerk, who had a wholesome respect both for his nose and the counter.

'Thank you,' said Geoffrey, and released him. 'Come on, Archie.' Without delay he made for the main staircase and, disdaining the lift, leapt up the shallow steps three at a time.

'Lunatics!' muttered the outraged little night-clerk, torn between a desire to leave his post which was strictly forbidden and a dislike of being kicked downstairs which he feared only too well might happen were he to follow. Finally he chose the better part of valour and, choking down his emotion as best he could, watched the purple dressing-gown disappear round the angle of the stairs.

'But why all this frantic excitement, old man?' panted Archie, toiling up the stairs in the dressing-gown's wake. 'You surely don't think anything can have happened to the young woman, do you?'

'I don't know,' Geoffrey replied, with a touch of grimness. 'But that's just what I'm going to find out.'

Arrived at the third floor, they hurried down the main corridor, Geoffrey watching the numbers of the doors as he passed them.

'Three twenty-three, three twenty-five, three twenty—hullo, the door's open.'

It was true. The door was standing slightly ajar and the light from inside was visible through the opening. Without hesitation

Geoffrey threw it wider and looked inside. The room was empty.

'Gone, has she?' remarked Archie with interest, peering over his shoulder.

'She's been to bed too,' Geoffrey frowned, glancing swiftly round the room. 'Been to bed and got up again. Archie, I don't like this. Let's see if—'

'Look out,' Archie whispered suddenly. 'Someone coming.'

They drew back from the open door. A girl was advancing along the corridor, in a shell-pink wrapper with a good deal of lace about it.

Geoffrey exclaimed with relief, 'Veronica! Thank goodness.'

'Hullo!' said Veronica cheerfully, as she caught sight of them. 'What on earth are you doing, Geoffrey? I didn't know you were going to change your hotel.'

'What's happened, Veronica?' Geoffrey demanded. 'I've been trying to get you on the telephone from the Hermitage, but the man couldn't get an answer. So we came round. Oh, by the way, Lord Bramber, Miss Steyning.'

'How do you do?' Veronica said perfunctorily and turned back again at once to Geoffrey. 'But Geoffrey, you surely didn't come round like that, did you?'

For the first time Geoffrey seemed to become aware of the purple dressing-gown. 'Good lord!' he exclaimed, not without surprise. 'I suppose I did. Well, I must have done, mustn't I?'

'He's mad, Miss Steyning,' Archie pointed out sadly. 'Always has been. Used to gibber at his nurse and probably mopped a bit in his spare time too, to say nothing of mowing—I was shouting at you to change it all the way down the stairs,' he added to Geoffrey, in tones of sorrow and pity.

'You want to improve that shout of yours,' Geoffrey said kindly. 'I never heard a word.'

Veronica obliged the company with a slight blush. The reason for Geoffrey's great haste was only too obvious.

'Well, I'm very glad you have come,' she said hastily, 'both of you. Because I've had another adventure. Wait here a minute while I make my room respectable and then I'll tell you. It's really rather exciting.'

VI

'I like this lady of yours,' Archie remarked with candour, when the door had closed behind Veronica and sounds as of drawers being opened and shut were coming from behind it.

'You leave the poor girl alone, that's all,' Geoffrey growled. 'She's got troubles enough on her hands without you adding to them.'

'Geoffrey!' Archie remonstrated in a pained voice. 'You are too modest. And she still doesn't know who you are?' he added maliciously.

'No, she doesn't. And don't you go telling her.'

'I must exercise my own judgment,' Archie returned smugly. 'I never was one to stand by and watch poor innocent girls being deceived, I wasn't.'

The opening of the door checked Geoffrey's reply, but from the look on his face it would have been a forcible one.

'You can come in now,' Veronica invited. She had slipped on a frock in place of the wrapper and the room behind her certainly looked tidier than it had.

Nevertheless Geoffrey hesitated. 'Had we better, do you think? Isn't there somewhere else handy? I mean . . .'

'Geoffrey, don't be old-maidish,' Veronica laughed and stood aside to allow them to enter. 'We're in Monte Carlo, not Surbiton.'

They entered.

'Now then, you'd better have the armchair, Lord Bramber, as the guest of honour. As a mere secretary, Geoffrey, and an ex-one at that, you have the trunk. I'll sit on the bed. Oh and please give me a cigarette, somebody. My nerves aren't used to this kind of thing.'

One of Archie's despised cigarettes found an appreciative home and Veronica embarked on her story.

'Well, I came straight up here after you left me, Geoffrey,' she began, hugging her knees, 'and it wasn't two minutes before I found out that you'd taken the wrong bag back to the Casino. I still had the Spanish woman's, you bright person. Did you know that?'

Geoffrey nodded. 'Yes, I'd guessed as much. Go on.'

'Of course, I'd looked inside before I realised it wasn't mine and even then I didn't tumble to it at once. There was a powder-puff, you see and a handkerchief and all that sort of thing and in the inside pocket was a piece of paper. I was feeling rather limp and sleepy and still not realising that it wasn't my bag at all, I opened the paper and looked at it, wondering what it was. It was covered with a jumble of letters and figures; and then, of course, I knew I'd got hold of the wrong bag.'

'Letters and figures,' Geoffrey repeated thoughtfully. 'I wonder if that was why they've been so remarkably anxious to get it back in such a hurry. Was there much money in the bag, or anything that looked valuable?'

'No, not a thing. That's the extraordinary part. And only a single ten-franc note. It couldn't have been for anything of that sort that they wanted it back so urgently.'

'It's funny,' Geoffrey mused. 'And they wanted it even more urgently than you know. I found a man in my room at the Hermitage calmly searching for it, if you please. He seemed to think I'd lodged the wrong bag at the Casino on purpose.'

'They told each other off most politely, Miss Steyning,' Archie put in irrepressibly. 'I stood between 'em and egged 'em on, but Fritz wouldn't fight. Well, what happened next?'

'Well, of course I thought I should have to go to the Casino first thing tomorrow, explain the mistake and change the bags. But I was saved the trouble. I went to bed and got off to sleep almost at once; it can't have been more than a few minutes later before I was wakened by somebody moving about the room. I switched on the light by the bed and saw a man standing by the dressing-table. I recognised him at once. It was the man who had spoken to me in the gardens when you'd gone back to the Casino, Geoffrey.'

'Not the husband—or Fritz, as Archie calls him?'

'No, no; not a bit like him. The one who I told you frightened me so much, like a snake. Well, of course I was petrified—far too petrified even to scream. He began to speak at once, quite calmly, something about having made a mistake in the room-number, thought it was his own room and all that; apologised stiffly but politely in perfect English for having disturbed me and marched out, leaving me gasping like a hooked fish. When I came to my senses I noticed that the bag, which had been on the dressing-table, had gone too.'

'Ah,' said Geoffrey.

'Aha,' said Archie.

'He may have been the rightful owner,' resumed Veronica, with some indignation, 'but there are ways and ways of doing that sort of thing and to break into my bedroom while I was asleep seemed to me decidedly a wrong way. I was so angry that I quite forgot how frightened I was of him. I jumped out of bed, jumped into my dressing-gown and ran after him.'

'That's the spirit,' Geoffrey agreed with enthusiasm.

'Unfortunately he'd got too much of a start. I'd heard him turn to the right outside my door, so I went that way. There's another smaller staircase at the end and I could have sworn I heard him running up it. I fled up goodness knows how many flights and explored about fifty corridors, but couldn't see a trace of him anywhere. Then I came back and found you here.'

Geoffrey lit another cigarette. 'It's all very queer,' he ruminated. 'There's obviously something very important, or something that these people consider very important, at stake. What do you think, Archie?'

'Oh, not a doubt of it. For an hour or so you two have evidently been a spoke in a rather nasty-looking wheel. No doubt you're well out of it; because of course that's the end, so far as you're concerned, now they've got their paper back. That's obviously what they were after. Well, it's been good fun while it lasted; but do you know, I can't help feeling it's rather a pity that Miss Steyning couldn't have managed somehow to give the bag back without the paper, just so that we could have seen what would have happened.'

'But I did!' Veronica exclaimed excitedly. 'I've been trying to tell you, but you would keep on talking. It looked so important that I took it out of the bag before I went to bed and hid it under my pillow. Here it is!'

VII

Veronica delved under her pillow, extracted a sheet of paper and handed it across to Geoffrey.

'Now that,' commented Archie, with a good deal more alertness than he had yet displayed, 'is what I call a piece of genius. I congratulate you, Miss Steyning. If the gods are with us, we're going to have some fun yet with that bit of paper.'

Geoffrey was busy examining the cabalistic signs with which the paper was covered and Veronica turned to the last speaker with a smile. She liked this languidly exquisite young man, who yet gave a hint that there might be something quite firm underneath his polished exterior. With him and Geoffrey between them she felt quite safe, even if, as Archie surmised, her abstraction of the document from the Spanish-looking lady's handbag led to 'fun'. And if she had felt any surprise in the ex-secretary of a millionaire introducing to her a full-blown lord as his friend and apparently an intimate friend at that, she had certainly not shown it. Perhaps since eleven o'clock that same evening surprises had ceased to exist for Veronica.

'I do believe you're hoping that it really does mean something exciting, Lord Bramber.'

'Am I not! Life is pretty dull in this hole, don't you think? I believe some people at home think Monte Carlo is wicked. I find it more respectable than Hull on a wet Sunday. If you've had the luck to project us into the middle of a real non-stop thriller, Miss Steyning, I shall be duly grateful. And so,' added Archie, with a completely innocent face, 'I'm sure, will Geoffrey.'

'Here, Archie,' observed Geoffrey, passing the paper across, 'stop talking for once and see what you can make of this. I'm blessed if I can make anything out of it.'

'Geoffrey,' Veronica remarked irrelevantly, as Archie studied the paper in his turn, 'I'm not usually nervous, but I do think that—'

'It's all right, Veronica,' Geoffrey interrupted soothingly, 'there won't be any *danger*, you know.'

'I wasn't meaning that,' Veronica retorted with dignity. 'And I hope there is, for Lord Bramber's sake. What I was going to say was that I'm not usually nervous, but I really do think you'd better not go on sitting on my trunk any more after all. It's the only one I've got and you're larger than I thought. Do you mind trying the floor?'

Geoffrey obediently transferred his muscular bulk to a more solid resting-place and Archie looked up from the paper.

'I can tell you what we must do with this,' he said, with unwonted seriousness. 'Of course it may be nothing, but on the other hand it may be rather important. As it happens there's one man in Monte Carlo at this moment who can tell us, my cousin, Bobbie Carruthers. I don't know whether you've ever heard, but he's one of the lads in the Secret Service, I believe, though naturally he doesn't want that generally known. I'm quite sure we ought to take this round to him at once.'

'Seems a pity to let it pass out of our hands,' Geoffrey

murmured with regret. 'I don't see why we shouldn't tackle it ourselves.'

'Because we don't know what it is,' Archie pointed out, 'and if it is of importance to Bobbie, we oughtn't to take any risks with it. Though if you ask me, I think he'll probably pass it up, in which case we can tackle it ourselves. Well?'

'I suppose you're right,' Geoffrey conceded.

'The Secret Service!' Veronica said raptly. 'Oh, yes, do let's. I *am* glad I came to Monte Carlo.'

And so it was decided.

Veronica insisted on accompanying the men on their mission, which in view of the activity of Fritz and his friends the two agreed would be the safer course and, for the same reason, it was decided that they had better set off at once. The men were thereupon promptly turned out of the room while Veronica made herself ready.

Right in the doorway they collided with the sallow-faced little night-clerk who, his apprehension apparently forgotten, spluttered at them indignantly. One gathered that all this was not only highly irregular, but a nasty smudge on the fair fame of the Magnificent Hotel. Mademoiselle would be requested to take her departure first thing tomorrow morning, while as for Messieurs, the little clerk must really insist that they leave the hotel at once. It was a positive scandal that—

'Why, Archie,' observed Geoffrey with the utmost geniality, 'here's something for us to play with while we're waiting.'

He picked the little man up by the seat of his trousers, walked briskly along to the staircase and, slinging him over the marble balustrade, held him suspended above the unpleasant void.

'Do you think he'd go off pop if I dropped him?' he asked his companion with interest. 'Or would he just squash flat, like a starfish?'

'I don't know, Geoffrey,' responded Archie, with no less interest. 'I should drop him and see.'

In this way the time passed pleasantly for all concerned, except the night-clerk, until at the end of five minutes or so a little man no longer sallow but white and not to say tinged with green, crept hurriedly down a back staircase, pondering no doubt on the maniacal ways of the brutal English.

'But why this exhibition of cruelty to animals,' Archie asked, as they strolled back along the corridor, 'so unlike your usual gentle nature, my dear Geoffrey?'

'Didn't you see?' said Geoffrey. 'The little blighter was listening outside the door. I'll bet you a hundred to one Fritz and Co. have got at him. I'm not sure that I ought to have let him go at all. He's probably scampered off to report what we're going to do.'

A muffled scream from inside Veronica's room intercepted Archie's reply. 'Geoffrey!' they heard her cry. 'Geof—'

As if with one mind both men hurled themselves at the door. It was not locked and opened to their touch. In the middle of the room Veronica was standing, in hat and coat. The French windows on the further side, which opened on to the usual balcony and had before been closed, were now open.

In the aperture stood a man, an automatic pistol in his hand.

VIII

All this Geoffrey took in at a glance, together with the fact that the man with the automatic was a stranger to him. The next instant he hurled himself forward.

There was a scream from Veronica and Geoffrey crashed to the floor. Archie had tackled him round the knees from behind.

'Idiot,' observed the latter, holding Geoffrey down by main force. 'Can't you see this chap means business?'

'Thank you, sir,' observed the stranger courteously. 'You at any rate appear to have the sense to see when you are beaten. You are quite right, I do mean business. I want that document which was taken out of the handbag by Miss Steyning. If I do not get it I shall shoot all three of you. Miss Steyning first. Kindly shut the door, Miss Steyning.'

With a brave attempt to look as if revolvers pointed in her direction were one of the ordinary things of life to her, Veronica crossed the room and shut the door. The two men had picked themselves up from the floor and stood, looking rather foolish, in the middle of the room.

'Now then, which of you has the paper?' remarked the intruder tentatively. 'You, sir!' he added without hesitation to Archie, as Veronica's glance flickered swiftly towards that gentleman and away again.

'Damn!' observed Archie with feeling.

'Don't give it him, Archie,' Geoffrey urged. 'Look here, if we go for him together he can't—'

'My dear Geoffrey, as our friend observes, I know when I'm beaten and I'm certainly not going to risk getting plugged for the sake of a piece of paper that means nothing in my young life.' He put his hand into his breast-pocket and pulled out the document. 'Here you are, sir. I suppose you won't gratify our curiosity by telling us what all the fuss is about?'

The man took the document at arm's length, glanced at it swiftly and put it into his pocket. 'Thank you. I'm glad that you at any rate have sense. Now back to the door, please, all three.'

He waited till they had obeyed, his pistol still pointing unwaveringly at Veronica, then with a swift movement stepped back, closed the French windows and vanished.

'Well, I'm hanged!' said Geoffrey bitterly. 'Archie, you shouldn't have given it to him.'

'We're all three alive now,' Archie returned equably. 'The lad meant business. Besides, it wasn't our paper after all and fair's fair. Likewise, honesty is the best policy.'

'I can't let him get away with it like this,' Geoffrey muttered. He ran across the room, threw open the windows again and plunged out on to the balcony.

'Geoffrey, do be careful,' Veronica implored.

Archie raised his eyebrows. 'Geoffrey always was one of the boys of the bulldog breed,' he murmured; but he too had hurried in the other's wake.

Veronica joined them and all three leaned over the balcony rail, to watch an agile figure rapidly descending the fire-escape almost directly beneath them.

'Veronica,' Geoffrey said softly, 'just bring me that water jug of yours.'

'My water jug?' Veronica repeated in surprise, but brought it nevertheless.

Geoffrey poised it for a moment and then hurled it almost vertically down. The man was actually in the act of stepping down from the last rung of the fire-escape. There was a crash, a tinkle, a thud and a sound as of rushing waters. 'Oh, pretty!' Archie exclaimed, craning over the balustrade. 'Oh, handsome.'

'That wins the cigar or toothpick, I fancy,' observed Geoffrey with satisfaction. He pulled off his dressing-gown and ran lightly, for all his size, down the fire-escape.

'What's happened?' asked Veronica, also leaning over the balcony. 'Surely Geoffrey didn't—hullo, what's that thing on the ground?'

'That's Hans,' explained Archie. 'Geoffrey pipped him rather neatly on the cranium. But I'm afraid he's dented your water-jug beyond repair.'

Veronica almost danced with excitement. 'And now he's gone down to get the paper back. Oh, good for Geoffrey! Isn't he splendid, Lord Bramber?'

'Geoffrey's a good old horse,' replied Archie, his words more casual than his tone. Archie was being very busy at the moment trying not to do anything so unBritish as show the excitement which was filling him. 'By the way, was that the cove who interviewed you earlier in the evening?'

'Yes, the one who frightened me so. Am I wrong, or isn't there something horrible about him? Did you feel it?'

'I did,' Archie said candidly. 'I've seldom met a cove I disliked more at first sight. In fact,' he added thoughtfully, 'that may have been why I gave in so weakly. I'm not always so feeble as I must have looked tonight. At least, I hope not.'

'Of course you weren't feeble,' Veronica said warmly. 'It was because I was there. I know that. When there are pistols and things about, the presence of a woman must be most superfluous. As a matter of fact I thought it was very brave of you to give in at once instead of trying to save your face, as most men would.'

'Oh, come, that's going a bit too far,' Archie laughed. 'Ah, Geoffrey's got the paper. Good! Now we're all serene-oh.'

Geoffrey, standing over the body, had waved the document to them to show that he had found it and was now climbing rapidly back up the fire-escape.

'Geoffrey!' Veronica called out softly. 'You—you haven't killed him, have you?'

'Not a bit,' Geoffrey replied from twenty rungs below them. 'Just dinted him a bit, that's all. I'm afraid he'll have a nasty headache in about half-an-hour, but nothing worse.'

He was climbing rapidly up towards them. He had in fact reached within a yard of the floor of the balcony when something happened which Archie, though he had said nothing to Veronica, had all the time been dreading.

From the shadows on the ground came the muffled report of a shot. Geoffrey, who had been in the act of stretching up to pull himself on to the balcony, seemed to collapse on himself. His hand left its grip on the rung above him and he fell.

IX

Veronica uttered a low little cry of horror. Archie only said, abruptly; 'Get back into the room, Miss Steyning.' Veronica did not obey. Together they leaned over the balustrade.

'*Oh!*' exclaimed Veronica, hardly believing what she saw.

Archie had seen the same thing. He straightened up, took Veronica by the elbows and ran her back into the bedroom. They had both seen Geoffrey arrest his fall by catching hold of a rung only three feet below him, hang on to it and then climb rapidly up to the balcony. The sound of another shot reached them from below, but almost at the same minute Geoffrey tumbled into the room, crouching forward. Archie sprang to draw the curtains.

'Geoffrey . . . ?' asked Veronica, her hand to her mouth.

Geoffrey beamed at her. 'Missed me, both times. The first bullet hit the wall six inches away from my head. I jumped nearly out of my skin.'

'But you fell?'

'Pretended to fall,' Geoffrey corrected her. He turned to Archie. 'Funny thing, isn't it? That's the first time I've ever been shot at in my life and yet I acted just on instinct. I pretended to fall, to make the blighter think he'd pipped me and when I judged he'd lowered his gun I shinned up again. It seems to have worked.'

'Good man,' Archie grinned. 'And you've got the paper?'

'I've got the paper.'

'Give it back, Geoffrey,' Veronica suddenly urged. 'Give the wretched thing back to them.'

'Give it back?' Geoffrey echoed in surprise.

'Yes. It isn't worth this kind of thing.'

'Are you weakening?' demanded Geoffrey.

'Yes,' Veronica acknowledged. 'I don't like you being shot at.'

'I don't mind him being shot at,' Archie said with equanimity. 'No, Miss Steyning, now we've got it again we can't give it back without another struggle. For King and Country, you know. Likewise, Peace with Honour.'

'In this case,' Geoffrey put in, 'a Strategic Retreat. In other words, we'd better leg it while friend Fritz is still busy with friend Hans. We don't want to be bothered on our way round to your cousin's, do we? In fact, we don't want them to know we're going round to your cousin's at all. So now's the time. You'd better come, Veronica. It'll be safer.'

'Oh, yes,' Veronica agreed, 'I'm coming.'

'And you, Geoffrey,' Archie said with interest. 'Are you going in your shirt-sleeves or your dressing-gown?'

'Shirt-sleeves, I think. Come along, children.'

Geoffrey opened the door, glanced down the passage and reported it empty. Treading delicately, like conspirators, the three passed out of the room and down the stairs.

In the hall the little night-clerk still lurked behind his desk and eyed them askance.

Archie regarded him with a thoughtful eye. 'Supposing you were right, Geoffrey, and that little creature does belong to the other side,' he said in a low voice. 'We don't want him to tell them we've gone out as soon as our backs are turned.'

'I'll biff him one and put him to sleep,' said Geoffrey comfortably.

'No, you idiot, we don't want him to guess even that we've gone anywhere important. We ought not to have brought Miss Steyning with us. Then he'd have thought we were just going back to our own hotel.'

'I'm not going to stay in my room alone, with that balcony,' said Veronica with decision.

'No, but what about the back stairs? Look here; you say goodbye to us here, very ostentatiously, then pop up to the first floor, find the service stairs and get out of the hotel that way. You may have to go through a kitchen or two, but no one will be about at this hour. It's nearly half-past two.'

'All right,' Veronica nodded. 'Where will you wait for me?'

Archie thought. 'The safest place is where the enemy won't think of looking for us and in this case I should say that's anywhere in the neighbourhood of the fire-escape. Did you see those ornamental gardens inside that little square? We'll be crouching under a bush there, looking out for you. Fritz is sure to think he's frightened us away from that side for good and all.'

'Very well and mind you do wait. Well, good night,' she added loudly. 'Thank you so much for coming round. It's been a delightful evening.'

They exchanged loud and earnest farewells and then Veronica ran up the stairs again. The two men linked arms, called a cheerful good night to the clerk, to which they obtained no reply and marched out of the main entrance. There they turned as one man and marched back into the hotel again. Fritz was waiting on the front steps.

'That man,' said Geoffrey, 'is becoming a nuisance.'

'Hush,' said Archie. 'Hi!' he called out to the little night-clerk. 'Where's the gents' cloakroom? *Où est la chambre aux manteaux pour les Messieurs?*'

The clerk sulkily indicated the direction. The two marched that way.

'Must have an excuse for coming back,' Archie explained, as they went on. 'And now we know where Fritz is. Well, that's very nice of him. All we've got to do now is to find a convenient window, this one for instance and hop out through it. Are you ready?'

'Half a minute,' said Geoffrey, taking down an overcoat from one of the pegs. 'I'll return it in the morning and it's less conspicuous.'

He put it on, Archie opened the window and reported the coast clear and they scrambled out into the street.

'Sing hey,' observed Archie. 'We're off.'

Cautiously they made their way to the little garden, vaulted the railing round it and crept under a bush. Apparently no one had seen them.

Twenty minutes passed.

Then Geoffrey, looking upwards, uttered an exclamation.

The figure of Veronica was plainly visible embarking on the descent of the fire-escape from the balcony outside her own room.

'Dash it,' muttered Archie, 'she's got pluck, this young woman of yours, but it's a bit conspicuous.'

As he spoke, a man came into view round the angle of the building. He looked up at the fire-escape and the two could see his profile clearly. It was Fritz. He moved towards the foot of the escape.

Unknowingly, Veronica continued to descend.

X

'What about it?' whispered Archie.

'Get his revolver, at all events,' Geoffrey whispered back.

In a few seconds they had made their plan. Archie was to saunter out in front, as if not knowing that the man was there, allow himself to be held up, at the point of the revolver if necessary, and engage the man's attention fully enough to allow Geoffrey to get up behind him and take him by surprise; the chance had to be taken that the revolver might go off, with Archie in front of it. Veronica was coming down slowly enough to enable them to carry this through before she reached the ground.

'By the way,' Archie whispered, just before they parted, 'I'd quite forgotten friend Hans. What's happened to him? You notice he's gone.'

Fritz carried him away,' Geoffrey suggested, 'or he may have come round. I hope not. For some reason I'd sooner tackle six Fritzes.'

Archie nodded emphatic agreement and they crawled their different ways. Emerging on the other side of the gardens, Archie jumped over the railing and made his way back towards the fire-escape. Out of the corner of his eye as he approached he saw Fritz hastily taking cover behind a projecting window. Still out of the corner of his eye he saw Geoffrey gain the shelter of the next projecting window, unperceived.

Everything went as they had planned. Archie strolled to the bottom of the fire-escape and looked innocently up at Veronica's descending figure. Fritz walked out on him from two yards away, revolver in hand, Archie, simulating great fear, hurriedly delved in his pockets for the document and then two muscular arms wound themselves suddenly and firmly round Fritz's neck, Archie dived under the revolver and grabbed it before it could go off and Veronica descended to meet an impotently kicking Fritz and Geoffrey's face grinning over his shoulder.

'So now perhaps,' Archie said with severity, 'you'll tell us why you disobeyed orders and came out of the hotel again, Miss Steyning.'

Veronica recognised that she was being given a cue for the benefit of Fritz. 'I was going to follow you to your hotel, to see if they could give me a room for the rest of the night,' she said quickly. 'I was frightened up there all alone.'

'I see,' said Archie with a terrific frown and winked as Fritz's head jerked the other way.

'Well, this is all very nice and jolly,' Geoffrey remarked, holding the struggling Fritz without difficulty, 'but what am I to do with this pretty thing? We want to get to bed sometime tonight, don't we?'

'Rock-a-bye, baby?' Archie suggested significantly.

'I suppose so,' Geoffrey agreed. 'It seems like murder, but I suppose so.' With a sudden jerk he twisted Fritz round and hit him accurately and scientifically on the point of the chin. Archie fielded him neatly as he fell.

'Touches the spot every time,' he commented amiably. 'Send your son to Cambridge. First-class education guaranteed. Never say a university education isn't worth while, Miss Steyning.

Geoffrey learned to box there and look how useful it's coming in now.'

'Oh, do let's get away,' chafed Veronica, who did not in the least feel like standing longer than was necessary on the pavement over a prostrate man.

'Up with his heels, Archie,' Geoffrey ordered.

Between them they lifted the unconscious Fritz, carried him tenderly to the railings round the little garden and decanted him neatly into a clump of bushes.

'That settles him,' observed Geoffrey, delicately dusting his hands. 'He'll be out of this world for at least an hour and, thanks entirely to you, Veronica, when he does come round he'll think we went straight to our hotel from here. So now perhaps we can get on with the job in peace. By the way, why didn't you come out of the back regions, as arranged?'

'Because I couldn't find them,' Veronica rejoined tartly. 'I don't know if you've ever tried to find the back door of a big hotel at three o'clock in the morning; because if not, I shouldn't bother. I wasted what seemed like hours and I was so afraid you'd start without me that I thought I'd better go down the fire-escape to avoid the night-clerk. You told me, Geoffrey,' she added reproachfully, 'that the fire-escape would be safe.'

'And so it was,' Archie put in irrepressibly, 'here you are amongst us without a bruise or blain, with never a weal nor a woe. Geoffrey saw to that. But I told him how to do it.'

'Idiot,' laughed Veronica happily.

They were walking quickly along the sea-front, in the direction of the villa in which Archie's cousin lived. In the little square behind Veronica's hotel everything had been deserted, but here people were still to be seen in spite of the lateness of the hour. The two men were keeping to the well-lighted routes, although this involved something of a detour; but with Veronica in their company this was the merest prudence. Archie had said that Monte Carlo always struck him as more respectable than a

London suburb, but now it was beginning to seem that in Monte Carlo one never knew.

The villa of Archie's cousin lay at the Monaco end of the town. It was a long walk and all three were keeping their eyes open for a taxi; but like all taxis all the world over, when one was particularly wanted it failed to materialise. They proceeded to make what pace they could on foot.

Veronica kept glancing behind her. After all their unexpected appearances she could not believe that neither Fritz nor Hans was going to bob up suddenly and present an entirely fresh revolver at them; but after a few hundred yards even she felt satisfied that no one was following them. She breathed a sigh of relief.

At the same moment Archie sighted a taxi crawling along behind them and hailed it eagerly. As if the driver really could not be bothered to hurry, it came up very slowly but reached them at last. Geoffrey opened the door for Veronica and Archie stepped up to the driver to give him the address of his cousin's villa, when he was startled by a cry from Veronica, who was gesticulating towards the interior of the taxi.

Geoffrey looked in through the door.

'Oh, my goodness,' he groaned. 'The Spanish woman!'

'*Dead?*' asked Archie incredulously.

XI

'Dead?' Geoffrey repeated. 'Of course not dead. Why should she be dead?'

'Sorry, I thought she was,' said Archie. He peered into the taxi's dim interior. '*Vous n'êtes pas morte, madame?*' he asked politely.

The lady leaned forward urgently. 'Monsieur, save me!' she implored.

Archie turned to Geoffrey. 'She's not dead. That's a nuisance, isn't it?'

'What did she say about saving her?' Veronica asked distrustfully.

'Ah, mademoiselle, I appeal to you, as one woman to another. I am in terrible danger. Only you can save me. Please, please get in here and let us drive to a café where I can tell you what it is you have done to me by taking my handbag. Please!'

Geoffrey and Archie exchanged glances. 'May as well hear what she's got to say,' suggested the former.

Archie acquiesced, though not altogether without reluctance and the three got into the taxi.

It was not difficult to find a café that was open all night and within a few minutes all four were seated round a table on a terrace overlooking the harbour.

The Spanish-looking lady plunged without hesitation into her story. The document about which all the fuss had been made was, she explained frankly, a code letter from a gentleman who was not her husband. It was, not to put too fine a point upon it, a love-letter. The Spanish-looking lady regretted that such things should be, but there it was. The man who had paid the call at Geoffrey's room was her husband. He suspected and he meant to get hold of the letter at all costs. Equally at all costs the gentleman who was not her husband was determined to prevent him, by getting hold of the letter himself and burning it. It had been for this purpose that he had obtained it at the point of the revolver from the three of them in Veronica's room at the Magnificent. Unfortunately, however, Geoffrey and the water-jug between them had prevented the success of this plan.

'I hope I didn't do the gentleman too much damage,' said Geoffrey courteously.

The Spanish-looking lady brushed the damage aside. 'It was nothing. It would take more than that to hurt *him*,' she said proudly.

'But why didn't he explain the situation, instead of brandishing a revolver?' Archie wanted to know.

'He did not think that it would be of any use. He thought you would not believe him. I do not know why. I told him to explain and, as men of honour, of course you should give the letter to him, but he said not. It was foolish. Ah!' The lady started dramatically. 'Here he is!'

Geoffrey and Archie stiffened and then rose. Their late opponent was making his way towards them, a deprecatory smile on his lips.

'I was sitting the other side and saw you come in. May I sit with you? It is very kind. You bear no ill-will, I see. Nor I.' With a slight smile he touched a piece of sticking plaster in his hair. 'It is nothing. A little headache, nothing. You have told them, my dear? Yes, yes. You see, gentlemen, we have all been making a great trouble about a small matter: small, that is, for you, but for us not. I could not tell you before, since a lady's name was involved; you will understand that. But now, you leave us no alternative. We throw ourselves on your mercy. Do not, we entreat you, restore the letter to this lady's husband.'

'We never intended to,' Archie said shortly, taking a sip of his drink.

'I am delighted. I thought you did. I do not even ask you to restore it to me. All I ask is that you burn it, here and now, so that this lady and I may know ourselves safe.'

'Sorry,' Archie said and his tone was undisguisedly sceptical. 'Nothing doing.'

'But why not? My dear sir, why not?'

'Yes, dash it,' Geoffrey put in. 'Why not? I'm all in favour. I'll burn the thing and have done with it.'

'Ah,' said the lady admiringly, 'you are a true English gentleman.'

'Oh, I don't know about that,' Geoffrey said modestly and, disregarding Archie's frowns and headshakings, drew from his pocket the cause of all the trouble. 'This is it, isn't it? he asked, showing it and yet holding it so that the other could not take it.

'That is it,' nodded the man.

'Then here goes,' said Geoffrey. Under the eyes of the other four he crumpled the thing into a ball, struck a match and lit it. Even a vicious kick on the ankle from Archie did not stop him.

The newcomer watched it burning on the stone floor till Geoffrey ground out the ashes with his heel.

'So!' he said, with undisguised satisfaction and producing his cigarette case, offered it round. Archie and Geoffrey exchanged glances. Both had noticed that the man's thumb was curiously twisted, so that the nail faced almost inwards. The malformation seemed oddly sinister.

For a few moments the ill-assorted party remained, talking a little stiltedly about the weather and other Monte Carlo topics and it was noticeable that the only one who appeared completely at ease was the man with the twisted thumb. Then, with an air of natural authority, he rose.

'It is quite time, my dear, now that our little business is settled, that you were getting back to your hotel. You are ready? So!'

Polite farewells were exchanged and the couple departed.

Geoffrey watched them out of sight. 'We'll give them five minutes, for safety,' he said, 'and then sing hey for Cousin Bobby.'

'Cousin Bobby?' Veronica said in surprise.

'Cousin Bobby!' Archie echoed disgustedly. 'What's the use of Cousin Bobby now that you've spoilt the whole thing? Of all the transparent yarns I ever heard! Fancy you being taken in by such stuff.'

Geoffrey grinned. 'I'm not quite such a fool as all that, Archie. Instead I took the lot of you in myself. Don't you remember my famous card-trick? Well, I palmed that document in exactly the same way. Here it is. What I burnt was an old bill for cleaning white flannel trousers.'

XII

'All right,' said Geoffrey as they got out of the taxi, 'I'll pay the man.' He went round to the driver's seat and gave him a note. The man took it. Geoffrey promptly seized him by the scruff of the neck, hauled him bodily out of his seat and hit him shrewdly on the point of the chin. The man collapsed on the pavement.

'Did you take a dislike to him?' Archie asked with interest.

'I suppose you didn't notice that the thumb of his left hand was twisted,' Geoffrey said. 'I think he's safer with us.' He picked the unconscious man up, slung him over his shoulder and carried him into the porch.

Considering the lateness of the hour, their ring was answered surprisingly soon and it was in a surprisingly short time afterwards that they were sitting in the Hon. Robert Carruthers' study, with the Hon. Robert himself, in pyjamas and a dressing-gown, listening carefully to their story. He was a slight, clean-shaven man, between forty and fifty, with a quiet manner and if he had felt any surprise at being called out of bed at such an hour he did not show it.

Geoffrey began the story, Veronica contributed her own part and Archie helped both of them.

'Um!' commented the Hon. Robert, when the story had been brought to a rather uneasy conclusion.

'Dash it all, Bobbie,' Archie said indignantly, 'you might say something more than "um!" There may be nothing in all this for you, but let me tell you that it's been quite hectic for us.'

The other smiled. 'Sorry, Archie; I was thinking. And I'll tell you at once that there's quite a lot in it for me. It's your remark about the man's thumb being twisted inwards which settles that. We've been after that man for a long time and if this document gives us one certain piece of information, you three have done a big piece of work. I'll get it decoded at once (we know their code, luckily), and let you know.' He picked up the paper and went out of the room.

'We're heroes,' said Archie fatuously to Geoffrey.

'And I'm a heroine,' asserted Veronica.

'You are,' said Geoffrey, with such warmth that for the second time that evening Veronica blushed: and Veronica did not blush easily.

Within a few minutes the Hon. Robert was back. He smiled at them happily. 'You've done it,' he said.

'Oh, we knew that,' said Archie. 'But what is it we've done?'

'That,' the Hon. Robert continued to smile, 'is precisely what I can't tell you.'

The three cries of protest which met his words, induced him to modify them to some extent.

'Well, it's a state secret and it involves two other powers, but I can tell you this. The man who represented himself to you as the lady's lover is known to our lot as the Man with the Twisted Thumb. He can disguise a lot, you see, but he can't disguise that. He's probably the most efficient international spy in existence. No one knows what his real country is, but he acknowledges none, except the one who will pay him highest. He used to work for us at one time; he sold us and went over to someone else; then he sold them and is working now for a third party and specifically against us.'

'And that's why you came here three months ago and took this villa?' Archie cried.

'That's why I came here three months ago. And for three months I've been trying to lay my hands on this fellow. But he lies very low. I knew at once that this paper of yours must be of the highest importance to have brought him out of his hiding-place.'

'But what about the other two—the lady and Fritz?'

'We knew all about the lady, but Fritz is a new one to us. The lady, you see, acts as a link between our man and his organisation. We knew that. But at the same time we'd never been able to trace her contact with him. There was another link between the lady and the leader and that link must have been Fritz.'

'Who at present is probably still lying in the bushes in those gardens,' said Geoffrey.

'And can go on lying there. We can't touch him or the lady but the joke is that we found out some time ago that the other man, the big noise, is wanted in France for a political crime committed years ago. France seems to have forgotten all about it, but it would be very much to France's interest to have him under lock and key for a few years. He's safe enough here in Monaco, but if only we could get him over the French border we could have him locked up at once. It's a pity,' added the Hon. Robert regretfully, 'that you couldn't somehow have inveigled him along with you. We can put a spoke in his wheel all right, through the information in that paper, but I would have liked the man himself.'

'You've got him,' Geoffrey grinned. 'I forgot to tell you that bit. He's dumped in your hall at this moment and he won't come round for at least a couple of hours.'

The Hon. Robert jumped up and things began to happen quickly. Looking extremely happy, the Hon. Robert announced that he was going to put the man into his car and drive him over the French border immediately and, almost before they knew what had happened, the others found themselves bundled out of the house and sent on their ways. 'You'll pick up a taxi somewhere,' he said kindly.

'Curse him,' said Archie feelingly. 'I'm not so sure. And you're too tired to walk, Miss Steyning.'

'I'm not tired a bit. And please call me "Veronica", won't you? I feel I've known you for simply ages.'

'I should love to. And it certainly is time for a few introductions. You and Geoffrey haven't really been introduced yet, for instance, have you?' Archie said, disregarding the latter's warning scowls. 'I'll do it now. Sir Geoffrey Grant, Miss Steyning.'

Veronica opened her eyes. '*Sir* Geoffrey Grant?'

'*Sir* Geoffrey Grant,' Archie repeated maliciously. 'He may have an explanation or two to make. I should ask him.'

'Taxi!' exclaimed Geoffrey. 'Hi—taxi.' A belated taxi was going rapidly past, but on Geoffrey's shout it stopped. He put Veronica inside, climbed in himself and shut the door.

'Here,' said Archie indignantly, 'what about me?'

Geoffrey leaned out as the taxi started.

'You'll walk,' he said firmly.

ANTHONY BERKELEY

Anthony Berkeley Cox (1893–1971) was a versatile author who wrote in a range of genres under several names. The importance of his contribution to the Golden Age of detective fiction cannot be overestimated, whether for the way in which he played with the accepted 'rules' of the genre or for the way he spearheaded the shift away from the *who* and the *how* of puzzle plots and on to the *why* of the modern psychological crime stories.

Cox began his writing career with short pieces of light fiction for *Punch* and other magazines before turning his hand to comic thrillers, including *Cicely Disappears*, published in 1927 under the title *The Wintringham Mystery* as a newspaper serial under his own name. 'The Man with the Twisted Thumb' belongs to this early phase of his writing, even though it wasn't published until 1933, eight years after his first detective story, *The Layton Court Mystery*. This and his second were published anonymously but the third, *Roger Sheringham and the Vane Mystery* (1927), appeared as by Anthony Berkeley, which Cox used for the remainder of his detective fiction. As Berkeley, Cox often showed contempt for his readers and he was in many ways a hack, openly admitting that his main incentive in writing was because it paid well. His best work, arguably, are the ten novels featuring Roger Sheringham, an amateur investigator who works sometimes with—and sometimes against—Scotland Yard. Sheringham has much in common with Cox. Both went up to Oxford and served in the First World War. Both became best-selling writers and both disparage their own fiction while being intolerant of others' criticism. Against this background, Cox's comment that Sheringham was 'founded on an offensive person I once knew' is likely to have been an example of the writer's often-noted peculiar sense of humour; another is the fact that he dedicated one of the Sheringham novels to himself and two novels of uxoricide to his first and second wives.

The best known of Cox's detective stories is *The Poisoned Chocolates Case*, based—like several others—on a real-life crime, in this case the attempted poisoning of the Commissioner of the Metropolitan Police in 1922. This is investigated by Sheringham and other members of 'The Crimes Circle' whose members suggest solutions that one by one are discounted. While the group was probably based on the Crimes Club, which focused on the analysis of historic crimes, it inspired Cox to create the Detection Club, a dining club for writers of crime and detective stories. Over the years, Cox would collaborate with Club members on fundraising ventures including an anthology of true crime and four round-robin mysteries. This and the fact that he founded the Club in the first place might suggest that Cox was a clubbable, convivial man, but this is contradicted by his contemporaries' recollections of him and his habit of basing his fictional victims and murderers on school friends and literary acquaintances, which in recent years has led to some unconvincing speculations about his true motives.

When Cox tired of playing with the detective story, he decided to take a new direction, and as Francis Iles wrote two powerful psychological mysteries—*Malice Aforethought* and *Before the Fact*—as well as a third less successful novel, before abandoning writing altogether. From the mid-1940s, other than a few propaganda stories featuring Sheringham, some other short fiction, a few radio plays and two collections of limericks, he focused not on writing crime fiction but reviewing it, which he did up until shortly before his death in 1971.

'The Man with the Twisted Thumb' was first published as a twelve-part serial between January and December 1933 in *Home and Country*, the journal of the Women's Institute, where it was discovered by the Cox scholar Arthur Robinson.

THE RUM PUNCH

Christianna Brand

MONDAY

Inside the house, the telephone rang. Sergeant Troot locked the garage door on the battered little car in its undercoat of reddish-brown, and ran in through the kitchen. Small hands clutched at his trouser legs. 'Daddy, Daddy, don't let it be the Inspector, saying you can't come on our holidays . . .' The car was a secret; he had bought it second hand and smuggled it in—it was to be painted bright yellow, all ready to go off to the seaside on Saturday.

But it wasn't Inspector Port on the 'phone, it was Mrs Waite.

'Oh, Sergeant, we're in such a muddle over the parking arrangements for our party tonight!'

Sergeant Troot rather liked Mrs Waite. She was a pretty woman, young to have a twenty-year old daughter. And an evening at the Hall would mean a nice fat tip towards the seaside holiday. 'I'll come along and do point duty for you, Ma'am.'

'You're an angel!' He could picture her blue eyes smiling as she rang off.

The two little girls were horrified. 'But, Daddy, suppose you're not back in time for Saturday?'

'Saturday?' he said. 'Don't be funny! The party won't last four days, you silly little clots.'

But that, alas, was where Sergeant Troot was wrong.

The housekeeper met him when he went up that evening to get things sorted out in advance. She was a faded little woman with a faded manner. He went back to the kitchen when he had arranged matters to his satisfaction and kindly helped her to sample her iced rum punch. This fortunately was to his satisfaction also. He made civil conversation. 'How are you liking it here, Mrs Bee?'

Mrs Bee thought it was lovely—a bit countrified for her taste, she was used to the town; but lovely. And Mrs Waite was a lovely lady. And Mr Waite was a lovely, lovely gentleman. 'All these snobby friends of hers say she married beneath her, but *I* can't see it.'

'Her first husband was a "Sir",' said Sergeant Troot, doubtfully. 'Or so they say; she didn't come to live here till after he died. Sir George Something. Research chemist. And very rich.'

'And very old,' said Mrs Bee tartly. She seemed to take it as a personal affront that Mrs Waite's snob friends considered her to have married beneath her.

Mrs Waite came into the kitchen in a flurry of charm, blonde hair fluffed out into the fashionable haystack. 'Oh, Sergeant—bless you for coming!' Her husband followed her—a dark, handsome man with a florid face; and yet, it was true, with something just faintly servile in his manner. And Miss Gina in a white and silver dress. Sergeant Troot saved it all up to tell to his Mary tomorrow. 'Hallo, Sarge,' said Gina. She'd known him since she was a kid. All the same, she didn't look too happy—indeed it seemed to him that they all looked rather strained. Just being rich—that isn't happiness, he thought to himself a bit smugly. Sergeant Troot needn't bother; he would never be rich.

He stood at the gate, big, broad-shouldered, beaming, ushering in the cars with practised ease. Timmy Jones hopped out of his Bentley and gave him a great whack on the back. He too had known Troot most of his life. He dived into a pocket. 'Get your Mary to buy the kids some buckets and spades or something.' Just like Timmy to remember that a seaside holiday was coming.

And here was Mr Butler—who, like Timmy Jones, was in love with Gina. Not such a good car; and not such a nice fellow either—rather smooth, with a dark, sallow, handsome face—Sergeant Troot always had an uneasy feeling that he ought to recognise him, that he'd seen him somewhere else. The village intended Gina to marry Timmy Jones; but it was said that her stepfather was all for this Butler—a 'business associate', though he seemed very young for anything so high-sounding.

The party had begun at nine. By ten the flow of cars slackened to a trickle and Gina came to the front door and beckoned. 'Sarge, Mummy wants you. Mrs Bee seems to have quite lost her head and everything's chaos, and now Papa wants to burst into speeches.' She called her stepfather Papa. 'You couldn't be an angel and come and buttle for us?'

Sergeant Troot was quite ready to forsake being an angel in a teetotal field and come and be an angel behind a bowl of punch. With much merriment they squeezed him into a white waiter's jacket. Mrs Bee was darting about, hen-headed, behind the trestle tables forming the bar in the great hall. She gave the punch a stir that sent it merrily swirling round in its bowl, poured out a last glassful for a clamouring guest and thankfully handed over the big silver ladle to the Sergeant. 'One for Mr Waite. Is that a clean glass, sir?'

'It's the one I've been using,' said Mr Waite, holding the glass across the bar to be filled by Sergeant Troot. 'I've hung on to it all the time—can't stand getting mixed up with other people's.' He refused a plate of tit-bits. 'No, thanks, I never touch those things.' Glass in hand, he walked across to the high marble fireplace, pausing on the way to take a big gulp of the punch. He said to his wife, who stood a little apart: 'Are we ready?'

'I don't think they are,' confided Mrs Bee to the sergeant, muttering. 'Been arguing all day. He wants to announce Miss Gina's engagement—or anyway, force it a bit, say how much he hopes it'll come off.'

'Oh, lor',' said Sergeant Troot, disgusted. 'What price poor young Timmy? She was all for him till this Butler came along.'

'She's young,' said Mrs Bee, shrugging. 'Got her head turned, I daresay; he fell for her the minute he set eyes on her. But she'd better have stuck to Mr Jones. This one's got no money.'

Timmy and Dal Butler, with Gina, had joined the little group at the fireplace. Sergeant Troot heard a voice say, 'Cigarette, sir?' and caught a glimpse of a man's hand proffering a case. Mr Waite said, 'Thanks.' As he lit up, he embarked upon his little speech, raising his voice. 'Ladies and gentlemen—please charge your glasses and we'll drink a couple of toasts together.' His voice changed. He had taken a drag on his cigarette and he glanced at the tip of it and tossed it into the fire. 'What have you been doing to this fag—doping it?'

Sergeant Troot gallantly filled up a glass for Mrs Bee who accepted it genteelly; and topped up his own, looking out over the big room filled with chattering guests, hoarding it all up to describe to Mary and the kids. Mr Waite said again: 'Ladies and gentlemen—my family and I drink first to: Our Guests!'

Am I a guest or the family? thought Sergeant Troot. He decided to his own satisfaction that he was both and got ready to drink all the toasts on either side. 'The Guests!' He raised his glass to his lips.

It never got there. Gina cried out suddenly, shrilly: 'Dad!' and then, again, 'Daddy!' and screamed once and went off into peals of hysterical laughter that ended in a storm of tears. Across the room, Troot saw the startled turn of Mr Waite's head towards his step-daughter. He, who was generally so florid, looked now very pale; his eyes were glassy. He seemed to be about to say something but no words came and he put his hand to his throat. Sergeant Troot forced a way through the guests towards him.

Mrs Waite had Gina by the hands, trying to calm her, Dal Butler stared, open-mouthed, Timmy was pressing forward, crying, 'Ginny, darling, what's the matter?' Mr Waite had sat down. He was paler than ever, sweat stood out on his forehead. The sergeant changed tack and went over to him. 'Are you ill, sir?'

He seemed again to be trying to speak, tearing at his collar as though to get breath. Sergeant Troot got down on his knees in front of him, pulled the tie loose, wrestled to undo a stud. Mr Waite's hands were clamped to the arms of the chair, his mouth opened and closed, he tried to speak but seemed powerless to get out a word. Yet his eyes were intelligent, thought still flowed, it was only his tongue that would not obey him. Sweat trickled down his face, he licked dry lips, his hands began to drum on the arms of his chair, dreadfully trembling. Sergeant Troot knelt there before him, helpless. What am I supposed to do? Should I move him, lie him down, leave him as he is?—whatever I decide is sure to be wrong. He called, 'Is there a doctor here?' but no one came forward. Into his mind came the thought, The chap's going to die, there'll be an inquest, fuss, enquiries, I'll never get through with it in time to take the kids away . . . He slapped the thought back as unworthy at such a moment and got up uncertainly to his feet. 'Keep back, please. I think Mr Waite must have had a heart-attack.'

Mr Waite's hands slackened, before the stare of a hundred horrified eyes he began to tip forward—tipped stiffly forward and before the sergeant could thrust out a hand to clutch at him, slowly, grotesquely bundled, slid out of the big chair and on to the ground. And as he died, his tongue at last with a final great effort obeyed him. He said one word. 'Poison!'

TUESDAY

Inspector Port stood among the ruins of last night's party. Sergeant Troot, his round face quite grey with fatigue and anxiety, came back from the telephone. 'All arranged, sir.'

'You've been a long time about it,' said Inspector Port.

Sergeant Troot was supposed to have been in a huddle about finger prints and plaster casts. In fact he had been talking on the 'phone to the kids at home. 'But Daddy, Daddy, you promised you'd be back by this morning and now it's only four days till Saturday and today's nearly gone already . . .'

'It's only just begun,' said Sergeant Troot gloomily.

'But Daddy, the holidays . . .'

And the car. He'd been going to give it the final coat tonight, the coat of primrose yellow to tone in with the russet covers that Mary was making for the seats. It was to have been drawn up, gloriously, at the front door when they woke up on Saturday morning. 'Oh, Daddy, the seaside will be horrid without you.'

'I'll be there, kiddos. Don't worry.' But he was worried himself. And now here was the Inspector, beefing. 'Right under your nose, Sergeant. The man was poisoned.'

'Yessir,' said Troot, listlessly.

'The first husband was a chemist. Well, research chemist, not a chap in a white coat selling hot water bottles. Drugs all over the place.'

'Yes, but not *this* place.'

'Easy enough to bring some along when she moved house.'

'What would she bring it for?' said Sergeant Troot.

'To murder the next.'

'You don't suggest, sir—?'

'The first left a lot of money; and she married again very soon after. It'll bear looking into,' said Inspector Port.

Mrs Bee, summoned, knocked timidly at the door and crept in, hands folded. Been here some weeks, no previous connection with the family, retired, lived at address given, had seen advertisement for this post and been tempted; lovely family, never regretted it, not until—until now. The poor gentleman! Mrs Bee put her apron to her eyes and wept a respectful tear. Taken so suddenly!

'Your master was murdered,' said Inspector Port, bluntly.

Mrs Bee gave a sharp barking scream, fell into a chair and fanned herself. Murdered! She couldn't believe it! She, who had always kept herself respectable, mixed up in a murder—Oh, get on with it, woman! thought Sergeant Troot, fuming with impatience. We shall never get through at this rate . . .

The poison would have acted swiftly, reported the police surgeon: within five minutes or so the symptoms would have begun. He had described them, Sergeant Troot confirming as he went along—pallor, constriction of the throat, rigidity, paralysis, collapse. Death probably within seven minutes of absorbing the poison. Inspector Port asked: 'What did he eat or drink just before the first symptoms?'

'Nothing. He ate nothing,' shrilled Mrs Bee, up in arms in defence of her pastries. 'The Sergeant can tell you. "I never eat these things," Mr Waite said; Sergeant Troot heard him say it.'

'That's right,' said Sergeant Troot, dispiritedly. For if not the 'eats'—what else was there but the punch? And he himself had served Mr Waite with the punch.

Mrs Bee described the business with the punch. ('Get on with it, get on with it, the Inspector's not asking for the recipe,' moaned Troot within himself.) Aloud he said impatiently: 'Dozens of people took the punch. I had some myself. There can't have been anything wrong with it.'

'Mr Waite's glass—?'

Sergeant Troot had told the Inspector a hundred times already about Mr Waite's glass. But they must waste another five minutes over it. Mrs Bee confimed. 'Mr Waite said he'd kept it all evening, he was always afraid of getting someone else's. He held it out, himself, to the Sergeant, across the table. The Sergeant didn't touch it; he just poured in the punch.'

'Like I told you,' said Troot, exasperated.

'This punch,' said the Inspector. 'Bits of fruit and cloves and such?'

'Certainly not. This was an iced rum punch,' said Mrs Bee haughtily. 'I've explained to you already. Quartered limes to commence with, yes, and the crushed ice; but all carefully strained.' She continued with her recital of events. 'I gave it a stir and passed the ladle to Sergeant Troot.'

'You gave it a stir, that's right,' said Troot, quickly.

'Yes, and then I—No, I tell a lie,' said Mrs Bee. 'First I poured out a glass for a guest, *then* I gave you the spoon.'

And the guest who had drunk from that glass was alive and blooming. Yet the very next person to be served had been Mr Waite. And Sergeant Troot himself had served Mr Waite. He hurried the Inspector away from the punch to the matter of the cigarette passed to the murdered man just before he died.

Inspector Port sent for Mrs Waite. She looked very pale, frightened and anxious and yet—not exactly heart-broken?

Troot went quietly mad while Port laboured through ponderous condolences. 'Now, Madam—who gave your husband that cigarette?'

No one had noticed. It had been 'one of the boys'.

'That is to say Mr Timothy Jones or Mr Dal Butler?'

And Timmy Jones made no secret of the fact that he resented Mr Waite's interference in the matter of Gina's marriage—that he knew that on this very evening Mr Waite had intended to force Gina's hand. Sergeant Troot didn't like it: in his pocket still burned Timmy's ten-bob note towards the children's buckets and spades. 'Yessir,' he said, in reply to the Inspector's command to go and fetch Mr Jones; but within himself he decided that Mr Butler should join the party also. That rather flashy young 'business associate'—what motive might *he* not have, that none of them there could know anything about . . . ?

But Mr Butler never did join the party after all. Mr Butler had departed—leaving no forwarding address.

Mr Waite's office, consulted, produced Mr Butler's home address. Sergeant Troot, cursing his own interference, plodded up to London. A small house in a neat suburb: Mr Dal Butler had lived there with his mother, it appeared, but it was now deserted. Sergeant Troot took a busy look round. An expensive young man. Souvenirs of a university education, tip-top schools; made-to-measure shirts, suits from a very good tailor . . . Everything of the best, in fact; but—a perfectly ordinary telephone. Sergeant Troot looked at it with longing, resisted temptation for a little while, gave in, picked up the receiver and dialled a number. A toll call. He fished in his pocket and honourably placed his pennies on the table. 'Mary?'

'Where are you?' said his wife's voice. 'What's happening? The kids are frantic in case you're not through with it for Saturday.'

'So'm I,' he said gloomily. He gave her a rapid resumé of events. 'Not a clue, so far. Not a suspicion. Let alone any proof . . .' His free hand played nervously with some object he had picked up from the table where the telephone stood. Out of the corner of his eye, he noted something shiny, something silver, something cool and hard to the touch. 'It's no good, Mary! I may as well give up, and you take them alone; at this rate, old Port'll never let me go. Not a clue—not in any sense; we just haven't got a clue . . .'

The something shiny was a photograph frame, a small silver frame with a rather faded snapshot: a snapshot of a man with a small boy, standing holding his hand.

Mary's voice went on and on, but Sergeant Troot wasn't listening. He was looking at the picture. After a little while he said: 'Look, Mary—don't worry. I think perhaps we may have a clue after all.'

For the man in the photograph was Mr Waite. Mr Waite wore, curiously, dark pin-striped trousers and a white linen jacket. And the boy with him was Dal Butler: and now Sergeant Troot knew why he had always had that feeling of having seen Dal Butler somewhere before.

For the boy in the picture was the dead spit and image of the man.

WEDNESDAY

Sergeant Troot, dog tired from the long, unrewarding search for Dal Butler, who, whatever his relationship with the dead man was still missing—rubbed sleep from his eyes and crept out to the garage. He could slosh a first coat of paint on the car before breakfast, anyway. Not that it would be any use—the kids must go off to the seaside prosaically by train, that was now all too certain; but at least they might have a glimpse of the primrose wonder and of joys to come. He worked feverishly for a couple of hours. At nine o'clock he trudged wearily up to the Hall where the Inspector was already pursuing his unhurried investigations.

Gina met him in the garden and drew him surreptitiously into a greenhouse. 'I want to talk to you, Sarge, and with all these leaves in here no one will see us.' She had been longing for him to get back from London, she said. 'That stupid old Port—he thinks Dal did it or Timmy and that I knew in advance and that's why I had hysterics too soon, as it were. I mean, I did, you know. Papa hadn't really begun to be ill yet when I screamed out, "Daddy!"'

'"Dad!"' corrected Sergeant Troot. 'You screamed out "Dad!" first: and later, "Daddy!" He eyed her keenly, and yet with a sort of protective anxiety. He had known her since she was a kid. 'Miss Gina—I've realised now it wasn't really "Dad!" you called out, was it? It was a name that sounded like Dad.'

She shrank back against the great, spreading leaves of some giant exotic plant. 'A name that—?'

'Your step-father was usually rather florid. Gone suddenly pale in the face like that—he reminded you of someone: didn't he?' She said nothing. 'Miss Gina—this young man that your step-father was encouraging you to marry, was almost forcing you to marry—you suddenly realised in that one moment who he was. It was "Dal!" that you cried out: wasn't it? Because you suddenly knew that Dal Butler was your step-father's own son.'

She did not deny it. Indeed, she seemed almost pleased that he should know it, eager about it. 'Because, you see what that means? Dal can't be suspected now. He'd hardly have killed his own father.'

'So why did he run away?'

'He . . . well, he's told me now, Sarge. You see, he and his father between them, they'd—they'd fiddled our money, my mother's and mine that my own father had left us. He'd left a lot: he was rich and he was heavily insured. He was a great believer in insurance, he taught my mother to be too: and a jolly good thing because she made my step-father take out a big insurance in her favour in case he died before her; and now that's all we shall have. All the rest's gone.'

'Mr Waite and his son have embezzled it?'

'Well, I don't know what they've done exactly, but they've spent it. It wasn't all Dal's fault,' she said, unhappily. 'He was only a boy when my mother married his father. It was all spent on giving him a terrific education, all the advantages his father hadn't had. Then, when he grew up, the two of them started gambling to repay it before it was found out. So they lost the rest; and then the only thing to do was to try to get Dal married to me before I came of age and it was all found out.' She flushed. 'Not very flattering, Sarge, was it?'

'Yet you forgive Mr Butler?'

'He was only a child when it started,' she said again. 'It was his father's influence.' But she suddenly looked at him surprised. 'How do you know I've forgiven him?'

'You continue to harbour him.'

'I?' she said, startled. 'Harbour him?'

'You've got him hidden somewhere—or when has there been time to explain all this to you?' And he looked round the greenhouse, casually, and said: 'All right, Mr Butler—you may as well come out now.'

Mr Butler came out with a rush that upset several large green plants but not Sergeant Troot. But it was not very nice of Mr Butler to have secreted a knife when Gina brought him his smuggled-in food, and to attack her friend, Sergeant Troot, with it. Troot caught at the stabbing hand and wrenched the knife away. Dal with his free hand picked up a pot of cactus, flung it through the wall of the greenhouse and snatched up a piece of broken glass resulting from the smash. 'Let me go or I'll slash your face with it.'

'Cor lummy,' said Sergeant Troot, astonished. 'What a nasty little brute you are!' He held the squirming young man off, quite easily, at the end of a long right arm as rigid as iron. But over his shoulder he said to Gina: 'Get outside, Miss.'

'Sarge, I can't—'

'Get outside Miss, please.' If there was going to be a rough house, it was a bind having women cluttering things up.

'I don't like to leave you—' she began, distressfully. But she stepped outside the door and stood uncertainly in the path. 'Now,' said Troot to the struggling Dal, 'chuck that piece of glass away. Come on—chuck it!'

Dal Butler chucked it—straight into Sergeant Troot's face. As Troot instinctively ducked, caught unawares, his hand for a moment lost its grip. In that moment Dal was outside and the door slammed in the sergeant's face. There was a further shower of broken glass, blinding him temporarily; he covered his face with his arms, thrust his shoulder to the wooden frame of the door and at once was free. But Butler had snatched up a second piece of glass and now, thrusting a terrified Gina before him, was tearing down the path in the direction of the garages. Gina's own car stood in the driveway. He shoved her in before him, the dagger of glass held close to her cheek. Sergeant Troot, chasing after them, saw the gesture and it brought him to a halt. Butler yelled: 'One step nearer and I'll use it!' You could see the words giving him confidence, giving him new hope. One foot half into the car he shouted again: 'I'll use it! If you follow me, if I find I'm being followed, tracked down—anything—I'll use it, I'll cut her to ribbons.' And it was true. Liable to heaven knew what charges of embezzlement and fraud and now to new charges for murderously attacking a policeman—nothing he could do to get free would be not worth the risking. Short of murder, perhaps; but the destruction of her beauty might be not so very much less terrible to Gina than death itself . . .

Sergeant Troot watched them out of sight and turned and ran into the house, and now he gave no thought to a little yellow car still not half painted, or to a seaside holiday for two young hopefuls.

Inspector Port's reproaches were hard to bear. He took over control himself and Troot found himself left all alone at the Hall, sick with anxiety, remorse and a terrible feeling of helplessness. Had Port really understood and appreciated that threat? And if he had not, and Butler found himself pursued, was it not all too certain that he would put it into action? What, anyway, would be his next move? For if to give chase would endanger Gina, then anticipation was the only chance. Troot sat with his head in his hands at the big kitchen table while Mrs Bee, anxious and trembling, plied him with cups of unwanted tea. 'If he harms her, if he kills her . . .'

'He won't kill her.'

'If he kills her, they'll hang him.'

'They won't. But anyway, it wouldn't help Miss Gina.' He lifted his sad head. 'What'll he do next, Mrs Bee? Go abroad?'

'Abroad?' said Mrs Bee. 'But no. If he turned up at the airport or the station, dragging the girl—?'

'He might get rid of her.' Mrs Bee gave a sharp scream and he shook his head impatiently. 'I mean, lock her up somewhere.' But where? 'If only one could work that out in advance and *be* there.'

'Yes.' She thought it over for a long time. She said at last, slowly, and all her faded foolishness seemed to be gone for a moment in this hour of sick anxiety: 'To go abroad he must have ready money.'

'He has no money.'

'No money in the big sense, perhaps. But a bit in the bank, I don't suppose he's as broke as all that, is he?' She said again in that slow, thoughtful way: 'And to get cash out in a hurry from the bank, he'd have to go there.' She looked him in the eye. 'Sergeant—he mustn't kill that girl. If I was you . . .'

Sergeant Troot was already halfway out or the kitchen.

But it was someone else who went—at Sergeant Troot's earnest suggestion—to Dal Butler's bank. Troot himself was on his way elsewhere.

So that when a white faced girl, whose male companion stood very close to her, dropped in at her bank to cash a cheque on her own account for as much as it contained—she found a curiously slow and delaying clerk behind the counter; and while he yet dillied and dallied, the swing doors opened and a man came in, breathing heavily as though he had been hastening—and two big hands grasped the young man's arms and jerked him violently backwards. And something fell from his hand that smashed into harmless smithereens on the stone floor of the bank.

THURSDAY

So Master Butler was under lock and key and there was at least one suspect eliminated from the unenviable distinction of being a murderer: for what Gina had said was true—there was no reason to believe Dal (ready though he might have been to kill Sergeant Troot), the destroyer of his own father. Gina, young and resilient, had by Thursday morning recovered from the shock and terror of her involuntary few hours 'on the run' with him. Sergeant Troot could feel pretty pleased with himself.

Inspector Port was hardly grateful, smarting, perhaps beneath the superior strategy of the Sergeant in having anticipated Dal Butler's forcing Gina to obtain cash from her bank. 'Twenty four hours skulking here in the greenhouse under your very nose: and then you're actually in there with him and you let him go.'

During those twenty four hours Sergeant Troot had been up in London and if Butler had been under anyone's nose it had been Inspector Port's. And if Port had had splintered glass held close to his eyes . . . ! But it would not encourage the Inspector to sympathy in the matter of Sergeant Troot's seaside holiday with the kids—even if all hope of getting off by Saturday had not by now perished. Moreover, Port was now assailed with advice and instruction from higher quarters, the question of calling in Scotland Yard nagged at him like an aching tooth. In some mysterious way, of course, it was all Troot's fault.

A wearisome morning followed of routine investigation and formalities. Troot applied a little strategy and sneaked half an hour for lunch at home. But he wished he hadn't! Mary had given up hope but two bright faces still shone with happy anticipation and in the garage Mary had been most nobly struggling with tins of yellow paint, and the little old second-hand car was as bright as a baby chick. A couple of hours on the internal economy of the chick and it would be ready to appear as planned on the morning of the holidays to the incredulous joy of the two little girls. But to what avail if Daddy wasn't there to drive them away in their chariot of gold?

Up at the Hall, Inspector Port pursued his unhurried enquiries. He had Timmy Jones in the toils when Sergeant Troot eventually arrived there, Mrs Waite and Gina sitting anxiously looking on. For a girl said to have so completely recovered, thought the Sergeant pausing in the doorway unobserved, Gina looked very sick and pale. Timmy was reiterating what he had quite evidently said already a hundred times. Yes, he had been fed up at Mr Waite's interference in the matter of Gina's marriage, and he didn't care who knew it. Yes, he had perfectly appreciated that Mr Waite had been within an ace of winning his way—a public reference to the intended engagement would have forced Gina's hand and Gina, he knew, had been—well, misled—and might well have given in. But no, he had known nothing before the party, or the proposed announcement: so why should he have come all prepared with a poisoned cigarette?—even if he had been able to possess himself of poison, which he couldn't.

'The fact remains,' said Port, that you and you alone could have passed him that cigarette.'

'I tell you, Dal Butler gave him the cigarette.'

'Dal Butler is out of this. Dal Butler had no reason to give Mr Waite—his own father, as it turns out—a doctored cigarette. And the cigarette *was* doctored. Mr Waite said it tasted funny and chucked it into the fire.'

'I daresay if you've just had a lethal dose of poison,' said Timmy, 'anything might taste funny.'

'Mr Waite had not just had a lethal dose of poison. Whatever he took must have been administered within seven minutes of the time he died. But he'd eaten nothing that evening, his glass had not been tampered with, there was nothing else that could have affected him but the punch. And there was nothing wrong with the punch. All the guests drank it, the bowl was stirred a moment before he was served, a glass was filled for a guest after the bowl was stirred and it was my sergeant himself who poured out the drink for him. After that—'

'Was his glass tested afterwards?' said Timmy. 'Because *I* don't believe it was.'

Sergeant Troot made himself as invisible as possible in his doorway. This was something of a sore point for in his acute anxiety at the time of Mr Waite's death, he had certainly not immediately possessed himself of the glass. When he had looked round for it, several glasses had presented themselves, standing about, half-finished, on the marble mantelpiece and on a small table near at hand—as, at parties, glasses do. Several had borne the dead man's fingerprints, among a confusion of others—he had, of course, handed glasses round among his guests. None bore his only, as one might have expected since he had declared that he'd 'hung on to' his glass all evening. On the other hand, no one could swear that in the confusion they had not picked up this glass or that to push it out of the way. 'No poison was found in any glass,' said Inspector Port stiffly. That would have to do for Master Jones. He put on a solemn face. 'Timothy—er—what's your second name?'

'Edward,' said Timmy, staring.

'Timothy Edward Jones, I am going to take you into custody and you will later be charged with—'

Sergeant Troot could stand there, an observer, no longer. Delighted though he would privately have been to allow his superior to make an ass of himself, loyalty and duty forbade. He stepped forward and the fine flow of Inspector Port's warning was interrupted. 'Well, Miss Gina?' said Sergeant Troot. Poor kid, it was bad to have to startle her so, to see her jump and throw that anguished look at him and go even paler. 'You can't let this go on, Miss' said the Sergeant, gently. 'Not even to protect—well, anyone. Can you?'

'Oh, Timmy!' said Gina; and burst into tears.

'Mr Timmy might go through with it, Miss—if he knew the

reason. But I can't let that happen, can I?' Said Sergeant Troot, almost apologetically. 'It wouldn't be right. Mr Timmy had nothing to do with it. You know that.'

'Why not?' said Inspector Port in a voice of doom.

'Because he wasn't present when Mrs Waite's first husband died,' said Sergeant Troot.

Inspector Port fluffled and flustered. 'What do you mean?'

'Miss Gina knows what I mean,' said Troot. 'It was she that called out when Mr Waite was taken ill. She called out, "Dal!" Well, that's been explained. But then a minute later she screamed again and she called out, "Daddy!"'

'She couldn't have,' said Mrs Waite, raising her head from where she had sat, sunk in a kind of terrified stupor. 'She didn't call her stepfather "Daddy". She called him by a sort of nickname, "Papa".'

'Exactly,' said Troot. He looked at the white faced girl. 'She had a bad couple of minutes then—two shocks one after the other. Her stepfather lost his high colour and she recognised his likeness to his son. But then as his condition got worse, as he grew glassy-eyed and began to clutch at his throat, not able to speak—well, then, a memory came up out of her childhood. She remembered when she had seen someone do that before; and she cried out, "Daddy".' He turned to Gina. 'Your own father, Miss Gina—he died the same way, didn't he? And all of a sudden, you realised. They had both been murdered.'

Mrs Waite screamed out, 'No!' and slid fainting to the floor.

The hours ticked by. You couldn't question a woman who lay on her bed moaning and weeping, half conscious. Gina, under the steam-roller tactics of Inspector Port, wept and protested. 'Of *course* I didn't know. Of *course* Mummy didn't know! Our doctor was at the party and he thought Daddy'd had a heart attack.'

'Your father died at a party too?'

'Yes, only it was a Christmas party. So I was afraid you'd' think that Mummy—' She broke off miserably. 'I knew Timmy couldn't really be suspected. My father died the same way, and he didn't smoke.'

'Why should you think we'd suspect your mother?'

'Well . . .' She said miserably: 'Her marrying Waite so soon after.' She flushed. 'Oh, sorry—I called him Waite out of old habit.'

And Troot recalled suddenly that faintly, faintly servile air that the man had had; remembered the odd dress in the photograph—the striped trousers worn with a white linen jacket. And the name of Waite's own son had been . . .

'Miss Gina,' said Sergeant Troot. 'Isn't it true that after your father's death your mother married—her own butler?'

The tall handsome butler, so pleasant and civil-spoken; standing behind the bar in some other room at some other long ago party. A Christmas party.

Standing behind the bar with one eye on the pretty, rich young widow-to-be, ladling out—a hot rum punch.

FRIDAY

Friday morning; and in twenty four hours it would be Saturday morning. And the little yellow car was ready: a couple of hours work on it and it could be round at the front door tomorrow morning. Sergeant Troot hoped at least that it would make up to the kids for the bitter disappointment of his not being able to go off with them to the sea. But it was surely hopeless now?

Conferences, experts, fingerprints, measurements . . . Inspector Port had twenty four hours grace before Scotland Yard moved in. Get on with it, get *on* with it, clamoured Troot's mind in respectful outward silence. At seven he crawled home to supper, at eight he was due again at the Hall. 'We must promise them an outing later on,' he said to Mary, over the two bright, innocent, pig-tailed heads. But it was all too dismal. 'Even if we made an arrest tonight that wouldn't be the end of it.' He went off bitterly depressed. All hope was over.

Mrs Waite, very glamorous, very frail and unhappy, was with Inspector Port in the big drawing-room. 'Let's all have a drink, at least, if we've got to spend the whole evening discussing it.' Mrs Bee brought a tray with whisky and soda and Sergeant Troot obliged by pouring out to specification. As she went out, Mrs Waite asked her: 'Where's Miss Gina?'

'I believe she's out in the garden with Mr Jones, Madam.'

'Spooning,' said Inspector Port bitterly. 'I passed them as I came in. Looked to me like a proposal. The young gentleman seems quite bowled over.' He had not forgiven Timmy for proving at the last minute, so dramatically not the culprit.

Spooning in the garden . . . Quite bowled over . . .

Miss Gina was spooning in the garden; and Mr Timmy seemed quite bowled over . . .

Sergeant Troot looked up at the clock and the clock said half past eight; and suddenly the hands began to spin, round and round and there was a little yellow car at the centre and Sergeant Troot was going to get home to fix that car for tomorrow morning after all. If only . . . If *only* . . . He got up suddenly to his feet. 'I'll go and get her,' he said abruptly, and opened the French window and went out into the garden.

He was back in a little while. She wasn't there. 'But she must be found,' said Sergeant Troot, very loudly and clearly, overriding the outraged protests of his superior. He gave the Inspector a look that said: I can't explain now but she simply must be found.

'I'll find her,' said Port, meekly, and marched off purposefully towards the greenhouses; he evidently considered that having harboured one young man there, Gina might well ensconce herself there with another. Mrs Waite, apparently infected with the prevailing desire to lay hands at once on her daughter, declared that she was probably indoors all the time and hurried away, upstairs and downstairs, to see. Sergeant Troot departed through the French windows again, and in the pleasant twilight, the big drawing-room with its chintzes and china was for a little while deserted and silent.

Or almost deserted; almost silent—save for the gurgle of liquid, the swish of soda, the tinkling of ice into glasses.

They all met again ten minutes later. Gina had been discovered in the billiard room with Timmy—and please to go away and not disturb them; and now that she was known to be safely sitting there, Sergeant Troot apparently lost interest in her. He and the Inspector and Mrs Waite returned to their whiskys and sodas.

You could hardly have a drink with a lady and at the same time get down to accusing her of murder. Inspector Port chatted civilly until he could turn back from guest into investigator. But after a little while, the Sergeant said to him a trifle anxiously: 'Are you feeling all right, sir?'

'Me?' said Port.

'You look a bit . . . I feel rather queer myself,' said Sergeant Troot. He shook his head muzzily, his eyes were fixed and staring. He said rather thickly: 'The whisky—'

'The whisky?' said Inspector Port, staring back. He too had gone pale, beads of sweat stood on his brow.

Sergeant Troot looked across at Mrs Waite. She sat bolt upright in her chair. She was very pale also and her hands were shaking. He opened his mouth, seemed to try to force out words, mumbled at last as, before him, a dying man had murmured a single word. Poison!

'Poison?' stammered Port. 'The—the whisky?' His tongue clove to the roof of his mouth, on the arms of his chair his hands began to shake, sickeningly. He tried to say more but he could not, his throat was dry and constricted. He too stared at Mrs Waite. She sat swaying in her chair. She cried out, dry-mouthed: 'Why are you both looking at me like that? You don't think that *I*—'

And gently the door inched open: and Mrs Bee came in.

They gazed at her, glued to their chairs, pale faced, sweating, trembling: speechless, only their sick minds racing. It was Mrs Waite who gasped out at last: '*You* killed him!'

'Yes.' She stood there, a little faded woman, looking back steadily at them. She said: 'He was my husband.'

If by profession you are a butler, it is quite ridiculous that your name should be Butler. So you change your name. And when, under your new name, you murder your employer and inherit the wealthy widow—it is easy enough to conceal the existence of any previous Mrs Butlers. 'All these years—playing second fiddle, him living here with this creature—' she threw out a contemptuous hand to Mrs Waite—'promising me that if I kept quiet and let him go through with it, we should be rich for life. And so we were rich: and what was the money spent on? All on the boy, every penny of it on the boy—bringing him up to have all that his father hadn't. And then when my turn came—broke, finished, spent the lot and in terror of being found out, the pair of them! They lay there trapped, unmoving, gazing on her as she stood lashing herself to fury, glorying in their helplessness to respond to her. 'You come up to the Hall,' he said, 'I'll fix you a job, at least you can live there in comfort.' In comfort indeed!—as her housekeeper! So I left my little home but I thought, My lad, your hour is striking. I watched while they tried to foist Dal on to the girl to hush it all up. But that wasn't going to work, she didn't really care for him; sooner or later it was all going to come out. And then what? Prison sentences for them—and for me, after all these years of waiting . . . ? Nothing. Nothing left. Or only one thing.' And she turned upon Mrs Waite and spat out at her in gruesome imitation of her own oft-repeated words: 'I've made him take out a simply huge insurance.' She repeated slowly: 'A simply huge insurance: in favour of—*his wife*.'

Mrs Waite's head fell forward, her eyes closed. Mrs Bee looked at her with cool interest. 'And I am his wife,' said Mrs Bee. 'His legal wife. With him gone, Dal and I would have done all right on the insurance. But then the fool had to go and blurt it all out to Gina. And when he ran away . . .' She mused over it. 'He's my son,' she said. 'I couldn't let him kill her and get himself hanged for murder. I had to stop that.' But there was no time for musing. She pulled herself together and from the pocket of her neat black housekeeper's dress took a scrawled note and dropped it by Mrs Waite's chair. 'Your confession,' she said. 'These two had found you out, believe it or not, dear, and so you silenced them with the same poison you used to murder both your husbands. And then I suppose it was all too much for your poor diseased brain and you killed yourself too.' She smiled dreadfully, glancing at the clock: the poison took seven minutes to work, they hadn't got much longer. 'And they *had* found out,' she said. She looked at the paralysed, gasping Troot. 'I saw your face when he said those two phrases, this fat fool here: "Spooning in the garden; and quite bowled over."'

Sergeant Troot's mouth opened and shut but no sound came. He lifted a leaden hand, and made a small, circular movement with his thumb.

Mrs Bee laughed, another of her dreadful laughs. 'Quite right,' she said. 'Move up to the top of the class. If you can move; but of course you can't, can you? Yes—that's how it was done. That's how he did it—my husband, her ladyship's butler—all those years ago. Just a wipe of poison round the bowl of the spoon as it's passed across to some innocent: and the stuff's washed off into the next glass served with it.'

Into the chill, sick silence, the clock struck the quarter. She looked up at it. 'Well, well—time's passing. Cue to come in now, I think, and find the two poor victims, and their murderer, dead by her own hand. But before I go . . .' She walked over to Mrs Waite, lying white and almost totally unconscious in her chair, and slapped her once, viciously, across the face. 'That's for all the years that you had with my precious husband!' She moved across to Inspector Port. 'And that's for you—with your drivel about "spoon" and "bowl" that gave the idea to this oaf of a sergeant.' She came over to Troot. 'And that's for you—'

'And this is for you,' said Troot, and jumped up and caught her and held her fast. He said to Mrs Waite: 'You can come to now, Ma'am. A jolly good show. You caught on like lightning when I winked at you.' To the Inspector he said civilly: 'Feeling better now, sir?'

'Eh? What? No poison—?' stammered Inspector Port.

'I saw that she knew that I knew. I made the opportunity for her to come back and poison the whiskys. I was hiding out on the terrace. Then I nipped back and tipped the stuff out and poured in some fresh.' He glanced up at the clock . Everything was going to be splendid. 'Of course sir, you knew? You were just pretending?'

'Of course, of course,' said Inspector Port hastily.

'Some people do—I mean, some imaginations are so lively . . .

Mrs Bee had gone limp in his arms and ceased to struggle. The Inspector hurried out to the terrace and blew shrilly on his whistle for reinforcements. 'You can hand her over, Troot. I'll deal with it all.' He too glanced at the clock. 'You put up a splendid show. For myself I—I just thought it best to—to give you a free hand, to—to go on pretending . . .'

'Quite so, sir,' said Sergeant Troot doubtfully. He looked at the clock again.

'So you hurry off home, my boy. Don't worry any more about it. I'll see to all the rest. You can leave it to me.' He said to Mrs Waite, benignly: 'A family man. Wants to get off on his holidays, you know, first thing tomorrow!'

But Sergeant Troot was halfway to the door: in splendid time to put the last touches to the little yellow car and drive her round to the front door, all ready for the morning.

CHRISTIANNA BRAND

Mary Christianna Milne, best known as Christianna Brand, was born in 1907 in what was then the British protectorate of Malaya.

While her earliest known crime story, *Death Goes Swimming* or *The Black Swimming Cap*, was written as a child, her first published short stories were light romantic fiction. It was not until after her marriage to the surgeon Roland Lewis, at the comparatively late age of 30, that she took up detective stories. Overcoming hatred of her father and coupling his middle name with her own, she became Christianna Brand. Her first book, *Death in High Heels*, featuring Inspector Charlesworth, was published in 1941 and it gave the young author a great deal of satisfaction by allowing her to 'kill' an obnoxious colleague. Brand's second novel was written during the London Blitz and for this mystery, *Heads You Lose*, Brand created a new character, Inspector Cockrill of the Kent police. 'Cockie' was based on her beloved father-in-law and the book sold well. Her third book, *Green for Danger*, was an even greater success and was filmed with the great character actor Alastair Sim playing Cockrill. A further five novels appeared before, for family reasons, Brand abandoned detective fiction for twenty long years. But, a writer to her soul, Brand did not—could not—abandon writing altogether, working on film scripts and producing more short stories and a series of novellas for women's magazines, as well as playing an active part in the Detection Club and the Crime Writers'

Association. Brand also wrote three books for children featuring *Nurse Matilda*, a nursemaid who also happens to be a witch, which were adapted by Emma Thompson for two films in which she played the lead role.

In the mid-1970s, Brand resumed her career as a detective novelist with a series of compelling mysteries. These late books include *The Honey Harlot*, a fictional exploration of the mystery and myths surrounding the *Mary Celeste*, as well as *The Rose in Darkness* with Inspector Charlesworth and *A Ring of Roses*, which was expanded from a short story and brought back Inspector Chucky, a memorable Welsh policeman who had appeared nearly thirty years earlier in Brand's excellent novel, *Cat and Mouse* (1950).

Renowned for her ingenuity and humour, Christianna Brand was one of the best writers of the Golden Age who, but for the hiatus in her career, would undoubtedly be better known today. At her death, in 1988, she left a mass of unpublished material including two novels, *Take the Roof Off* and *The Chinese Puzzle*, featuring Cockrill, as well as a Charlesworth novella and many more criminous short stories, which will form the basis of a second posthumous collection to be published in 2020.

The story included in this collection, 'The Rum Punch', was originally planned as a newspaper serial and this is its first publication.

BLIND MAN'S BLUFF

(Being another adventure of Max Carrados, the celebrated blind detective)

Ernest Bramah

This play was written in 1917–1918 and some characters use offensive language or otherwise behave in a way that reflects the prejudices and insensitivities of the period.—T.M.

CHARACTERS

HUGH DARRAGH: Age 40. Polished, plausible, clean-cut man of the World. An adventurer.

VIOLET DARRAGH: Age 25. His wife, passing (for Hulse's benefit) as his sister. Assumes a vivacious attitude in Hulse's presence. Afraid of Darragh and has a timid, repressed style when with him alone. Undecided in her attitude towards Kato.

KATO KUROMI: A Japanese. Age 30. Rather under average height, strongly built. Pleasant, genial, smiling, amused and amusing. A little contemptuous in an undemonstrative way of Darragh of whom he is not afraid.

JOHN BERLINGER HULSE: Age 28. An American attaché, genial, blunt, unsuspicious but not dense. Temporarily in love with Violet and taking all her people on trust as a matter of course.

MR TIMS: Elderly. A tailor's machinist. Deferential and depressed. Seedily dressed.

POLICE CONSTABLE

And:

MAX CARRADOS: the blind detective, temporarily employed by the American government to keep Hulse out of danger, unknown to him.

Scene: a drawing room in London
Time: nine p.m., some time after the declaration of war by the United States

(*Curtain rises on Darragh, Violet and Kato. DARRAGH is reading an evening paper. He has a cold and distant air. VIOLET is watching him in anxious and timid expectancy. KATO is observing them both as he studies the position of half a dozen pieces on a chess board. A clock strikes nine*)

DARRAGH: Hulse was meant to be here at nine o'clock.

VIOLET: (*with a start*) Oh, yes, Hugh—about nine.

DARRAGH: (*with a deep breath*) And Tims promised that he wouldn't be a minute later than eight with the coat complete. Good Lord! That I have to depend on such rotten tools! (*crushes the paper in his hand with dull passion*)

VIOLET: I . . . I . . . (*stops timidly*)

DARRAGH: (*with deadly politeness*) Yes, Violet? You were about to say . . . ?

VIOLET: Nothing, Hugh. Really, nothing at all.

DARRAGH: (*in the same vein*) Oh yes, Violet. I am sure you had some helpful little suggestion to make . . . The situation, Kato, to put it bluntly is this. If that wretched tailor Tims isn't here with that coat before young Hulse arrives, a month's patient shadowing and preparation, our ingenious plan, all our careful rehearsing and the best chance mortal ever had of landing a veritable fortune at one scoop simply go to the devil! And Violet is about to remark that perhaps Mr Tims has forgotten to wind up his watch or poor Mrs Tims' cough is worse . . . Go on Violet, don't be diffident.

KATO: (*making a move on chess board*) Pawn take White Queen and Check given in one move . . . (*to DARRAGH as he replaces chessmen in box*) If it is written to be, it will be, my friend. Who says? Perhaps.

(*DARRAGH makes a gesture of annoyance and contempt and is moving towards the door*)

VIOLET: (*getting up and crossing towards window*) Perhaps I can see . . .

DARRAGH: (*stopping and calling sharply*) Good heavens, Violet, do have a grain of sense! You know how strict the police are with the lighting regulations here. Open the blind an inch and we shall have the police in on us. Do you understand, the *Police*, and the devil knows what they may find out then. Oh, come away, idiot and sit down.

(*VIOLET returns to seat*)

DARRAGH: (*as he goes out, scowling*) You make me tired!

(A*s DARRAGH closes the door after him KATO's good-humoured face changes to a look of indignant resentment. He slowly rises to his feet with clenched hands and takes a step towards the door as if irresistibly drawn on*)

VIOLET: (*laughing a little with bitter mirthlessness from the sofa on which she has seated herself*). Is it true, Katie, that you are the greatest ju-jitsuist outside Japan?

KATO: (*becoming gentle at once*) Polite other people have say so.

VIOLET: And yet you cannot keep down even your own little temper.

KATO: (*crosses towards Violet and regards her for a moment*). I can keep down my temper so admirably that I—whose ances-tors are samurai, that is great nobleman and most high princes—have been enabled to become thief and swindler and . . . and . . . low down dog to laugh at it. What matter anything with me connected? Perhaps, (*seriously*) but there are *three ideals* above me at which I do not laugh. My Emperor (*inclines his head slightly*), my country and you, beautiful white lady (*becoming everyday again*) . . . and so, on three occasions, my temper slightly get the better of me.

VIOLET: Poor Katie—or poor me. I wish things might have been different. But there (*hardening*) we're all of a colour, my good man—a gang of crooks and I'm as crooked as any of you.

KATO: No. No. It isn't so. It isn't you of yourself. Is we bad fellows around you. Your husband ought never to have brought you into these things—and then to allow you—to compel you to—ah that is why, as you say, my temper ju-jitsues me. This time it is the worst of all—this young American, Hulse, for whose benefit you pass as the sister of your husband. Oh, how any mortal possessing you—

VIOLET: (*lighting cigarette*) Business, my dear man, strictly business. We aren't a firm of family solicitors. Jack Hulse had to be fascinated, and I—well, if there's any hitch, it isn't exactly my fault! (*smiles on him bewitchingly*)

KATO: (*fascinated*) Yes. Infatuated has become that so susceptible young man until you lead him about like pet lamb at the end of blue ribbon. Business. Perhaps. But how far must you have gone to find out all that you have done? (*torn by jealousy at the thought*). Violet, you have been so successful with this Hulse that I tremble at the thoughts that will rise up at me although I know how good and true you are at heart. And your husband—Darragh—he—(*laughs scornfully*)—business—very good business—and he *forces* you to do this so shameful thing and make mock of you for the pains!

VIOLET: Kato—

KATO: (*thoroughly wound up*) I am what your people say—

Yellow man—and you are beautiful white queen of my dreams—dreams—dreams that I would not stir a finger to spoil by making real. But if I were he (*nods towards door*) not ten thousand times the ten thousand pounds that Hulse carries would tempt me to *lend* you to another man's arms.

VIOLET: (*pettishly*) Oh, Katie, how horrid you are!

KATO: Horrid of me to say, but 'business' for you to do! Violet, you have found out for us that Hulse carries this packet of securities with him night and day, that he has them in the left breast pocket of his coat. You have learned exactly the shape and size that the packet makes and you have even discovered that for safety he sews up the pocket so that it cannot possibly be picked. Good. Business. Your husband cares not for anything so long as we succeed. But I, *Kato Kuromi, care* (*raising his voice*) *How, how* have you found this out? Now, *unless you and Hulse—*

(*DARRAGH is heard off right*)

VIOLET: (*in consternation*) Sssh

KATO: (*controlling his passion in his usual soft accents*) Oh. Yes, the views in the valley of Kedu are very fine and the river—

DARRAGH: (*he has entered at the last words. He comes in briskly and in a much better temper than when he went out. He notices nothing.*) It's all right. Tims is here (*speaking to someone outside through the door which he has left open, still at the door*). Come in, Tims, come on, hurry up.

(*Enter TIMS carrying a brown paper parcel*)

DARRAGH: (*again thro' doorway*) And, Harris, when Mr Hulse comes, show him into the morning room at first. Not up here, you understand? (*closes door*) Now, Tims.

TIMS: (*as he unfastens the parcel*) I'm sorry to be a bit late, Mr Darragh. I was delayed.

DARRAGH: Oh well, never mind now.

VIOLET: Is Mrs Tims well?

TIMS: (*turning his back on them all, still untying*) No, miss. She's better now. (*He swallows a sob*) She's dead, died an hour ago. That's why I wasn't quite able to be here at eight.

(*VIOLET gives a little moan of sympathy. KATO regards Tims with tranquil curiosity*)

DARRAGH: Devilish lucky you were able to get here by now in the circumstances, Tims.

TIMS: Well, sir, you see I shall need the money all the same now—though not quite for the same purpose as I had planned. There (*shakes out a dinner jacket which he has now taken from the parcel*). I think you'll find that quite satisfactory sir.

(*DARRAGH takes the jacket and passes it to VIOLET with an enquiring air. She lightly examines it and seems satisfied*)

DARRAGH: Exactly the same as your people made for Mr Hulse a week ago.

TIMS: To a stitch, sir. A friend of mine up at the shop got the measurements, and the cloth is a length from the same piece.

DARRAGH: But the cut, Tims? The cut is the most important thing. It makes all the difference in the world.

TIMS: Yes, sir, you may rely on that, I used to be a first class cutter before I took to drink, Mr Darragh, sir. I am yet, when I'm steady. And I machined both coats myself.

DARRAGH: That'll be alright then. Now, you were to have—?

TIMS: (*apologetically*) Ten guineas and the cost of the cloth you promised, sir. Of course, it's a very big price, sir, and I won't deny that I've been a bit uneasy about it from time to time.

DARRAGH: (*hurrying him up*) That's all right—

TIMS: I shouldn't like to be doing anything underhanded—anything wrong, sir. And when you stipulated that it wasn't to be mentioned to anybody—

DARRAGH: Well, well, man, it's a bet, didn't I tell you? I stand to win a clear hundred if I can fool Hulse over this coat. That's the long and short of it.

TIMS: I'm sure I hope it is, sir. I've never been in trouble for anything yet. It would break my wife's 'eart—(*stops suddenly as he remembers. His voice breaks. Then without another word he makes shakily for the door, covering his face with one hand*)

DARRAGH: (*as TIMS disappears*) Pay him, Kato, and let him out. I'll square up with you afterwards.

KATO: (*following TIMS*) All right-o!

DARRAGH: Now, Violet, slip into it. Hulse will be here at any moment now, and we don't want to keep him waiting. (*takes small packet out of a drawer and hands it to her*) Have you got the right cotton? Here's the dummy packet. Here you are.

VIOLET: (*slipping dummy packet into left breast pocket of coat and beginning to stitch it up quickly with a needle and cotton she has produced*) Yes, Hugh . . . and, Hugh—

DARRAGH: (*impatiently*) Yes, yes?

VIOLET: I don't want to know all your plans, Hugh, but I want to warn you. You are running a most tremendous risk with Kato.

DARRAGH: Oh, Kato. Pooh!

VIOLET: It is serious, Hugh. He is patriotic before everything else, and your scheme—well, *our* scheme—makes him unwittingly a traitor to his own country. When he learns that the packet which we have lifted from Jack Hulse contains not ten thousand pounds but a report of the most confidential nature from America to France, connected with the entire strategy and details of the American forces there, that you are selling this—that you have already sold it—to agents for Germany, something *terrible* may happen.

DARRAGH: It might, Violet. And therefore I haven't told him. Furthermore, I'm arranging it so that he will never know. Cheer up, Violet there will be no tragedy. All the same, my girl, thanks for the warning (*lays a hand carelessly on her shoulder*). It shows a proper regard for your husband's welfare.

VIOLET: (*affected by this unusual mildness*) Oh, Hugh, Hugh, if only you were more often—

(*The door is opened quietly but very quickly and KATO re-enters. Closes door*)

KATO: Here's a pretty go. Hulse has come and brought someone with him.

(*All stand aghast for a moment*)

DARRAGH: Damnation. That ruins everything. What ghastly muddle have you made now, Violet?

VIOLET: I? I don't know. I never dreamt of such a thing (*To Kato*) Are you sure?

KATO: (*nodding*) Slow man. Fellow who walks . . . (*stretches out his arm and walks a step with slow deliberation*)

VIOLET: Blind! Its Max Carrados. They've been great friends lately. Hulse has told me all about him. Carrados is most awfully clever in his own way but stone blind. Hugh, Hugh, don't you see? It makes no difference after all. Carrados can be in here and yet with all his sharpness he won't have a suspicion of what is going on!

KATO: True, if he is blind.

DARRAGH: (*hurrying out*) I'll make sure, Kato—(*indicates finished coat to the Japanese*)

(*KATO makes a gesture of assent and proceeds to change his coat for the new one, first rumpling the latter slightly to take off all the edge of its newness. His own coat he puts carefully away. This is complete comfortably by the time DARRAGH is heard returning with his guests. Enter DARRAGH. He waits at the door and while there he throws a swift and significant glance to Violet and with emphasis points to the buttonhole in the left lapel of his coat, trying to indicate that someone who is coming has a flower in their buttonhole, and at the same time jerking his head backwards towards the passage outside. The meaning of this is seen an instant later for when HULSE appears he is wearing a flower in his buttonhole*) (*turning and speaking through the doorway*) Take your time, Mr Carrados.

(*Enter CARRADOS and HULSE*)

Violet, a new friend for you—Mr Carrados. Mr Carrados, my sister.

(*VIOLET and CARRADOS bow*)

CARRADOS: Not to see you, exactly, Miss Darragh, but nonetheless, I hope, to know you as well as if I did.

HULSE: (*who has meanwhile shaken hands with Violet*) I wanted you to know Max before I went, Miss Darragh, so I took the liberty of bringing him round.

VIOLET: You *are* going, then?

HULSE: Yes. I've got the orders I've been waiting for. Twelve hours from now I hope to be in Paris. I should say 'I dread to be in Paris' for it may mean a long absence, but Max is going to write to me whenever he meets you—or meets anyone who has met you—or—well, so forth, just to cheer me up.

VIOLET: Take care, Mr Hulse, gallantry by proxy is a dangerous game!

HULSE: That's just it. Max is the only man I shouldn't be jealous of—because he can't see you!

(*VIOLET smiles and is leaning slightly forward. She delicately smells the flower in his buttonhole. With an enquiring look—an unspoken 'Will you accept it?' HULSE unpins the flower and offers it to her. She takes it and arranges it in her dress. DARRAGH meanwhile has been slowly crossing the room towards Kato but slyly observing the others with backward glances. The moment he sees Hulse touch the flower to remove it he is up to Kato, speaking decisively*)

DARRAGH: It's alright. We carry on.

KATO: According to programme?

DARRAGH: Exactly as we had arranged. Come across now (*DARRAGH turns to the group with KATO. As he nears them*)

I don't think either of you know Mr Kuromi—Mr Hulse, Mr Carrados.
(*They shake hands*)

HULSE: I am particularly anxious to meet Mr Kato. Miss Darragh has told me what a wonderful master of ju-jitsu you are.

KATO: Oh well—Little knack, you know. You are interested?

HULSE: Yes indeed. I regard it as a most useful acquisition at any time, and particularly now. I only wish I'd taken it up when I had the leisure.

VIOLET: Let me find you a chair, Mr Carrados. I am sure *you* won't be interested in such a strenuous subject as ju-jitsu. (*she takes his arm*)

CARRADOS: Oh yes, I am though. I am interested in everything.

VIOLET: But—surely—

CARRADOS: I can't see the ju-jitsuing? Quite true, but do you know, Miss Darragh, that does not make a great deal of difference after all. I have my sense of touch, my sense of taste, my hearing—even my unromantic nose—and you would hardly believe how they rallied to my assistance since my sight went, I often think you seeing people rely too much on your eyes. For instance (*they have now reached the chair that Violet had destined for him. To guide him into it, she has taken both his hands in hers. CARRADOS has gently disengaged his right hand and is lightly holding her left hand between both of his*). Hulse and I were speaking of you the other day—forgive our impertinence—and he happened to say that you disliked rings and had never worn one. His eyes, you see and perhaps a thoughtless remark of yours. Now I *know* that until quite recently you undoubtedly wore a ring, broad and smooth, possibly a wedding ring, on this finger. (*holds up her wedding ring finger*) (*The other three men have dropped their conversation and are listening. HULSE stares incredulously. DARRAGH and KATO are momentarily disconcerted. VIOLET is embarrassed*)

HULSE: Oh-ho, Max, you've come a cropper this time. Miss Darragh has *never* worn a ring (*to Violet*) have you?

VIOLET: N-o.

(*CARRADOS continues to smile benignly on her*)

DARRAGH: (*doubtful if they can carry it off and deciding to nip any rising suspicions by frankness*) Wait a minute, Violet, wait a minute. Didn't I see you wearing some sort of old ring a little time ago? I really believe Mr Carrados may be right. Think again.

VIOLET: (*taking the lead*) Why, yes, of course—how stupid of me! It, it was my mother's wedding ring and I wore it to—keep it safely. That was how I found out I disliked the feel of one and I soon gave it up.

DARRAGH: (*genially*) Ah—ha. I thought that we should be right.

KATO: (*crossing to Carrados*) This is really much interesting. I very greatly like your system, Mr Carrados.

CARRADOS: (*good naturedly*) Oh, scarcely a system—it's almost second nature with me now. I don't have to consider, say 'Where is the window?' If I want to open one. (*He has never taken the seat and now he goes unerringly towards the window*) I know with certainty that the window is here. How? Well it is ten degrees cooler outside than it is in here, so that's very simple. Was I right? (*He now lays his hand on the blind and lace curtains as he stretches it out in the direction of the window*)

VIOLET: (*hurriedly*) Yes—but, oh, do be careful, Mr Carrados. The police are most awfully particular about the light here and there is a policeman on point duty always, just opposite. We live in constant fear and trembling lest a glimmer should escape.

(*CARRADOS smiles and nods and leaves the window*)

CARRADOS: Then there is the electric light, heat at a certain height, of course.

KATO: True, but why *electric* light?

CARRADOS: No other light is noiseless and odourless—think:

gas, oil, candles, all betray their composition yards away. Then (*moving on again*) the fireplace—I suppose you can only smell soot in wet weather? And by the way, when you last had a fire here, it was mixed coal and logs. The mantelpiece (*touching it*) Petworth marble with its characteristic fossil shell markings. The wallpaper (*brushing his hand over it*) arrangements of pansies on a criss-cross background (*touching his tongue with one finger*)—colour scheme largely green and gold—

HULSE: (*mockingly as he points at a picture*) Engraving of Mrs Siddons as the Tragic Muse, suspended one for seven inches from the ceiling on a brass headed nail, supplied by a one-legged ironmonger whose Aunt Jane—(*all laugh except KATO*)

CARRADOS: You see what contempt familiarity breeds, Miss Darragh. I look to you, Mr Kuromi, to avenge me by putting Hulse in a variety of undignified attitudes on the floor.

HULSE: (*to Kato*) Oh, I shan't mind if you put me up to a wrinkle or two.

KATO: You wish?

HULSE: Indeed I do. I've seen the use of it. When I was coming across, one of the passengers held up a bully in the neatest way possible. It looked quite simple, something like this, if I may? (*KATO nods smiling assent. HULSE grabs his left arm under KATO's right and with his left hand grips KATO's collar*) 'Now' he said 'struggle and your right arm snaps.' I expect you know the grip.

KATO: (*politely amused*) Oh, yes. Therefore, it would be foolish to struggle. An expert in ju-jitsu never struggles. He gives way.

(*KATO appears to be falling helplessly away from Hulse sideways. HULSE is compelled to follow. KATO saves himself by his left arm while his bent left leg is an obstacle that brings HULSE to the ground. KATO is immediately upright again and politely assists HULSE to rise*)

Probably the bully did not know of that. But if he was so careless as to allow your friend to take him by the hand, this would have been better thing to do.

(*He approaches HULSE who has recovered his breath. HULSE gives him his right hand and KATO, grasping the fingers in his own right, lightly presses the tip of his thumb into the slack flesh between Hulse's thumb and first finger. HULSE at once doubles up in a helpless attitude*)

(*releasing him*) Then, in addition, there are several other ways for disposing of assailant who attacks as your friend did. The one I showed was very mild and would scarcely be used serious. The others are more violent. (*offering his hand for attack again*) Perhaps you would wish me to show you them?

HULSE: (*holding back*) Well, if it's all the same to you, I'd rather you showed me something—something where I downed the other fellow.

KATO: Oh, but you would—only for now *you* represent the other fellow.

DARRAGH: But this is all mere ABC, surely, Kuromi? I've seen ordinary gymnastic instructors do it. We understood that you were a master of the art.

KATO: Oh, well, I never say so.

VIOLET: No, that's why we thought you were. Haven't you some wonderful secrets that you keep for an emergency?

DARRAGH: Yes. I seem to remember hearing about secret grips and so on that were known and handed down in families for generations. They were said to be regarded as valuable heirlooms and were never taught except by father to son.

VIOLET: Oh, how exciting! I'm sure there must be some in your family, Mr Kuromi?

KATO: (*apparently disinclined to pursue the subject, turning away*) Oh yes. Perhaps.

VIOLET: Oh, do show us.

HULSE: I should very much like to see something of the very real thing, Mr Kuromi.

VIOLET: We won't breathe a word.

KATO: (*returning to centre*) Oh, that matters nothing because you could not possibly have any idea of the secret hold to tell. No. I don't like, as you say, showing it off.

VIOLET: Oh, just this once.

HULSE: (*they are speaking together*) As a great favour.

DARRAGH: Nonsense, man.

KATO: Well, as you all wish it so. (*Chorus of assent*) This is not only hold, it is (*thinks for a word*)—control. It is not known to me alone only. Of course, in reality I could make use of it not often for it would depend on my being able to secure the exact conditions, which with a practised opponent would be unlikely. But for now Mr Hulse will please allow me to do so. (*encouragingly*) It is not violent, this one.

(*KATO has removed his coat as he speaks and now stands expectantly as HULSE does nothing*)

(*smiling*) Will you so? (*points to his shirtsleeves*)

HULSE: (*hesitating and betraying some little concern*) Oh—is it necessary?

KATO: Please, yes. Or I shall be unable.

(*HULSE takes off his coat, first touching the outside of the left breast pocket as he has a betraying habit of doing. KATO has laid his coat already on a chair behind him. HULSE now does the same, using a chair on his side. KATO takes the action further down stage, away from the chairs. DARRAGH moves casually to a convenient spot. KATO now takes Hulse's right hand in his own right, puts his left hand round Hulse's right wrist and slowly pushes his left hand up as far as Hulse's elbow*)

(*pleasantly*) The object of the control is not only to reduce a person to helplessness but to be able to make him do exactly as one would wish against his will. All these master holds have their particular names and this one is called—literally—'The Thunderbolt in a Silk Package'.

VIOLET: Your countrymen are so romantic!

KATO: And yet so practical! Mr Hulse is now in condition to do exactly as he is told, he can move no single limb or joint except by my permission. Mr Carrados will have his revenge. I will tell Mr Hulse what to do and he will do it—or, yes, perhaps it will be more amusing if I *compel* him to do just what I tell him *not* to do. Well, do *not* put out your left arm, Hulse. We see.

(*HULSE's left arm goes rigidly out. This is DARRAGH's cue. He knows that Hulse is inflexibly rigid and he rapidly but coolly proceeds to change the positions of the coats, transferring the ordinary contents of Hulse's pockets to the pockets of the substituted coat. Meanwhile*)

(*smilingly*) Now turn your head and look round.

HULSE: (*with an effort and in an altered voice*) I cannot. I am held in a vice.

KATO: (*pleadingly*) At all events, Mr Hulse, do not stand on your left leg and pirouette with your right—it is so undignified! (*HULSE executes this movement*) And finally, do not box my ear for my pain.

(*HULSE swings his left hand violently round. KATO releases him and ducks agilely, thus avoiding the blow and bringing the demonstration to an end*)

HULSE: (*feeling his arms and neck*) Crumbs! That was an experience! I felt—well, I don't believe that I was half there. And yet I knew all the time what I was doing. (*is putting on his coat—which is the wrong coat. Touches his pocket, feels the dummy packet and is satisfied*) Now I don't suppose, Kuromi—(*turns and finds that KATO has moved off to speak quietly to Violet and Darragh and learn that all is right. He therefore crosses to Carrados*)

You old scoundrel, Max. it was you who put him up to that. Have a cigarette all the same.

(He offers his case to Carrados. CARRADOS leans forward to take one. It is now that he strikes upon the change of coats, though not yet fully understanding the details. For a moment his action is arrested in doubt and incredulity—then he leans still moreover and while affecting to pick out a cigarette—touches the cloth. Then, rising and standing between Hulse and the others he smells the lapel of the coat)

CARRADOS: (*with rapid intensity*) You wear a gardenia, Hulse?

HULSE: Yes, but I—

CARRADOS: (*still masking the action and conversation under the detail of taking a cigarette*) There has never been a flower in this coat! Be on your guard, man. By Heavens, we're in a nice fix!

HULSE: (*not yet grasping the full necessity*) What—

(*All through this there is business of lighting cigarettes and putting the box away*)

CARRADOS: Don't speak aloud. There is some treachery here. 'MIDNIGHT SUN'!

HULSE: 'MIDNIGHT SUN'! The password! Godfrey Daniel! Then you must be the man the Government told me would be put on to look after me!

CARRADOS: That's why I'm here now. Take no particular notice of me. Carry on just as usual and raise no suspicions. Move away now. (*CARRADOS sits down again*)

(*HULSE moves off towards the others. VIOLET turns as he approaches*)

VIOLET: Was it a very dreadful experience?

HULSE: Well, curious certainly. Yes, curious. The more I think of it the more—(*fears that he is getting too significant, though as yet his ideas on the situation are far from collected*) You've never seen it done before?

VIOLET: Oh, no. It is a great honour to get Mr Kuromi 'show it off' as he says.

HULSE: (*with deadly simpleness*) Yes, I should say so. I quite feel that.

VIOLET: And are you really going so soon? A month hence—a week—and the memory of this—of me—will all be a dream?

HULSE: Never! If I live to be a hundred—yes, if by any oversight I live to be a thousand. I shall never forget this evening!

VIOLET: Oh, this *evening*! Not poor me!

HULSE: This evening is you—very largely. And a little of Mr Kuromi, perhaps.

KATO: (*hearing his name and turning to them*) Yes, you say me, Mr Hulse? It is all understood? You bear me no ill malice?

HULSE: I won't go so far as to say it's quite all understood but the malice in any composition wouldn't fill an egg-cup. (*It is at this moment that the full nature of the plot dawns on CARRADOS. In his moment of discovery he incautiously brings down his right hand on his right leg with an emphatic slap. They all look at him, slightly startled*)

CARRADOS: (*divining the feeling*) Only a little catastrophe with the hot end of my cigarette. Yes, thanks, it's all right. I knocked it out. Hulse, I'll trouble you again.

(*HULSE crosses over, taking out his case*)

DARRAGH: (*to the other two, resuming interrupted conversation*) No, there's no need to hurry them. Better not, in fact. We're absolutely safe now.

CARRADOS: (*taking cigarette*) Thanks, old man, (*as he gets a light from HULSE*) I've got it. We may be able to carry it through. Play up to me for all you're worth.

HULSE: Sure!

DARRAGH: (*advancing by way of table, from which he picks up a box*) Cigarettes, did you say, Mr Carrados? Won't you try one of these?

CARRADOS: Thanks but I've just taken one of Hulse's (*humorously*) I felt I had to be nice to him, you know.

DARRAGH: (*grinning*) Oh, I understand that we're all forgiven. A pity you should miss so wonderful a feat.

CARRADOS: (*with slow deliberation and gradually raising his voice so that Kato shall not fail to hear*) Still I think I can imagine it all . . . As a matter of fact, the trick of that grip was known to me long ago.

KATO: (*hearing and hastening to the men, to confront CARRADOS with some acerbity*) Trick! And known to you! Oh, but impossible!

CARRADOS: Perhaps 'The Thunderbolt in a Silk Package' is not quite so exclusive a possession as you imagine, Mr Kuromi. It was shown to me by a Turk in Cairo many years ago—before I lost my sight. He not only demonstrated it but, for a consideration, showed me the dodge and made me quite proficient myself.

KATO: Dodge, you say! Oh, with difficulty I restrain myself quite politely. Well, Mr Carrados, since the Turk so proficiently showed you, perhaps you can return the table on me to my discomfiture.

CARRADOS: (*smiling and shaking his head*) You know very well that my dead eyes would be a fatal handicap now. But as you are proposing a return match I will put up Hulse against you and under my direction. We shall see if *he* can't make *you*—say—well, comb your hair with your left foot (*To add jealousy to Kato's already rising pique and to ensure his acceptance of the challenge CARRADOS adds*) I'm sure that he is pining to shine again in Miss Darragh's bright eyes.

KATO: (*in the desired mood*) Oh, yes. Come on. We'll try.

HULSE: (*in very modest tones*) Well, I'll do my level best.

CARRADOS: (*finessing DARRAGH out of harm's way*) And Mr Darragh shall sit here in my place and judge impartially.

(*DARRAGH is induced to take the seat and the other three men go further up stage towards the window. They stand much in their original positions. CARRADOS is behind them and nearer to the window. They remove their coats and place them as before without comment.*)

CARRADOS: Are you well under the light, Hulse? And with it shining as much as possible into Kuromi's eyes? (*This induces the two to move a little further away from him—and their coats*)

Now you know the position, take his right hand in yours—quite firmly and suddenly—like this. (*CARRADOS's right hand goes quickly out and comes into contact with the blind cord. There is a pull, a crack and the blind comes bodily down, displaying the unguarded window*)

(*CARRADOS stumbling forward from the window with groping hands he encounters the sofa and in a helpless confused way pushes it forwards on its easy castors so that it more effectively cuts off the two chairs, the coats and that part of the room from the others*) Good Heavens! What have I done? What has happened?

CONSTABLE: (*voice outside window, peremptorily*) Put out that light!

(*There is a pause of stupefaction all round. The next moment*)

VIOLET: Better, Hugh . . .

KATO: (*moving towards switch*) Shall I?

CONSTABLE: (voice outside window, *still sharper*) Put out that light at once. *Do you hear?*

DARRAGH: (*springing to the switch and jerking off the light*). Curse the thing!

(*The room is totally dark. CARRADOS is now seen by the audience to re-change the positions of the coats, so that the coat with the dummy packet is where Hulse's real coat was and vice versa*)

DARRAGH: Fetch that candle reading lamp out of my room. Be quick. We can do nothing till we have a light.

CARRADOS: I'm most terribly distressed. Did I really do it?

KATO: (*ironically*) We think you must have done. You cannot have been quite—quite proficient.

(*Re-enter VIOLET with a lamp or candle with its shaded hood*)

DARRAGH: Bring it carefully up here, Violet. Now Kato, help me with this table.

(*Lighted by VIOLET they move a table to beneath the window and DARRAGH quickly fixes the blind. The light is again turned on.*)

CARRADOS (*To VIOLET*) I hardly know how to apologise after your warning, Miss Darragh. My unfortunate over-confidence (*sighs*).

VIOLET: Oh, don't think so much of it, Mr Carrados, it might have been worse.

DARRAGH: It was damned unfortunate all the same.

KATO: (*back in his position in the centre of the stage*) I am still expectantly ready.

CARRADOS: No. No. I withdraw my man. I'm too distressed to be able to do anything of the sort now (*They resume their re-changed coats and, by a curious preoccupation, not only HULSE but KATO also touches the outside of his coat over the packet and is satisfied*) Mr Darragh is right. A catastrophe like this breaks up the harmony of our evening, we all feel it, much as we may regret the fact. Besides, Hulse, you haven't much time to spare.

HULSE: (*looking at watch*) That's true. I have a lot to do yet.

DARRAGH: Of course if you think that you must—

CARRADOS: I really think that we must. And if, through my clumsiness, it hasn't been altogether a pleasant evening, it has certainly been an instructive one.

DARRAGH: (*sardonically*) Perhaps after all we shall profit by the experience.

CARRADOS: (*shaking him warmly by the hand*) You put it so admirably! (*this in an admiring tone*)

(*CARRADOS shakes hands with KATO, and HULSE, following him, shakes hands with both the men*)

DARRAGH: Violet, will you go down?

(*VIOLET nods and prepares to escort the men out. HULSE opens the door for her, and she passes out. He follows. CARRADOS, in the act of going out, turns round at the door and seems to look sadly at the window*)

CARRADOS: (*shaking his head*) Dear, dear me. (*He sighs heavily and exits*)

(*DARRAGH and KATO stand for a moment listening to the retiring footsteps*)

KATO: Now to reap the reward of industry (*goes to where he has concealed his own coat, takes it out and changes*)

DARRAGH: And intelligence, Kato. It was my plan.

KATO: It wasn't bad plan. I always say so. Of course all depended on me though.

DARRAGH: It was a perfect plan, It couldn't go wrong.

KATO: So long as I did my part. (*preparing to rip open the sewn pocket of what he thinks is the coat Hulse has left behind*)

DARRAGH: (*restraining him*) Wait a minute, Katty. They have to get their things, remember. We mustn't risk Hulse coming up again for anything.

KATO: No, well. But we must all be clear out from here in half an hour now.

DARRAGH: That's just it, we mustn't dawdle counting the notes and things like that. For Heaven's sake, man, let's get on with necessary matters.

KATO: Quite well so. But it will take a minute only to make sure. I like not this way of yours, Darragh?

DARRAGH: Oh nonsense, Katty. You don't think that I want to bolt, do you? A third is yours and you shall have it (*KATO meanwhile has been picking open the sewn pocket and is about to withdraw the packet*) Look here, take the packet and put it in this drawer and you shall have the key.

KATO: No, I like not that either, Darragh. There are two keys.

DARRAGH: (*angrily*) That's an infernal insulting thing to say. If you weren't a Jap I should take it seriously. Kindly remember that in details of management I give orders and you obey.

KATO: (*holding the coat away from Darragh*) Oh, no, I think— (*he has his hand on the packet now*) But this is strange. We seem to have done ours up in exactly the same paper as the real one.

DARRAGH: How on earth—? (*They disclose the packet fully and stand regarding each other blankly with the packet between them. Words and wild incoherencies tremble on their lips but they cannot frame the horrible misgivings possessing them both. Then with an effort DARRAGH pulls the packet out of Kato's hands and rips off the outer covering. An evening newspaper is displayed!*):

DARRAGH: Damnation! Our Dummy! (*a moment's pause of mutual satisfaction*) What have you done, you fool?

KATO: Me? I? A fool? Oh, good, good. Why, you are the fool, you muddle up the coats yourself—

DARRAGH: I see it! That blind humbug Carrados, when he had us in the dark—when you were fool enough to be led into showing off with your wretched ju-jitsu again—he re-changed the coats. I might have known the Government would shepherd young Hulse till those despatches were safe—(*breaks off, recollecting that he is on dangerous ground, turns round and affects to be occupied with things on the table*).

KATO: (*sharply*) What, what is that Darragh? Government despatches—What despatches you say of?

DARRAGH: (*offhand*) Oh, nothing, Katty. Lend a hand, there's a good fellow. We have to clear out all the same, you know.

KATO: No. I think not until I know more. You speak of Government despatches to be made safe—from us. I liked not your way about the packet just now—I think there is something funny, queer in this business, Darragh. Hulse is an American, going to Paris. America is an ally and sending troops to France. (*with rising excitement*) And who was that fellow Krantz you used to meet?

DARRAGH: Kindly mind your own business, Kato. What the devil has it got to do with you?

KATO: Of me, myself, it matters nothing, but of my country and my Emperor and my country's Allies—everything. Can you deny that this Krantz was a German spy and that your business was to sell him those plans? (*DARRAGH is silent*) It is easy to guess—a man who is faithless to his wife and treacherous to his friends would be a fitting tool to betray his country.

DARRAGH: (*with venom*) You yellow dog—

KATO: (*advancing threateningly*) You dare to call me that, you who—

DARRAGH: (*drawing pistol*) Keep off, you fool, keep off or I'll—

(*KATO knocks Darragh's wrist and the pistol drops. Then he seizes his wrist in a lock grip and with one hand begins to push back his head slowly but irresistibly*)

DARRAGH: (*in a strangled voice*) Stop—stop, Katty, my neck—

KATO: (*grimly*) It is you who are going to stop—Darragh—to stop forever.

(*The door opens and VIOLET enters*)

VIOLET: (*suppressing a scream*) Kats—Hugh—what is it? (To someone beyond the open door) Do—do come and stop them.

(*Enter a CONSTABLE very deliberately*)

CONSTABLE: Here, what's this all about?

(*KATO releases DARRAGH who stumbles back into a chair*)

KATO: (*pleasantly*) Only a little friendly ju-jitsu, officer.

CONSTABLE: Jug-itsu? Can't say I know much about it, but I *do* understand the Lighting regulations. Now, a short time ago, there was a light coming through that window—

DARRAGH: The lighting now! The light Carrados bluffed us

over—and you want to fine me for it! Go on, ask anything—do anything. This is the limit.

(*The CONSTABLE takes out a large notebook and opens it leisurely, looking at Darragh the while*)

CONSTABLE: Now, about that there light that was a comin' thro' that window—

ERNEST BRAMAH

Ernest Bramah Smith was born in 1868 and brought up in Lancashire where he attended Manchester Grammar School. After leaving school in 1884 he worked on a farm, an experience that provided the material for his first book, published that year as by Ernest Bramah. Smith next took up journalism, first working alongside Jerome K. Jerome at *Today Magazine*. He also started writing short stories, and in the late 1890s he created the character that was to make him famous, Kai Lung, an itinerant storyteller whose tales and proverbs help him to outwit brigands and thieves in ancient China. While many modern readers would dismiss these stories as literary yellowface, they were immensely popular and, although Smith never visited China, his portrayal of the Chinese and their customs was accepted as a guide to a country about which most of his readers and contemporary reviewers knew very little. However, the character has dated badly and Smith's purple prose, replicating what he and others considered 'Oriental quaintness' and 'the charm of Oriental courtesy', means that the Kai Lung stories are seldom read today.

In 1913, Smith created his other great character, Max Carrados the blind detective, for a series of stories for the *News of the World*. Carrados was immediately hailed as something new and the stories were extremely popular. While he owes something to Sherlock Holmes, Carrados's nearest contemporary would be the preternaturally omniscient Dr John Thorndyke, the creation of R. Austin

Freeman, and there are many similarities between the characters of Carrados's household and their equivalents in Freeman's Thorndyke stories. More than one contemporary critic also suggested that Carrados might have been inspired by the career of Edward Emmett, a blind solicitor from Lancashire, who achieved some celebrity towards the end of the nineteenth century. As well as Carrados, Smith's stories feature some economically drawn but memorable characters, such as the detective's amanuensis, Parkinson, who has an eidetic but erratic memory, and the self-described 'pug-ugly' Miss Frensham, once known as 'The Girl with the Golden Mug'. And the stories often feature contemporary concerns like nationalist terrorism, Christian Science and suffragacy. However, Carrados's hyper-sensory brilliance can sometimes appear unconvincing, no more so than when he is able to detect by taste traces of whitewash on a cigarette paper that has been fired from a revolver.

A little after the outbreak of the First World War, in 1916 Smith enlisted in the Royal Defence Corps. This led to his writing non-fiction pieces for various magazines on a wide range of subjects but he continued to write stories about Kai Lung and Carrados and also completed a few stage plays, including adaptations of two of the Carrados stories as well as an original play, *Blind Man's Bluff*, written in 1918 for the actor Gilbert Heron. The previous year Heron had had great success with his own adaptation of another Carrados story; *In the Dark* had been very successful not least for its 'great surprise finish' when the final scene was performed in absolute darkness. Both plays originally featured on a variety bill and, as well as detection, Smith's play accommodates an on-stage demonstration of ju-jitsu.

The final stories about Max Carrados appeared in the 1920s, followed by a single full-length novel, *The Bravo of London*, in 1934—but Smith would continue to write from time to time about Kai Lung, up to his death in Weston-super-Mare, in 1942.

Blind Man's Bluff was first performed at the Chelsea Palace of Varieties on 8 April 1918. This is its first publication.

VICTORIA PUMPHREY

H. C. Bailey

The Pumphreys came over with the Conqueror and did very well out of it. For many centuries they continued to prosper. Then they became respectable. The cause of this unfortunate change in the character of the family is not known. The result was that the estate which had made the fourteenth Baron Pumphrey the richest man in the Midlands dwindled till the eighteenth (and last) Lord Pumphrey left his only daughter nothing but her name.

Priddle, Finch and Pollexfen did not come over with the Conqueror. Probably they were here before. Other lawyers who have had to do business with them declare that their methods were formed in the Stone Age. They have been family solicitors as long as families have had solicitors. Young Mr Pollexfen (he is not much turned sixty) had a great battle with Mr Eldon Finch before he was allowed to bring a woman typist into the office.

You are now to behold Miss Pumphrey wondering why she ever asked for the job. A large, fair, benign girl, she sat doing nothing in the corner of a musty room, also inhabited by three aged clerks and a small boy. It was her usual occupation after lunch. She looked very inappropriate. The firm is not of those which spend money on premises or furniture. In the precincts of Gray's Inn there is no office more decrepit. And the Hon.

Victoria Pumphrey is rather like an apple-tree flowering in sunshine.

Into that office came a grave man, who said mournfully that he was Mr Wilson Ellis. He had little grey whiskers; he wore a frock-coat as if he was born in it; he might have been a statesman of Queen Victoria's bright youth. He saw the Hon. Victoria Pumphrey and was deeply affected. He blushed like a nice boy, but horror seemed to be what he felt most. He gobbled a little. And Miss Pumphrey smiled upon him and he was led away to the presence of young Mr Pollexfen and stayed till closing-time.

But when he came out he looked still more unhappy. Victoria, emerging in her hat from the cupboard which she used as a cloakroom, gave him another smile of consolation. This sort of thing makes some women nasty about her. Mr Wilson Ellis murmured and made way for her and opened the door for her.

Upon the dark and creaking stairs he coughed, as one who humbly desires attention. Victoria waited for him. 'I beg your pardon, Ma'am,' he purred. 'If quite convenient, could I speak to you?'

'Do speak, Mr Ellis,' said Victoria.

Mr Ellis bowed and murmured and held up his cane to a taxi. He crowded himself into one corner, giving Victoria all the seat. He looked at her with deferential devotion and sighed.

Mr Wilson Ellis has been called by an employer mourning his retirement the last of the butlers. Others may have as much of the technique; none so much of the spirit of that noble profession. While he was making the Marquess of Gloucester the happiest of men, Lord Pumphrey and his daughter were often at the house and won that devotion which Mr Ellis always had to offer to an old title and a fine woman.

'I beg your pardon, Ma'am. I don't exactly know how to begin. I have got something in my mind, but I don't quite see my way. If you wouldn't mind taking tea in my little place—'

The taxi stopped at a large new stone building behind Piccadilly, a block of service flats. Victoria was escorted into a room on the ground floor which was a copy of Lord Gloucester's famous Adam library. She gazed about her with big, wondering eyes, and turned them on Ellis, and Ellis murmured that his gentleman had always been very kind and perhaps he had been a little fortunate, and it was drawn out of him that he managed the whole place—in fact, he owned it. He gave her tea—very much the butler. And Victoria, who had not been so beautifully served for years, shone upon him and wondered what on earth the old fellow had up his sleeve.

So, after the last of the potted char sandwiches: 'I didn't know you were a client of Mr Pollexfen's, Ellis,' said she.

'Rightly speaking, I'm not, Ma'am.'

'Did you come there to look for me?' Victoria smiled.

'No, Ma'am. I had no idea. It gave me quite a turn.' He wrung his hands. 'If I may say so, it don't seem right to me.'

'One must live, Ellis.'

'You and that Mr Pollexfen—begging your pardon, Ma'am!'

'But he's quite a harmless little man.'

Ellis sighed. 'I put him down as having no feelings, Ma'am. No fine feelings.' He shook a mournful head.

Victoria laughed. 'Well, what are you going to do about it, Ellis?'

'I should judge there could be something more fitting,' he coughed, 'and more remunerative.'

'My dear man, do you want a typist?'

'I wouldn't suggest it, Ma'am.' Ellis was horrified. 'I don't rightly see my way. But I'd be very thankful for your advice. And I don't know but what something might lead to something. Maybe you happen to remember the Madans, Ma'am? The Hereford Madans. Very old family.'

'I thought they were extinct.'

'Oh, no, Ma'am, not at all. Mr Oliver Madan, he must be quite an old gentleman now—matter of seventy; he's always been a kind of hermit, so to speak. He's never had his health. A martyr to rheumatoid—rheumatoid arthritis: a kind of gout, so I understand, Ma'am.'

'I remember! Very gouty indeed. Twisted and peppery. He's the only Madan extant, isn't he?'

'In a manner of speaking, Ma'am. He's the head of the family, and he never married. But there is a young lad who comes of a younger branch, such a nice boy, son of a naval officer who was killed at Jutland. His mother died giving him birth. He's quite alone, poor child, and the father left him very little.'

'What's Mr Oliver Madan doing about it?'

Ellis shook his head. 'It's been very difficult to approach Mr Madan. I'm afraid he's rather hard, Ma'am. He wrote that he could admit no claim.'

'Dear fellow. And who's looking after the boy, Ellis?'

Ellis looked profound. 'After all, he's generally thought the heir to the Madan property. I consider it in the light of a speculation, Ma'am.'

'Where is the boy?' said Victoria. Ellis murmured the name of a most exclusive and expensive preparatory school. 'You do the thing handsomely, don't you?'

'Oh, no, Ma'am, I assure you. It's just business with me—strictly business.'

'Then let's come to it.'

'Well, Ma'am, the trouble is there's another Madan cropped up, as you might say. Last month there was a gentleman came to Mr Oliver Madan and said he was his grand-nephew from Australia.' Ellis put his finger-tips together and looked at them sadly, and over them at Victoria. 'That is what I went to see Mr Pollexfen about Ma'am.'

'Help!' said Victoria. 'It's like a telegram sent by someone saving money. I suppose it means something, but it doesn't make sense. You've left out too many words, Ellis. First question: where does Oliver Madan live? Secondly: how on earth do you know about this man coming to him? Thirdly and lastly, my brethren, what do you want to do about him?'

Ellis smiled. 'So kind of you to take an interest, Ma'am,' he murmured. 'Mr Oliver Madan has a house at Babraham Hoo, near Peterborough, in the Fen country, I understand.'

Victoria said: 'My hat!'

'Quite a fine old house, I'm told. There is a friend of mine with Lord Thornley in the neighbourhood who is so good as to let me know if anything occurs.'

'Deeper and deeper yet. You've been having him watched?'

Ellis shifted in his chair. 'In a manner of speaking. Just in the interests of the boy, you understand, Ma'am. Now, you see, if this gentleman from Australia who says he is Frank Madan, really is, then he would be the heir and—'

'And that's an end of your little speculation.'

'Exactly so, Ma'am. You see, there certainly was a Madan who went to Australia. Quite a while ago, in the gold rush. And, of course, he may have married and—'

'And this man may be his lawful descendant, as right as rain. Bad luck, Ellis.'

'Very bad luck for the boy.' Ellis looked at her. 'Such a nice boy, Ma'am.'

'Ellis,' said Victoria sternly, 'don't be sentimental. I am not, but far otherwise. Has old Mr Madan accepted this heir from Australia?'

'My information is that he has received him.'

'Well, what about it? If the head of the family is satisfied, that's that.'

Ellis coughed. 'Mr Oliver is a very old gentleman and an invalid. I couldn't say I'd take his judgment. There's been claimants to estates before, Ma'am, and from Australia, too. And old folks have accepted them.'

'What, like the Tichborne claimant? He came from Wagga Wagga or somewhere, didn't he? Deeper and still deeper.'

'Just so, Ma'am. That was why I called on Mr Pollexfen. His firm are the lawyers to the Madan family. They have been for generations.'

'Well, did it cut any ice?'

'None at all, Ma'am. On the contrary, Mr Pollexfen was extremely difficult.'

'You surprise me.'

'He seemed to me to suggest that I was impertinent,' said Ellis sadly. 'I put it to him, Ma'am, that I was only there in the interests of the boy—such a nice boy!—and the real interests of the family. I'm afraid he has not the feelings of a gentleman. He kept on telling me it was all quite irregular. He won't do anything.'

'That seems quite like our Mr Pollexfen,' Victoria admitted. 'But what about it, Ellis? Where do I come in?'

'I had hopes that you might be willing to undertake a little—er—a little commission,' he hesitated over the word. 'Something quite correct, Ma'am. I mean to say, if you could see your way to go down and take a look at things at Babraham Hoo and this Australian person it would be a great kindness to me and the boy—such a—'

'Don't say that again or I shall scream. My good Ellis, how on earth can I go to Oliver Madan's house?'

Ellis smiled. 'You always had such tact, Ma'am. And you have met Mr Oliver Madan, to be sure.'

'Centuries ago. When I was a schoolgirl. What of it? How can I tell if his Australian is genuine or spurious?'

'Oh, Ma'am!' Ellis smiled. 'That's just what you would know. A lady like you. If you could see your way, it would be the greatest service. And, of course, any fee—I should be only too happy—and the matter of expenses—I do assure you, Ma'am, it would be worth anything you please to me to get your opinion.'

Thus, Miss Pumphrey is wont to say, was she launched on her present profitable career of crime. But she considers that she always had a bent for it.

In the morning Mr Pollexfen received a telegram which said that Miss Pumphrey had influenza, while an express was carrying her to Peterborough. The well-fed Bradford merchant in the other corner of her carriage, faced by a large and comely woman who was continuously amused, became uncomfortable. He deceived himself. The smiles and little gurgles of Miss Pumphrey were not caused by any interest in him, but by concentration of thought, which often has this effect upon her. She was endeavouring to make up her mind whether she was playing the fool. Why she had accepted Ellis's commission she knew very well. Six months of typing for Mr Pollexfen had made her ready to do anything that might become a woman for a change. Whether Ellis was the simple, sentimental philanthropist he seemed, or the speculator he pretended, she had no opinion, but his rise to awful opulence impressed her. Ellis seemed to be a man worth following by one who wanted a good bet, and Miss Pumphrey did. She was very tired of being poor. And, on consideration, the job did not seem so crazy as it looked at first.

She made herself comfortable in a hotel at Peterborough. She lunched wisely and well (Miss Pumphrey likes to take her time). She ordered a car and drove out to Babraham Hoo. Miles of country lay flat as a floor, a melancholy country under the grey March sky, black earth without a hedge or a tree on it, marked geometrically by broad drain-cuts through which the fen water flowed, slow, slimy and turbid. 'This is priceless,' said Miss Pumphrey. 'Like the works of the late Mr Euclid painted in mud colour.' A windmill stood with unmoving sails, a giant scarecrow, and leered at her. A scrap of wild marsh broke the tilled land and, beyond it, stunted birches stood white amid yellow moss and pools of oily, dark water, an uncanny goblins' wood. The car checked, turned, and swung into the moss-grown drive of Babraham Hoo.

It stood among dense shrubs, a square house of yellow brick, like a box with windows cut in it. Miss Pumphrey rang and rang again a bell which had to be pulled hard and sounded far away. After minutes, a plump maid opened the door and stared vacantly. Miss Pumphrey said that she wanted to see Mr Oliver Madan, and gave her card. The rustic maid read it, and the name of the Hon. Victoria Pumphrey, or the regal presence, startled her. She gaped, she hesitated, she led Miss Pumphrey to a drawing-room, and left her without a word.

It was a large room, but stuffy with the smell of yesterday's cigars. It was not convenient: a smoky fire burnt ineffectually in a vast, absurd grate, ancient paraffin lamps of china were the only lighting, and Mr Oliver Madan had not been thorough with his furniture: much of it was dingy and uncomfortable in the austere taste of Queen Victoria; the rest of a modern and gaudy luxury.

Victoria had leisure to study it before a man came in. He was rather red and rather bald; he was in respectable black. His name was Price; he was Mr Madan's secretary, which seemed to Victoria a pretty word for valet, for such was his manner. He was afraid that the doctor had forbidden Mr Madan to receive visitors. Victoria hoped it was nothing serious.

'Mr Madan has been an invalid for a long time,' the secretary said reproachfully. There was a felt pause. 'You didn't know, Madam?'

'I knew his health wasn't good. Doesn't he ever see anybody now?'

'I'm afraid not, Miss Pumphrey.' The secretary did not conceal that he thought her inconsiderate, but was anxious to oblige. 'Can I do anything for you?'

'I should like you to take him my card.'

'Oh, you know Mr Madan?'

'I think he will remember me.'

'Yes, yes, of course.' The secretary's eyes said that no man could possibly forget Miss Pumphrey. 'Certainly, I'll take him your card. I'm sure he would like to know you called. And if there's anything else—I mean to say, if you would tell me the nature of your business—perhaps something could be arranged.'

Victoria smiled on this obliging person. 'You see, my business is rather vague.' She smoothed down her dress.

Amazement was written on secretary's red face. 'Vague?' He repeated.

'I'm writing a book,' said Victoria modestly, 'about Herefordshire—the old families, you know—and I wanted to ask Mr Madan some questions about the Madans.' She clasped her hands. 'Do you think you could arrange it, Mr Price?'

Mr Price stroked his back hair, which was all the hair he had. He really did not know. He didn't think it was at all possible. He would see Mr Madan, but he really didn't think—and, still talking, he slid out.

Victoria was left alone long enough to grow very tired of that drawing-room. She wandered about. She felt that she could make an inventory of its ugly contents, and another man came in. He was big enough every way to make two of Mr Price and less than half his age, a dark fellow with a swagger and an engaging grin.

''Morning. Put you in cold storage, what?' The fire leapt asunder in clouds of smoke as he poked it. 'Say, this house wouldn't be warm if you set fire to it.' He had a faint Cockney twang, yet not the true Cockney.

'A real English house,' said Victoria.

'Oh, English! And then some.'

'So am I,' said Victoria.

'I should say so.' His keen dark eyes examined her with approval. 'I'll tell the world there's nothing better when it's good.'

'That's very kind of you, if you're not English.'

'Australian. English pedigree stock. I'm a Madan, of sorts. Frank Madan. He grinned broadly. 'Very pleased to meet you, Miss Pumphrey.'

'Thank you, Mr Madan.'

'The thanks are on me. You don't know what it's like to see a human woman in this place.'

'Of course I don't,' Victoria admitted.

'Kind of puts in the central heating. I say, are you staying in these parts?'

'I wasn't thinking of it. But I really don't know. You see, I want very much to have a talk with Mr Oliver Madan.'

'Oh, God!' said the Australian.

'That's not very encouraging,' said Victoria.

'Well, I mean to say, what's the matter with Mr Frank Madan? I'll talk all you want.'

'How nice of you! But do you know much about the history of the family, Mr Madan?'

'Sure, lady. Sit down and hear the story of my life.'

'Please be serious,' said Victoria with dignity. 'I am writing a book.' Mr Madan again appealed to his creator. 'About your native county,' Victoria went on severely. 'I want Mr Oliver Madan to help me with some points about his family. Don't you think he'll be able to see me?'

'He can see all right,' the Australian admitted, 'but he don't talk. Not so you'd notice it. He only groans. He's got his, you know, and got it bad. Gout, rheumatoid something. He don't show.'

'I wonder if I can come down again,' Victoria said sadly.

'Do you live in London? Say, I run up sometimes. I wonder if we could make a date?'

The door opened to let in Mr Price. He looked respectfully surprised at the Australian, who was rather near Miss Pumphrey and earnest about it. 'Mr Madan sends his compliments, Madam. He is much obliged to you, but he does not find himself equal to seeing anyone.'

'I'm so sorry,' said Victoria. 'Perhaps I might call again.'

'Sure,' the Australian grinned.

But Mr Price was less encouraging. 'Really, I couldn't say. I shouldn't like to promise. You know, if you could write, Miss Pumphrey, I might be able to get the information you want. I'm sure that would be the best way.'

Victoria thanked him prettily, and, with a hand tingling from the grip of the Australian, went back to Peterborough.

Before the fire in her bedroom, placid in the comfort which comes from a bath and a dressing-gown, she considered things. She likes to put business out of her head before she goes to dinner. She has some manly instincts.

She is never in a hurry. She did not write to Oliver Madan. She stayed in Peterborough and waited. On the second day, as she was going to lunch, she saw her Australian come into the hotel and ask questions at the office. Two minutes later he was swaggering across the dining-room to her table. 'Miss Pumphrey! Well, that's fine! May I have the honour?' He sat down grinning. 'I say, this is on me, you know. I've been in about a horse and I was just coming here for a spot of lunch. And here's you! Some lunch. Well, what's the best they've got? That's all right. It's honest to God stuff they give you here. And a bottle o' bubbly'll make it go. What say?' He gave the order before she said. 'So you reckon to stay and have another try for the old man?'

'I do want to see Mr Oliver Madan.'

'Sure you do. You aren't here for your health.' His small brown eyes gleamed.

'Dear me, no,' Victoria smiled. 'I shouldn't come here for my health. Would you, Mr Madan?'

'Not. Many nots. If there's anything slower than these parts I guess it's hell.' The champagne came and he grasped at the bottle. 'Say, we've earned this.' He filled her glass. 'You put that where you need it, Miss Pumphrey. Here's luck.'

Victoria smiled at him over the wine. 'What luck do you want, Mr Madan?'

'You go on looking like that.'

'You didn't come to Babraham Hoo to see me.'

'If I'd known where to find a peach like you I wouldn't have come to the old ash-pit. Gee! To think you spend your time writing books!'

'And how do you spend your time, Mr Madan?'

'I'd hate to tell you, sister. I haven't got going since the war petered out. Pa went west while I was with the Light Horse, in Palestine, and my little grey home was bust. I've been knocking about—Kenya, the Cape. Couldn't strike it. So I kind of drifted back to Blighty to try my luck with old man Oliver. He's got the stuff, you see, and I could do with a bit.'

'Yes, I see,' said Victoria rather slowly.

'Well, it's got to come to me some day,' the Australian protested. 'What's the matter with a bit on account?'

'Dear me, Mr Madan, I am not one of the family.'

'You know all about us, don't you?' the Australian grinned.

'Only about the past, Mr Madan.'

'I thought you knew old man Oliver.'

'I used to. But he is only one. I wanted him to help me about the others, you know. The bygone Madans.'

'What's the matter with 'em?'

'They had a way of vanishing, Mr Madan.'

'Most folks do—underground.' He pointed downwards and grinned.

'Underground,' Victoria repeated, 'as you say.'

'My grandpa went out to Sydney in '49. Died up country prospecting. Pa took up land—sheep. He went out in '17. I'm the one they left. Not much to write a book about in that. What do you reckon to put into your book, sister?'

'Just history, Mr Madan. Family history.'

'Don't sound like a best-seller to me. Any money in it?'

'Thank you,' said Victoria, 'I do very well.'

'I should say so,' the Australian agreed. 'I wonder, can't we do anything together?'

Victoria laughed. 'What does one do here, Mr Madan? Shall we go and look at the cathedral?'

'I don't think,' said the Australian. 'But say, sister, I'd love to make a date in London.'

'Is there nothing doing at Babraham Hoo?'

The Australian looked at her queerly. The Australian hesitated.

'Perhaps we shall meet there again,' Victoria smiled. 'Goodbye, Mr Madan.' She left him at the table. As she went out she saw him drinking up the champagne. He seemed to want it.

Meditation in a long chair before her bedroom fire assured her that she was satisfied. The Australian had plainly come to Peterborough to look for her and to pump her. That meant he was frightened of her. And he would not be frightened unless he were a fraud. Yes, she had done very well. Their little conversation frightened him more. He would have something to think about at Babraham Hoo, if he went back. Yes, the business was clearing up . . . But she was rather sorry. Of course the fellow was an outsider. And yet—well, she was sorry . . . She did not quite see her way.

She is never in a hurry. It was not until the next afternoon that she drove out again to Babraham Hoo. Her chauffeur, a large and chatty youth, took a friendly interest in this second expedition. It seemed that no one ever went to Babraham Hoo.

The door of the yellow house was opened more quickly this time. The rustic maid had an embarrassed air. Mr Madan could not see anyone, Ma'am. He was too ill. Mr Price? Oh, she thought Mr Price was out.

'I will wait for him,' said Victoria, and swept in. She was left in the hall.

But Mr Price was in. He was in that cavernous drawing-room with the Australian. Victoria heard their voices, which were not friendly, but the Australian, when the maid took in her name, began to laugh. The maid came out again looking scared, and held the door open for Victoria.

The Australian was sprawling before the fire, Mr Price on his feet, fidgeting with his coat, with his back hair, with his collar. 'Come again, sister!' The Australian flung back his head to look at her with a grin.

'Really, Miss Pumphrey, this is quite useless, you know, quite useless,' said Mr Price.

'No; I don't think so,' Victoria smiled.

'You can't see Mr Madan. He's much too ill.'

'But I'm afraid I shall have to,' said Victoria sweetly. 'You see, I have found out something he—'

'What's that?' The Australian stood up.

'I thought you wanted to ask him questions,' said Mr Price.

'Not now,' Victoria smiled. 'This is something he'll have to be told. About the Madan family. I said I was making enquiries, you know.'

The two men came towards her. She drew back to avoid them, but she was brought up by one of the big pedestal lamps.

'Let's have it, sister,' said the Australian, close upon her.

'What do you mean?' Mr Price snarled.

'It's a matter for Mr Madan.'

'I act for Mr Madan,' said Price.

'And this gentleman—for whom does he act?'

Price licked his lips and looked at the Australian. 'Ah, get to hell out of here!' the latter cried, and jostled him aside. 'This is my show.' Price scowled at him and slunk out. The Australian grinned. 'Yellow, ain't he? Yellow all through. Now, my dear, what have you got?' He came still nearer.

Victoria started away. The big lamp went down into the grate and crashed into potsherds. The fire caught the oil and a flood of flame streamed over the floor. Victoria swept out into the hall to cry: 'Fire! Fire!'

Mr Price, who was half-way upstairs, came tumbling down again. 'What is it? What's happened, Miss'?'

'The house is on fire!' Victoria screamed.

An oily smoke poured out of the drawing-room. The Australian was heard stamping and swearing and shouting for water. The rustic maid ran into the hall and fled again, screaming 'Fire!' and Price looked into the room and gasped and coughed and hurried after her. There were more screams from the kitchen, a clatter of pails and pouring of water. And the smoke grew thicker and Victoria cried 'Fire! Fire!'

A man came running downstairs. He was grey, he was small, but he was very agile. Victoria stood aside and watched him. He called for Price as he came. He hesitated, looked at the smoke pouring from the drawing-room, and made a dash for the hall door. He flung it open and stood panting, confronted by Victoria's car and her bewildered chauffeur.

She swept through the smoke and joined him. 'Mr Oliver Madan?' she smiled.

The little man looked at her with unsteady eyes. 'Another time, another time,' he muttered, and turned away. 'Price, damn you, where are you, Price?'

Mr Price, shuffling along with two pails of water, heard him, saw him, flung the pails into the drawing-room, where the Australian received them with oaths, and hurried out. 'What did you come down for?' he gasped.

'How was I to stay up there with the house afire?'

'You didn't ought to come. You know that. You get back quick.'

'But you're very harsh, Mr Price,' Victoria smiled. 'You're very curt. Isn't this Mr Oliver Madan?'

Price did not answer. He stared into her wide eyes.

She turned to the little man. 'Mr Madan?' she enquired.

'Well, what do you want?' he muttered.

'It was delightful to see you run downstairs. When I saw you last you were quite a cripple.'

'You made a mistake. You never saw me before. I don't know you.'

'How horrid of you to forget! I am Victoria Pumphrey. When

I saw you last you were Mr Madan's valet. Sant, isn't it? Yes, Sant.' She ceased to smile. She looked from the pallid little man to the crimson Price. 'What have you two creatures done with Oliver Madan?'

'It's all a mistake, Ma'am,' said Price eagerly. 'I swear it is. Of course this isn't Mr Madan. Mr Madan's not at home.'

'I believe you,' Victoria said.

The Australian, hot and singed and smoky, strode out with the invincible grin on his smudged face. 'All clear,' he said. 'That was neat work, sister. You sure got to see him.'

'This is Mr Oliver Madan, is it?'

'Why, yes. That's old man Oliver all right. How goes it, Uncle? Found you could skip when you got warm?'

'This creature is Oliver Madan's valet,' Victoria said.

'The hell he is! He's the only Oliver Madan here. Say, what have you boys been giving me? Where's my uncle? What have you done with my uncle?'

'Your uncle!' Price snarled.

'Ain't you been standing in with us?' the valet cried. 'You know you have, ever since you came.'

'I thought so.' Victoria turned away to her chauffeur, her ecstatically interested chauffeur. 'Police is what I want—the nearest policeman.'

'That's right, Miss!' He jumped into the car and pressed the starter.

'Here, Miss Pumphrey. don't you do that!' The little man caught at her. 'We have done nothing wrong, I swear we haven't. The old man died natural, quite natural. I have only been acting for him.'

'Where did he die? When?'

'In Droitwich, it was. Three years ago. I'll tell you—'

'You can tell the police,' said Victoria, and got into her car.

'You win, sister,' the Australian said, and kissed a black hand to her.

When a village policeman had understood enough of the story to be persuaded to come to Babraham Hoo, no one remained there but an hysterical maid and a prostrate cook, who complained that their wages had not been paid.

Miss Pumphrey went back to London by the next train.

Mr Wilson Ellis was at home. Mr Wilson Ellis, in evening dress, is the exquisite, ideal butler. He wished to know if Miss Pumphrey had dined. He could hardly bear it when she said she didn't know. He said vain things about soup and cutlets.

'You may give me,' said Victoria, 'one cheap American cigarette.' She laid herself on a couch in his little Empire drawing-room and sighed satisfaction and smoke. Ellis was afraid she had had a distressing time. 'My dear man! The time of my life.' Ellis hoped that everything was all right. 'You're all right. You and your nice boy. He's the heir of all the Madans, safe enough.'

Ellis was heard to murmur: 'Thank God!' Then he asked if she was quite sure.

Victoria laughed. 'Don't worry. You've backed a winner. I suppose you always do.'

'I've been very fortunate,' Ellis murmured. 'Then this Australian, Ma'am, you're sure he is an impostor?'

'Oh, the Australian is an extra turn. He wasn't in the programme. I always thought that. Didn't you?' It was obvious that Ellis did not.

'Oliver was the mystery. Would Oliver let a young nephew come and live with him, genuine or spurious? I think not! Why did he? I went after Oliver. And he was invisible. Very interesting and suggestive. Do you know his man?'

Ellis gasped a little. 'That would be Price, Ma'am? Not to say know him. He is not well liked.'

'You surprise me. What about Sant?'

'Sant is dead. He died three years ago.' Ellis shook his head. 'I don't want to say anything unkind, but Sant wasn't straight. He did what he liked with Mr Madan.'

'Poor old thing,' Victoria sighed. 'Well, I was saying I went to Babraham Hoo and Mr Oliver Madan wouldn't see me. He was too ill. But I got him downstairs today. I had to set fire to the house to do it. No wonder he didn't want to show! He wasn't Oliver Madan. He was Sant.' Ellis made vague noises. 'Don't you see? It wasn't Sant who died three years ago: it was Oliver Madan. These two beauties, Sant and Price, they had him sick in a strange place. They called him Sant and buried him as Sant, and Sant lived on as Oliver Madan and drew the income. He never had to appear. The old man had been an invalid and a hermit for umpteen years. Only a matter of forging his signature. It was too easy—till the Australian blew in and spoilt it. I don't know whether he got wind of something queer or whether he was just trying his luck. He is a dashing rascal, worth ten of Sant and Price. He must have seen through them quickly enough. They say he's been standing in with them. I dare say he bluffed them out of a good share of the swag. I hope he did.'

'Well, upon my word!' said Ellis. 'But this must have been very unpleasant and dangerous for you, Ma'am. I am extremely sorry. I had no idea. I—'

'My dear man, I loved it!'

'God bless my soul!' said Ellis. 'Pray, Ma'am, where are they now?'

'Bolted. I told the county police, of course. They're about as quick as a glacier. You'd better take your solicitor to Scotland Yard in the morning. I'll go too. Then we'll call on Priddle, Finch and Pollexfen and make them sit up. Little Mr Pollexfen won't like it at all. You'll prove Oliver Madan's death and your nice boy will come into the estates. But I don't think I shall be going back to Priddle, Finch and Pollexfen.'

'No, Ma'am?' said Ellis, a little short of breath. 'I—I am sure I hope not. Something more becoming. If I could be of any assistance, I'm sure I—I should be proud.'

'You can. I shall set up on my own. The Hon. Victoria

Pumphrey: Friend of the Family: relations discovered or destroyed; domestic quarrels made or settled; family skeletons a speciality.'

For this is how Miss Pumphrey entered upon the profession of which she is the most distinguished practitioner.

H. C. BAILEY

Henry Christopher Bailey (1878–1961) created one of the most popular detectives in Britain in the 1920s, Reginald Fortune, referred to by his friends as 'Reggie' and by others as 'Mr Fortune'. Between 1919 and 1948, Reggie appeared in nine novels and over eighty carefully plotted long short stories that are peppered with humour and full of originality. Fortune is a gentleman detective, a surgeon who acts as a medical consultant to Scotland Yard in the shape of, for the most part, the Honourable Stanley Lomas, chief of the Criminal Investigation Department, and Superintendent Bell. While the stories have become damaged by the detective's mannerisms, as well as by some regrettable racist and anti-Semitic references, Fortune is a likeable, well-rounded character and his cases tackle themes that rarely occurred in crime fiction of the period. As well as Fortune, Bailey created Joshua Clunk, a Dickensian lawyer, who has a cameo in one of Mr Fortune's novels, while Fortune plays a minor role in two of Clunk's cases. And, less unusually than might be thought would be the case for detective fiction of the Golden Age, both Clunk and Fortune are prepared to take the law into their own hands.

After graduating from Oxford in 1901 with a first-class honours degree in 'Greats', Bailey became a journalist, joining the *Daily Telegraph* where he stayed for over forty years fulfilling a variety of roles including drama critic, crime journalist, war correspondent and editorial writer. While at University Bailey had begun writing well-regarded historical novels, often set in the Middle Ages and sometimes with criminous elements, but in the late 1910s he turned to detective fiction. While Bailey continued to write historical fiction until the 1930s when his thirtieth book, *Mr Cardonnel*, appeared, he is best known for his richly atmospheric and entertaining detective stories in which Fortune—or Clunk—unravels a crime, and sometimes a conspiracy, from apparently insignificant clues.

Though they do not always conform fully to the 'rules' of fair play, Bailey's detective stories explore psychology and detection, unusual for the genre, and they often probe themes that are considerably darker than those investigated by Fortune and Clunk's contemporaries, for example corruption among politicians and the police, child abuse and miscarriages of justice. Such originality won Bailey the admiration of his peers as well as readers. Despite—or perhaps because of—his career, working for the most conservative of Britain's newspapers, Bailey also used detective fiction gently to satirise class-consciousness and other 'traditional' values, thereby mildly lampooning precisely the kind of person who might be thought to read the *Daily Telegraph.*

'Victoria Pumphrey' was first published in *Holly Leaves*, the Christmas number of the *Illustrated Sporting & Dramatic News* in December 1939.

THE STARTING-HANDLE MURDER

Roy Vickers

When a man of high intelligence steps outside the law, he pits his cunning against that of the police and the Public Prosecutor. Like the fox, who, we are told, understands the technique of hunting, he runs with discrimination and often gets away.

But the simile breaks down on the Department of Dead Ends—unless you can think of some fussy old gentleman who sets out with the vague intention of following the hounds on foot and accidentally stumbles headlong over the fox.

The Department, one must admit, was not animated by a sporting spirit. Its purpose was to catch the law-breaker not by a keen duel of wits, but—just anyhow. It is possible to contend that all its successes were flukes. And so, by all the rules of detective work, they were. But if the Department had not logic, it had a sort of philosophy—that a law-breaker will walk into prison if you open enough doors for him.

It cared nothing for psychology nor the criminal mentality. This blindness was partly responsible for its success in the Hartways murder. For the murderer had no criminal mentality. The Department of Dead Ends caught him because he was a gentleman. Not a gentleman crook—but a gentleman in the rather formidable Edwardian sense of the word, meaning a man of more or less aristocratic lineage who might work but was not compelled to do so, who was eligible for any of the best clubs, and whose manners and morality were strictly within the code of his own class.

Except, of course, for the murder.

Lionel Anstruther Tracington Cornboise was not quite the typical young man of the period. He was intended for the Diplomatic Service, but while at Oxford was offered a probationary commission in the Guards, and accepted. One of his brother subalterns was young Hartways (the man he subsequently murdered), an old school friend, whose first name also happened to be Lionel. But there does not seem to have been any confusion—because at home, at school, and subsequently in the Army, and even eventually by his wife, Hartways was always called 'Balmy'.

Throughout his boyhood Hartways had a slightly eccentric manner and a penchant for practical jokes at which he would laugh inordinately. In the light of subsequent events it may be regretted that the eccentricity was so mild that it rather endeared him to people and earned him the affectionate prefix. For no one guessed the real trouble until it was too late.

As small boys they had joined in energetically despising Hilda Cressnal, the daughter of a retired Indian Colonel who sat for the Borough. They were severally guilty of tweaking her fiery red plaits. As hobbledehoys they had blushed about her. In junior subaltern days she was writing innocent little notes to both of them in the dainty-genteel style of the period. Each of them had a fairly substantial income, and it was understood that they were friendly rivals.

Motor-cars were coming into general use, though they were still frowned upon in the mess, because it was commonly believed that they would put an end to hunting. Hartways was the first of the mess to buy one. This gave him the advantage of being able to ignore train services. The indirect result was that when they were all twenty-four Hilda accepted him.

Cornboise was best man. If he suffered he did not show it—for at this stage all young officers owed something of their mental make-up to Mr Kipling. Moreover, this was the heyday of the strong, silent man.

For the next year Lionel Cornboise was an occasional guest at Hartways Manor—'a ring-fence, deer-park' place on the South Downs. Hilda played the game, so Cornboise had no idea that there was anything wrong. In fact, the first suspicion came to him when he and Balmy were in barracks.

Since his marriage, Balmy had been rather progressively living up to his nickname. With that nickname he was a licensed wag. But there were limits to the licence. There was a practical joke played on the juniors that came under the head of 'tagging' and got into the papers. There was no court-martial, but the adjutant gave a pretty stiff warning and, in effect, withdrew the licence.

For three months Balmy Hartways simmered down. Then, just at the beginning of the London season, he broke out again. On a guest night. The incident was not talked about, and it will be sufficient to say that the Colonel saw him that night and on the next day Balmy Hartways sent in his papers.

Within a week Cornboise was dining with the Hartways at their house in Bruton Street. Balmy Hartways referred openly to the fact that the Colonel had told him what to do—he made a good story out of it.

In those days the ladies withdrew, even if there was only one of them, and left the gentlemen, if not to their port, at least to their brandy liqueurs. Pretty soon Balmy asked Lionel to go up to the drawing-room, saying he would join him presently. Afterwards Lionel guessed that Hilda had demanded the arrangement, and it struck him as a little pathetic that Balmy should have agreed.

The scene that follows reads like the rough notes of a play by Mr Sutro. Measured in years, it is such a short time ago. If Balmy were alive at this moment he would hardly admit that he was elderly. But the key to the social relationships of this period has been trampled in the mud of the Great War, and cannot be found even in the memory of the middle-aged survivors.

'Let me give you some coffee, Lionel. I have no doubt Balmy will join us in a minute.'

'Thanks, Hilda! If you will allow me to say it, you are not looking quite your normal self.'

At this point, we imagine, Hilda 'shrugged her shapely shoulders'. As a matter of fact, they really were shapely, as was the rest of her. There is a published photograph headed 'A Gibson Girl in Society', and Hilda had the same high coiffure, wide eyes, retroussé nose, prominent chin, narrow waist of the type popularised by Mr Charles Dana Gibson.

'Oh, it's nothing, Lionel! Please don't speak of it.' With the words, I am afraid, was a brave little laugh.

'There isn't much a fellow can say.' The brave little laugh was making Lionel's voice unsteady. 'At your wedding, Hilda, I made a bit of a speech. I felt rather a fool making it. But I happened to mean what I said.'

'You said you were Balmy's friend—and my friend, if I would let you be . . . Oh, Lionel, I want to tell you everything, but I don't know how to begin . . . Those silly little jokes. He plays them at home—constantly. Not so much here, but at Hartways. It's—awful. He gets moods—and then he's awful, like another person. When he's not playing the jokes he's his old charming self. He's never cruel to me—at least, he never means to be. But, apart from me, he does all sorts of things. He has bought Lord Doucester's yacht. It costs seven thousand a year to keep it up, and, as you know, we have barely ten. I believe—I believe he'll get into debt.'

'Good God!' said Lionel, and did nothing. There was, of course, nothing that he could do. But he did not accept their invitation for the yacht that August.

In September rumours about the Hartways reached him. Later he received two extremely cheery invitations from Balmy, but was able to plead duty as an excuse for both. He felt that he dared not face Hilda's tragic eyes, because he knew that the Hartways were 'dropping out'.

We know at least what he meant by that. Those were the days of 'Society', when phrases like 'a leading hostess' and 'a well-known clubman' had real meaning. This Society may have been easier for a rich man to enter than in the Victorian days. But for some lost reason those that were in seem to have attached far more importance to their position than in any previous period of history. If you were in, you spoke of a friend who had dropped out much as nowadays you might speak of a friend who had been sent to Devil's Island. It was as if they regarded the society of non-fashionable doctors, lawyers, business men and the like—in short, the whole middle class, cultured or otherwise—as being uncivilised and intolerable.

Cornboise was worried, too, about their financial position. He knew that the yacht had been offered for sale at a very considerable loss. There was a tale, too, about a very surprising deal at Christie's by which Hartways had bought a diamond necklace and two Old Masters.

In February came another invitation from Balmy, and by the next post a letter from Hilda begging him to accept. He went down the following week, but before he left Town he heard that Balmy was doing funny things on horseback. There was, in fact, a sort of horseback series of practical jokes.

He had ridden upstairs in his house—which, after all, did not matter very much. But there was a nasty little incident with the local innkeeper's daughter. Passing her on the road in the middle of the afternoon, he had leant down, tossed her across the saddle and galloped into the village, where he had set her down by the inn. He had kissed her once on the cheek as part of the programme, but it was not an amorous exploit. It was just a silly practical joke, like the one that had ended his career in the Guards. But no one took it as a joke except Balmy. The girl had prosecuted him. The Bench had given him a month, and he was out on bail pending an appeal to Quarter Sessions.

When Cornboise arrived there were half a dozen other men guests—very queer birds. One, called Beeding, was a jockey who had been warned off the Turf. They behaved quite decently and were positively deferential to Lionel. But the topics that interested them eluded him. Balmy liked them immensely, and Cornboise wondered what Hilda thought about it.

He does not seem to have seen Hilda alone. It was a queer visit, with a queer atmosphere in the house, and it is difficult to fill in the gaps and discover how they grouped themselves and passed the time. But it is clear that one night all the men were together, drinking in the gun-room round about midnight, after Hilda had gone to bed.

Around the walls of the gun-room was a well-known series of sporting pictures depicting the first steeplechase, in which men were riding clad in white nightshirts and nightcaps. In one of the pictures was a background of a village and a church with a steeple, which looked faintly like the village and church of Hartways.

Cornboise records that he saw Hartways staring at the picture as if he saw it for the first time—so was almost prepared for the sudden whoop of insane joy.

'I say, you fellows, these fellows were sportsmen, eh what! How would you like to do a cross-country by moonlight in a nightshirt?'

'Don't wear 'em!' giggled Beeding, the jockey. 'It will have to be pyjamas for me.'

'You can get 'em off the servants,' said Balmy. 'I'll get mine from Hilda. *Hoicks!*'

Cornboise tried to glare the others out of it, but they were all pretty drunk, and the deference had worn thin, for, at heart, they thought him a dull dog.

Balmy bolted upstairs and the others scattered in quest of white nightshirts or, as a substitute, nightdresses. Cornboise, after some hesitation, followed Balmy. His room was just beyond the Hartways'. Through the door he heard Balmy whooping.

'Well, if you won't tell me where you keep 'em I'm going to have that one. *Whoops!* By God, Hilda, you must come too! Come like that! As Godiva. We'll make history all over again, and later on we'll have a pageant—please the village, what! Come on! You look fine like that! You needn't mind the boys. They're all the best of fellows.'

'Balmy! Balmy—give me my dressing-gown.'

'Oh, rot, I say, what! You can't have Godiva in a dressing-gown. All right, wear it to come down in.'

'Yes. Yes. I'll wear it to come down in. It's a fine idea, Balmy! I'll ride Daphne. Go and see that she's saddled for me and I'll join you.'

'Good girl! Always said you were a good old sport.'

Balmy lurched out of the room, leaving the door open, and when he had gone Cornboise showed himself.

'Why did you say you would go?'

'Oh, I always agree when he's like that. And in a minute or two he forgets. Dr Treadgold said I must always agree.'

'The doctor told you that, did he? . . . What else did the doctor tell you, Hilda?'

(*'She was out of breath and her eyes were fixed, almost glazed, and I was very alarmed and thought it better to bully the truth out of her.'*—This statement was made at the subsequent trial.)

The truth, anyhow, came tumbling out. Something like this:

'Treadgold said he must have had it all his life. And it's quite incurable and he'll get worse. And Treadgold thinks that when he surrenders to his bail at Quarter Sessions they will have him examined. And Treadgold says he will be certified. And, if not then, it's bound to happen later.'

There is a break here, and the next thing we know is that Cornboise confronted the steeplechase party on their return. They were a tough lot, and could have paid him out, but he sent them all to bed except Balmy, whom he pushed into the gun-room.

Balmy became nervous and defiant.

'Afraid you're rather bored with the little party, old man! Never mind! There'll be a church parade on Sunday.'

'I'm not exactly bored, Balmy. But I shall have to leave tomorrow.'

It was a life-long friendship, Balmy remembered this and became morbid.

'If you must go, dear boy, I'll come with you. We'll go up in the eleven-twenty. I've got to go up anyway and sell that dashed necklace—getting devilish hard up. Mustn't be robbed, for I forgot to insure it. You can be the bodyguard. And I tell you what—I'll take the jolly old starting-handle off the car in case of an attack. Jackie Beeding says it's the safest thing to carry nowadays.' He used an imaginary starting-handle in the guise of a bayonet. 'Where was I? Oh, yes—I'll give you lunch at the club and we'll talk about old times, what! No, no, I've resigned. Tell you what—'

'Balmy, you and I are friends.' (*'When I said this I put my hands on his shoulders and looked very hard at him. He looked back at me, and I was sure then that he was quite sane while I was speaking to him, and when he answered me his voice was like it used to be.'*—Again I quote from the trial.) 'I want to ask you something, old man. Don't you feel that during the last year or so there's been something wrong with you?'

'Yes, I do, Lionel. I don't know what I'm doing, fooling about like this. I must try and pull up.'

It was a preposterous setting for a tragedy. For a lucid minute Balmy faced the facts about himself—in the gun-room at midnight, flushed and ridiculous, with Hilda's night-dress torn and mud-bespattered over his dinner-jacket and riding-boots.

Then the soldier acted on the doctor's words in a way that would have horrified the doctor.

'Balmy, old man, you can't pull up—ever. It's like having an incurable disease. If I could have it instead of you I would. But, of course, I can't. I'm thinking of Hilda.'

'Then what d'you think I ought to do?'

'You've got a revolver in that drawer, Balmy. Use it like a gentleman.'

(*'And after I had said that he went silly again and roared with laughter, and I knew he would never do it. So I said I would go by an earlier train, and when I got to my room I admit I cried like a woman, because I had always been very fond of Balmy.'*)

Hartways Station is built at the mouth of the Starcross tunnel. There is the end of the platform—ten yards to the signal-box and another five yards to the tunnel. Cornboise, we must suppose, spent the night thinking about the tunnel. There is no word of the actual preparations he made for the murder.

He left by the eleven-three—a dangerously pointless thing to do, because the eleven-three is local and peters out at Stortford Mills. If you want to go by the eleven-three from Hartways to Victoria you have to get out at Stortford Mills and wait on the same platform until the eleven-twenty comes along. So you might just as well catch the eleven-twenty to start with and save yourself a wait on Stortford Mills platform.

Cornboise was driven to the station in the car, which then returned for Hartways.

In the pocket in the door was the spare starting-handle—a normal precaution in the days before the self-starter. Cornboise slipped it into his Gladstone.

He boarded the eleven-three. When the train entered the tunnel, at a speed that was well under ten miles an hour, he opened the door, stepped on to the footboard, shut the door behind him and dropped on to the track.

For this operation he needed both hands. His Gladstone bag was looped on to his elbow by means of a cord. He was wearing a raincoat which he had buttoned right up to the throat, and in the pocket of the raincoat was Hartways' revolver.

Now, it is easy enough for an athletic man to board a train going at about ten miles an hour, if he can reach the handrail. Cornboise had made a pretty good calculation of the distance and knew that he would miss the handrail by about a foot and a half.

That was where the starting-handle came in.

When the eleven-twenty entered the tunnel he caught the handrail easily enough with the starting-handle and swung himself on to the footboard.

He had chosen the second coach, where the first-class compartments would be. He had ascertained that no one else was going up with Hartways, and it was a safe bet that on that line there would be no other occupant of the first-class.

The bet came off. Hartways was alone in a first-class smoker. Cornboise steadied the Gladstone on the footboard, opened the door and got in.

He shot Hartways through the heart, and almost in the same moment threw him out of the open door into the tunnel. He threw the revolver after him.

From opening the door to throwing the body on the line had taken him about nine seconds. He had shot through Hartways' overcoat. Even so, there was a large splash of blood on the seat. He picked up the cushion and reversed it. Then he reversed all the cushions so that the black waterproof side was uppermost. He wiped the starting-handle and left it on the cushions.

With the Gladstone once more on his arm, he crawled along the footboard to the next compartment, a first-class non-smoker.

He was in the compartment the better part of a minute before the train left the tunnel. In the daylight, he inspected himself in the mirror. His face was covered with smuts, which he removed with eau-de-cologne from his Gladstone. He unbuttoned the raincoat. His collar was unsoiled. The bottom of the Gladstone bag was caked with grit. He removed it by rubbing it vigorously on the mat.

When the train stopped at Stortford Mills he stood up, put the Gladstone on the rack and behaved as if he had just got into the carriage.

Before the train started the porter ushered two ladies into the compartment with him and they travelled together to Victoria. The three of them slipped into a casual conversation concerning the opening of a window. One of the ladies lent Cornboise a paper.

An hour later he had passed through the barrier at Victoria and returned to his rooms in Knightsbridge.

All his leather was kept polished. In the absence of his man he cleaned and polished the Gladstone. He cut the raincoat into small pieces and burnt them in the open fire in his sitting-room.

The evening papers carried the story. He had just finished reading it when a couple of juniors from Scotland Yard called to ask him some more or less pointless questions.

He told them that he must go at once to Mrs Hartways, who might have need of him, and he talked to them in a four-wheeler to Victoria.

He had, he told them, travelled on the eleven-three to Stortford Mills and there waited for the eleven-twenty. He had taken the earlier train for the express purpose of avoiding his host's company. And, for this reason, at Stortford Mills he had entered a non-smoker. He told them about the nightdress steeplechase. In reply to a question he said he believed Hartways was carrying a valuable necklace, but was not sure.

And then Cornboise had his first shock.

'He was carrying it all right, sir. And we don't need to look far for the motive. It was in his pocket when he left his house. Mrs Hartways testifies to that. And it was missing when the body was found in the tunnel.'

'It's an extraordinary thing, but he was almost expecting to be robbed. He said he intended to carry a starting-handle—as a weapon of defence,' said Cornboise, and the juniors thanked him and wrote it all down.

In the train Cornboise tried to figure out how the necklace could have disappeared. Then he concluded with military simplicity that it was no concern of his. The detectives thanked him for giving them what amounted to no information whatever and left him at Victoria.

When he got down to Hartways the jockey party had only just left, having been detained for questioning by the police.

Hilda had 'taken to her room', but she received him—in a little dressing-sitting-room (the 'boudoir'). She was in one of those accordion-pleated tea-gowns. She was white and haggard, but to him she was pathetically beautiful. At sight of him she cried a little and he said nothing.

'I'm crying because I'm so glad to see you,' she told him. 'It's terrible, Lionel, and I'm terribly sorry for poor Balmy. But the most terrible part is that I myself—I—oh, I'm a beast!'

'Rot! It's a blessed release. And we both know it, Hilda. For God's sake let's be honest with each other!' He made her drink some sherry and eat an omelette. Before he went she sobbed again a little and he took her in his arms and kissed her on the forehead. And he said: 'Be brave, little woman.'

Then he went to the inn to spend the night.

On the way out he had a word with the butler in the hall. Some of the older servants were hovering, for it was no time for discipline. For a minute or two he talked sympathetically to them all. He had the odd impression that they knew perfectly well that, necklace or no necklace, he had killed Hartways. They knew that he had been in love with their mistress and probably was still. They had tacitly sympathised with him over the appalling company that had been brought to the Manor. He had come down, disapproved—and then had happened the only solution to the Hartways tragedy.

Cornboise did not care. Everyone—with the possible exception of Hilda—might be morally certain that he had killed Hartways. But he knew now that he had made no slip. Already Stortford Mills station would have been combed. He knew, in fact, that the crime could never be brought home to him.

A few minutes after he had gone, the Scotland Yard men wanted Hilda again. Could she give them a detailed description of the necklace? She could do better than that—for Balmy had had an exact copy made in paste.

She gave them the paste copy and they insisted on giving her a receipt for it, though she protested she did not want to see it again, as she would never, in any circumstances, wear it. The Edwardian lady had a deep-rooted horror of imitation jewellery.

'Was it a valuable necklace, madam?'

'My husband paid six thousand guineas for it at Christie's. It used to belong to the Riverstoke family.'

The paste necklace was sent on the next train to Scotland Yard. The detectives went over their facts. The only one of the house-party who had not a perfect alibi was Beeding, the jockey. It was known that he had fussed round Hartways, helped him on with his overcoat, and then followed the car on his motorcycle as far as the station, and had then 'gone for a spin.'

'Suppose he didn't go for a spin? Suppose he stopped by the hedge at the end of the station there and slipped between the signal-box and so into the tunnel? Then what if he jumped and hooked himself up with that there starting-handle and—did the trick?'

Next day they put this theory to a practical test and came to the conclusion that, though just possible, it was too far-fetched. Beeding had admitted that he had advised Hartways to carry a starting-handle for protection. This had been subsequently confirmed by Cornboise. The starting-handle, therefore, had nothing to do with the crime.

The inquest revealed no new facts. Hartways had been ingeniously murdered by a person unknown, the motive being the very valuable necklace.

The starting-handle and, six months later, the paste replica of the necklace drifted to the Department of Dead Ends.

Twelve months and one week after the death of Hartways the engagement was announced between his widow and Lionel Cornboise, who had now stepped into the baronetcy. They were married in April.

Hartways Manor and the house in Bruton Street had been sold, but even so there was very little left of the Hartways estate. And Hilda had been staying with an aunt at Brighton.

The following autumn Hilda's father died and left to his daughter some two thousand a year and, in effect, to his son-in-law his seat for the Borough. Cornboise resigned his commission, and a year later, in the Liberal landslide, managed to hold his seat by a tiny majority.

On his being returned to Parliament, Cornboise bought a house in Queen Anne's Gate. In the meantime Hilda had presented him with a red-headed replica of himself. Hilda became 'one of our younger hostesses'. The scandal and misery of her first marriage were officially forgotten.

But not by Hilda, for the memory added salt to her present happiness. Lionel did not quite understand this point of view, and would become strong and silent whenever she referred to Balmy.

They had been married over five years when she dropped a newspaper and asked him:

'Do you remember that horrid man Beeding? He was a jockey or something. He has got into the papers. They found him lying unconscious in a side-street off Holborn. And there was a starting-handle lying beside him, but he had been stabbed. The police think it was a race-gang.'

'The devil gets his own sometimes,' grunted Lionel, and went off to the House of Commons.

While Beeding lay unconscious in a private room in St Seiriols' Hospital, Superintendent Tarrant, of the Department of Dead Ends, offered the information that they had a starting-handle which had been one of the clues in the Hartways murder five years previously. Detective-Inspector Rason sent back a minute with a polite denial that the starting-handle had ever been a clue to anything. It had long ago been decided that the presence of the starting-handle in the first-class compartment had no bearing on the crime.

As for the second starting-handle, when Beeding recovered consciousness he admitted it was his. He was, he said, carrying it from the garage to the agents' depot for repairs. He did not know who had attacked him, nor could he guess the object of the attack. He had not, he said, been robbed.

Now, in Beeding's pockets there had been found small change only. But the proprietors of the garage, a tumble-down stable, had handed Beeding a ten-pound note on behalf of a ready-money bookie and had seen Beeding put it in his pocket-case—a few minutes before the attack.

Beeding stoutly denied this. Rason was puzzled, but Tarrant jumped on it.

There on his table were the two starting-handles. The first one had been carried, so the notes ran, because Hartways had feared attack. And Beeding had advised him to carry it for that purpose. The second starting-handle did not seem to be in need of repair.

Beeding, then, believed in carrying a starting-handle as a

weapon of defence, in case he might be attacked, when he was carrying something especially valuable. There was, Tarrant had to admit, no logical connection between the two crimes. But that did not matter in the least. He inquired from the doctor about Beeding's condition. The doctor described the nature of the wound, then:

'Officially, he is making good progress. He is quite clear-headed and feels no pain. He may be like that for a week, six months, a year. But if you want an unofficial opinion I should think it extremely unlikely that he'll ever get out of that bed.'

A week passed and Superintendent Tarrant, with a couple of clerks and a bag, went to have a chat with Beeding.

The conversation began by seeming to be directed to the question of Beeding's possible assailants, and Tarrant produced the starting-handle.

'This was your starting-handle, wasn't it, Mr Beeding?'

Beeding had a good look at it.

'No.'

'Ever seen it before?'

'Not as far as I know.'

'Ah! I've had that starting-handle for five years. It was the one that was found in the train when Hartways was murdered. And you've never seen it before?'

'Oh, I saw it at the time when your fellows were carting it round, I suppose. But why are you bringing all this up?'

'I just thought you might be inclined to make a yarn of it!' The Superintendent smiled. 'I'm going to show you something else in a minute, Beeding. You were friendly with Hartways, weren't you? Let's see, what did they call him?—Balmy Hartways, wasn't it? Went to stay with him and taught him a few things about horses, didn't you, Beeding? Did you ever happen to see his missus wearing the—the Riverstoke necklace?'

'What are you getting at?'

'Nothing, Beeding. You don't have to tell me anything you'd rather keep quiet about. Never give evidence against yourself. Perhaps I'd better not ask any questions until you're out and about again. But maybe I've got a bit of good news for you and maybe I haven't . . . What would you say if I told you we'd got the man who knifed you?'

'Tommy rot!' said Beeding so quickly that Tarrant became fairly sure of his ground,

'The man who knifed you *and* robbed you, Beeding.'

Beeding stayed mum. Tarrant dived into the bag and dangled before Beeding's eyes the paste copy of the Riverstoke necklace. Beeding became profoundly excited.

'Cor! You've got him, and I know who it was. Chalky Saunders. He's been hanging round Polly and she gave him the tip, the dirty little slut. My God, I'll pay her for that when I get out!'

Superintendent Tarrant put the necklace away.

'When you get out! . . . When you get out, did you say, Beeding? You're reckoning on getting the sentence commuted, then?'

Beeding dropped his jaw and gazed at the wholly irrelevant starting-handle.

'I took the necklace from Balmy before he ever went on the train!' he cried. 'While I was helping him on with his overcoat in the hall I picked his pocket.'

'Kept it a long time, haven't you, Beeding?'

'Well, none of the fences would touch it when there was a murder tacked on. And just lately I had the chance of planting it on a new man—never mind who. I'd mentioned it to Polly and told her I was taking it up on the chance. Cor! . . . But I had nothing to do with the murder, Mr Tarrant. That was done in the train, and how could I have got in the train?'

'Didn't happen to slip along to the tunnel and hook yourself up on to the handrail by means of this starting-handle, did you?'

'No. I swear I didn't. I tell you I took it off him—'

'All right, Beeding! I believe you, and I dare say, if you get a good man, the jury will, too. But we can't promise to keep Polly out of it now you've mentioned her name.'

Tarrant left Beeding a few minutes before twelve. By one-thirty the whole of the diamond trade, legitimate and otherwise, knew that the Riverstoke necklace was being hunted by the whole pack. By three-fifteen it was brought to Scotland Yard by a terrified fence with a very weak explanation—which was accepted.

Lionel Cornboise had as yet no aspirations to Cabinet rank. He had made one very military maiden speech and for the rest contented himself with a very zealous obedience to the Whips. He was told that he could go home for tea, and was there informed that Lady Cornboise was in the dining-room with an official from Scotland Yard.

In those days Scotland Yard held no more secret terror for him than it holds for you and me. He supposed that Hilda had lost an umbrella and was therefore surprised to see two large diamond necklaces laid out on the dining-room table.

'Lionel, isn't it splendid? They've found the Riverstoke necklace after all these years. And they're not allowed to tell me where they've found it. This other one's only the paste one. I was just going to sign a receipt when you came in. This is Mr—er—'

'Tarrant,' supplied Tarrant, and smiled. Lionel made polite conversation while Hilda signed the receipt.

'I don't think I want any tea—I'd rather have a drink. Join me in a whisky-and-soda, Mr Tarrant?'

'Thank you, Sir Lionel!'

In those days, when men had a drink women retired. Hilda retired with the necklaces.

'Funny your finding it after all these years! The long arm of the law and all that! I understand I'm not allowed to ask how it all happened.'

'Well, Sir Lionel, one has to guard one's tongue with the ladies. Of course, there can't really be any secret about it, because we've got the man and Lady Cornboise will be a witness, I'm afraid. Did you ever hear of a man called Beeding?'

'Yes. A racing tout of some sort. Half a minute, though! If he—stole—the necklace—'

'*Quite* so, Sir Lionel!' The Superintendent, we may suppose, appeared to mellow under the influence of the whisky. 'And I don't mind telling you I know just how it was done. You remember there was a starting-handle found in the carriage that seemed to have nothing to do with the murder. Now, either I'm a Dutchman or Beeding had that handle under his coat when he was following Hartways' car on his motor-bike. He rode on when the car stopped at the station—and then I'll tell you what he did. He rode on a bit and hid his motor-bike. Then he came back, cut through the hedge, slipped past the signal-box and hid himself in the tunnel until the eleven-twenty came along. He's a little man, but they're very wiry, those jockeys—oh, very wiry! You'd be surprised! When the eleven-twenty came along he made a jump for the train, using the starting-handle to shorten his jump—hooked it into the handrail. Then he shot Hartways with Hartways' own revolver, which he had stolen from the house, and there you are! He found the market a bit too hot for that necklace, especially as it was so well known, being the Riverstoke necklace, and he had to hold it.'

'H'm! Has he confessed?'

'No. He put up a silly little tale about picking Mr Hartways' pocket before they started off. But that's too easy. You know as well as I do, Sir Lionel, that Marshall Hall himself couldn't do anything with such a fool defence. We've got him—like *that*. And we'll hang him—you see if we don't.

'The part I don't like,' continued the Superintendent, 'is the girl he's living with. Decent enough little thing called Polly. Funny how these fellows often get very nice women. As she was helping him hide the necklace we shall have to charge her as accessory to the murder. But, of course, they won't hang her—probably let her off with five years.'

Lionel went upstairs and found Hilda.

'Oh, Lionel, isn't it splendid! You know, poor Balmy gave six thousand for it at Christie's. And it wasn't insured. So the money will be ours. All right! I was going to say we'll sell it and make a trust for David.'

'You always say "poor Balmy" . . . Do you wish it had never happened, Hilda?'

'No.' Then she echoed his own words from the past. 'I think I'm honest with myself about that, Lionel. It was a blessed release.'

'I'm not sorry it happened, either,' he said. He suddenly kissed her and said goodbye, but she just thought he was going back to the House of Commons.

A gentleman might conceivably commit murder if he were utterly and absolutely convinced that by so doing he ensured an increase in the sum of human happiness. But a gentleman could in no circumstances allow another man, however intrinsically worthless, to pay the price of his own crime. To say nothing of allowing an innocent woman to go to prison for five years.

It was six o'clock when he reached Scotland Yard. But Superintendent Tarrant was still there. It was almost as if he were waiting for Sir Lionel Cornboise.

'I've come to tell you that you're barking up the wrong tree,' he said, in that clipped military voice. 'Beeding had nothing to do with the murder of Hartways. I killed him myself. I don't want to talk about it. Let me sit down here and I'll write a circumstantial confession.'

That night Beeding died.

ROY VICKERS

William Edward Vickers (1889–1965) wrote under several pseudonyms, including David Durham, Sefton Kyle and John Spencer, but it is for his work as Roy Vickers, in particular the short stories featuring the Department of Dead Ends, that William 'Duff' Vickers is best remembered today.

Vickers was born in Wandsworth and boarded at Charterhouse School, and on completing his schooling he went up to Brasenose College, Oxford. For reasons that are unclear, he left Oxford without completing his degree but was admitted in January 1909 to Middle Temple, one of the Inns of Court. As at Oxford, Vickers left Middle Temple prematurely and, perhaps planning to follow in the footsteps of his publisher father, began work as a journalist, writing extensively for a number of newspapers. His first short story, 'The Stolen Melody', was published in 1913 and a steady stream of others followed, appearing in *Detective Story Magazine, Topical Times* and elsewhere. His first full-length work was a biography of the former Commander-in-Chief of the British Army, *Lord Roberts*, which was published shortly after the eminent soldier's death in 1914.

In August 1916, Vickers enlisted as a Private in the Durham Light Infantry and he spent the next three years in Greece, including a stint writing for *Balkan News*, a newspaper for the British Salonica Force which was fighting on the Macedonian Front. After the First World War, Vickers took up writing full time, with his first novel,

Bonnie Mary Myles, appearing as a newspaper serial in 1919. By the end of 1930, Vickers had written twenty-five more novels, under various pen names; among them was *The Mystery of the Scented Death* (1922), his first crime novel. Vickers was astonishingly prolific, producing more than seventy novels in the thirty years between 1920 and 1950; many are light, rather forgettable romantic thrillers but all of them are characterised by an easy style and economically drawn but compelling characters.

In September 1934, 'The Rubber Trumpet', the first of Vickers' Department of Dead Ends stories, was published in *Pearson's Magazine*. The Department is an imaginary section of Scotland Yard where what a contemporary critic described as 'the flotsam and jetsam of unsolved crimes' are stored, awaiting illumination by Inspector Rason, a cold case specialist who always unravels the truth. Vickers wrote many other short stories, including—as David Durham—a series about Miss Fidelity Dove, 'the smartest crook in London, in the world, in history', which were gathered in the collection *The Exploits of Fidelity Dove* published in 1924.

One of Roy Vickers' most famous short stories is 'Double Image', which in 1954 won first prize—equivalent to £10,000 in today's money—in a short story competition run by *Ellery Queen's Mystery Magazine*; the story was adapted into a popular comedy thriller that opened in London's West End in 1956 with Richard Attenborough and Sheila Sim.

One of only a handful of uncollected stories about the Department of Dead Ends, 'The Starting-Handle Murder' was first published in *Pearson's Magazine* in October 1934.

THE WIFE OF THE KENITE

Agatha Christie

Herr Schaefer removed his hat and wiped his perspiring brow. He was hot. He was hungry and thirsty—especially the latter. But, above all, he was anxious. Before him stretched the yellow expanse of the veldt. Behind him, the line of the horizon was broken by the 'dumps' of the outlying portion of the Reef. And from far away, in the direction of Johannesburg, came a sound like distant thunder. But it was not thunder, as Herr Schaefer knew only too well. It was monotonous and regular, and represented the triumph of law and order over the forces of Revolution.

Incidentally, it was having a most wearing effect on the nerves of Herr Schaefer. The position in which he found himself was an unpleasant one. The swift efficient proclamation of martial law, followed by the dramatic arrival of Smuts with the tyres of his car shot flat, had had the effect of completely disorganising the carefully laid plans of Schaefer and his friends, and Schaefer himself had narrowly escaped being laid by the heels. For the moment he was at large, but the present was uncomfortable, and the future too problematical to be pleasant.

In good, sound German, Herr Schaefer cursed the country, the climate, the Rand and all workers thereon, and most especially his late employers, the Reds. As a paid agitator, he had done his work with true German efficiency, but his military upbringing, and his years of service with the German Army in Belgium, led him to admire the forcefulness of Smuts, and to despise unfeignedly the untrained rabble, devoid of discipline, which had crumbled to pieces at the first real test.

'They are scum,' said Herr Schaefer, gloomily, moistening his cracked lips. 'Swine! No drilling. No order. No discipline. Ragged commandos riding loose about the veldt! Ah! If they had but one Prussian drill sergeant!'

Involuntarily his back straightened. For a year he had been endeavouring to cultivate a slouch which, together with a ragged beard, might make his apparent dealing in such innocent vegetable produce as cabbages, cauliflowers, and potatoes less open to doubt. A momentary shiver went down his spine as he reflected that certain papers might even now be in the hands of the military—papers whereon the word 'cabbage' stood opposite 'dynamite', and potatoes were labelled 'detonators'.

The sun was nearing the horizon. Soon the cool of the evening would set in. If he could only reach a friendly farm (there were one or two hereabouts, he knew), he would find shelter for the night, and explicit directions that might set him on the road to freedom on the morrow.

Suddenly his eyes narrowed appreciatively upon a point to his extreme left.

'Mealies!' said Herr Schaefer. 'Where there are mealies there is a farm not far off.'

His reasoning proved correct. A rough track led through the cultivated belt of land. He came first to a cluster of kraals, avoided them dextrously (since he had no wish to be seen if the farm should not prove to be one of those he sought), and skirting a slight rise, came suddenly upon the farm itself. It was the usual low building, with a corrugated roof, and a stoep running round two sides of it.

The sun was setting now, a red, angry blur on the horizon, and a woman was standing in the open doorway, looking out into the falling dusk. Herr Schaefer pulled his hat well over his eyes and came up the steps.

'Is this by any chance the farm of Mr Henshel?' he asked.

The woman nodded without speaking, staring at him with wide blue eyes. Schaefer drew a deep breath of relief, and looked back at her with a measure of appreciation. He admired the Dutch, wide-bosomed type such as this. A grand creature, with her full breast and her wide hips; not young, nearer forty than thirty, fair hair just touched with grey parted simply in the middle of her wide forehead, something grand and forceful about her, like a patriarch's wife of old.

'A fine mother of sons,' thought Herr Schaefer appreciatively. 'Also, let us hope, a good cook!'

His requirements of women were primitive and simple.

'Mr Henshel expects me, I think,' said the German, and added in a slightly lower tone: 'I am interested in potatoes.'

She gave the expected reply.

'We, too, are cultivators of vegetables.' She spoke the words correctly, but with a strong accent. Her English was evidently not her strong point and Schaefer put her down as belonging to one of those Dutch Nationalist families who forbid their children to use the interloper's tongue. With a big, work-stained hand, she pointed behind him.

'You come from Jo'burg—yes?'

He nodded.

'Things are finished there. I escaped by the skin of my teeth. Then I lost myself on the veldt. It is pure chance that I found my way here.'

The Dutch woman shook her head. A strange ecstatic smile irradiated her broad features.

'There is no chance—only God. Enter, then.'

Approving her sentiments, for Herr Schaefer liked a woman to be religious, he crossed the threshold. She drew back to let him pass, the smile still lingering on her face, and just for a moment the thought that there was something here he did not quite understand flashed across Herr Schaefer's mind. He dismissed the idea as of little importance.

The house was built, like most, in the form of an H. The inner hall, from which rooms opened out all round, was pleasantly cool. The table was spread in preparation for a meal. The woman showed him to a bedroom, and on his return to the hall, when he had removed the boots from his aching feet, he found Henshel awaiting him. An Englishman, this, with a mean, vacuous face, a little rat of a fellow drunk with catchwords and phrases. It was amongst such as he that most of Schaefer's work had lain, and he knew the type well. Abuse of capitalists, of the 'rich who batten on the poor', the iniquities of the Chamber of Mines, the heroic endurance of the miners—these were the topics on which Henshel expatiated, Schaefer nodding wearily with his mind fixed solely on food and drink.

At last the woman appeared, bearing a steaming tureen of soup. They sat down together and fell to. It was good soup. Henshel continued to talk; his wife was silent. Schaefer contented himself with monosyllables and appropriate grunts. When Mrs Henshel left the room to bring in the next course, he said appreciatively: 'Your wife is a good cook. You are lucky. Not all Dutch women cook well.'

Henshel stared at him.

'My wife is not Dutch.'

Schaefer looked his astonishment, but the shortness of Henshel's tone, and some unacknowledged uneasiness in himself forbade him asking further. It was odd, though. He had been so sure that she was Dutch.

After the meal, he sat on the stoep in the cool dusk smoking. Somewhere in the house behind him a door banged. It was followed by the noise of a horse's hoofs. Vaguely uneasy, he sat forward listening as they grew fainter in the distance, then started violently to find Mrs Henshel standing at his elbow with a steaming cup of coffee. She set it down on a little table beside him.

'My husband has ridden over to Cloete's—to make the arrangements for getting you away in the morning,' she explained.

'Oh! I see.'

Curious, how his uneasiness persisted.

'When will he be back?'

'Some time after midnight.'

His uneasiness was not allayed. Yet what was it that he feared? Surely not that Henshel would give him up to the police? No, the man was sincere enough—a red-hot Revolutionist. The fact of the matter was that he, Conrad Schaefer, had got nerves! A German soldier (Schaefer unconsciously always thought of himself as a soldier) had no business with nerves. He took up the cup beside him and drank it down, making a grimace as he did so. What filthy stuff this Boer coffee always was! Roasted acorns! He was sure of it—roasted acorns!

He put the cup down again, and as he did so, a deep sigh came from the woman standing by his side. He had almost forgotten her presence.

'Will you not sit down?' he asked, making no motion, however, to rise from his own seat.

She shook her head.

'I have to clear away, and wash the dishes, and make my house straight.'

Schaefer nodded an approving head.

'The children are already in bed, I suppose,' he said genially.

There was a pause before she answered.

'I have no children.'

Schaefer was surprised. From the first moment he saw her he had definitely associated her with motherhood.

She took up the cup and walked to the entrance door with it. Then she spoke over her shoulder.

'I had one child. It died . . .'

'Ach! I am sorry,' said Schaefer, kindly.

The woman did not answer. She stood there motionless. And suddenly Schaefer's uneasiness returned a hundred-fold. Only this time, he connected it definitely—not with the house, not with Henshel, but with this slow-moving, grandly fashioned woman—this wife of Henshel's who was neither English nor Dutch. His curiosity roused afresh, he asked her the question point blank. What nationality was she?

'Flemish.'

She said the word abruptly, then passed into the house, leaving Herr Schaefer disturbed and upset.

Flemish! That was it, was it? Flemish! His mind flew swiftly to and fro, from the mud flats of Belgium to the sun-baked plateaus of South Africa. Flemish! He didn't like it. Both the French and the Belgians were so extraordinarily unreasonable! They couldn't forget.

His mind felt curiously confused. He yawned two or three times, wide, gaping yawns. He must get to bed and sleep—sleep—. Pah! How bitter that coffee had been—he could taste it still.

A light sprang up in the house. He got up and made his way to the door. His legs felt curiously unsteady. Inside, the big woman was sitting reading by the light of a small oil lamp. Herr Schaefer felt strangely reassured at the sight of the heavy volume on her knee. The Bible! He approved of women reading the Bible. He was a religious man himself, with a thorough belief in the German God, the God of the Old Testament, a God of blood and battles, of thunder and lightning, of material rewards and dire material vengeance, swift to anger and terrible in wrath.

He stumbled to a chair (what *was* the matter with his legs?); and in a thick, strange voice, suppressing another terrific yawn, he asked her what chapter she was reading.

Her blue eyes, under their level brows met his, something inscrutable in their depths. So might have looked a prophetess of Israel.

'The fourth chapter of Judges.'

He nodded, yawning again. He *must* go to bed . . . but the effort to rise was too much for him . . . his eyelids closed . . .

'The fourth chapter of Judges.' What was the fourth chapter of Judges? His uneasiness returned, swelled into terror. Something was wrong . . . Judges . . . Sleep overcame him. He went down into the depths—and horror went with him . . .

He awoke, dragging himself back to consciousness . . . Time had passed—much time, he felt certain of it. Where was he? He blinked up at the light—there were pains in his arms and legs . . . he felt sick . . . the taste of the coffee was still in his mouth . . . But what was this? He was lying on the floor, bound hand and foot with strips of towel, and standing over him was the sinister figure of the woman who was not Dutch. His wits came back to him in a flash of sheer desperate fear. He was in danger . . . great danger . . .

She marked the growth of consciousness in his eyes, and answered it as though he had actually spoken.

'Yes, I will tell you now. You remember passing through a place called Voogplaat, in Belgium?'

He recalled the name. Some twopenny-ha'penny village he had passed through with his regiment.

She nodded, and went on.

'You came to my door with some other soldiers. My man was away with the Belgian Army. My first man—not Henshel, I have only been married to him two years. The boy, my little one—he was only four years of age—ran out. He began to cry—what child would not? He feared the soldiers. You ordered him to stop. He could not. You seized a chopper—ah God!—and struck off his hand! You laughed, and said: "That hand will never wield a weapon against Germany."'

'It is not true,' cried Schaefer, shrilly, 'And even if it was—it was war!'

She paid no heed, but went on.

'I struck you in the face. What mother would not have done otherwise? You caught up the child . . . and dashed him against the wall . . .'

She stopped, her voice broken, her breast heaving . . .

Schaefer murmured feebly, abandoning the idea of denial.

'It was war . . . it was war . . .'

The sweat stood on his brow. He was alone with this woman, miles from help . . .

'I recognised you at once this afternoon in spite of your beard. You did not recognise me. You said it was chance led you here—but I knew it was God . . .'

Her bosom heaved, her eyes flashed with a fanatical light. Her God was Schaefer's God—a God of vengeance. She was uplifted by the strange, stern frenzy of a Priestess of old.

'He has delivered you into my hands.'

Wild words poured from Schaefer, arguments, prayers, appeals for mercy, threats. And all left her untouched.

'God sent me another sign. When I opened the Bible tonight, I saw what He would have me do. *Blessed above women shall Jael, the wife of Heber the Kenite, be . . .*'

She stooped and took from the floor a hammer and some long, shining nails . . . A scream burst from Schaefer's throat. He remembered now the fourth chapter of Judges, that dramatic story of black inhospitality! Sisera fleeing from his enemies . . . a woman standing at the door of a tent . . . Jael, the wife of Heber the Kenite . . .

And sonorously, in her deep voice with the broad Flemish accent, her eyes shining as the Israelite woman's may have shone in bygone days, she spoke the words of triumph:

'This is the day in which the Lord hath delivered mine enemy into my hand . . .'

AGATHA CHRISTIE

The name of Agatha Christie (1890–1976) is synonymous with the Golden Age of crime and detective fiction. While her first novel was not published until she was nearly 30 years old, she encapsulates its guiding principle, that of fair play detection, as well as being responsible for some of the finest examples of the genre, particularly in the 1930s which saw the publication of titles including *Peril at End House* (1932), *Murder on the Orient Express* (1934), *Hercule Poirot's Christmas* (1938) and the book now titled *And Then There Were None* (1939). Christie created Hercule Poirot and Jane Marple, two of the best loved and most enduring characters in detective fiction, and all of her books remain in print. Whatever some may think, the so-called 'Queen of Crime' is not yet ready to relinquish her crown, not even forty years after her death.

In what she later termed 'my age of innocence', Christie wrote poetry and plays—as well as a few short stories and a romantic novel that remains unpublished—before she became attracted by what she called 'the fascination of crime and its lure'. To those who reproached her for abandoning 'serious' writing, she told them: 'I have a sordid mind. There is no money in poetry, and lots in criminals and their ways—provided you have a sense of humour.' While she had written her first novel, *The Mysterious Affair at Styles*, 'as the result of a bet', the book was an immediate success and, as she said in an interview to promote her second novel, 'When once you adopt crime it's difficult to give it up, I know I can never do so.' And countless readers are grateful that she never did.

Given her sales figures, there has been much speculation about Agatha Christie's 'secret'. It was even subject to media speculation in 1923, when she was reported as having said that 'she framed her final chapter first and then worked backwards, covering up her tracks as she went'. That of course is only part of the story and fortunately we now have two essential, wholly fascinating studies of how she wrote her books, *Agatha Christie's Secret Notebooks* and *Agatha Christie's Murder in the Making* (subsequently combined into the one-volume *Complete Secret Notebooks*), in which the Christie scholar John Curran also reveals how extraordinarily prodigious her imagination was.

As well as a best-selling novelist, Christie was an immensely successful playwright responsible not only for the longest-running play in history, *The Mousetrap*, but a string of other thrillers including *Witness for the Prosecution*; again, there is now a detailed study of Christie's theatrical life, the engrossing *Agatha Christie: A Life in Theatre* by Julius Green.

'The Wife of the Kenite' was probably written in South Africa in 1922 when Christie accompanied her husband Archie to promote the British Empire Exhibition, which ran from 1924 to 1925. It is an unusual story but features a scenario to which she would return throughout her career, most notably in the stage play *Love from a Stranger* and in the novel *Five Little Pigs*. 'The Wife of the Kenite' was first published in Australia's *Home Magazine* in September 1922.

ACKNOWLEDGEMENTS

'The Inverness Cape' by Leo Bruce reprinted by permission of Peters Fraser & Dunlop (www.petersfraserdunlop.com) on behalf of the Estate of Leo Bruce/Rupert Croft-Cooke.

'Dark Waters' by Freeman Wills Crofts reprinted by permission of The Society of Authors as Literary Representative of the Estate of Freeman Wills Crofts.

'Linckes' Great Case' by Georgette Heyer copyright © Georgette Heyer 1923.

'Calling *James Braithwaite*' by Nicholas Blake reprinted by permission of Peters Fraser & Dunlop (www.petersfraserdunlop.com) on behalf of the Estate of Nicholas Blake.

'The Elusive Bullet' by John Rhode copyright © Estate of John Rhode 1936.

'The Euthanasia of Hilary's Aunt' by Cyril Hare reprinted by permission of United Agents.

'The Girdle of Dreams' by Vincent Cornier copyright © Estate of Vincent Cornier 1933.

'The Fool and the Perfect Murder' by Arthur Upfield copyright © 1979 William A. Upfield.

'Bread Upon the Waters' by A. A. Milne copyright © A. A. Milne 1950, reprinted with permission of Curtis Brown Group Ltd, London.

'The Man with the Twisted Thumb' by Anthony Berkeley reprinted by permission of The Society of Authors as Literary Representative of the Estate of Anthony Berkeley Cox.

'The Rum Punch' by Christianna Brand copyright © Christianna Brand 2018. Reprinted by permission of A M Heath & Co. Ltd Authors' Agents.

'Victoria Pumphrey' by H. C. Bailey copyright © the estate of H. C. Bailey 1939.

'The Starting Handle Murder' by Roy Vickers copyright © the estate of Roy Vickers, reprinted with permission of Curtis Brown Group Ltd, London.

'The Wife of the Kenite' by Agatha Christie copyright © 1922 Agatha Christie Limited. All rights reserved. Agatha Christie® is a registered trade mark of Agatha Christie Limited in the UK and elsewhere.

Every effort has been made to trace all owners of copyright. The editor and publishers apologise for any errors or omissions and would be grateful if notified of any corrections.